Will You Love Me Again?

SHERI KEYES

PAGE PUBLISHING
Conneaut Lake, PA

First originally published by Page Publishing 2022

ISBN 978-1-6624-8254-0 (pbk)
ISBN 978-1-6624-8262-5 (digital)

Printed in the United States of America

CHAPTER 1

(Author's note: the first section of this chapter serves to inform those who have *not* read *May I Love You?* of its major events, or to refresh the memories of those who have.)

Sean Wallach and Jenny Weaver met in October at a diner in the small northeastern New Mexico town near where she lived. They instantly felt comfortable with each other, quickly fell in love, and after a mere three weeks got married at the rim of the canyon where they had had their first date. Having grown up on a reservation, she had lived in New Mexico her entire life. But Sean, a helicopter pilot, was on an extended vacation from his native Scotland, touring the USA on a leased Harley-Davidson.

The couple enjoyed a honeymoon in Durango, Colorado. Sean soon accepted a position flying choppers for the Albuquerque Police Department (APD), changed his citizenship, and bought a house on three acres northeast of town for his new bride. For their first Christmas together, he bought a new SUV for Jenny and later relinquished the Harley and bought a slightly used truck for himself.

Sean and Jenny began attending church and developed warm friendships with several couples there. Because they now lived near Albuquerque, Jenny was able to spend more time with her sister, Janice, who was married to Tarak and had two children, Alicia and Adam, and her brother, Jack, who held a prominent position at a software development company. This more than made up for losing the privacy she had enjoyed in her rural mobile home prior to meeting Sean.

On her birthday, February 3, Jenny learned she was pregnant. She shared the news with Sean that night when he took her to dinner at their favorite restaurant in Santa Fe. He was utterly thrilled and cried unashamed tears of joy as he held Jenny in his lap and fed her French silk pie.

His parents, Andrew and Eileen, were able to visit for a week at the end of February. On Sean's days off, the four of them took a road trip to visit Grand Canyon National Park. At their wedding reception—which had been planned to coincide with his parent's visit—Sean quite unintentionally gave a speech in which he shared some of the highlights of his and Jenny's very untraditional courtship and marriage.

Though Sean was an extrovert and was gifted with the ability to put people at ease, Jenny was introverted and less comfortable in even small groups. Nonetheless, she stood at his side and contributed to the tales Sean shared with their friends and families. They laughed as he told them about meeting Jenny while wearing his kilt and how Sean had surprised her with a helicopter ride, where he exchanged their temporary wedding rings with the custom-designed ones that couldn't be ready for their wedding on such short notice.

Sean and Jenny had agreed not to tell the guests about the baby, but bolstered by the smiles of the attendees, Sean faced Jenny and stated, "My love, we have dated, married, honeymooned, and bought a house and cars. The next step, I believe, is children." In a moment filled with emotion, he informed the guests that he and Jenny were expecting a baby.

Several months later after an uneventful pregnancy, Jenny's labor began suddenly. Sean drove her to the hospital with a police escort where she very quickly delivered a healthy baby girl whom they named Elise. Their life together was almost like that found in a romance novel.

A little before Elise's third birthday, Jenny got pregnant again but suffered a miscarriage at nearly four months, which sent her spiraling into a deep depression; for over a month, she refused Sean's attempts at loving or even consoling her. This crushed his very soul. Just when it seemed as if they were in the beginning phase of piecing together their shattered hearts and lives, Sean's father passed away unexpectedly, necessitating Sean's traveling to Scotland for nearly two weeks. Desperate for the chance to talk to someone about his tangled emotions, Sean had a near-encounter with an ex-girlfriend (only a kiss, born of rage at his circumstances rather than passion).

He ultimately turned to his mother for counsel, and she shared experiences from her and Sean's father's past while offering him a lifetime of wisdom and good advice. He arranged for his flight home—hopeful but with a great deal of doubt about the future of his marriage.

When he returned home to Albuquerque, Jenny, having spent Sean's absence very introspectively, apologized to Sean for having shunned him and treated him so poorly. Sean, committed to having no secrets, then divulged his indiscretion while in Scotland. Jenny, understandably upset and unsure if she could ever trust him again, couldn't determine if she even wanted to continue in the marriage. But Sean, certain that if Jenny could just remember the love they once shared, held her tight as she wept and tried to escape from him until she finally relaxed in his arms. They prayed and talked all through the night and then very slowly and gently reacquainted themselves with each other just before dawn.

***** (End of review of *May I Love You?*) *****

Sean and Jenny's love rebounded stronger than ever, and their life continued as before. While engaged in pillow talk one night, they revisited the dark times they had experienced after the miscarriage.

Sean held Jenny closely and began, "I pray that we never again have to struggle in our love for each other. If a problem of some type *does* develop, let's agree that we will talk to each other and work it out together. We simply *cannot* shut the other out. We *must* be on the same team."

Jenny added, "Agreed. I know some emotions can get very strong, but we have to have faith in God and trust in our love for each other and continue to put those things ahead of everything else."

Sean wanted more because he *never* wanted to go through times like those few weeks again. "Should we have a code word so that if needed we can remind the other person of what we have decided here?"

"Maybe *unity?*"

Sean pondered Jenny's suggestion. "I like that."

*****

In order to enhance their savings for college funds and a wedding for their daughter, as well as retirement, Sean had begun doing contract work with a company that offered helicopter rides to the public, much like he had done in his native Scotland years before. This would also serve to replenish some of the savings he had used when he made a down payment on their house. For the same reason, and also because he wanted his wife and child to always be safe and comfortable in their travels, Sean was adamant about having their vehicles serviced regularly as he knew that maintenance was cheaper than a monthly loan repayment.

Jenny had completed the online coursework to obtain her associate's degree and then passed the various exams to become a dental hygienist. She and Sean had decided that while she might seek employment after Elise began school, until then she would be a stay-at-home parent to their precious daughter.

Elise, now nearing four-and-a-half years of age, had really enjoyed her most recent Christmas because she was old enough to better understand it. Sean and Jenny took turns handing her gifts and helping her to unwrap them while the other took plenty of pictures and videos to send to Sean's mom and his brother, Colin, back in Scotland. The little family was happy and healthy, which was all anyone could hope for.

Sean and Jenny continued their daily walks with each other as often as possible, and Jenny had taught herself to make many delicious meals full of healthy and fresh ingredients. Sean had created and planted a small garden in the backyard during their second spring at their home. Jenny was familiar with tending it because of the garden her parents had maintained when she was a child. As Elise grew, Jenny taught her about the plants, their flowers, the importance of the pollinators, and how to tell when the fruits and vegetables were ready to be harvested.

The three of them attended church weekly and had strong friendships with several of the other families. Small and sometimes larger groups enjoyed meeting and being entertained in the homes of the various members. Get-togethers at the Wallach home were especially favored as it had a large fenced yard, and kids could run and play freely. Sean's hamburgers were legendary, and Jenny was famous for the various delicious salads she prepared using ingredients fresh from her garden.

At a recent gathering in the home of a family that owned a piano, Sean unexpectedly sat at it and began to perform. Everyone was shocked because he had never before played or even mentioned that he knew how to tickle the ivories. Jenny in particular sat open-mouthed at the beautiful songs he played completely from memory. When asked about it, he shared that his mother had taught both her sons about music and that they had owned a small upright on which they both learned. He said that he had also, like so many other teens, played the guitar and drums in a garage band with some friends while they were in high school.

On the ride home that night, Jenny informed Sean that on his next day off, they would be going to buy a piano for him to play.

"Why?" he asked.

Jenny answered with astonishment that he would even question the idea, "Because you play so beautifully!"

"I guess it just wasn't that important to me," he asserted. He glanced over at his sweet wife and grinned. "I can ride a bicycle too, but I don't think we need to go buy one."

"Just think of the joy you can bring to others when you play those beautiful songs! And what about Elise? Wouldn't you want her to learn something that you could teach her?"

"I didn't think of that. I guess it *would* be easier to teach her and oversee her practice than to pay someone to give her weekly lessons."

"Since we have not yet bought a dining table, we could put a piano in the dining room. If we decide to do something different in the future, we will deal with it then. But I want to hear you play for me every day!"

Sean turned his head to look at his beautiful wife and smiled. "Okay!"

The rough and emotionally distant times they had experienced after Jenny lost the baby made him appreciate the good times even more, and he was amenable to anything to keep her happy. As his dad had often said, "Happy wife, happy life!"

They arrived at their home. Sean backed Jenny's SUV into the garage (so it was easier for her to load Elise into her car seat and also so she didn't have to back out into the street) and then carried the very sleepy Elise to her bed. They skipped their usual nighttime prayers with her, but Sean offered a silent supplication as he tucked her in and wished her sweet dreams.

Jenny went straight to the dining room to try and visualize a piano. She heard Sean walking in behind her after he finished in Elise's room. He draped his arm around her shoulder.

Jenny asked, "Do you think we could make a baby grand fit in here? They are so much prettier than the uprights."

"I guess so. They come in different sizes." Sean turned to look at her. "But it will be a *lot* of money, Jenny."

"Money well spent," she insisted. "You deserve to have something! You work so hard all the time for Elise and me. Plus we would get to hear you play! I *insist* that we do this!"

Sean just shrugged and nodded his head. *Happy wife, happy life, no money*, he thought.

Then Jenny did what Jenny always did. She turned to him and gazed up at him while hugging him in a way that left no room for doubt as to what the rest of the evening entailed.

*****

It was the morning of Sean's day off. Jenny had called a local warehouse and made an appointment for eleven o'clock to view their inventory of pianos. After breakfast, Sean strapped Elise into her car seat, and the three of them traveled into town.

Jenny favored the models that were black in color. Sean cared more about the sound and the feel of the keys. Together, they settled on a five-foot, five-inch baby grand that had the firm feel Sean preferred and the ebony satin finish Jenny desired; because it was slightly used, it had a price tag that was more palatable for both of them. (Jenny didn't realize that pianos could cost from around $3,000 to more than $40,000.) Delivery arrangements were made for the following week.

Since they were already in town, Sean and Jenny decided that they would treat themselves and Elise to lunch and then some family enrichment. They went to a nearby *panaderia* where they shared an exquisitely prepared pizza that had been cooked in a wood-fired oven. Because Elise had been so well-behaved while they shopped for the piano, they allowed her to choose the toppings. In addition to the pepperoni and black olives she chose, Sean and Jenny had mushrooms added to half of the pie.

Next, they drove to the Indian Pueblo Cultural Center. Elise was excited to look at the exhibits on farming and plants. Sean asked her many questions, pretending to know nothing about gardening. Jenny had taught her well because she was able to answer all her daddy's questions and even told him some things he truly did not know. They read all the informational displays and learned how the indigenous people had managed to grow a variety of thriving crops in very arid conditions and also that other wild-growth plants were harvested for a myriad of uses.

Jenny was mesmerized by the dances that were performed by Native Americans wearing traditional costumes. Though these were Pueblo Indians and she was Apache-Comanche, she still felt a kinship with them. She knelt beside Elise and pointed out the beaded moccasins and the bells, feathers, and shells worn by the dancers. Elise loved all the diverse types of bells and the distinctive sounds made by each. Jenny pointed out the drummers and chanters and patted the rhythm on Elise's little hands. Jenny stood, and Sean picked up Elise so she could better watch the dance. Jenny explained to her husband and daughter the importance of the drum and how it represented the heartbeat of the animals whose skins had been used as well as that of Mother Earth. She told them that the drummers sat in a circle that represented the circle of life and that the rhythm facilitated healing and realignment of the mental, spiritual, emotional, and physical realms of human existence.

Sean particularly enjoyed the art displays. The variety of pottery especially captivated his attention. There were pots of every shape, size, color, and purpose. Some of the decorations on them were bold and simple, and some were so intricate and precisely executed he could scarcely believe they could have been done even in modern times, much less more anciently. Pieces were painted, etched, and carved. The fact that the wealth and depth of color were achieved using only what was provided by Mother Earth was astounding to him. When they proceeded to look at the more modern art (mostly on canvas), Sean and Jenny agreed that the use of brilliant color was very moving and that it represented a vibrant and dynamic people.

On the ride home, they listened to a CD that Sean had secretly purchased which contained songs and chants similar to those they had heard while watching the dancers.

"You are *so* funny!" Jenny told him.

"Why?" he asked innocently.

"You have a history of buying CDs that are very ethnic or are for a very specific purpose!"

Sean feigned being hurt. "Well, I *liked* the music." He glanced over at his wife. "And I was thinking that maybe someday you might want to teach some of the dances to Elise."

Jenny pondered the idea, tilted her head to the side, and nodded. "I hadn't thought of that." She smiled at her loving husband. "Thank you." Then she bent over to him and kissed him on the cheek, lingering there just a moment more than was necessary for a show of thanks.

Jenny stated, "I think we need to make sure and expose Elise to Scottish traditions as well." (This was more of an order than a suggestion.)

Duly noted, thought Sean, pleased that his wife wanted to expose their daughter to both of her ethnic heritages.

*****

Sean was at work when the piano was delivered, but he and Jenny had discussed where and in which direction to place it (facing the window), so that when he arrived home it was in position for him to play as he serenaded Jenny. He hadn't realized how much he would enjoy being able to play again. Jenny sat nearby with her eyes closed and smiled as he played and sang song after song.

8

He ordered some music books so that he could begin teaching Elise how to play. Meanwhile, nearly every day he held her in his lap and showed her middle C, the pattern of the black-and-white keys, and the repetition of the notes A through G. He also taught her some simple but recognizable songs. She was at the age when she loved learning, and Sean loved teaching her. He knew that time spent with children is time spent developing the future.

*****

And so life went for the Wallachs. With the exception of the miscarriage and a short period of time after it, their life together had been nearly charmed. Sean had a good-paying job he loved, Jenny had the home of her dreams with only a small mortgage (due to Sean's large down payment from the money he had saved before he came to the United States), their relatively new cars were paid for, and they had a precious daughter who was a joy to them. Everyone that knew Sean and Jenny stood in awe of their visible love and adoration for each other, the quiet calm and positivity they possessed, and their excellent relationship-building and parenting skills. And, of course, Jenny was gorgeous and Sean was handsome.

CHAPTER 2

Sean was on the morning shift; this was his favorite because he was able to sleep with and hold Jenny all night. However, because he had to get up and leave so early, he was frequently quite tired in the evenings, and he didn't want to miss these precious years in Elise's life. So every afternoon when he got home, he would spend time with her doing whatever she desired. Sometimes she wanted Sean to read to her, other times she requested time with her flashcards or "computer," and still other times, she wanted to draw pictures with him. Her favorite, though, was learning about the piano and how to read music.

Jenny was appreciative of these blocks of time because they gave her an uninterrupted opportunity to prepare dinner, do laundry, or finish whatever else she might not have completed during the day. In fact, because Sean was *so* helpful, sometimes she was even able to spend a little time enjoying a book or pampering herself.

Both parents knew that mealtime as a family was important, so that was nearly nonnegotiable if Sean's schedule allowed it. After dinner, Elise would usually play in her room while Sean and Jenny caught up with each other on their day as they tidied the kitchen. Then it was time for her bath, story time, and bedtime. The two of them usually took turns directing these nighttime routines although occasionally they would participate together.

On Sean's days off, Jenny was careful to let him sleep as late as he could. On this particular late March morning, Sean awoke to the unmistakable smell of bacon sizzling in a hot skillet. He quickly showered and dressed then joined her in the kitchen. When she had finished flipping the pancakes on the griddle, he touched her arm, turned her to him, then gave her a *very* appreciative kiss while holding her close to himself. Elise was at the table with her crayon set and giggled at them. Sean turned to face her.

"Do you like seeing Mommy and Daddy hugging each other?"

"It's funny!" Her dark eyes were shining brightly.

Sean cocked his head to the side. "Why is it funny?"

"Because Mommy goes like this, 'Mmmmm, mmmm'!" Elise closed her eyes, protruded her lips, and twisted her head from side to side as she groaned, mimicking her mother kissing her father.

Jenny blushed, Sean laughed, and Elise returned to her coloring.

"Do you think she's scarred for life?" Sean quietly asked, his serious tone a thin veil for his sarcasm. They chuckled. He opened the refrigerator and retrieved the orange juice. "Would you like me to pour some juice for everyone?"

"Yes, please. Ask Elise if she wants milk or juice with her pancakes."

Elise chose milk, and Sean prepared drinks for his family. He carried the glasses to the table and asked Elise to move her art supplies to the coffee table. He promised to draw with her after breakfast. Then he put plates and silverware on the table.

Jenny asked Sean to set trivets on the table so she could carry the hot platters of pancakes and bacon that had been kept warm in the oven to the table; of course, he gently removed the oven mitts from her hands and carried the platters himself. She quickly served and cut Elise's pancakes into bites. Sean seated her, they offered a prayer of thanks, and then enjoyed a wonderful breakfast together.

As Elise played in her room and they quickly cleaned up the kitchen, Sean asked Jenny what her agenda held for the day.

"Everything's in good shape here at the house, so I was wondering if you wanted to take a drive to the mountains north of here and carry a picnic lunch. I've got leftovers we can heat for supper."

Sean answered with a big grin. "I can't think of a better way to spend my day off than enjoying God's beautiful scenery with the two ladies in my life!"

With the passage of time, Jenny had become even more aware of how appreciative she was of her wonderful husband. He was always cheerful, helpful, and supportive. He was an excellent father to little Elise, and she adored him. Jenny was especially grateful for Sean and

Elise's relationship because she knew if a girl had a good rapport with her father, she was less likely to make bad decisions as a teen.

Jenny directed, "Why don't you look at your maps while I make some quick ham and Swiss sandwiches? While you decide on a route, I'll also take care of packing a bag for Elise."

"Can do!"

Jenny made three sandwiches, placed them in baggies, and put three pickles in another baggie. She also moved several stems of grapes into a larger bag and sealed it. She filled their water containers and went to the laundry room to get the picnic basket from the top shelf. Sean heard her and jumped up from the table to get it down for her. He patted her on the bottom as she walked away with it. When she turned to look back at him—and he knew she would—he smiled and winked at her.

Jenny placed the food in the basket and left it on the counter for Sean to carry to his truck. She went to Elise's room, and they picked out two books, a doll, and an extra set of clothes for her to take along. Jenny helped Elise put her things in her purple backpack.

Sean's girls came out of Elise's room and into the living room. Sean stood and stated that he had chosen a potential course for them to follow. He showed it to Jenny, and she agreed it was well-planned. Then he knelt down to speak to Elise.

"Sweetie, I know I promised to draw with you after breakfast, but Mommy thought we might enjoy a picnic in the mountains today. Does that sound like fun?"

"Uh-huh!"

"So I will draw with you either later today, or if we get home too late, we will do it tomorrow, okay?"

"Okay, Daddy!" Because both of her parents made it a goal to keep their promises as often as possible, Elise was never anxious or argumentative when plans were changed. She knew they would come through if at all possible.

They loaded everything in Sean's truck, including his guitar. (He had so enjoyed being able to play the piano again that he also bought himself a guitar.) He filled the tank with gas, smiled at each of his girls, and they were on their way toward the mountains of northern New Mexico.

*****

The little family thoroughly enjoyed the early spring day in the sun and fresh mountain air. Elise chased butterflies in a meadow while Sean strummed his guitar and sang love songs to Jenny; he made it a point to sing "Danny's Song." Jenny leaned back on the soft blanket, savoring the smell of the pine trees and the peaceful wind blowing gently through them.

They arrived home in time to eat the leftovers Jenny had mentioned, and true to his word, Sean got on the floor with Elise, and they drew pictures together while Jenny heated the food and made a quick salad with tomatoes and cucumbers from their garden. Jenny took pictures of father and daughter and sent them along with the ones she had taken in the mountains to Sean's mom. Later, Jenny bathed Elise while Sean rinsed off the dishes and loaded them in the dishwasher. Then he read a bedtime story to the now sleepy Elise. Jenny and Sean both knelt with her for her prayers, gave her hugs, and wished her sweet dreams.

As they left Elise's room and softly closed the door, Sean grabbed Jenny and began softly but passionately kissing her. Life had been so busy with Elise, Sean's friends from work, and their friends from church that they had not had a nice long evening in a while. He pulled back to look at her and realized his attentions had left her nearly breathless. One more kiss like that and he would need to carry her to their bed. So kiss her he did. When he picked her up, she closed her eyes, nuzzled his neck, and enjoyed the scent of her man.

Sean was extremely attentive to Jenny, and she was subsequently very responsive to him, so their lovemaking was always spectacular. She treasured the way he looked at her—right into her soul—as he loved her. He enjoyed her warm arms wrapped around his neck while they kissed and her strong hands firmly running down his back and arms when he brought her.

Afterward, Sean held her closely as their breathing slowed. Jenny lightly traced her fingers on his chest as they quietly talked. Right before she drifted off to sleep, he made certain that the sheets and blanket were straightened and that she was comfortable. With her needs met, he could then sleep.

*****

Just before daybreak, Sean awoke with a great need for his wife. He turned to her and began kissing her shoulders and neck as she slept beside him. Her eyes fluttered open in the dim light, and her sultry smile let him know she was definitely willing. He gently turned her over, and his soft lips and warm breath worked their magic on her. Sean was somehow as gentle as a lamb and as ferocious as a lion all at the same time. As he met her, Jenny thought there was no better way to be awakened than this.

When their pounding hearts returned to normal, Sean asked, "Did you enjoy my love songs to you yesterday?"

"Umm, *very* much!"

"Did any of them stand out to you?" Sean tried to keep his voice neutral.

Jenny raised her head off Sean's shoulder and looked at him, trying to remember what he had sung. She felt bad that she hadn't paid more attention.

Sean realized that her answer was no; he didn't want her to feel bad, so he said, "It's okay. You were relaxed and enjoying the day, and that is what was important!"

"Well, tell me what you sang, and I'll try to give you an answer anyway!" Jenny offered.

Sean named off several of the songs he sang, being careful to include "Danny's Song" in the middle of the list.

"Oh, I really like 'Danny's Song.' Who sings that?" Jenny asked as she put her head back on her warm husband.

"Loggins and Messina."

"Yeah…," Jenny said dreamily, a slight smile softening her face. Then she realized what Sean had done. She raised back up and looked at him, her mouth slightly open.

Sean's face was blank, but he was looking up at her expectantly. "Are you thinking…," Jenny began but couldn't finish.

"Yes."

Jenny put her head back on Sean's shoulder. He felt her shiver, so he pulled the covers snugly around her. As he did so, he wondered if she were cold or afraid. He let several moments pass then kissed her on top of her head.

Sean exhaled slowly. "Jenny, I know we haven't talked about this together in quite some time. But I also know we had wanted to have more than one child. The song was just an invitation to see if you wanted to begin the discussion."

He felt her tremble slightly, turned to face her, and held her tightly in his arms. He felt her tears drop on his shoulder. As always, he gave her time to release her emotion and then to collect herself.

When she drew back to search his face, Sean said, "Talk to me, my lady."

"I know we need to discuss it. It was so easy to not mention it and just let time pass. But Elise *is* getting older."

Sean nodded slightly. *He* wanted another child. But not at the expense of his wife's sanity.

"Is it even a possibility? I just want to know where we stand. If you say no, then I'll not bring it up again. But if you think even maybe, then perhaps we should begin talking and praying our way through it."

Jenny smiled at Sean with a mixture of sadness and hope.

He smiled back at her and gently suggested, "We could meet with Dr. Hoffman and maybe let her examine you and then give us advice."

Jenny took a deep breath. "I think that's a good idea." She wanted to be brave for Sean, but right now, she just needed his strength.

Sensing that, Sean continued to hold her close. "I'll be with you every step of the way."

"Especially the first part, right?" Jenny laughed.

Sean chuckled. He was proud of his wife for boldly moving away from the comforting veil of silence.

"Would you like me to call and make an appointment, or would you rather do it?" he offered.

"I'll do it. And I'll call later today. Do you have a preference for a day or time?"

"Let's aim for one of my off days. That way we have more time to talk and work through any kinks."

"Okay." Then Jenny added, "I love you, Sean. And I appreciate you."

"Ohhh." Sean chuckled as he rubbed Jenny's arms and shoulders. "I love you too, Jenny. And please know that this is *your* call. I'll not force anything on you unless you are comfortable with it."

"No! Just in these few moments, I'm realizing it's time to have this conversation. So thank you for trying to bring it up so sweetly by singing to me!"

The two of them held each other a little longer then moved to the shower. All the talk of making babies had an effect on them, and they took advantage of the quiet time of the early morning to add a new verse to their song.

CHAPTER 3

Jenny's early afternoon appointment with her gynecologist, Dr. Hoffman, went well. No problems were found that were a cause for concern about Jenny having another baby.

Sean asked how long they should expect to wait before getting pregnant after ending birth control ("up to twelve months") and if there were any things they should or should not be doing ("continue with healthy habits and use common sense") then paused to look at Jenny. Not wanting to upset her, he haltingly asked, "Does...having one miscarriage...in any way...increase the likelihood of having another?" Though he was looking at Dr. Hoffman as he spoke, he glanced at Jenny a couple of times to make sure the question didn't cause her discomfort.

Dr. Hoffman knew that Jenny had experienced a particularly difficult time emotionally after her miscarriage, so she wanted to be as reassuring as possible. "In *any* pregnancy, there is about a 20 percent chance of having a miscarriage. That risk does not change after having had just *one*. Jenny, you and Sean are both healthy and at a good age, so don't let that event cause you concern. If you *must* think about the past, think about Elise and what a wonderful pregnancy and delivery she was!"

She wrote Jenny a prescription for vitamins and told the couple to just relax and let nature take its course. She also told them to continue taking their daily walks as that was so important for so many reasons.

Sean and Jenny thanked Dr. Hoffman and left her office. Elise was staying overnight with her cousins, Alicia and Adam, so the couple had the remainder of the afternoon and the night to themselves. After Sean helped Jenny into his truck and then seated himself, he asked if there was anything she would like to do.

Jenny turned sideways to face Sean. "Do you remember our first date when we were at the canyons?"

"Yes. Very well." Sean was looking straight ahead, wistfully remembering that day.

"I remember we were hugging and kissing but had decided not to go any further." Jenny was leaning against the door, smiling radiantly.

"Yes. It was among the hardest things I've ever done in my life. I wanted you *so* badly that day." He looked over at Jenny and realized he would do *anything* to keep that smile on her face.

"And I you," she returned lustily.

Sean knew what he had to do. "Maybe that snake has crawled away by now!" he posited as he started the engine.

They both laughed. Sean looked at his watch. Two o'clock. It would take nearly three hours to get there, but it would still be daylight. They could work at making babies for a while and then return home at a reasonable hour (and perhaps work at it some more!)

Sean fastened his seat belt and told Jenny to fasten hers, backed out of the parking lot, then began the drive eastward.

They held hands much of the way, and Sean occasionally raised Jenny's fingers to his lips while sneaking a commanding glance at her. Jenny's specialty may have been creating lots of anticipation and tension in Sean, but his was lots of preparation. By the time they reached Highway 39 to turn north, he wanted to finish the prep work. He pulled over onto the shoulder, unfastened his seat belt, and reached to wrap his arms around her as he overwhelmed her with a hot-blooded kiss. When he pulled back, he knew she was ready. He gave her a final look that let her know *he* was in charge on this day, put the truck in gear, and blazed down the road to their destination.

Sean always kept a blanket and other emergency items in his truck, so once he pulled off the road at the canyon, he retrieved it from behind the seat, walked to Jenny's side to open her door, and held her hand as she stepped down. As they walked, he set the blanket on the ground near a small bunch of trees where they would later sit. They moved to the rim to look across the great expanse of land and rocks and brush. He stood behind her and enveloped his arms around her. They, as before, listened to the wind rushing through the canyons and the trees. Sean began kissing Jenny on the side of her neck, moving her hair out of the way as he followed a path around to her back and shoulders. When she could no longer ignore his attentions, she turned to him and pulled his face to hers. When they stopped to look at each other, the connection between them was nearly palpable.

Sean walked backward toward the blanket while holding Jenny's hands. She followed with great docility. Neither ever broke the gaze they had on the other.

Sean shook out the blanket and spread it on the sand a good distance away from the hiding place of any reptiles. "Sit, my love," he decreed. Then he walked to his truck to retrieve a bottle of water and a flashlight, just in case.

He lay on the blanket beside her propped up on one arm. He looked up at her. She was his, and he knew it. He patted the blanket in front of him and quietly directed, "Lie here, my lady."

Jenny obediently prostrated herself before her husband, who gently tucked her windblown hair behind her ear. It was Jenny's turn to squirm, wondering when Sean was going to stop looking at her like that and make his move.

In direct opposition to the speed at which he had driven to the canyon, once there, everything Sean did was slow and *very* purposeful. First, he removed his shirt. Jenny breathed in deeply and smiled subtly as she eyed him. Sean had a really nice physique—just the type she liked—that was not overly bulky but had good definition. Next, he began unbuttoning her blouse, kissing her chest and belly as he went. She actually thought she might erupt into flames from all his attentions to her.

The remainder of their clothes were slowly removed and laid to the side. Sean wanted Jenny as he had before—in fact, maybe even more so because their love had grown over time. His hands moved slowly over her, and his lips were warm. Jenny couldn't control the numerous small moans that escaped her.

Sean always made sure Jenny was completely ready for him before moving to her. He took great care to bring her before allowing his own pleasure. Today, out in nature, he was especially full of desire for this beautiful woman who had given herself to him. When he knew she was nearing her finish, he gave in to his need. Their euphoria was, as always, intense and shared.

Sean held her close, breathing in her scent in the clean air of the desert. Her head lay on his shoulder, and she dozed in and out, completely relaxed and happy.

After the sun fell low in the sky and the temperature began dropping, they replaced their clothing and gathered the blanket, water, and flashlight. They walked slowly to Sean's truck, arm in arm.

"What do you think of a bowl of green chili stew from Joe's Diner?" Sean asked.

Jenny smiled up at him. "That sounds *great!*"

Sean helped Jenny into the truck, and they traveled to the diner where they had met nearly six years before.

CHAPTER 4

Another year had passed. As Sean continued his employment with the APD, he began developing close friendships with some of the police officers. Occasionally, different ones would get permission to go up in the chopper with him. Sean learned more about the work done by the patrolmen, and they learned more about the things Sean could do to help them. As he became a more integral part of managing crime, he was included in more of their off-duty socializing.

Recently, several of the men—both single and married—had begun going to a karaoke bar that served great food. It quickly became a monthly event, and even the wives started attending. Sean was invited, and, even though neither he nor Jenny drank alcohol, they decided they could eat the food, enjoy the camaraderie, and maybe even sing a tune or two.

One evening, a large group was in attendance, and as good buddies will do, bets were made as to who could sing best, who could most accurately portray the artist, and who was willing to perform most outrageously. This led to other wagers, such as who could remember the most words without looking at the screen, who was the best backup singer, etc. Smiles and laughter abounded, beer was flowing freely, and money was flying around the table like bats outside a cave at sundown.

Though it initially took some convincing, Sean agreed to go onstage to sing the Eagles' "Take It Easy." (This, in fact, is what led to the bets on who could remember the most words; Sean seemed to have an encyclopedic memory of nearly every lyric he had ever heard.) Once he had gotten past his initial jitters, he realized that he had enjoyed himself so much that he was easily challenged to perform again and again.

Sean actually had a very good voice as he had grown up singing in both his church and school choirs. Jenny glowed as she watched her husband singing melody after melody, sometimes alone and sometimes with one or more of the guys, depending on the song. On some of the more intense love songs and ballads, Sean would lock eyes with and sing directly to his sweetheart.

As the evenings wore on, the women would usually move to sit together, leaning into and elbowing each other while laughing at the various performances by their husbands and boyfriends. It was during such a time that Sean performed a brilliant rendition of Bruce Springsteen's "I'm On Fire." He managed all the emotional intensity of the original, and he sang it as if Jenny were the only other person in the room. The other wives watched with a twinge of jealousy and chastised their husbands to sing to them "like Sean did to Jenny."

The women decided to join in the jocularity; Jenny was coerced (with a great deal of support from Sean, of course) to join two other women in singing first the Pointer Sisters' "Fire" and later "Slow Hand." At the outset, she was extremely nervous, but Jenny ultimately loosened up and had a great time, even singing some of the solo parts. Toward the end, the women were dancing and flirting with their men; they did such a good job they received a standing ovation from the entire crowd for their performance. Jenny returned to her seat beside Sean, sweaty, smiling, and ready for the post-outing entertainment to be had back at home. Later, her compadres motioned for her to join them and help choose the next song they would perform.

A stranger who had been sitting alone at a corner table and watching the evening's antics stood and approached the group. "This table seems like the place to be! You guys sure know how to party!"

Being naturally wary, many of the patrolmen lowered their heads and quietened their demeanors as they looked sideways at each other.

Finally, Matt, one of the younger officers replied, "Oh yeah. Everything we do is full tilt!" (His roommate was the designated driver, so Matt had consumed a good bit of liquid imbibement.)

The stranger cocked his head and asked, "Are you guys police officers?"

Derek, who was quite large and was one of the supervisors, straightened. In a very official voice, he questioned, "Who's asking?"

The stranger grinned broadly. "I knew you were! My name is George, and I was a cop in a little town in Florida. I quit to come out west and be closer to my brother who lives over in Farmington. I'm just here tonight hoping to meet a few people."

"How long did you work?" asked Derek, his face still showing his skepticism.

"I was there just over two years. My brother said he really liked the dry climate here, that there were no hurricanes, and also that the cost of living was lower. So I decided to take his advice. I'm going to headquarters tomorrow to fill out an application to work here."

As he was talking, several of the men watched him closely for signs of dishonesty or bad character. He stood calmly and non-aggressively with his shoulders lowered, and his smile seemed genuine. Remembering news videos of hurricanes striking the Florida coast, they also thought his story to be quite believable.

Satisfied that all seemed well, Derek motioned with his hand and said, "Why don't you sit with us? Grab a chair!" He pointed to two of the men. "James, Bill, make room between you two there!"

"Gee, *thanks*, fellas! It's good to meet some fellow officers!" said George. He sat and immediately struck up conversations with those around him.

"Those three women were pretty good!" he said to James.

"Yeah." James was making a serious dent in the burger he had ordered.

George continued, "Just curious. Are any of them single?"

James looked over at George. The hairs on the back of his neck tingled slightly. But he was hungry, and besides, his buddies were acting as if all was well. "Naw, man. All the women with us are taken."

George knew he needed to downplay his question. "Oh well! I guess it never hurts to ask, especially when you are new to town and don't know anybody!" To further indicate his question had been an innocent one, he immediately asked, "About how much should I expect to pay for an apartment here?"

James wiped his mouth, took a sip of his beer, and responded, "It depends on what you want and what part of town you're in." He realized the guy was new in town and had no other way to learn than to ask. He then told George a range of prices and shared information on some of the complexes where he or his friends lived.

At the end of the evening, George walked to the long table where most of the ladies were sitting and told them he had been impressed with their singing. He also asked what he needed to do if *he* wanted to sing a song the next time he was there. "Of course, I could never pull off sounding as good as *you ladies* did, but I'd still enjoy trying!" Mostly, he just wanted to get a closer look at the beautiful Jenny and try to get a read on just *how married* she was.

Everyone had had so much fun that they all agreed to meet every two weeks instead of monthly. There was a core group who attended religiously, others appeared regularly, and still others had a more sporadic presence. A few of them began dressing up to mimic their favorite musical artists, even wearing wigs or makeup.

Sean enjoyed the outings so much, in fact, that one night—with Jenny's consent, of course—he wore tight leather pants, a silver concho belt he found on eBay, and a loosely fitting but tucked-in white silk shirt, buttoned-down just enough to pull off a look that made women swoon. In a *molto blique* (very burlesque) move, Sean removed his leather bomber jacket and tossed it to Jenny as he sang the Doors' "Light My Fire" followed by "Touch Me." The crowd roared its approval, and Sean thereafter was referred to as "Mojo" by his buddies.

George now knew who his competition was.

*****

One weekend in early April, Sean and Jenny invited the group for a backyard BBQ and sing-along around the firepit. Sean had met and visited briefly with George and decided it would be a nice gesture to invite him, as well, since he was new to town. George thanked him earnestly and shook his hand. "I really appreciate your kindness. I know I'll get my life settled soon, but in the meantime, it's pretty lonely at my little place." (He was careful not to use the word "apartment" because if anyone tried to verify his residence, they would learn he had lied. Nor did he want to say "motel room;" he knew that, though it was accurate, it would raise red flags.)

"I know you would do the same if you were in my place." Sean smiled. He gave George their address and told him the time to arrive.

Sean made it a point to introduce George to each of the attendees. He also asked for George's help in manning the two grills where Sean cooked a variety of meats and vegetables. Jenny prepared couscous, pasta, and vegetable salads, and each of the other women brought either a dip or a dessert. Jenny made sparkling cranberry lemonade, and the guests were encouraged to bring any other drinks they preferred.

Sean had been practicing daily on his guitar. The department's other pilot, Tim Wilson, also played guitar, and he was asked to bring his instrument. (Tim had been in on Sean's unique plan to switch his and Jenny's temporary wedding bands with the custom ones while in the helicopter flying over Albuquerque.) Between them, they knew many songs. As they were both quite skilled, they could easily learn from each other. During most songs, they were able to successfully pull off one of them rhythmically strumming the chords as the other played various riffs and licks.

The party lasted late into the night. Sean had made sure they had a large store of firewood; everyone enjoyed standing around the firepit as the evening wore on and the temperature dropped. Jenny had, over time, purchased a number of blankets and wraps and stored them in a large cabinet in the laundry room. Individuals, husbands and wives, and small groups of people who were engaged in conversations appreciably joined under the warmth that the various blankets provided. Around eleven thirty, the women began helping Jenny put away the leftovers. Sean brought out a large trash can and began to gather all the plates and cups from the table, countertops, and porch. Everyone considered it to have been a terrific party and hoped to have others like it over the course of the coming year.

*****

Tim Wilson and Sean, especially, had formed a strong friendship. Sean was about seven years older than Tim and also had more flight experience, so Tim looked up to him.

One late afternoon, as Sean and Jenny sat together on the sofa discussing which was better—flying Sean's mother to Albuquerque or flying to Scotland with Elise—Sean's phone rang. It was Tim.

"Hey, Sean. I was wondering if you were busy."

"Hi, Tim. What's on your mind?" Sean could hear the despondency in Tim's voice.

"I was hoping I could come by your house and talk to you if that's okay. But if you're busy, we can do it another time."

Sean looked at Jenny; because they were sitting so close to each other, she had heard the conversation. She indicated her agreement with a nod.

"Sure! Not a problem. Do you remember how to get here?"

"Yeah. I'll be there in about half an hour. And, Sean, thanks."

"Sure, buddy. See you then."

Sean and Jenny looked at each other and shrugged.

Jenny stood to walk to the kitchen. "I'd better check to make sure I have enough to feed all of us. I may have to whip up another side dish really quickly."

"I'll check on Elise. She's been playing really well in her room."

As Jenny peeled some sweet potatoes to roast, Sean stepped into the doorway of Elise's room. She was lying on her stomach on the floor with her feet waving in the air, "reading" *Bubba and Beau, Best Friends* to her favorite doll, Amber, who was propped up against the bed. (The book had been written by a friend of the family and was signed by the award-winning author, Kathi Appelt.)

"What's my little girl doing?" Sean asked with a voice full of love.

"Reading." Elise, facing away from Sean, never looked up. She, like her father, was very "straight and to the point."

"May I join you?"

"Sure!" Elise jumped up, grabbed a different book from the shelf, and waited near the chair for her daddy to sit in it.

"Can you read this to me?" Her eyes were shining with the beautiful expectation of a child who is nurtured and loved.

"I don't know. That one looks hard. Do you think I can?"

"Sure you can, Daddy! I'll help you!" Elise crawled into Sean's lap and leaned back against his strong chest.

"Okay then. But you will have to help me with the hard words."

Elise chastised her father, "*Daddy!*" Then she stated with utter confidence, "You told me words aren't hard! All you have to do is try and then think what word makes sense!" She opened the book. "I'll read the title to you."

"Okay. I promise to try."

Elise, who was now more than five years old, pointed at the words as she "read" the title from the book's cover: *The Horse That Swam Away*. (Elise was actually able to recognize and read many words due to her parents' frequent reading sessions with her.)

"*Ooohh!* I wonder what this one is about?" Sean looked at his sweet daughter who was giggling at her silly father.

"I think it is about a girl who makes snowmen!"

Elise, still giggling, touched Sean's nose with her little index finger. "Boink!"

Sean gave Elise a nose boink in return as he smiled down at her.

Then her face grew more serious. "I read the title to you, Daddy," she stated precociously. "It is about a boy and his horse that live by the ocean."

"Oh! I get it. The title sometimes tells you what the book is about!"

"Uh-huh. Now, let's turn to the first chapter."

Sean's arms encircled his daughter, and he held the book open as Elise turned the pages. When she got to the Table of Contents, Sean asked, "What is this?"

Elise tilted her head to the side, raised her eyebrows, and looked up at Sean. "Daddy, I think Mommy told you because she told me. This is how we know what pages the chapters are on!"

"Oh, yes, yes. I forgot." Sean's goal as a father was to raise a child who was confident, who was willing to ask questions, and who could think through things. Every interaction he had with Elise was with these goals in mind. And he did it in a way that was playful and loving so that she enjoyed time spent with him.

They turned to chapter 1 on page three, and Sean began reading to Elise. Sometimes, he would ask her questions, like "What do you think might happen next?" or "Why do you think...?" In this way, Elise's skills were always being developed and good habits were forming.

Sean had read about three pages to his daughter when he heard the doorbell ring.

"Do you want to go with me to answer the door?"

"Yes! Let me put my book back on the shelf. We can read more later!" Sean smiled with pride at his second favorite girl in the world.

He and Elise walked to the front door and opened it. Tim was standing solemnly on the porch, looking as if he had lost his last friend.

"Hi, Tim," Sean said warmly as he reached to shake Tim's hand. "Elise, say hi to my friend, Tim, then run back to your room to play for a while before supper. Daddy and Tim are going to sit and talk for a little bit."

"Hi, Tim. Do you work with my daddy?"

Tim squatted so he could speak at eye level with Elise. "Yes, I do. I fly helicopters, just like your daddy."

"Okay. I'm going to go read to my doll, Amber!" Elise turned and skipped away.

Sean called after her, "Mommy will let you know when supper is ready, sweetie."

Sean then put his left hand on Tim's shoulder and used his right hand to point toward the two sofas in the living room. "Let's have a seat, and you can tell me what's on your mind."

Tim sat in the corner of one sofa, and Sean sat in the middle of the other. He leaned forward with his elbows on his knees and waited patiently for Tim to begin.

CHAPTER 5

Tim took several deep breaths, looked toward the window, and then finally straight at Sean. He shrugged as he stated, "I want what you have."

Sean controlled his facial expression, trying not to show his utter confusion.

"Not the house, the cars, the job, and all that." Tim shook his head from side to side as his hand made a swiping motion to dismiss those ideas. "I can get that. We make practically the same salary. What I want is your happiness, your confidence. But most importantly, I want a relationship like you and Jenny have." Tim turned his head to the side, embarrassed by his request.

Sean nodded his understanding as he, too, took a deep breath before speaking. "Do you have someone in mind? Because Jenny is taken!"

They both chuckled. The ice had been broken, and they both relaxed.

"I just broke up with the girl I was dating. She was just so...so selfish, so immature. She expected me to adore her, give her everything she wanted, and take care of her, but she also wanted to be able to sit around my house doing nothing and then flirt with other men when we were out. And when it was just the two of us, she spent most of the time on her phone texting or talking to her friends." Tim continued to shake his head. "It was like I was just a convenience to her." Tim's face and shoulders were drooping, clearly showing the despondency he felt.

Sean listened intently as Tim shared his situation, nodding that he understood. "Well, to be sure, you must begin with a quality woman and then work to build and maintain the relationship." He shrugged. "If either person is unwilling, the whole thing is thwarted."

"It's the same story, time after time. I meet a girl, she seems interested, we date a few times, we end up living together, and then begins the inevitable trip down the slippery slope." Tim used his upturned hands to emphasize his disillusionment.

"Do you mind if I ask where you go to meet people?"

Tim rolled his eyes and sighed. He had heard this before. "Sometimes at bars, sometimes at the gym. Once at a grocery store."

Sean held his tongue. He didn't want to be the next person to state the obvious. He was looking at Tim with great intensity and drawn lips.

Tim, slightly uncomfortable, acknowledged, "I know everyone says these aren't good places to meet your future wife. But it *does* work for *some* people—I *know* some." He seemed rather adamant about defending his choice.

Sean's father had taught him a great deal about thinking through a situation. So he usually *asked* a lot of questions as opposed to *giving* answers, which is usually what the other person wanted. But *his* way usually helped them to ultimately arrive at the answer on their own.

"Let me ask you this. When you go to a bar, what is it you are seeking?"

Tim was mildly irritated but responded to Sean's question nonetheless. "I don't know. I'm looking for a good time, looking to kill some time in the evenings, looking for a hookup. And *maybe*, if I'm lucky, finding love."

Sean nodded in agreement. "And the other people there—particularly the women—what is it you think *they* are looking for?"

"The same things, I guess."

"I think you're probably correct." Sean paused, hoping to give Tim time to recognize the apparent conclusion to the stated obvious.

"So then let me ask you this. If you were in the market for, let's say a cow, would you go to the movie theater?" Sean knew Tim was smart and knew also if they could get the salient points behind them, they could make faster progress toward finding a solution to Tim's anguish.

Tim's face first showed disillusionment, but it quickly turned to the beginning of hope as he realized the point Sean was trying to make.

Sean smiled. "Tell me what you're thinking."

"If I want a good relationship, I need to be looking where there are people who want the same thing."

Sean's eyes sparkled, and a smile of satisfaction accompanied his nodding head. *Now we can get somewhere!* he thought.

"So where are those places?" Tim asked with outspread hands. "And don't tell me church." Tim was shaking his head fervently. "I don't go to church."

Sean's smile faded. He sighed as he realized this conversation might need to last many hours.

"Okay. I won't. After all, Jenny and I met in a diner." Sean looked at the painting of the girl at the canyon (he and Jenny had bought it on their second weekend together) as he thought about what he would say next. "I'm not saying that nice women don't go to bars and gyms. But I *am* saying that their objective for *that* evening—and perhaps their lifestyle in general at *that particular time* in their lives—*might* not be to find a long-term relationship."

He studied Tim's face to see if he seemed to understand. He continued, using his hands to emphasize his words. "Even if marriage *is* an ultimate goal for them, the mere fact that they are *at* a bar on *that* night means you aren't catching them in the right mindset. And I don't think that many are able to make the switch from looking for a hookup to deciding on a husband in such a short amount of time."

Tim was nodding in understanding. "So—where?" he asked with a look of concern.

Sean shrugged. "What kind of things do you enjoy, Tim? What do you do in your spare time?"

"I don't know. I play video games, I like sports, I golf—typical guy stuff."

Woo, boy! Sean surmised to himself. *This is going to take some work!* "Do you think *you* are ready to settle into a longer-term relationship?" Sean asked matter-of-factly.

"Well, that's why I'm here. I told you," Tim shrugged. "That's what I want."

Jenny had walked over from the kitchen and stood at a polite distance at the edge of the living room. "Excuse me, guys. I wanted to let you know supper is ready whenever you are."

"*Excellent* timing, my love!" Sean stood. "I'm starved! How about you, Tim?"

Tim tilted his head to the side, wrinkled his face, and shrugged his shoulders. "No offense, but I'm not particularly hungry."

Sean motioned for Tim to come with him toward the kitchen. "You simply *must* try Jenny's new chicken dish. What is it again, my love?"

"Chicken piccata. I'm serving it over buttered egg noodles with steamed broccoli and roasted sweet potatoes."

Tim chuckled nervously. "Okay. That sounds too good to pass up!" he admitted.

"I'll get Elise," Jenny said over her shoulder as she walked toward the hallway to the bedrooms.

Soon the four of them were seated at the table, which Jenny had already set with service for four. Now over five years of age, Elise was able to feed herself quite well and no longer needed a high chair. The food was on serving platters, and Jenny had made a glass of ice water for each of the adults and poured a cup of milk for Elise. A pitcher for refills sat on the counter nearby.

"This looks *delicious*, my love!" Sean smiled at Jenny.

"Wow! I feel like I'm at a nice restaurant!" Tim added.

Sean looked directly at Tim and quietly stated, "Tim, we normally offer a prayer of thanks at each meal. You don't have to participate if you don't want to."

"That's fine. Thanks." While Tim was grateful for Sean's trying to make him feel at ease, he still felt a little awkward.

Jenny held Sean's hand, and he held Elise's. "Dearest Heavenly Father, we are grateful for this beautiful day, and thankful for the delicious food you have provided us, as well as the talented hands that prepared it. We pray that our home will always welcome those in need and that you will guide us in offering hope to those in despair.

We pray, too, for continued health and happiness in our family. In Jesus' name we pray, Amen."

Sean smiled first at his wife and then his daughter, then he stood to serve their plates. He reached for Jenny's dish first as he told her, "Go ahead and eat. I'll cut Elise's food." He next served Tim and finally Elise. After cutting her food, he made sure it had cooled enough so as to not burn her mouth then placed her plate in front of her.

"Thank you, Daddy."

"You're welcome, sweetheart. Be sure to let Mommy know how much you appreciate her cooking this delicious food for us!"

"I will! I want to taste it first!"

Sean served his own plate then sat to enjoy it.

"Thank you, Mommy. I like this chicken. Will you make it again for us?"

"Certainly! I'm glad you like it!"

Tim echoed Elise's sentiments. "This is *really* good! I've never had it before, but I hope to again some time!"

It was Sean's turn. "This is *excellent*. How did you learn of this recipe?" He looked at Jenny with great admiration.

"I was looking through the Italian cookbook that I ordered. It seemed to be a perfect dish to serve on a warm spring evening."

They continued to eat, making small talk between bites. Sean kept an eye on Elise in case she needed any help.

Feeling slightly embarrassed, Tim cautiously asked, "I know I said I wasn't very hungry, but I guess good cooking can bring on an appetite! May I get some more, please?"

"Sure!" Jenny encouraged. "Help yourself!"

Tim was glad that Jenny had said that last part. He had been taken aback at Sean's serving everyone's plates as he had never witnessed that before. He scooped himself a little bit more from each of the dishes.

Elise had nearly cleaned her plate. She drank the last of her milk then asked if she could be excused.

"Here, let me wipe your mouth." Sean used his napkin to wipe her little rosebud lips. "Go wash your hands and then you can play for a little while longer before your bath."

Elise climbed from her chair and skipped off to her bedroom.

Sean looked to Jenny who, with a small hand motion, indicated she was finished.

"I guess you will have yummy leftovers for lunch tomorrow," Sean said as he beamed at his lovely wife.

Jenny offered, "Why don't I take care of the dishes while you guys go back to the living room?"

Sean hated to leave her alone to both cook and clean up afterward, but he understood her question to mean that he should take care of his guest and that she would be fine. He was also glad he had spent time earlier in the evening with Elise because with Tim there, he probably wouldn't be able to help bathe her, say her prayers with her, or tuck her into bed. He made a mental note to do something a bit special for Jenny tomorrow.

"Okay. Thank you, my love." Sean bent to give her a quick kiss on the cheek.

"Thanks again, Jenny. That was the best meal I've had in a long while!" Tim's voice was full of sincerity.

"You're quite welcome, Tim. I'm glad you enjoyed it. Now you guys go and finish your visit." She used her hand to swoosh them away.

The two men stood, pushed in their chairs, and walked back into the living room.

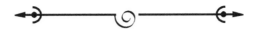

CHAPTER 6

Tim and Sean sat as they had before supper.

Tim looked at his watch and asked, "Is it getting too late for you? I can leave, and we can talk another time."

"No, no. We're fine. I'd like to try and help you." Sean, ever the problem solver, was intent on aiding Tim in resolving his relationship dilemma.

Tim reiterated the question Sean had asked before supper. "So I think you had asked me if I was ready for a long-term relationship and I said that that is what I wanted."

"Well, Tim," Sean rubbed his hand back and forth across his jaw and chin as he chose his words, "I'm wondering why, then, you are going to bars if your objective is different from that of the women who are there."

Tim waved his hands to indicate to Sean he could move on in the conversation. "I can see now that I need a different approach, and thank you, by the way. But I don't know *where* to go." Tim shrugged.

As tactfully as possible, Sean asked, "But…you also said you watch TV, you entertain yourself, you live a fairly carefree life. Am I correct?"

"Yeah. What's wrong with that?" Tim retorted.

Sean drew in his lips. Lines of concern crossed his forehead. Tim was his friend, and he didn't want to hurt his feelings. But to him, Tim needed to make some fundamental changes in *himself* before he would be ready to bring a quality woman into his life.

"If you want a woman to treat you like a king, you will need to treat her like a queen. This means you will have to be her *partner*, not *just* her spouse." Sean watched Tim's face; this was an underlying concept, and there was no need to explain more if he didn't understand it. He could see Tim's cognitive wheels turning.

Sean continued, "While it is true that there are women who will tolerate a great deal of being ignored or even treated badly, they won't be happy. They won't greet you at the door each evening with a smile, and they won't make sure you are happy to be there with them. Everything they do will be out of duty, not love."

"So are you saying I need to put on an apron?" Tim challenged.

"No. I'm not. I *am* saying that her job doesn't end after a shift of eight hours, and neither should yours. This is whether both of you work or only one of you."

Tim seemed quite uncomfortable.

"Tim, you said you wanted what I have. I'm telling you that anything worth having is worth working for, and *hard*. If having good things were easy, everyone would have them."

"I understand that," Tim said matter-of-factly.

"You don't have this great job and make lots of money because you just got by or settled for something easily obtainable. You had to learn many things—things not just everyone is willing to work at to learn—and then you had to prove your worth. The result is that your hard work landed you a better-than-average salary and greater job satisfaction."

Tim was nodding in agreement.

"You must know then that a good relationship is much the same. You must be willing to let her know that the two of you are partners. With few exceptions, there are no 'he' jobs or 'she' jobs, just tasks that need to be completed."

An idea came to Sean. "Excuse me just a moment, please."

Sean heard Jenny and Elise in the bathroom. He wanted to check on them to make sure all was well, but he also wanted to ask Jenny about his idea.

He told Elise he loved her and that he was talking to his friend but that he would check on her later that night after she had gone to sleep.

"Will you leave me your heart?" Elise asked.

Sean's face broke into a big smile. "Of course, sweetheart!" (A few months ago, while Sean was on the evening shift and got home after Elise was asleep, Jenny would tell her at bedtime that her daddy always checked on her when he got home. "How can I know he does that?" she whimpered. "Because your daddy wants to make sure you are safe. And he loves you *so* much! His heart is always with you." When Jenny shared this with Sean, he decided that he would always draw a red heart on a piece of paper and leave it on Elise's bedside table every time he checked on her after she was asleep. She liked it so much it had become a tradition.)

He kissed Jenny, thanked her for all her hard work this evening, and invited her to join him and Tim in the living room after she finished getting Elise to bed.

"No problem!" She smiled at her husband and knew from his look that she would receive extra attention later that night.

Sean walked back to the living room and told Tim that he was getting himself a glass of water; he asked if Tim would like one as well.

"Yes, thank you."

Sean returned, handed Tim his glass, and sat where he had been before. His arm was draped comfortably across the back of the couch.

"Tim, I've asked Jenny to join us in a few minutes after she gets Elise to bed. I hope you don't mind, but I feel like she can offer to you the female perspective."

"No, that's fine. It's actually a good idea."

"My father respected my mother very much. And he demanded that his two sons do the same. We were taught to say thank you to her for doing our laundry or cooking our meals. It's such a simple and easy thing to do, and it meant so much to her. Tim, people just want to be recognized. It took less than a second for us to say those two words, but it made her feel like what she did was noticed and appreciated. And *those* types of things are part of what I'm talking about."

"That makes sense. But there *has* to be more."

"There is. But it's all the same idea. Treat others the way you want to be treated. Mother never opened a door or pulled out a chair for herself her entire adult life. With a husband and two sons, she didn't have to. It was a small and simple thing we could do that subtly told of our respect for her, that showed her that we wanted to do things for her just as she did things for us."

Sean looked intently at Tim. "You noticed I served the food at supper."

Tim nodded in agreement.

"Mom cooked the food. But Dad wanted to in some way do something for her. So he took it upon himself to serve her plate. It seems corny, but it was the way I grew up. I adopted it myself because it is a way for me to *literally* serve my wife in return for her cooking. It's like...being waited on at a fine restaurant."

Tim nodded again and was happy to learn about what had seemed to him a very unfamiliar situation.

Sean continued, "Sometimes the woman does more things, sometimes the man does harder things. But if *both* are aware to help where they can and then show appreciation, I *promise* you, life gets really good."

Tim scratched the side of his head and looked very pensive.

Sean leaned forward as he spoke as if he could "push" his words into Tim's psyche. "When I am at home, even on my workdays, if I see something that needs to be done, I do it. Things like taking out the trash, sweeping the floor, doing the dishes, starting a load of laundry, cleaning the bathroom, or even shopping. And *certainly* helping with Elise. I know these are considered to be 'women's work'"—Sean made quote signs in the air—"but I don't agree with that. When I get home, Jenny has been here alone all day with Elise. I would *rather* that she spend time with Elise, loving her and teaching her, than spend time making the house look perfect. She does much of the shopping and cooking and cleaning because that makes the most sense in our situation. But there are only so many hours in a day. By my helping out, she can go from *trying* to complete that which has *no* end so as to please me to knowing that both partners do their best and leave the rest. The result is that she is much more at ease, and we can enjoy each other's company."

"But what if the woman is just sitting around watching TV and checking her phone? That's what that last girl did." Tim's face showed utter despair and confusion.

"Well, first of all, Tim, I started with a quality woman. I *know* that is not Jenny's nature. Second, I can *see* she has spent time nurturing Elise because the child is clean and fed and she is so happy and well-adjusted. Finally, absolutely as often as she is able, Jenny makes sure I have at least one home-cooked hot meal each day. She takes great care of me, Tim. The least I can do is return the favor."

"But you work, Mojo, you bring home the bacon," Tim stated as he rubbed his eyebrow.

"Yes, I do. But as I said earlier, her work doesn't end after an eight-hour shift. I work eight hours to earn money, she works eight hours doing all she can during that time to take care of managing our home life. What's left after that must be shared between us."

Jenny rounded the corner from the hallway. Sean stood. "Come join us, my love!" As she approached him, he put his arm around her in a quick hug, and then they sat together, holding hands. He turned to face her. "Is Elise all tucked in?"

"Yes. She knows you'll check on her."

"Aye. Thanks again for taking care of the entire evening. I will need to make it up to you." Sean winked at his wife.

"It's okay, it all works out in the end," Jenny stated with a gracious smile.

"Aye." Sean smiled at her, glanced at Tim, and then continued, "I was hoping you, or even we, could share with Tim some of the things we do in order to make our relationship really good."

"Of course." Jenny looked across at Tim as she began to speak but frequently turned her head to look at Sean for affirmation of what she was saying. "First of all, we early on decided that after God, *our relationship* was the *single* most important thing in our lives. Next came any children. I know that doesn't seem to mesh with how a lot of people think these days, so do you have any questions about that?" Jenny raised her eyebrows and cocked her head to the side.

Tim looked confused. "Well, yeah. I thought the kids came first."

"Children are important," Jenny continued. "But realize this. If *all* of your time, money, and attention is centered on the children, the adult relationship can wither and die. Relationships, like everything else, must be maintained. If they aren't, bad things can happen, like affairs where one or both of them are seeking the attention they crave, or constant battling over details they *should* have spent time talking about as a couple. If the marriage ends, do you think the kids are then getting the best deal?"

"No. I see your point." Now Tim was *really* confused.

Sean interjected, "It's like the directions they give you on a plane. If the oxygen mask falls from the ceiling, breathe for yourself first *then* take care of any children. If *you* aren't well, *how* can you take care of the children?"

Tim responded, "That's a good analogy."

Jenny continued, "Our wedding was officiated by a doctor I used to work for. He was a great father figure to me, and that is why we chose him. We told him he could say some things if he wanted, and he did. He said, *'Take responsibility for making the other feel safe, and give the highest priority to the tenderness, gentleness, and kindness that your union deserves.'* To emphasize her words, Jenny's hand was moving as if she were aiming a dart at each word. "He also said, *'If each of you takes responsibility for the quality of your life together and compassion for the needs of the other, your lives will be marked by abundance and delight.'* We found those words to be so important that we had a calligrapher write them on pretty paper and then we framed them. They hang in our bedroom so we can see them every day." Jenny smiled at her husband as she stated the last sentence.

She paused. "Tim, we *both* take those words *very* seriously because we know he offered them in wisdom."

Tim nodded. "I like that. The second one, especially, seems to reiterate what you both have been telling me."

"I have a friend. I feel so sorry for her. Her impression from her background and also from her husband is that *everything* in the house or with the kids is *her* responsibility. Her husband works and takes care of the yard. Once those things are completed, he thinks he's finished. He sits and watches TV endlessly. He goes golfing with his buddies almost anytime he wants, and he considers 'family time' to be everyone loading up to go watch *him* play softball with his friends. Tim, she is *worn out.* And she's miserable. She keeps on going 'for the kids,' but she doesn't even enjoy that anymore. She feels unappreciated and worthless. And what is even *worse,* despite *all* that she does, her husband complains that the house is not clean enough or that the food isn't good enough or that she's fat (she's not)." Jenny shook her head. "*When*, Tim, does she have time to exercise if, according to him, nothing is good enough and she needs to work harder? He claims she's not trying. He's always commenting about other women having a nice tan or pretty fingernails and manicured feet. *When*, Tim, can she do these things? And *what* would he say about the money being spent on herself?"

Sean added, "Honestly, I don't believe he's happy either. Despite having everything as he *thinks* he wants it, if he were happy, he wouldn't be complaining so much. And unhappy people just love to share all their displeasure with others and take it out on those close to them."

Jenny continued, "I have another friend. Her husband began having affairs even before they got married. Every time she learns of a new mistress, he buys her something. She drives a really nice car, they have a beautiful home, and she is dripping with jewelry. The gifts are given out of guilt, not love, and she knows it. But she stays for the material things. Her heart has stopped aching, and now she has affairs too. I can't imagine the coldness of their hearts."

"So, Jenny," Sean interjected, "perhaps it would help Tim to hear what it is that I do that you like or value the *most*? And don't ask me the same question because I would have to list off about one hundred things that are all tied for first place!"

Everyone chuckled and then waited for Jenny's response.

"Well, similarly, I'm not sure I can come up with only one thing. But knowing that you recognize my efforts and appreciate them is *huge*. You *always* make me feel good with a hug or a smile or a kind word. And you make sure I know I come first. You open doors and pull out chairs for me, you take my car to be washed and serviced, and you compliment me. And *every* day you tell me you love me, and *you look me in the eye* when you say it so that I know you mean it. In fact, you look me in the eye and give me your full attention all the time, especially if I'm talking to you. I have *never* had to compete with the TV or anyone else. You're respectful to me. I know I don't have to worry about you flirting with or even looking at other women."

Jenny turned to look Sean in the eye. Even though he didn't fully know what she was about to say, they had such a connection he knew that the mere fact she was consulting him meant that she was sensitive to his needs, his dignity, his very manhood. His eyes sent back to her encouragement that it was okay for her to continue.

Jenny looked directly at Tim. "Even when we are alone in our bedroom, he looks at *me—in my eyes*—not my body parts. I feel *so* respected. And I know he loves *me* and not just my body or the act itself."

Sean added sheepishly, "Once things get going, it's a bit different." Everyone grinned.

Then, more poignantly, Sean added, "But I believe that if a woman *truly* knows her husband loves and respects her, she will be the best wife she can. *Both* partners will just want to be better and better for the other."

"So here is what I'm hearing. It's a lot of small things that matter, maybe even more than the big ones," Tim concluded.

"*Yes!*" Jenny and Sean replied in unison.

Sean expounded, "If you tend to the small things, the big things usually take care of themselves."

"But you still haven't told me *where* to find a good woman."

Jenny moved to the edge of her seat, indicating her intention to rise. "I'm sure you and Sean will come up with something. But first, I'd like to ask Sean what it is he most appreciates about me—even though he told me not to!" Jenny raised her shoulders, scrunched her nose, and smiled to indicate her embarrassment at having ignored his request.

Sean thought for a moment. "It's how you make me feel. When I am with you, I am ten feet tall and bulletproof. You make me a very happy man. And I want you to stay happy so you can keep making *me* happy! Like me dad said, 'Happy wife, happy life'!"

Jenny looked directly at Tim. "Does that help?"

"Yeah. Actually, it does. You two have given me a lot to think about." Tim glanced at his watch. "It's getting late. Sean, I thank you for welcoming me into your home. Jenny, the food was some of the best I ever ate. I *do* feel better though there are many more questions I have. Maybe we can get together again soon?"

"Absolutely!" Sean agreed.

The three of them stood, and Sean and Jenny walked Tim to the door. Sean shook Tim's hand, and Jenny gave him a friendly hug.

"Just call anytime! You know my schedule!" Sean called out as Tim turned to walk to his car.

Sean closed and locked the door then turned his full attention to his wife, who smiled up at him.

CHAPTER 7

Always looking for ways to keep things interesting, on the next karaoke night, Sean proposed that everyone sing songs *only* by artists whose name or band began with the letter "A." Though they thought it a bit odd, all their group agreed to the caveat.

Sean began with the Allman Brothers Band's "Melissa," but instead of singing "Me-lis-sa," twice he sang "Sweet Jen-ny." His wife glowed at him as he crooned to her.

George, eager to get started bonding with his new group of friends, followed with another Allman Brothers Band's hit titled "One Way Out." (For the unfamiliar reader, this song is about a man caught upstairs with another man's wife, and climbing out the window is the only way out if he doesn't want a confrontation.)

One of the wives sang Adele's "Rolling in the Deep." She had never before taken the stage, so everyone was shocked at her *fantastic* rendition of this highly favored song. The entire crowd stood and cheered for a long while. It was several minutes before anyone was brave enough to follow her act.

Finally, Tim broke the silence with America's "Horse with No Name." He brought his own guitar to the stage with which to accompany himself. Most of the crowd was well-familiar with the lyrics, so they sang along with him. Smiles abounded with, what was for many, a walk down memory lane.

Sean, guitar in hand, approached Tim and quietly consulted with him. When he turned to face the crowd, the two of them played and sang America's "Ventura Highway" in perfect harmony.

George, not to be outdone, asked Sean to accompany him with the Allman Brothers Band's "Ramblin' Man."

Someone who was not of their group performed Bryan Adams' "Summer of '69." A rookie patrolman quickly trailered with "Run to You" (also by Bryan Adams).

The evening continued, with songs by Ambrosia, Aerosmith, Atlanta Rhythm Section, and others. Some were *really* good, others were, well, less than that.

After Sean and George finished "Ramblin' Man," Sean asked George if they could go to a quieter area and talk. He caught Jenny's eye and pointed to the table in the corner where he and George were going to sit. Sean thought that since Jenny was having fun with the other wives at their own table, it would be a good time to get to know George a little better, especially since he was trying to get a job at APD.

George took the initiative and asked Sean where he was from; upon learning the answer, he asked him how he had ended up in New Mexico.

Sean patiently answered George's questions. Then he asked George about where he had been born and his work in Florida. He noticed that George became quite tense and was evasive in his answers. He quickly directed a question back at Sean. "What is life like in Scotland?"

Again, Sean, in his easygoing manner, was informative. But he wanted to know more about this man who *might* not be what he was initially perceived as. "Did both your parents work?"

"Nah. My mom was sick a lot and didn't have steady work. I don't know where my old man was. How 'bout you?"

Sean told him about his parents, going to church, and his playing in a garage band as a teen. "Did you have brothers or sisters?" Sean asked.

"Naw, it was just me. I didn't have it easy like you with two parents who cared about me." Sean could sense the disdain in his voice. "My mom just wasn't cut out for motherhood, I guess." George's lower jaw jutted out as he turned his head to the side.

Sean pressed on. "How did she manage to keep food in the house?"

Quite unintentionally, George glared at him *just* long enough for Sean to notice, then he caught himself and quickly smiled. "I'm not really sure. Maybe she got food stamps...who knows?" He knew his answer about siblings had been rough and that Sean had him on the ropes. He needed to circle back to easy answers he was more familiar with and do a bit of damage control. He looked directly at Sean. "That's part of why I wanted to become a police officer. I wanted something better for myself. I wanted to be respectable and to help people. So as soon as I turned nineteen, I turned in my application."

Something about George's answers didn't *quite* ring true, but without evidence to the contrary, Sean wanted to give him the benefit of the doubt. "Did you live with her while you were waiting to submit your application? How did you support yourself?"

"I flipped burgers, worked at the car wash, sold plasma...whatever I could find." He laughed. "They loved me at the Red Cross because I was 'O negative' which, you probably know, is the universal donor."

"Well, it's good that you were able to achieve your dreams. I wish you the best of luck at getting hired on here. But for now, I had better get my wife and then go get our daughter from the babysitter."

George stood with Sean and extended his hand to him. They each smiled and nodded to the other.

Sean decided not to pass judgment on George, given that he had no hard facts to consider.

George hoped that he had recovered quickly enough from his derisive answers that Sean wouldn't get too inquisitive and try to check up on him. "Nothin' I can do about it now," he mumbled under his breath.

*****

Sean pulled up to the babysitter's house; she and her family attended church with the Wallachs. He put Jenny's SUV in park and said, "I'll be right back!"

Once inside, he drew cash from his wallet, paid the lass, and picked up his sleeping daughter from the couch. Since their neighborhood was very quiet and they only lived two blocks from the babysitter, he put Elise in Jenny's arms.

At home, Sean took his daughter from Jenny and carried her to her bed. He pulled the sheet up to her shoulders then stood for a moment in awe of the beauty of a sleeping child. As always, he drew a heart and left it on her nightstand.

In his own bed, Sean's sweet Jenny asked about his song to her. "Who is Melissa and why did they write a song about her?" she taunted.

"She is his only love as you are mine," he said as he moved to her.

Jenny's eyes were burning with desire for her man. "Prove it."

"As you wish, my lady."

CHAPTER 8

On a beautiful late April morning, Sean awoke thinking of Joe and Lucy at the diner in Mosquero. After a light breakfast, he asked Jenny if she would be interested in driving over there for a nice lunch. She agreed and quickly got herself and Elise ready for the day trip.

The drive to the diner took about three hours. As they pulled into the parking lot, Jenny recognized the car that she and Sean had sold to Lucy (one of the waitresses there) and her mom. The mother, Peggy, had five children, and Lucy had been forced to quit school to babysit her four younger siblings while her mother worked. They both had been walking to and from their jobs in all kinds of weather and at all times of the day. Because Sean had given Jenny a new SUV for their first Christmas together, they decided to sell her old car to Peggy for $250 (even though it had a value of about $2,500). They also anonymously sent cash to them in the mail each month to help out with groceries.

"Look! Lucy is here!" Jenny exclaimed. "It'll be good to see her and catch up on how things are for them!"

Sean smiled. Lucy and Jenny had spoken on the phone occasionally, so he knew Lucy had been able to enroll in an online program so she could finish high school. He had spoken to her brother, Jessie, several times, offering him advice and encouragement. As an incentive, Sean told Jessie he would take him on a flight in a helicopter once he graduated from high school.

Sean offered his hand to Jenny as she stepped out of his truck and then removed Elise from her car seat. He held the door open at the diner as his wife stepped inside and followed behind her to the table in the corner where they had shared their first conversation.

The aromas wafting from the kitchen confirmed their remembrance of the delicious food served there.

Lucy's face immediately lit up when she saw them. She quickly finished delivering an order to one of the tables and then rushed to speak to them. Sean deposited Elise in a chair, seated Jenny, then sat across from them.

"Hi!" Lucy smiled enthusiastically. "It has been too long since I saw you! How are things?"

"Great!" Jenny replied with a smile while making sure that Elise was comfortable and sitting quietly. "We just decided to drive over for a bowl of Joe's green chili stew. I'm *so* glad you're working so we could see you!"

As she and Lucy visited and interacted with Elise, Sean noticed that Lucy did not look so tired and sad and that she had also put on some much-needed weight.

"Were you able to finish school?" he asked.

"*Yes!* I finished just last month! And Jessie is going to graduate in a couple of weeks!" It was rewarding to see her quick and easy smile.

Sean and Jenny both grinned with delight and responded positively to the good news.

"I checked with Joe on the way over here. We have plenty of green chili stew. Is that what you both want, or would you like something else?"

Sean and Jenny both noticed that Lucy had also gained a new measure of confidence. They were thrilled in the changes they were seeing in the once shy, thin, exhausted girl.

Sean sought Jenny's eyes then told Lucy that yes, they would both be enjoying their usual today.

"Two Cokes?" Lucy asked.

"Absolutely!" Sean replied. "Elise will have a kid's cheeseburger and fries." He turned to look at the apple of his eye. "Elise, would you like a small strawberry milkshake with your meal?" She nodded excitedly. Sean looked back to Lucy, and she indicated that she had written the order on her pad. Sean continued, "And if you get a free moment, come let us know about the rest of your family."

"Sure thing!"

In a few moments, Joe delivered two bowls of his steaming specialty. Sean stood to shake his hand, and Jenny offered hers as well.

"Joe! It's so good to see you! How's business?" Sean inquired.

"Things are good. Once in a while, someone will come in and tell me you recommended my stew. I guess you know a lotta people!"

It was true; in many conversations, Sean had told of the delicious fare to be had at Joe's Diner. He had no idea people had actually taken his advice.

"Well, I'll let you and your family eat. Still wearin' that kilt?" Joe asked in his gruff voice.

"Oh, absolutely." Sean leaned toward Joe as if he were going to divulge a great secret. "My wife loves it!"

Joe reared his head back and laughed with gusto. "Well, I'd better get back to my grill. I've got a fresh-made pecan pie, ready for cuttin' if you want some later!"

Sean smiled at Joe. "Mmmm. We may have to do that!"

Lucy arrived with their drinks and Elise's plate of food. "Thanks, Joe," she told her boss. "Elise, I'll bring your milkshake in *just* a moment."

She asked, "Is there anything else you guys want besides fry bread? Joe was getting some ready before he brought your stew over."

"I think we're fine," Sean smiled up at Lucy.

The little family hungrily indulged themselves with Joe's famous fare. Lucy dropped off Elise's milkshake and a plate of fry bread on her way to deliver drinks to another table.

Once she had taken care of the other guests, Lucy came back to the Wallach's table.

"I may not have very long, but I wanna let you know that my mom got a promotion at work and a raise too. My little brother and sisters are doing well in school. And we *might* be moving soon to a better house." Lucy saw a customer motion for her. "I need to go, but I'll talk to you again before you leave."

"Super!" Sean smiled.

"I am *so* happy for her and her family!" Jenny told Sean.

"Yes. Sometimes people just need a leg up in this world. I feel great joy about selling them that car at an affordable price and sending that money each month." Sean was well-aware that acts of charity provided more to the giver than to the receiver. "Elise, how is your food, honey?"

"It's delicious!" She was so cute with her hair up in pigtails; a bit of ketchup was on her cheek. Jenny noticed and wiped it off.

Just as they finished their stew, Lucy arrived with a piece of pecan pie and two forks. Sean looked over to Joe who was grinning at him. Sean gave him a thumbs-up and a smile of thanks.

"On the house!" Lucy smiled then hurried away to greet three customers who had just entered the diner.

Sean nodded at Jenny. "I'm really happy we came here today. This has been nice!"

They both cut bites from the pie and were quite audible in their approval. "We need to get his recipe!" noted Jenny.

The couple finished the pie, took a last sip of their drinks, and rose to walk to the cash register to pay their tab. Sean reached into his wallet and left a twenty-dollar bill at the table for Lucy as Jenny wiped Elise's hands and then picked her up.

As he paid, Lucy told them that her mom wanted to talk to Sean and that she had a new phone number. She wrote it on the back of their receipt.

"I think she wants to talk to you about Jessie." Lucy paused as she counted Sean's change. "You know, things are really going so much better for us than they were. We think that you guys kinda gave us a jump start." Lucy smiled sweetly at Sean and Jenny.

"Everyone, at some point, needs a little help," Sean assured her. "It was *truly* our pleasure." Jenny and Sean looked at each other and smiled with great satisfaction. Sean reached for Elise so Jenny could put the receipt in her purse.

Lucy gave the Wallachs a final smile. "I've gotta go, but it was *really* great seeing you. I hope you come back again. And maybe I can come to Albuquerque some time!"

"Give us a call if you do! We'd love to have you over for lunch or dinner!" Jenny told her.

The two women hugged each other as Sean walked over to Joe and handed him a twenty-dollar bill. As was his way, Joe tried to refuse it, but Sean was insistent.

"I want you to still be in business next time I come over here!" Sean grinned at him.

"Well, thank ya." Joe nodded, his solemn eyes showing great appreciation. He lightly pinched Elise's cheek, and she grinned back at him.

Jenny joined Sean and told Joe how delicious their meal had been. "As always!" She smiled.

"You kids be safe out on that highway now."

"We will!" replied Sean.

He softly placed his hand on Jenny's lower back to guide her toward the door. Sean opened Jenny's door to the truck then put Elise in her car seat. They settled themselves in and began the three-hour drive back home.

Once there, the family took a long walk through the neighborhood, smiling and waving at neighbors who were in their yards. They even stopped and talked to a few of them.

Later that night, after Elise had been put to bed, Sean put some nice slow-dance tunes on the stereo. He and Jenny held each other in the dimly lit living room while swaying to the music and gazing at each other. Jenny rested her head on Sean's chest and breathed him in. He then slowly maneuvered them down the hallway to their bedroom, where the dance changed significantly.

CHAPTER 9

On his next day off, Sean called Jessie's mom, Peggy. She wanted to know if he really meant what he had said about giving Jessie a helicopter ride when he graduated.

"Oh, absolutely!" Sean grinned.

"Okay. I'm glad you were serious because Jessie has been talking about it *a lot* recently. He really admires you."

"Well, *thank you!* Jessie is a great lad, full of promise." Sean then lowered his volume and changed his tone to a more serious one. "I have great respect for you, Peggy. I know it must have been difficult for you with five kids and no husband, yet you have done a wonderful job raising your children to be courteous, respectful, and hardworking. I believe that at this point, if Jessie receives the proper inspiration, motivation, and direction, he will be able to do great things."

"Thanks, Sean. I've tried to do my best, but the struggle is *very* real."

"Everyone knows you have. When I have visited with your children, they each speak very highly of you. Kids know when they are loved and cared for, even if it's not all caviar and lobster!"

Both of them chuckled. An uneasy moment followed as Peggy began her next question. "Sean, I don't really know how to ask this, but...um...I really don't have the time or money to get Jessie to you, and I *hate* to have to ask you to come get him." She was near tears.

"No problem, Peggy! Would you be willing to let me get creative with a solution?"

"Sure!"

"Then let me look into a couple of ideas. I'll get back with you in the next day or so and let you know what I've learned."

"Well, I know you will come up with something incredible!"

*****

Sean found his wife sitting in her wicker rocking chair on the small porch outside their bedroom, reading a collection of short stories she had recently purchased. It was a beautiful day, so she and Elise had decided to enjoy the fresh air. Elise was practicing her writing skills on a tablet.

"How are my two beautiful ladies on this lovely morning?"

Jenny looked up at her husband and smiled. "We are fantastic! How was your call with Peggy?"

"It went well. Jessie has been talking about the flight I promised him, and she wanted to check with me."

"Daddy, look at my numbers and letters!" Elise stood and held up her tablet for Sean to see.

"Those are *really* good, Elise! I can see you have been working very diligently on them!" (Sean and Jenny had long ago decided to use their full vocabulary with Elise; she could—and did—ask questions about words she didn't understand.)

Elise brushed her hair back from her face and asked, "Do you want to see me write my name?"

"Absolutely! Can you write both your first *and* last names?"

Elise quickly sat on the patterned rug Jenny had placed there for her and began her task.

Sean continued with Jenny, "Peggy was upset because she was short on time and money and couldn't get Jessie over here. I told her I would check on some things and get back with her."

"Do you have anything in mind?"

"My first thought was to fly over there and land, let him climb aboard, and fly him around over the desert and canyons. Then I could refuel before flying back. My second idea was to go get him and bring him here to our house. I could take him for a flight the next day and then take him home that day or the next. He could stay in the spare bedroom. But I wanted to check with you first."

Elise was standing nearby, patiently waiting for her parents to finish their conversation. They had been very conscientious about teaching her to not interrupt when others were talking.

Sean smiled at her and squatted beside her. "Let me see your name."

Elise confidently handed the tablet to her daddy, leaned against him, and put her little arm around his neck. "This is *so* good, Elise. I'll bet you have also been practicing your numbers."

"Uh-huh! Mommy showed me how to make my plus sign too!"

"Is that so?" He winked up at Jenny. "Can you show me two plus three?"

"Okay!" Elise grabbed the tablet, sat, and quickly began writing.

"When you finish doing that one, I'd like you to make up your *own* addition problem, okay?"

"You *got* it!" Elise looked down at her work, the tip of her tongue peeking out between her lips as she concentrated on her penmanship.

Sean looked over at Jenny, anxious to hear her thoughts.

"I think both of those are good ideas, Sean. I like the second one a little more because it would give you two a chance to spend some time together, and you could give him some counsel on plans for his future."

"Well, he's a great kid despite the hardships their family has faced. Peggy has really tried hard to be a good parent."

"He's lucky to have you. Teenage boys need a positive male mentor in their corner with them."

"Do you have any plans in the next couple of weeks?" Sean did not want Jessie's visit to interfere with anything Jenny had already scheduled.

"No, I'm open. Do you want to shoot for next week on your days off?"

"Sounds great! I'll pick up an air mattress tomorrow while I'm in town." Sean scratched the side of his neck where a mosquito had bitten him. "Do we have sheets for a twin bed?"

"No, but I'll get a set when I make my shopping run. This is exciting! When you talk to Peggy, ask her what he likes to eat, okay?"

"Sure thing. Thanks, my love!" Sean reached down and patted her on the knee. Then he turned to Elise who was standing at his side again.

"Honey, this is perfect! Read me the problem you wrote."

"It says three plus three!"

"Correct! Can you write the answers to both of those problems while I make a quick phone call?"

Elise nodded and sat to complete her assignment.

Sean called Ron, the owner of the helicopter services business for whom he piloted to make extra money. He wanted to make sure a chopper was available on the day he and Jenny had discussed. He explained his plans, and Ron verified that that flight time was available. He also told Sean that he would give him an employee discount. "Thanks, Ron. I'll see you then!"

Elise handed the tablet up to Sean then reached for her sandals nearby. "Daddy, can we go look in the garden?" she asked as she slipped into them.

"Of course, sweetheart! You can show me what you and Mommy planted!" He looked at the tablet, checked her answers, and stated, "You will be a great mathematician someday!"

*****

The day was beginning to warm, so after Elise and Sean looked at and watered the garden, they decided to go back into the house. They sat together at the piano while Jenny prepared lunch for the family. Father and daughter were working on a duet from one of the music books. She had practiced quite a bit while Sean was at work each day and had nearly perfected her part; he was so proud of her. He hugged her tight against his side, and she giggled with joy.

Jenny finished getting lunch ready and stood next to the piano as they played their song one more time. With eyes full of love, she clapped her hands and exclaimed, "Bravo!" Elise was excited. She hopped down from the piano bench, wrapped her arms around her mommy, and smiled up at her. Jenny smiled back and said, "That was so good I think we might need to have a popsicle after lunch!"

Elise's eyes widened as she happily jumped and clapped her hands. "Yea!"

The family sat to eat tuna salad in pita pockets with cool cucumber slices and halved cherry tomatoes. The sweet grapes on the side were both beautiful and delicious. And, of course, the icy popsicles brought smiles and brightly colored lips and tongues to all their faces.

As was the norm, Elise went to her room for quiet time after lunch, and Sean and Jenny quickly brought the kitchen back to order. Jenny prepped some chicken breasts and created a marinade for them. Sean called Peggy to tell her about the plans he and Jenny had made to include Jessie in their home for a couple of days.

When Sean asked Jenny's question about Jessie's food preferences, Peggy replied, "Oh, he'll eat anything! He's a teenage boy!"

Sean laughed, remembering that his parents used to feed him and his brother sandwiches before they went for supper at the homes of friends. "Well, we will do our best to fill him up!" Sean told her the day and time he planned to arrive and asked her to send him with enough clothes for a total of three days and two nights. "Thanks for letting me do this with him. I think it could have a positive influence on his future."

"No, Sean, thank *you* for taking time out of your life to take him under your wing! He's really quite fond of you."

After he ended the call, Sean found his wife in their bedroom, putting away recently laundered clothes. "How 'bout a quick little poke?" he asked her, emulating Gus from *Lonesome Dove*.

"Hmmmm. What about our ever-inquisitive daughter?"

"I'll go talk to her. Be back in a minute!"

Sean returned and assured Jenny that Elise understood her mommy and daddy were going to be in their bedroom having a quiet discussion with the door closed. She was to remain in her room and read or play quietly with her dolls, and he would come get her when they were finished.

When she looked up at him, Sean knew that Jenny would be complicit in their ruse.

CHAPTER 10

The following week on his first day off, Sean kissed Jenny and Elise goodbye after breakfast, gassed up his truck, and began the three-hour trek to Mosquero to pick up Jessie. After a short visit with the family, the two of them enjoyed a long conversation as they made the return trip to Albuquerque.

They pulled into the driveway at around three in the afternoon. Sean and Jessie found Jenny and Elise on the back porch, planting some periwinkles in several large terra-cotta planters. Jennie removed her gloves and hugged Jessie. Sean introduced him to Elise, then they walked back inside; he showed Jessie the room where he would be sleeping and could store his bag. (He had bought and pumped up the air mattress, and Jenny had bought, washed, and put new sheets on it.)

Jessie grinned. "Wow! A bed all to myself! And a bathroom too! This is *nice!*"

Sean smiled in return. He hoped that as Peggy's kids graduated from high school, they would pursue education and careers and could enjoy a bit more prosperity than they had known while in their youth. "Jenny will have supper ready around six. Are you hungry? Would you like a snack?"

Jessie *was* hungry but didn't want to ask for food. He said, "No, but thank you. I bet your wife cooks up some really good meals in that nice kitchen."

"Yes, she *does!*" Sean replied. "Let's go sit in the living room. I'll get my laptop, and we can look up some of those things we talked about in the truck."

During their drive, Sean had asked Jessie about his plans for the future. He had received good grades while in high school, so getting into college was a definite possibility. They had discussed several fields of study, among them mechanical engineering, chemistry, and hydrology.

They went online and looked at graphs that showed the differences between incomes with everything from no high school diploma all the way up to post-doctoral studies. The two of them were astounded at the discrepancy from the lowest level to the highest.

Jenny quietly entered the living room and set a small platter containing apple slices, grapes, two types of cheese, and a variety of crackers on the coffee table. She winked at Sean as he smiled up at her. (They had discussed how hungry teenage boys could get.)

Sean nonchalantly stated "Help yourself!" as he reached for a slice of cheese and a cracker.

Sure enough, Jessie reached first for one treat and then another until ultimately the platter had only two grapes and one apple slice remaining. Sean instructed him to go ahead and finish it off "so Jenny won't have to put away leftovers." (Sean ate very little because he wanted to be hungry for whatever Jenny was preparing.)

While snacking, the two of them looked at average starting salaries based on having a degree in a range of fields of study. Sean counseled, "You need to think about and find a compromise between several components before making your final decision. Salary is, of course, important. But you don't want to have a job you hate just so you can make a lot of money. Also, you need to think about geography. It might be difficult to be an oceanographer if you are living in, say Albuquerque or Denver. Think, too, about what is probably going to be necessary for the future. The need for computer programmers is not likely to go away anytime soon. Water shortages are going to be increasingly common, so any job that would facilitate alleviating that problem is going to command a good salary. Finally, it might help to think about what kind of lifestyle you'd like to have and if a specific job would help or hinder that. For example, teachers work *long* hours. If you plan to spend a great deal of time, maybe golfing, you might not want to consider that career!"

Jessie asked, "What about jobs that *don't* require a college degree, like your job?"

"I know there are a number of careers like that. Welders, auto and diesel mechanics, and machinists are some that I know of that pay quite well. Many of them have special technical schools you must attend."

"How did you decide to be a helicopter pilot?" Jessie inquired.

Sean chuckled. "My parents sent me off to college with hopes of my becoming a lawyer. I learned in the very first semester that that was *not* for me. Don't get me wrong, I had very high scores on many different tests, so intelligence was not the problem. I just didn't see myself being happy in that line of work. In fact, I realized *any* desk or indoor job was not going to hold my interest. I had always been fascinated with flying, so I worked three jobs for the next year, saved my money, and then continued to work while going to helicopter flight school. Let me tell you, I didn't get much sleep during that time! I also had to take on a bit of debt but quickly paid it off once I secured a position."

Jessie's face showed concern. "How much did it cost?"

"It was well over fifty thousand dollars. To do it now can be as much as eighty thousand." Sean didn't want to discourage Jessie, but he wanted to be realistic.

Jessie fell silent for a few moments as he contemplated all that he and Sean had discussed. *So much information! So many decisions to be made! So much cost!*

Sean sensed that Jessie could use a break, so he suggested that they walk outside and look at the garden. He also showed him the spot on the far side of the yard where he wanted to build a chicken coop so Elise could gather fresh eggs each day for the family to eat while learning the responsibilities associated with taking care of things.

"Maybe you could help me build it! I would, of course, pay you for your time."

"That would be *great!*" Jessie responded with a smile.

The two continued to walk around the property. Sean asked Jessie about his friends, if he went to church, and if there were any special girls in his life.

"Mosquero is really small. My mom really tried hard to make sure me and my brothers and sisters stayed out of trouble, so she kept a close eye on who we hung out with. I've got a couple of pretty good friends. We ran cross-country for our school, but we didn't ever win anything."

Sean looked over at Jessie. "Did you do your best?"

"We ran together all the time. I think we just didn't have that good of a coach to teach us all we needed to know."

"Sounds like you learned discipline though."

"Oh yeah. Some mornings I just wanted to stay in bed, but I didn't want to let my friends down." Jessie was walking with his hands in his pockets and his head down.

Sean elaborated, "You know, I have noticed that people who do *anything* regularly, like running or swimming, are not only more healthy in general, but they tend to be more successful in life because they understand discipline and perseverance."

"Well, at least I've got *that* going for me!" Jessie chuckled.

Sean stopped walking. Jessie stopped as well and raised his head to look at Sean.

"Jessie, you have a *lot* going for you. You just don't recognize it. You are well-mannered and courteous, you are smart, you've got discipline, *and* you've got your *whole* life in front of you." Sean was looking directly at Jessie, squinting his eyes and nodding his head for emphasis, almost as if he were trying to drive the words into the young man's brain.

Jessie smiled shyly and looked down at the ground.

"Jessie, look at me." He did. "Confidence is one of the most difficult traits to master. It seems as if the world is always against you. And unfortunately for some, confidence often morphs into its very negative cousin, arrogance." Jessie nodded in agreement. "There's a reason I asked about church." Sean paused for Jessie's mind to catch up and perhaps make some kind of connection. The look on the young man's face let Sean know that that hadn't happened.

"I am guessing that with your dear mother's busy work schedule and all the demands on her for raising five children by herself, you did not go to church very often."

"No, we didn't. One of my buddies and his family came and got me several times during our senior year, but that was about it."

Sean glanced at his watch. It was almost five forty-five. "Let's go back inside and wash up and cool off before supper. I probably should see if Jenny needs any help."

"Okay."

The two of them walked inside and each went to his own bathroom. They both exited into the hallway at about the same time. Sean invited Jessie to sit in the living room and continue to explore on the computer or watch TV while he checked on his wife.

Sean eased up beside his sweetheart, wrapped his arm around her torso, and smiled down at her.

"Well, hello, husband! How are things going?"

"Quite well, I think. We've covered a lot of topics. How are *you* doing?"

"I've almost got everything ready. Would you mind checking on Elise, or would you rather set the table?"

"I'll do *both!*" He grinned confidently as he reached into the cabinet for plates.

"*Mmmm.* That's why I married you—for your multiple talents! Well, that and your kilt!" She smiled over at Sean who was basking in her verbal attention to him as he placed the plates on the table.

He sidled up to her and kissed her behind her ear while whispering, "I'm going to rock your world later tonight." As he opened the drawer to gather utensils, he winked at Jenny then set silverware at each place on the table. That completed, he walked to Elise's bedroom to check on her.

"Hello, sweet girl! What have you been up to this afternoon?"

"Mommy got me these beads and strings, and she showed me how to make jewelry with them. I'm making a necklace and a bracelet! Mommy will have to help me with the last part to make the knots."

"Let me see that!" Sean reached out to touch that on which his daughter had been furtively working. "This is really pretty, Elise! I like how you have a pattern going here!"

Elise smiled up at her father. "I can make one for you *too*, Daddy!"

"I will wear it with pride!" Sean smiled at his charming child. "Mommy has supper almost ready. Find a good place to stop then wash your hands and come join us in the kitchen, okay? Remember, Jessie is here and will be staying with us for a couple of days."

"Okay, Daddy. I'm almost finished with this one. I'll come to the kitchen in a few minutes."

"Super! I love you, Elise." Sean paused a moment at the door to smile at the second girl to win his heart.

"Love you too, Daddy!" she returned without raising her head. Her little fingers were working furiously, picking up and stringing the beads.

Back in the kitchen, Jenny asked Sean to set trivets on the table. He then used the hot pads to remove the casserole from the oven and place it on the trivets. He sniffed the aroma rising from the dish. "Mmmm! I can't *wait* for whatever this is!"

"It's shepherd's pie! I usually make it in a pie shell, but this time I decided to do it more like a casserole. I also melted a little cheddar on the top." Jenny was slicing a loaf of fresh French bread as she spoke. Then she arranged the slices in a basket with a fresh cloth resting in the bottom. She folded the edges over the top and handed it across the counter to Sean so he could place it on the table. "I'll get the salad out, and we will be ready!" She had added pepitas, Craisins, and walnuts to some crisp romaine then sprinkled it with a lemon and thyme vinaigrette she had quickly made using a lemon from their tree in the backyard and thyme from their garden.

Right on time, Elise emerged from her room, and Sean told Jessie to "come and get it!" Everyone took their seats, and Sean quietly told Jessie that they would have a quick prayer. They all bowed their heads.

"Our dear Heavenly Father, we are grateful this day for the bounty with which you have provided us, for our health, and for our safety as Jessie and I traveled today. We pray that in the next few days, Jessie can zero in on a plan for his future and that he will receive good advice from all those whom he contacts. We know that you have a plan for all of us, Heavenly Father, and we pray that we are able to hear the Spirit whisper softly to us. We give these thanks and ask for these blessings in the name of thy Son, Jesus Christ, Amen."

Jessie felt an odd mixture of pride and embarrassment. No one had ever prayed specifically for him like that. But he admired Sean and decided that the prayer was surely a good thing.

The food was delicious, as always, and Sean complimented Jenny with gusto for her talents in the kitchen. Jessie was encouraged to eat until he was stuffed; a warm meal, especially one with meat, was not common in his mother's house.

As everyone began to finish, Jenny announced, "I made dessert!"

Sean and Jessie looked at each other, raised their eyebrows, and smiled in anticipation, while at the same time wondering where they were going to put a plate of dessert in their already stuffed bellies.

"My love, you should have forewarned us! We are already so full we can hardly move!"

"We can have it a little later if you'd like," she suggested.

Again, the two fellows looked at each other. Sean knew Jessie was far too shy to state his choice, so he suggested, "Why don't we clean up the kitchen, watch a rerun or two, then enjoy your treat?"

"Okay!" Jenny agreed.

Jessie followed Sean's lead and helped to carry the dishes from the table to the sink where Jenny had begun rinsing them off and loading them in the dishwasher. Sean dampened a clean cloth and handed it to Elise. "Sweetie, would you please wipe the table?"

"Yes, sir!" She was a happy child and always willing to help. Sean and Jenny liked to think it was because she knew she was loved, they had regular routines, and they had the expectation that everyone helped out according to their ability. Smiles were always the order of the day, and anyone with a frown was encouraged to share their situation through honest conversation and was offered empathy and wise suggestions designed to help restore balance.

The four of them settled onto the sofas and watched two episodes of a favorite sitcom, then Jenny arose to retrieve the homemade dessert from the refrigerator. It was a lemon icebox pie with raspberries on top for decoration and texture. She cut four slices, put them on small plates, and called everyone to the table for their treat.

After dessert, Jenny went with Elise to her room for her bath. She was increasingly encouraging Elise to bathe herself as much as was possible, though Jenny still washed her hair for her. Once finished, she dressed in her favorite gown with pink flowers and a little bow at the neck, and Jenny stepped to the doorway and asked Sean if he wanted to read the bedtime story.

Sean told Jessie he could continue watching TV and that he would be back soon. Then he walked into Elise's bedroom, sat in the comfortable and familiar rocker, and waited as Elise chose a book.

Jenny told them that she would take care of clearing the dessert dishes during story time but that she would be back in time for prayers and hugs.

True to her word and with exquisite timing, Jenny returned to join her husband and daughter for nighttime prayers. Sean had been encouraging Elise to say a small prayer each night, then he followed with a more substantial one. Everyone shared hugs and kisses, then Jenny turned off the light, and she and Sean stepped into the hallway as they closed the door to their precious daughter's room.

Sean reached for Jenny's hand and nodded with his head, indicating he'd like her to join him in the living room with Jessie.

"Let me go to the bathroom real quick first!"

Sean sat on the couch opposite Jessie and smiled at him. "Jenny is going to join us here in a moment. We'd like to visit with you some more if you are not too tired."

"No, I'm fine! Sometimes I stay up pretty late."

Jenny took a seat beside her husband and he began, "Jessie, when we were outside, I asked you about church." Jessie nodded his head.

"I'd like to share a few things then maybe ask you a question or two. Would that be all right? I don't want to embarrass you or put you on the spot."

"That's fine. I'm okay."

"When I met Jenny, she, like you, had seldom been to church." He glanced over at his wife, who was nodding in agreement. "I, on the other hand, had attended all my life, even during my teenage years. Quite honestly, I don't know how I would have survived life if it had not been for that. I wasn't a *bad* teenager. I didn't get involved with drugs or other illegal activities, but I was just a typical little rebel, and I questioned *everything*. I wanted to try things that were not normal, like skydiving and scuba diving. I even have a fourth-degree black belt in tae kwon do. I played drums, guitar, and keyboards for a little garage rock band. I stopped doing things that I knew were good for me spiritually, like reading scriptures and praying and practicing charity and forgiveness. But in the end, I returned to the truths I knew all along."

He had been watching Jessie, who seemed comfortable so far. He took a deep breath and continued, "We spoke earlier about confidence. For me, knowing some things that you may not yet know helped me with that. I knew *where* I came from, *where* I want to go, and *how* I will get there."

A furrow began to form in Jessie's brow.

"Let's start with the basics. Do you believe in God?"

"I guess so." Jessie shrugged.

Sean was looking directly at Jessie, not to be intimidating but to try to get him to gather his wits and focus.

For the next hour or so, Sean explained to Jessie about faith, hope, charity, and love. He told stories from the scriptures. Jenny shared her experiences as a person who had not known these things before Sean told them to her. And they did it in a way that caused Jessie to want to know more by using questions and following a logical path of thought.

Sean did not want to overburden Jessie's brain, so he stopped before he had stated all he wanted to. He told Jessie that he'd like to have him come spend some more time in Albuquerque and go to church with them. Jessie responded that he'd like that.

"We've talked about a lot of things today! I hope I haven't scared you off!" Sean said as he stood and gave Jessie a fatherly smile.

"No, you're good. I'm going to think about all of it. And I *would* like to come here again soon."

"Well, there are towels in the cabinet in your bathroom. Feel free to bathe or shower. There should be some soap and other things you might need in there as well. Did you bring something to sleep in?"

"Yes, sir."

"Okay. Well, we will see you in the morning then. Our flight is scheduled for eleven. We'll have time to get up, eat breakfast, and drive over there without feeling rushed. I hope you sleep well!"

Jenny stood. "Good night! Let us know if you need anything!"

*****

Sean was concerned. He sat on the edge of the bed with his elbows on his knees wondering if he had said enough, afraid he had said too much. "I wish I had spent more time with him the last two or three years. He needs guidance so badly."

Jenny sat beside him, rubbing his shoulders. "Sean, honey, you do so much. You work full-time at APD and fly part-time for Ron, you are the *best* husband and father on the planet, you help your friend Tim and would probably help anyone else who knocked on the door!"

She leaned forward, looked at her husband with a smile, and kissed him on the cheek. "I think you said something about rocks or maybe rock and roll later tonight?"

Sean let out a low growl as he reached for his wife.

CHAPTER 11

The next morning, Jessie could barely contain his excitement about getting to go skyward with Sean. He sat politely at the breakfast table, cleaned his plate of the three bacon, egg, and cheese tacos Jenny made for him, and had a second serving of *papas fritas.* (Sean ate two tacos and *no* potatoes; he could scarcely remember a time when he could eat like Jessie just had.)

Jenny asked Jessie if he had told any of his friends about his upcoming flight.

"Yes, ma'am. I've got two friends I hang out with. They're really jealous!" He smiled shyly at her then looked back at his plate.

Sean turned to his daughter. "Elise, today Daddy is going to go fly, and Jessie is going to go with me. One day when you get a little older, I'll take you up in a chopper too!"

Elise's eyes danced with joy at the idea of watching her daddy fly a helicopter and seeing the ground fall away from her as he took her higher and higher in the sky. (She tried to visualize this because he had talked to her about it many times when she asked questions about his work.)

When it was time for the guys to leave, Jenny handed each of them a container of water. Sean was grateful that she remembered to do this for him each day he worked. In the sky, there are no water fountains. He hugged her appreciably, and she hugged him even more so (he had, indeed, rocked her world last night).

Sean and Jessie loaded into his truck and began the drive to the helicopter flight services location where he did contract work for the owner, Ron Ensley.

As Sean parked his truck, he saw the mechanic, Pete McElroy, walking back from the craft he would be flying today. "All fueled up?" he called.

Pete was wiping his hands with a cloth as he approached Sean. "Oh yeah. I've looked her over, and she's ready to go. It's a good day for flying—high visibility and not much wind. You guys have a great flight!"

"Thanks, Pete." Sean smiled as he extended his hand.

He called Jessie over, introduced him, and then began his own preflight check, explaining everything to his young student as he went. Sean had Jessie climb in, and he followed. He instructed his charge to fasten his harness snugly. Finally, it was time to fire up the engine. They both pulled on a headset; Jessie's almost couldn't fit around his big smile. As the engine and various fluids warmed up, Sean explained some of the gauges and other instrumentation and showed Jessie how he used the stick to control the craft. When everything was ready, Sean looked over to Pete, gave him a thumbs-up, then slowly brought the skids off the ground. Jessie's eyes widened along with his smile. He leaned over toward the window to watch as the ground got further and further away. After a few minutes, his cheeks were actually hurting.

Sean had decided that he would fly over to the Rio Grande and follow it for a few miles then head north to get closer to some of the mountains. On the way back into town, he flew over and pointed out his house. Finally, he flew around Albuquerque and pointed out various major roads and buildings. When the hour was up, he made a smooth landing and went through the shut-down procedure, again explaining everything to Jessie.

The two of them disembarked. Jessie was so excited he was certain his feet were barely touching the ground. Sean went into the office and spoke with Ron, made arrangements for payment, and then together they climbed back into Sean's truck to drive to his house.

"I've decided what I want to do for a living," Jessie stated with finality.

Sean looked over at him quizzically. *Surely the lad has not gone from chemistry or hydrology to flying helicopters. What about all those good grades in science and math?* "And what might that be?"

Jessie stared straight ahead as he spoke. "I wanna fly Apache helicopters for the army."

*****

Once back at home, Sean retrieved his laptop from his bedroom and brought it into the living room. Elise had talked Jessie into watching an animated cartoon; since he had younger siblings, he interacted very well with her.

Sean researched the requirements for becoming a chopper pilot for the US army. He was shocked to learn that any recruit could request it. Boards regularly met to look at the attributes of the various candidates. Letters of recommendation were of great value, particularly those from other military personnel.

"Jessie, come look at this."

Jessie smiled at Elise then walked to the other couch and sat near Sean, who passed the laptop to him. Sean could see his eyes quickly scanning the site as he scrolled through it. A smile was growing on his face.

Suddenly, he looked over at Sean. "I can *do* this!"

"I believe you can!" Sean smiled back. "Have you and your mother ever discussed your being in the military?"

"No, sir. She doesn't usually have much time to talk about hardly anything. She works a lot."

"Would you like me to talk to her?"

"I don't know. Do you think it'll help?"

"I think if she learns that they will pay you and train you, then she might be all for it."

Jessie's eyes grew distant as he visualized himself zooming through the air in an Apache. His smile continued to grow.

Sean tapped Jessie on the arm. "Hey, if you become an Apache pilot, you'll have to give *me* a ride!"

The two of them laughed together. Sean stood, looked over at the table, and saw that Jenny had their lunches ready. (She and Elise had eaten leftover chicken soup earlier.) She had used the remaining bacon from breakfast to make BLTs and reheated the leftover *papas fritas* in the oven to crisp them.

He motioned for Jessie to follow him; they sat at the table, and Jenny brought them each a cold glass of lemonade. "Guess what Jessie has decided he wants to do?"

"What?"

"Tell her, Jessie!"

"I want to fly Apache helicopters for the army!"

"Oh my! That doesn't sound *anything* like what you guys were looking up yesterday."

"Yeah, but then I rode in a helicopter!"

"Why Apaches rather than something more civilian?"

"I don't know. They're kinda badass, I guess." Jessie blushed and looked down at his plate.

Sean interjected, "Well, I know *I'd* love to fly one, just one time! An Apache is to a civilian chopper what a Corvette is to a minivan!"

They each ate their lunches. As they finished, Sean said, "Jessie, I'd be *happy* to give you a letter of recommendation. But you need to start seeing who else you can get them from. If you spend more time here, I can introduce you to a few of the officers who served in the military."

"That would be fantastic. Thank you!"

*****

Lunch was over, the kitchen was clean, and Elise was in her room for quiet time. Jenny sat in one of the chairs in the living room, continuing to peruse the collection of short stories she had recently begun reading.

Sean and Jessie sat at the table, formulating a plan and thinking of questions to ask and to whom to ask them. Sean had given Jessie a notebook and pen with which to jot down their ideas. Jessie knew he would need to talk to his mom; he thought she would probably initially be against the idea, imagining the worst-case scenario of him being killed in combat. Sean again offered to speak with her, if necessary.

They also decided that on their way out of town tomorrow, they would stop by the recruiter's office to pick up any forms, applications, or printed information available. With each passing moment, Jessie was more firmly convinced that this was the path for him.

After a while, they retired to the living room, where Sean resurrected the conversation on religion from the previous night. He had decided that today, he would have Jessie ask questions and he and Jenny would answer them. He emphasized that he was not trying to push anything off on the young man but rather that he was trying to offer something in which he had found great comfort and power.

Jessie was more interested than Sean could have hoped for, and he asked many really good questions. In the end, Jessie was excited to attend church with Sean and his family at the next possible opportunity.

While Jenny checked on supper (she had made potato salad while the guys were gone, and now she was slow-baking some glazed ribs in the oven), Elise quietly slipped out of her room and into her daddy's lap. She smiled up at him, her eyes twinkling, and his heart melted. He was glad at that moment that she was not sixteen years old and asking for a car.

The little group decided to watch *Ghostbusters*. Elise continued to sit in Sean's lap, holding on to him during the scary parts and shaking them both with laughter during the funny parts. Sean couldn't help but notice that Jessie looked relaxed; he was quite pleased about the events they had shared and decisions they had reached during their time together.

After the movie ended, Sean moved to the kitchen to help Jenny get supper on the table. Jessie again ate until his tummy was bulging. But *this* time, they all saved room for leftover lemon pie!

*****

At the recruiting office the next day, Sean stood to the side and gave Jessie the opportunity to take charge. He was glad that they had taken the time to think of and write down questions to ask. His heart swelled with pride as he watched the lad taking legitimate steps toward becoming a man.

Once back in the truck and headed east, Sean asked Jessie if he had any girlfriends.

"There's a few I talk to, but everybody there is kinda recycled. Mom has talked to me about how I need to focus on getting *out of* Mosquero before thinking about hookin' up with anybody. Most of the girls there will have had two or three kids in the next five years and probably will get married and divorced several times over the years. Mom wants all of us to have a better life. I know she speaks from experience."

Sean was impressed that Peggy had been able to share her wisdom with Jessie in a way that he had actually internalized it. "Your mom has taught you well," he noted.

As they continued their drive, the conversation flowed easily. Jessie was grateful for Sean's guidance, and Sean was grateful that this young man was so receptive to good advice.

Once they arrived at Peggy's house, everyone ran outside to say hello. The kids were excited that their brother was home from his big adventure. Peggy knew that it had probably been a life-changing experience for her son, and her eyes teared up as she spoke with Sean.

They went inside, and everyone crowded onto the little bit of furniture in the small room. Knowing that Jessie was probably nervous about telling his mom his decision, Sean began, "I think Jessie may have something to tell you."

Jessie blushed, but, following Sean's example, he squared his shoulders and shared his plans with the family.

As expected, Peggy was against her son being in the military despite the perks. Sean quietly explained to her how many people held positions that paid rather well because of their military training. Air traffic controllers, pilots, and mechanics topped his list. "It's like going to college without having to pay tuition."

Emboldened by Sean's calm and logical explanation, Jessie attempted to drive home the point by stating, "Mom, I love and appreciate you and all you've done for all of us. One of the things you taught us was to have a desire for a better life. I can get that by doing this. And it's what I really want to do for the rest of my life."

Meanwhile, the younger children had gotten bored and scattered to other parts of the house to play. Sean, Jessie, and Peggy continued to quietly discuss Jessie's future.

Ultimately, the two men convinced Peggy. Jessie had been sitting beside her, and he reached over and hugged his mom and told her he loved her. She cried on his shoulder, but when they pulled back, she smiled at her oldest son and said, "I'm so proud of you, Jessie!"

"It's all on you, Mom. You've done your job well!"

Sean smiled at the warm scene between mother and son. He glanced at his watch, took a deep breath, and said, "Well, I guess I'd better be heading back to my little family." He stood and extended his hand; he and Jessie looked into each other's eyes as they shook on the success of their time together.

*****

Once back home, Sean asked Jenny what she thought of either giving or selling their extra couch to Peggy and her family. "We never intended to keep it long term anyway. We've just been fortunate to have the room for it while we waited for an idea of what to do with it." He went on to explain that Peggy didn't have much furniture, and what she did have was well-worn.

Jenny squinted at her husband and responded, "I think you continue to amaze me with your generous heart. I know that *we* will be the ones who benefit the most from giving it to her because the Lord wants us to love and be charitable to others. By being obedient to that, *we* will reap blessings of happiness from giving it to her, and *they* will get what is essentially a new couch to sit on!"

"I'll call her and ask if she wants it. I'll just tell her we aren't using it and would appreciate her taking it off of our hands. I'll also try to set up a time when Jessie can come back over and spend a few more days. When I go pick him up, I'll just load it in my truck and take it over to her." Then Sean hugged his wife, happy to be at home and in love.

CHAPTER 12

Sean was a man of action; as such, he called Peggy the next week. "I was wondering if I can come get Jessie again. He agreed to help me build a chicken coop."

"Sure, Sean. I think he can learn a lot from you," she replied.

"Okay. I'll come get him tomorrow. Oh! I almost forgot. Jenny and I have this extra couch just sitting around taking up space. I was wondering if you might be able to use it?"

"Oh, Sean. I'm *so* embarrassed! You have done so much for us already!"

"Peggy, it's nothing fancy. It was just something to sit on in our first duplex when we first got married. We would *really* appreciate not having to keep heating it in the winter and cooling it in the summer! Once it's gone, we will have room for a dining table. Come on now! It would really help us out a lot!"

"Okay. But let me pay at least a *little* something!"

"No way! I'm getting cheap labor from Jessie to build my chicken coop! And you really will be doing us a favor by getting it out of our hair."

"Well, I guess that's okay then. But don't pay him. We owe you."

"Peggy, it will all work out, okay?"

"All right. You are an angel here on earth."

After the call, he went to the lumberyard to purchase all the necessary supplies for building the chicken coop. At the chosen location in the backyard, he made several measurements, hammered in some stakes, and ran string around them. In that way, he and Jessie could begin building right away after they got back home.

The next morning, since the couch was inexpensive and, therefore, fairly lightweight, Sean allowed Jenny to help him load it into

the bed of his truck but only after she *insisted* that she could handle it. (She thought it was ridiculous for him to call someone to
come over and help him. "I'm not a weakling, you know!" she stated
emphatically.)

He hurried over to Mosquero. He and Jessie carried the couch
into the house, and they quickly began the trip back to Albuquerque.

Jenny made sure to have plenty of food on hand and told Jessie
to help himself with all the fruit, cheese and crackers, and brownies
he wanted. She shared that supper would be pulled-pork enchiladas
with queso sauce, charro beans, and saffron rice with vegetables.

Jessie thanked her sincerely, grabbed a banana and a brownie,
and headed into the backyard to help Sean, who was looking over the
rough blueprint he had previously drawn of the structure.

Their first task was to dig holes and set corner posts. (Sean let
Jessie do the bulk of the digging, as young men don't seem to feel as
achy the next day!) They wanted to get the poles set in the cement
so it could cure overnight. They also discussed the various tasks to be
completed the next day and the order in which they would be done
so that they wouldn't waste time.

"Perfect planning makes for pretty projects!" Sean exclaimed.

The men showered then ate Jenny's delicious supper. Afterward,
the three of them played dominoes. Elise sat in Sean's lap and paid
close attention to Sean's instructions to her about how the game was
played. She was delighted to place the dominoes as Sean chose them.
Later, he even let her choose some of the plays. If her choice was not
the best one, he would whisper to her why it wasn't and then allow
her to correct her selection.

There's nothing like hard work to bring on a good slumber in a
teenager. Weary, clean, and well-fed, Jessie fell asleep within moments
of flopping onto the air mattress.

The next morning, after a hearty breakfast of omelets, biscuits,
and fruit, the men returned to the backyard. Jenny and Elise checked
on them frequently, bringing them refreshing glasses of iced water
along with apple slices and brownies.

By lunchtime, the framing was complete. After a meal of sesa-
me-glazed chicken strips, roasted veggie skewers, and fried rice, the

men returned to the backyard to put the roof on the structure. Jessie took his shirt off and used the ladder to climb on top of the roof beams. He hammered the tin sections as Sean handed them up to him. Next came the sides, and finally, they stretched chicken wire across the front. They quickly built a door and attached it with hinges.

While the men were working, Jenny and Elise went online to choose and order some baby chicks, as well as the other supplies that would be needed. (She and Sean had previously researched and discussed what to purchase.)

Sean opened the patio door and stuck his head inside. "Why don't you two ladies come see where the chicks will live."

Elise was *very* excited that they would soon have chickens for her to feed each day. After they matured, she would be able to gather their eggs.

Jenny was impressed with the sturdiness of the structure and how cute it looked. She told Sean and Jessie that she was very amazed at how quickly they had been able to get it completed.

The men went inside to clean up. Jenny wrapped ears of corn and large russet potatoes in foil. She cooked bacon and crumbled it, grated cheese, and sliced scallions to put on the potatoes.

Sean and Jessie went back outside to light the grill while Jenny rinsed, dried, and seasoned the three large rib eye steaks (since they were so large, she and Elise would split one). As Sean cooked the food, Jenny cut a watermelon.

"You always cook such delicious food, ma'am," Jessie observed. "I really like coming here!"

"Thank you, Jessie! I enjoy cooking for people that appreciate my efforts. But I am *especially* thankful that you came and helped Sean build our chicken coop!"

"I learned a lot from Sean. Maybe one day when I get married and have kids, I can use some of that knowledge to make stuff for *my* family."

Sean was quite tired from laboring in the heat, but he grinned at Jessie's thoughts of someday having a family.

The next morning, the four of them dressed for church and drove to the meetinghouse. On their drive back from Mosquero, Sean and Jessie had talked more about religion, so Jessie was eager to attend.

The group returned home, changed clothes, and Jessie loaded his bag into Sean's truck. After lunch, Sean drove Jessie home.

On the way, Sean pulled his wallet out of his hip pocket. He removed two one-hundred-dollar bills and extended them to Jessie, who seemed confused. (Sean had calculated five hours of work on the first day and eight hours on the second day, all at a rate of fifteen dollars per hour.)

"My mom said that the work on the chicken coop was to pay for the couch."

"Okay. If that is how you and she want to look at it, that is fine with me. Just call this my contribution to your future. I had told you on your previous visit that I would pay you to help me. I could not have done it without you, Jessie. So put it deep in your pocket and save it for an emergency or to buy something you really want or need. You earned it. Your mom doesn't need to know about it." Sean waved the money toward Jessie. "Here, take it."

Jessie was embarrassed, but he reached for the two bills. "Are you *sure?* Because this is a *lot* of money."

"I've only been more sure about two things in my life, and that was to obey the Lord and to love my wife."

"Well, *thanks,*" Jessie managed. He wasn't sure which emotion was stronger, his gratefulness or his embarrassment.

"You earned it. You paid attention to my instructions, you labored diligently, and you did good work. I'm proud of you!" Sean looked at Jessie and smiled.

Jessie felt like a man.

*****

Jessie kept those two bills hidden deep in his wallet for many years, even after he achieved his goal to pilot Apache helicopters. When on furlough and visiting his mom, he always took time to travel to Sean and Jenny's house. Usually, he and Sean would drive to the mountains or the river so they could walk and talk. Sean was so proud as he considered Jessie to be his "adopted" son.

Jessie finally used the money on the day he bought a wedding ring for the woman he would ask to marry him. He, like Sean and Jenny, did not buy an expensive diamond engagement ring as Jessie and Cassandra also had a very short courtship of just five weeks.

Sean performed the ceremony—at the canyons where he and Jenny had gotten married years before.

CHAPTER 13

Sean and Jenny had for some time been considering the possibility of homeschooling Elise. They always had the luxury of tabling the discussion because there was plenty of time to make a decision. But now that Elise was nearing her sixth birthday, they felt an increasing amount of pressure to choose between public, private, and at-home schooling. (In Albuquerque, children must be *at least* five years old by 12:01 a.m. on September 1 to attend school; since her birthday was on September 16, Elise could not have attended last year even though that would probably have been their preference if using public school.) Both Sean and Jenny had asked various friends and relatives to share their thoughts on the matter, but their responses were too diverse to help. Since they both had been very involved with Elise her entire life, they were leaning toward homeschooling; whatever they were doing seemed to be working really well as Elise was clearly further along developmentally than other children her age.

While rinsing the dishes after supper, Sean broached the subject and suggested that they ask Elise what *she* preferred. Jenny shrugged with her lips but after a moment of thought stated with admiration, "You are always able to zero in on the most simple and commonsensical approach!"

"I just want what's best for my ladies!" Sean smiled and leaned to kiss his sweetheart on the cheek. She finished wrapping the leftovers and set them in the refrigerator then waited for Sean to dry his hands. They walked together into the living room.

Sean directed, "Take a seat, my love. I'll get Elise."

The three of them sat together with Elise in Sean's lap. He began, "Sweetie, you know you've reached the age when you will be starting school soon."

Elise nodded.

Sean continued, "Mommy and Daddy know that you might not have thought much about it. Has your cousin Alicia talked to you about school?"

"Yes. She likes it."

"Okay. When you go, would you like to go to a school like Alicia or stay here at home and let Mommy and Daddy teach you? And we think you need to know that because you were born shortly after September first, you will be among the oldest in your class."

Elise was being raised to be strong, brave, and independent, so Sean knew that if she chose homeschooling, it wouldn't be because she was afraid to step out into the unfamiliar.

Elise thought for a moment. (Sean loved that Elise, like her mother, always considered the question at hand and then answered honestly.) "I'd like to go to school. Alicia says it's fun."

Sean and Jenny looked at each other, raised their eyebrows, and smiled. This conversation was going quite well!

Jenny asked, "Do you have any questions or concerns?"

Elise turned her head to look up at her daddy. "Can I get a new backpack?"

"Of course, you can, sweetie," chuckled Sean. "I'll tell you what. Mommy and Daddy are going to talk more about this tonight after you go to bed, then we can all talk about it some more in the next few days. Why don't you think about it, too, okay? We still have plenty of time to decide, so it's okay to change your mind if you want to."

"Okay, Daddy!"

"Why don't you go take your bath. Mommy will check on you in a few minutes." (As she was getting older, Sean and Jenny had decided that it was no longer appropriate for him to be a part of Elise's bath-time routine.)

"Yes, sir." Elise climbed down from Sean's lap and skipped away to her room.

The two parents looked at each other. Sean was the first to speak. "Well, what do *you* think? Are you ready for her to start, regardless of *where* it happens?"

"We will have to go shopping for school clothes and supplies, but, yes, I could do it. It *will* be strange without her here though. She's been my little companion!"

Sean reached his arm around her shoulders, pulled her closer to him, and kissed her on her temple. "We can talk more tonight, but I think she's ready. And she's *so* smart. I wonder if they might consider advancing her a level at some point."

Jenny offered, "We can have Alicia come over soon for a sleepover. They can set up a tent in the backyard if they would like to. We could get them talking about school and see how she handles that."

"Good idea! You are such a wonderful mother!"

"Well," Jenny laughed, "I'm just trying to stay caught up with *you!* You're the *best* father, ever!"

During pillow talk later that evening they discussed the details of what tasks would need to be completed, who would be responsible for each one of them, and a timeline to guide all of it.

*****

A few days later while Sean was at work, Jenny and Elise drove to her sister Janice's house for a visit. Though Alicia was almost four years older than Elise, the two of them played very well together. Sometimes Adam would also play with them, but usually he liked to stay in his room and create things from the various sets of building blocks he had.

Jenny asked her sister about the possibility of Alicia spending the night with Elise on one of Sean's days off (so he could set up the tent and manage the firepit).

"I'll ask Tarak, but I'm sure it'll be fine."

Jenny explained, "We thought we might get the girls talking about school and see if Elise wanted to go to public school or have us teach her."

"That's a good idea," Janice agreed.

Once Jenny had moved to Albuquerque and was able to visit more frequently, the two sisters had grown quite close. They consulted each other on nearly everything and frequently shared recipes, coupons, and information about sales at various stores.

Jenny glanced at her phone. "Elise and I had better head on home. I need to finish up with dinner. Afterward, Sean and I are going in the backyard to work in the garden and do a bit of cleanup."

The sisters hugged. Jenny called for Elise to come from Alicia's room, and the two of them drove back home.

"Mommy?" Elise called from the back seat.

"Yes, my love?"

"I can't wait to start school!"

Jenny looked into the rearview mirror at her precious companion of the last nearly six years. A pang of sorrow struck her as she realized that she would soon have to adjust to a lonely house each day.

"We will need to go shopping for school clothes and a new backpack and all your supplies!"

"Great!" Elise smiled and looked out the window at the world whizzing by.

*****

Once Sean got home, Jenny placed the pizzas she had created earlier into the hot oven. She had roasted a variety of vegetables and sliced some leftover smoked pork tenderloin. She smeared pesto on the dough, spread the meat and vegetables all around, and placed thick slices of fresh mozzarella across the top. She had made two of them, with the intent of there being leftovers for her and Elise's lunch the next day. As was typical, they also enjoyed a fresh, crispy salad made with ingredients from their garden.

As they were enjoying the delicious creation, Jenny told Elise to share with her daddy what she had told her mommy in the car.

"I can't wait to go to school!" She smiled brightly at Sean, who was glowing with pride as he looked at his beloved daughter.

Once the meal ended and the quick cleanup was finished, the three of them donned gloves and boots, and Sean brought a rake, a hoe, and a shovel from the garage. They spent the remaining daylight hours pulling up plants that were no longer producing, pruning others, and plucking the weeds that are the bane of every gardener.

Later that night, the two lovers discussed what plants they would next add to their little vegetable patch.

*****

Now that the decision about school had been made, Jenny and Janice were in frequent contact with each other about school clothes and supplies. They took turns going to stores that were having sales and bought supplies for both girls. If one of them found a cute item of clothing or a good buy, she took a picture and texted the other to see if she wanted it also. By the time the schools were ready to open their doors, the girls were ready to enter them.

And Elise had a new backpack.

CHAPTER 14

It was karaoke night. Some of the attendees had begun bringing various games to play while they listened to the music—backgammon, checkers, sets of dominoes, and decks of cards. They decided that the loser of a game would have to sing a song of the victor's choice, which was almost always difficult or embarrassing to perform. The group laughed raucously as the performer good-naturedly struggled through the ordeal.

On a sultry June evening, Sean (aka Mojo) very atypically lost in a first-to-five-points game of backgammon. The winner, a rookie police officer who had repeatedly lost to Sean in previous attempts, went full throttle in his choice of songs—"Emotional Rescue" by the Rolling Stones. Always willing to "put it out there," Sean pranced around on the stage like Mick Jagger as he belted out the falsetto strands of the tune. Once finished, he breathlessly bowed as the crowd—who were also breathless from laughing—gave him a standing ovation. A few of the patrons suggested that he assume the new moniker of "Mick."

A couple of weeks later, someone proposed a "winner-take-all" three-round tournament of first-to-five backgammon in which each competitor paid ten dollars to participate. Eight players quickly ponied up the fee and wrote their names on the bracket lines. As this was one of his favorite games—and he was normally quite adept at it—Sean was one of them.

During the first round, four pairs of players sat at different tables, rolling dice and moving their checkers around the board; four victors quickly emerged, among them Sean. By the second round, the trash talk had begun. Sean remained quiet, choosing instead to intimidate his opponent by playing rapidly and often aggressively then staring coolly at him as he contemplated various move options. Sean's countenance bore his confidence, and the slight grin that accompanied it was unnerving for the other player. Sean won easily, five to nothing.

The final round was between Sean and the rookie patrolman who had recently beaten him. The crowd gathered around the table to watch. Once again, Sean silently stared down his rival, who occasionally glanced up at him nervously. Sean doubled and went on to win the first game, earning two points; the rookie won the next, earning a single point. In the next game, the rookie doubled, and Sean immediately redoubled. Playing without compromise, Sean kept the rookie on the defensive and was able to gammon, thus receiving twice the value on the doubling cube or eight points. Sean, therefore, won, ten to one.

The money was awarded to Sean, who immediately found a waitress and ordered several baskets of various appetizers for all the participants and observers to share. He also gave the overworked lass a very generous tip.

*****

It was Sean's day off, and Jenny had several errands to run and a good bit of shopping to do. To make things easier on his sweet wife, Sean volunteered to take Elise to the park so that Jenny wouldn't have to put her in and then take her out of the car seat so many times in the scorching heat. This would save her time and energy, and Sean would get to have "Daddy time" with his darling daughter. They agreed to meet for lunch at a sandwich shop owned by one of their friends from church. (And, even better, they also served ice cream!) Sean and Elise then went to the post office to pick up their delivery of baby chickens while Jenny finished up with her shopping. Once she returned home, Sean unloaded her SUV while Jenny deposited all the various items in their proper places—but not until after Elise dragged her out to see the baby chicks that she and her daddy had gently placed in their new home.

Jenny always involved Elise when putting away groceries as it was an excellent time to work on math and other skills. "How many cans of tuna did Mommy buy?" or "We had three cans of soup, and Mommy bought two more, how many do we have now?" She also taught her how to put the newer items in the back so that the older items could be used first, how to face the labels to the front so they could easily see what was in the pantry, and how to put like things together. On this day, Sean stood nearby, smiling and watching his two ladies. The day-in and day-out work Jenny did with Elise was invaluable and had far-reaching benefits. His heart swelled with pride for his little family.

Elise's sixth birthday was approaching, and Sean and Jenny needed to discuss her party and a few upcoming changes. So after a morning of playing at the park, an afternoon of helping Mom, and an early bath and supper, the three of them snuggled together on the couch and watched *Frozen*, Elise's favorite. Sean and Jenny put their pooped daughter to bed then sat together at the table to make plans for Elise's party.

Jenny proposed a *Frozen* theme for the decorations. With Elise's "help," she would prepare chocolate cupcakes with snowy white frosting and lots of sprinkles. Many small individual pizza crusts would be made ahead of time. On the day of the party, one would be provided to each attendee; a variety of toppings would be available. Once each person had finished creating his or her pizza, Sean would quickly bake them on his gas grill in the backyard. They would also make old-fashioned ice cream so the kids could watch. Sean agreed with all her ideas and thanked Jenny for all the thought she had put into having a nice birthday party for Elise.

"What are you thinking about for a birthday gift?" Sean asked.

"What about a little bicycle with training wheels?"

"I like that." Sean smiled as he pictured himself running alongside Elise to help her after he removed the training wheels at some point in the future. He walked to the kitchen to get a glass of water, returned to the table, and offered the drink to Jenny.

After she took a sip and returned it to him, Sean drank from the glass as well then began, "I think it is time to begin assigning small chores to Elise and also to begin giving her an allowance."

Jenny looked at her husband with a thoughtful expression. "I hadn't thought of that before. Tell me what you're thinking."

"I believe she is capable of doing some small tasks that contribute to the family in addition to the ones you are already having her do, like picking up after herself with her toys and books, putting her dirty clothes in the basket, and making her bed."

"Do you have something specific in mind?" Jenny queried as she massaged the side of her neck.

"I was thinking she could set the table for our family meal each evening. Later we can add other things."

Jenny contemplated Sean's proposal and visualized Elise placing a napkin and silverware at each person's place. "I think she can handle that pretty easily. When she gets a bit older, she can manage the plates and glasses as well."

"Agreed." Sean smiled as he, too, visualized Elise performing her assigned task with a great sense of importance. "I also think we should begin giving her an allowance of six dollars per week, which is one dollar for each year of her age. What do you think of that?"

Jenny tilted her head and responded with a quizzical expression, "She doesn't have a need for money yet."

"That's true, but we can use this as a time to teach her about saving money for something she might want in the future. We can also start telling her about saving 10 percent for future needs or even retirement. We don't want her to be like your friend who retired with no money in the bank and only her monthly retirement checks to live on!"

Jenny's face relaxed as she was now on board with Sean's notion. "Yeah, that's a good idea. We could even teach her about tithing."

Sean smiled at his wife, who was always quick to catch on to his ideas and then to implement them. "Sometime after her party, we can sit down with her and explain it all."

"Sounds good," Jenny replied. She was grateful that Sean always had such good suggestions, was so willing to be involved in Elise's life, and was able to teach her things in such a loving and protective way.

They both yawned and, realizing they had had a very full day, decided to move toward their bedroom. Sean couldn't resist sneaking a peek into Elise's room on the way. Jenny waited at the door while he pulled the sheet up to the little girl's shoulders and then bent and kissed her on the forehead. He also pulled open the top drawer of her nightstand, retrieved a sheet of paper and a pen, then drew a red heart which he placed on top of the nightstand for Elise to find the next morning. As he quietly closed the door to her room, Jenny looked up at him and said, "How about we work at making a little brother or sister?"

Sean was only too happy to accommodate his wife's request.

CHAPTER 15

Because Jenny's sister, Janice, had so many times been willing to accommodate Sean's and Jenny's need for a babysitter, they decided that they should return the favor in some way. After a lengthy discussion, they decided to take little Elise and Janice's two kids—Alicia, now nine, and Adam, now seven—to the zoo for the day and then to keep them overnight.

Jenny, always careful with her husband's hard-earned money, prepared sandwiches, chips, and juice for lunch and fruit and cookies for snacks, along with plenty of water. Sean helped her to pack it all into a cooler, and he loaded it into the back of her SUV. They drove to Janice's house and went inside to visit with her briefly.

"What are you going to do with all this free time, Sis?" Jenny inquired.

"I've scheduled an appointment for a massage, then a manicure and pedicure, and then I'm getting my hair cut!" Janice was ecstatic about the chance to spend some time on herself.

"That sounds amazing!" Jenny was excited for her sister who had been such a help to her for the last few years.

"Do you and Tarak have any plans for this evening?" Sean asked.

"Yes, but I don't know what they are. He's keeping it a secret. But he told me to also buy a new dress while I'm out."

"Ooo-la-la!" Jenny teased.

Sean, too, was happy for Janice and Tarak. It had been his idea to keep Alicia and Adam overnight so that his sister- and brother-in-law could have some couple time together. "We don't want to keep you from your big day. Are the kids' bags ready? I'll take them out to the car."

"Yes. Kids, go get your suitcases from your rooms and bring them to Uncle Sean," Janice directed.

Alicia and Adam scampered to their rooms. They were eager to get to go to the zoo but even more enthusiastic to spend their first night away from home. They emerged and handed their overnight bags to Sean, who unlocked the SUV and opened all the doors so the heat could escape. He started the engine and turned on the air conditioner then put the small suitcases in the back beside the cooler. Janice brought Adam's car seat from her car, and Sean strapped it into the back seat next to Elise's. Alicia would sit in the third-row seat.

Janice kissed her children and reminded them to be on their best behavior while at Uncle Sean's and Aunt Jenny's house. The moms loaded Adam and Elise into their seats. Sean made sure that Alicia's seat belt was fastened, then he seated Jenny before returning to the driver's seat.

"Wave bye-bye to Mommy!" Sean told Alicia and Adam. Alicia blew a kiss to Janice, who returned the gesture. Then the little group rolled slowly down the street to begin their adventure.

Once they were moving along the freeway, Sean asked, "Alicia, what are you most excited about seeing at the zoo?"

"The lions. I think they are beautiful!"

"Adam, how about you? What would you like to see first?"

"I like bears."

Remembering the carved wooden bear they had bought on their honeymoon, Sean and Jenny smiled at each other.

"I'm going to guess what Elise wants to see." Sean glanced into the rearview mirror to see his daughter's face. "I think she wants to see the crocodiles."

"Nope! Guess again!"

Sean loved teasing his daughter and encouraging her to think and make conversation. "Oh, I know! You want to see the giraffes!"

Elise giggled. "Daddy, you are so funny! You *know* I like the monkeys!"

"Oh, yes! That's right! I forgot." Sean smiled at Jenny. "What do you think Mommy wants to see the most, Elise?"

"Hmmm. I...think...Mommy wants to see...the *zebras!*"

Sean glanced into the rearview mirror again. "Why do you think she wants to see the zebras?"

"Because they look like horses, and Mommy likes horses, silly!"

They continued to talk about things they wanted to see and were soon turning into the large lot full of cars. Sean couldn't find any shade in which to park, but he did notice that there were some picnic tables under some trees. He parked as close to them as possible so he wouldn't have to carry the cooler very far when they came out for lunch.

Once everyone was out of the car, Sean and Jenny told the kids about the importance of staying together and reminded them to always be within six feet of the adults. (Sean stood to the side to show them what that looked like.) He locked the car, pocketed the keys, and they were off to explore all that the zoo had to offer.

One of the first exhibits inside the entrance was the apes. Sean, sensing that Adam might be intimidated by their size, knelt down beside the kids and asked, "Don't their eyes look like human's?" Alicia, especially, was enjoying watching how they moved. Adam stayed quite close to Sean, but when an orangutan made a funny face at him, he giggled out loud and began making faces back at it. Jenny picked up Elise so she had a better view. Two of the gorillas were running on all fours while chasing each other. Jenny loved seeing the look of awe on her daughter's face.

They moved on and, much to Elise's delight, came to the monkeys in the Tropical Americas exhibit. She could not get enough of watching them swing through the trees. Sean relieved Jenny of holding her. When the monkeys began shrieking, he could feel Elise's upper body shake as she laughed. He realized that for him, the joy of the day was in seeing the faces of the children.

Adam saw the sign for the polar bears and wanted to go there next. What a show! There was a large ball in the water; the bear would jump in on top of the ball then roll over while in the water with it. Next, he would climb out of the pool and very forcefully shake his whole body, sending great sprays of water in all directions. He did this over and over. Everyone in the crowd was laughing at and taking pictures of his antics.

The group walked next to the big cats exhibit where Alicia smiled radiantly. She announced to the group, "I'm going to become a veterinarian and work at a zoo someday." When the big male lion yawned, the crowd gasped at the size of his mouth and the huge teeth inside it. They moved along, spending time at each of the different sections. Sean asked Adam which of the cats he liked the best. He, like his sister, preferred the lions.

Jenny asked the group if they were ready to go outside and eat lunch and get a cold drink. Everyone agreed that that was a good idea. On the way, they used the restroom and washed their hands. Jenny took the kids to the picnic table while Sean retrieved and rolled the cooler over to them. Jenny handed each person a paper plate and doled out the food as Sean helped the little ones unwrap their sandwiches and chips. Jenny opened a drink for each of them, and then she and Sean also sat to enjoy their meal. The temperature was nice in the shade, and everyone was relaxed and smiling. It had been quite a while since breakfast, and everyone was hungry, so lunch was quickly finished. Sean gathered the trash and carried it to a nearby garbage can. Then he encouraged everyone to take a drink of water since the afternoon summer sun would be really hot. He rolled the cooler back to the SUV, locked the doors, and then they all headed back into the entrance of the zoo.

"Who's excited to see the elephants?" Jenny asked.

"Me!" all three kids responded excitedly.

They walked around the loop past the exhibits they had already seen and on to the Asian exhibit, where elephants and camels walked about freely. Though she had indicated she wanted to see them, Elise was initially intimidated by the size of the elephants. Sean held her in his arms to give her a sense of support and security and encouraged her to recognize that they were ignoring her; he also explained that God had created all kinds of creatures, both large and small. Sean didn't want to let Elise walk away while she was fearful, and he knew that if he could change her focus to that of being curious, she could overcome her apprehension.

Sean pointed toward the large pachyderms. "Look at their feet! They have toenails like you!"

Elise raised her head from her daddy's chest and craned her neck to see. But her face showed she was intimidated; she returned to hugging him closely.

"If you could paint their toenails, what color would you use?" Sean deftly asked.

Elise leaned back and scowled at Sean. She was not buying this line of questioning.

"I think I would use orange or maybe green." Sean nodded emphatically.

Elise took the bait. She again leaned back and responded with vigor, "*No, no, no!* You have to use purple."

"Purple? Why purple?"

"Because it looks good with gray!" Elise was certain in her answer. And she was no longer clinging tightly to her daddy.

"Purple it is then." Sean smiled at his young daughter. "Why do you think they have such big ears?"

Elise looked over at one of the massive animals. "So they can hear well!"

Sean chuckled at his daughter's straightforwardness. "Well, they *do* need to hear well so they know if a lion or tiger is nearby. But look how they flap their ears. Why do you think they do that?"

Elise was studying the movement of the huge beasts. "It's like a fan. And maybe like stegosaurus so they can cool off."

"Yes!" Sean glowed at Elise's recall of previous discussions about the plates on the dinosaur being used to regulate their temperature.

Sean told Elise a few more things about the elephants. After she became comfortable and regained her confidence, she squirmed to be put back on the ground.

"Look at those camels!" Sean exclaimed to Adam. "How would you like to ride one of those?"

Adam smiled up at his uncle, his eyes squinting because of the bright sunlight. "They're really big."

Sean asked Alicia if she knew why this exhibit had camels with two humps.

"These are Asian camels. The one-hump camels are the ones we usually see in the Sahara Desert of Africa."

"Good!" Sean had been impressed with Alicia's knowledge of animals and thought she might very well achieve her goal of becoming a veterinarian someday.

The group moved on to see other exhibits, with Elise skipping merrily along. Sean and Jenny smiled at each other. Their next stop was at the African exhibit. Everyone was familiar with all the animals there as they had seen them on various wildlife shows. Jenny thought the zebras were cute with their wagging tails and big ears. Sean was amazed at the sheer size of the giraffes. He explained to the kids that they had the same number of bones in their necks as humans did, just bigger ones.

"A neck massage would take all day!" Jenny quipped.

Sean laughed heartily at his wife's wit.

Sean lifted Elise onto his shoulders so she could see the large exhibit. Additionally, her little legs had had to work twice as hard as his, and he thought that she might be getting overly tired, especially with the intense heat. They continued walking down the path and saw ostrich, buffalo, rhinoceros, warthogs, and hippopotamuses.

When everyone was ready, they moved on to their final exhibit of the day—the seals and sea lions. Like the polar bear, they put on quite a display. One of the keepers was standing near the water with a bucket of fish. She threw them in, one at a time, and the seals would slide into the water and wiggle their way toward the treat. Elise giggled at how they moved, and Adam commented that they were really fast in the water.

"Have you guys had a good time today?" Sean asked, signaling that their time at the zoo was drawing to a close.

"Yes, sir!" replied the trio in unison.

"Does anyone need to go potty before we head home?" Jenny asked as they passed the restrooms. She took the girls into the ladies' room, and once they were out of sight, Sean put Adam on his back and ran to the gift shop. Sean made a quick purchase, stashed it inside his shirt, and he and Adam were waiting for the girls on a bench outside the doors when they exited.

"Everybody ready?" Sean asked.

Everyone nodded and began the trek out to Jenny's SUV. Sean told Jenny to take the kids to the picnic table while he fetched the fruit, cookies, and water. While at the car and since they were nearby, he rolled down the windows so it could begin cooling off. He also removed the sack he had stuffed in his shirt and placed it under the kids' bags. Everyone enjoyed crunchy apple slices, sweet grapes, and chewy homemade cookies. Sean told them all to be sure to drink plenty of water.

Once finished, they walked to the SUV. Sean and Jenny secured the kids in their seats, and they began the ride home. The couple discussed what their plan of action would be once they arrived. Sean pulled into the garage, the kids were unloaded, and everyone entered the house—happy for the day's adventure but also grateful to be in the air conditioning.

CHAPTER 16

Sean brought in the cooler and the kids' bags while Jenny showed them where they would be sleeping. Sean and Jenny had decided that Adam, being the only male, would sleep on the air mattress in the bedroom they hoped would again be a nursery someday and that Alicia would spend the night with Elise in her bed.

Elise wanted her cousins to see her new chickens. Sean quietly stood nearby as she explained to Alicia and Adam about her daily feeding and watering tasks. She also answered their questions about how big the chicks would get, if they would be able to fly, and when they would begin laying eggs. Sean was so proud of her *he* nearly crowed like a rooster!

Next, Jenny had Alicia get out a clean set of clothes from her suitcase and then took her into Elise's bathroom and showed her where the towels were kept. After making sure Alicia had everything she needed, Jenny told her to shower and then went into the kitchen to begin supper. Sean did the same with Adam, telling the lad to call him if he needed anything.

He checked on Jenny, who was making a quick dinner of tacos. He asked what he could do, and she directed him to chop lettuce and tomato and grate cheese while she continued with preparing the meat. She also put some leftover macaroni and cheese in the microwave to serve alongside the tacos.

Alicia emerged from Elise's bedroom freshly showered. Jenny left the meat on low heat while she went to supervise Elise's bath time. Sean turned on the TV for Alicia then went to check on Adam, who had just finished getting dressed; Sean told him to join his sister on the sofa while he returned to the kitchen to heat the taco shells.

When Jenny and Elise came out of her bedroom, Sean told Jenny that he would finish dinner while she took a shower.

"Are you sure?" she queried.

"No problem, my lady. I've got this. If you'd like to take a nice soak, that's okay too."

Jenny didn't want to desert Sean with all three kids and the cooking for *too* long, so she quickly showered, dried off, and donned a floral dress with a snug bodice and a flouncy skirt. She took a moment to put just a touch of Sean's favorite scent behind each ear. She returned to the kitchen feeling quite refreshed.

Meanwhile, Sean had placed the warmed taco shells on a platter and was putting the seasoned meat in them. He had finished dicing the tomatoes, shredding the cheese, and chopping the lettuce and had also set the table.

Jenny told Sean that she would finish prepping the tacos while he showered and that they would eat when he finished. They quickly kissed, and he followed her suggestion. The enticing scent his wife was wearing did not escape his attention…nor did the flirty little dress.

Jenny had made a fresh pitcher of lemonade the night before and was pouring it into glasses when Sean returned to the kitchen.

"It smells less like a zoo in here now!" Sean quipped. He eased up behind his wife, who had taken the time—as always—to make herself extra appealing to him. He placed his hands on her hips and breathed in her scent as he left lingering kisses on her ears and neck with warm, soft lips. Since extra kids were in the house, she blushed.

He called the kids to the table and seated Jenny, Elise, and Alicia. Since their table only had space for four, he stood at the nearby counter. Jenny questioned him with her eyes, but with a wink and a thumbs-up, he assured her he was fine. He told the kids to bow their heads while he offered a prayer of thanks for their happy day at the zoo and for the delicious meal Jenny had prepared.

Sean gave each child two tacos, and Jenny placed some macaroni and cheese on everyone's plate.

"Here is a bowl of picante sauce if anyone wants to add some to their tacos," Jenny directed.

After everyone seemed settled, Sean served his plate.

"These are *delicious*, my love! Did you get these tomatoes from the garden?"

"Yes. They're really producing well this year. Elise helped me pick some yesterday, and then we made the picante sauce."

"You made this?" Sean asked Elise.

"Uh-huh! Mommy helped me!"

Sean loved the confidence his daughter had. "Elise, have you forgotten something?"

Her eyes opened wide as her little mouth formed into an oooh. "Thank you for supper, Mommy. I really like these tacos!"

"You're welcome, sweetheart!"

Sean smiled at his little family. They had had a good day. "Which movie would you like to watch after supper? We have *Shrek* and *Toy Story*."

"Which ones?" Alicia wanted to know.

"We have the first two of both of them."

Alicia and Adam looked at each other and said in unison, "*Shrek!*"

After everyone finished eating, Sean directed the kids to carry their plates into the kitchen. "Run to the bathroom and wash your hands and faces while I get the movie ready!"

Jenny began cleaning up while Sean loaded the movie and adjusted the volume. The kids came into the living room and settled onto the sofa. Sean asked them if they wanted pillows or blankets.

"Yes, please!" the three kids answered.

Sean went into the laundry room, retrieved some light blankets from the cabinets there, and dropped one into each child's lap. He reached into the lower shelves of the cabinets on the side of the fireplace for some pillows which were kept there for just this reason. He tossed them across the room to the kids, who thought this was great fun. Then he joined Jenny to help her finish cleaning up the kitchen. Since there were no leftovers, it was a really quick task. They exited the kitchen, turned off the lights, and joined the jumble of kids on the couch. Alicia lay her head on Jenny's shoulder and Elise crawled into Sean's lap.

Adam was the first to succumb to the combination of the day's exertion and the hour on the clock. Elise fell not long after. Sean arose and carried his beautiful daughter to her bed then returned for his nephew. By then, Alicia was yawning. Jenny asked her if she wanted to go ahead and go to bed. She agreed. She walked with her to Elise's room and made sure all was well with the two girls. Then she checked on Adam. She decided it would be okay for them to sleep in their clothes; this would also make the morning easier because they wouldn't have to be told to get dressed.

She had heard Sean turn off the movie so she knew he had gone to their bedroom. When she entered, she had to cover her mouth to keep from laughing out loud.

Sean was standing naked in their bed, beating his chest and wearing a gorilla mask. He began grunting.

"Sean, where and when did you get that?" Jenny laughed.

"At the gift shop at the zoo! I figured it might come in handy someday for something. Tonight seems to be the right time!"

"Come down from there, you beast!"

The gorilla cocked his head sideways and grunted.

"Let me see if I can entice you," Jenny offered in a lusty voice. She looked down and began unbuttoning her bodice while casting her eyes upward at her beast.

The creature beat his chest one last time then climbed down from his "mountain." He grunted and took over the task of unbuttoning Jenny's dress. Then he removed the mask, tossed it to the side, picked up his Beauty, and placed her softly on the bed.

"It was Beauty that enticed the Beast," Sean whispered as he began a full-frontal assault on his captive maiden.

*****

Jenny had set the alarm for six thirty the next morning so she could get breakfast in the oven before the kids arose. She had made potato, bacon, egg, and cheese tacos the evening before the trip to the zoo, wrapped them in foil, and placed them in the refrigerator. Once she had them heating, she returned to their bedroom to get dressed for the day. From their bed, Sean saw her and grunted as he smiled hopefully in her direction.

"I don't know when Alicia and Adam wake up!"

Sean frowned and whimpered.

"Such a sad beast!" Jenny said as she bent to pat him on the head. "You know, patience *is* a virtue!"

"Yea, well I'm not feeling particularly virtuous right this second," Sean stated matter-of-factly.

"Good things come to those who wait!" Jenny said brightly.

"Things may come to those who wait but only the things left behind by those who hustle!" Sean countered.

Suddenly he burst from the bed, planted a big kiss on his lovely wife, and said, "Just kidding!"

Sean quickly dressed and brushed his teeth then asked, "What can I do for you today, my lady?"

Jenny smiled at her husband. She loved how he tried to always keep things fun. "I sure am happy I decided to marry you!"

"*Decided?* You make it sound like it took you a while to choose!" Sean exclaimed.

"It did! I had to stop laughing, swallow, breathe, and then say *yes!* That was like…a whole four seconds!"

They laughed as they hugged each other, then together they made their bed and walked down the hall holding hands.

Once in the kitchen, Jenny asked Sean to set out plates and pour juice for each person while she retrieved the picante sauce from the refrigerator and sliced a new container of strawberries.

Sitting at the table with his chin resting on the palm of his hand, Sean asked, "Do you think we should wake them up? I mean, if I have to wait because of them, then they need to get on up!" he teased.

"You *are* a beast!" Jenny countered.

About that time, Adam came out of the hall and into the living room, rubbing his eyes as he walked.

"Hey, buddy! How did you sleep?" Sean asked.

"Fine. I'm hungry."

"Aunt Jenny is cooking breakfast now. Why don't you go to the bathroom and wash your hands and face? By then the food will be ready!"

Jenny said, "I'll get the girls. Do you want to go ahead and pull the tacos out of the oven? We can help them unwrap them at the table."

"Sure thing!" Sean replied.

Moments later, everyone was at the table enjoying the fruits of Jenny's labors. Sean was really proud of her for having thought to do some work ahead of time so things wouldn't be so stressful while Janice's kids were with them.

Cleanup was quick and easy, and soon everyone was in the living room. The kids wanted to finish the movie they had started last night, so Sean moved it through the scenes until everyone agreed it was the correct place to begin. Jenny went into the bathrooms to gather the kids' clothes and put them in the washer. Later she would launder the sheets and also wash a load of towels.

When *Shrek* ended, Sean asked if they wanted to watch *Toy Story*.

"Yes!" The kids were unanimous.

Sean got the movie running for them then went looking for Jenny. He found her in their bathroom, leaning over the toilet.

She looked up at him. "I guess I don't have to spend the money on a pregnancy test."

Sean grabbed a washcloth, wet it, and wiped her face. His joy was overshadowed by the fact that poor Jenny was not feeling well, but he could not hide his smile.

"What can I do for you?" he offered.

"I think I'm okay now. Let me stand up."

"Go slowly, my love." Sean moved closer to Jenny to assist her if necessary.

She took a deep breath. Sean gently wiped her face again.

"Thank you. I think I'm good. I didn't have this with Elise, so I need to do some reading to learn more."

"Why don't you lie quietly in bed and do some research on your phone. I'll go sit with the kids. If you can go to sleep, do. I can take the kids home after this second movie ends."

"I can go with you!"

"Let's see how you are feeling once the movie is over." Sean walked beside Jenny to the bed. He knew she was strong and independent and didn't want to be coddled, but he wanted to be nearby to catch her if necessary. He lay beside her and held her for a moment, kissed her on the forehead, then stood and arranged the pillows so she could lean back on them.

"How's that?"

"That's great. Thanks, Sean."

"I'm going to get you some water. I hope you didn't overdo it yesterday." Sean looked at her intently for signs of distress.

Finding none, Sean went to the kitchen and got a fresh glass of iced water for Jenny. He also grabbed a package of crackers. "I'm going to take this to Aunt Jenny and then I'll be right back. Are you guys okay?"

"Yes!" they all replied.

Sean quietly entered the master bedroom and set the water and crackers on the nightstand. "I think the kids will stay reasonably quiet through the movie. Rest if you can. I'll check on you later. If you are asleep, I will just take the kids home and come right back, okay?"

"Well, hopefully I won't sleep *that* long!"

Sean sat on the edge of the bed and held Jenny's hand. "I love you so much, Jenny."

"I love you too, Sean. Everything is going to be fine. Don't worry, okay?"

"You just rest. I'll check on you later."

Sean rose, walked to the door, and quietly closed it behind him.

In the living room, Elise asked, "Where's Mommy?"

Sean said, "She's taking a little nap. So let's not make too much noise, okay?"

The kids all nodded of their intent to comply. While they continued to watch the movie, Sean moved their clothes from the washer to the dryer; later, he folded them.

Once the movie ended, Sean asked Alicia and Adam to bring their suitcases to the living room. He handed them their folded clothes, and they put them in their bags. "Check around the house and see if you have left anything behind. I'm going to peek in on Aunt Jenny. I'll be right back and then I'll take you guys home, okay?"

Sean opened the door to the bedroom as quietly as he could. Jenny was sleeping. He could see that she had eaten some of the crackers and drank some of the water. He closed the door equally as quietly then went to the kitchen and opened one of the drawers. From it, he retrieved a piece of paper on which he drew a heart with a red pen. He put the pen back in the drawer and the piece of paper in his shirt pocket.

"Kids, let's go out to the car. Quietly, please!"

Sean told Alicia to sit in the front seat, and he strapped Adam and Elise into their car seats. He reminded Alicia to put on her seat belt.

"I'm going to get your suitcases. I'll be *right back!*"

Sean removed the paper from his pocket and slid it under the door to the bedroom where Jenny was sleeping. He went into the living room and picked up the two small suitcases then walked out to the garage and put the bags in the back of Jenny's SUV. He pressed the button to open the garage door, started the car, and asked everyone if they were ready. He glanced at Alicia and checked to make sure her seat belt was properly fastened then pulled out of the garage. He closed the garage door and drove to Janice's house to return her children to her.

Once there, the kids burst into their house shouting, "Mommy!" They excitedly told her about all the animals they had seen then scurried to their rooms. Elise ran with Alicia to play with her many dolls.

Sean told Janice that all had gone well and that her children were very well-behaved.

"Where's Jenny?"

"She's taking a nap. I told her I could handle bringing them home. How was your night out? And I *like* your haircut!"

"Oh, thanks!" Janice unconsciously reached for her hair. "We went to a dinner theater and had a *great* time. Thank you so much, Sean!"

"No problem. I'd better get back, though, because I promised her I wouldn't be gone long."

"Okay. Tell her I love her and thanks!"

"I will." Sean walked to Alicia's room and told Elise it was time to go. She stood and reached for Sean to pick her up. He carried her to the car, strapped her in, and drove home to check on the epicenter of his world.

CHAPTER 17

Sean rushed into the house and discovered Jenny was in the kitchen making a fresh pitcher of lemonade (she frequently made it because they had so many lemons from the tree in their backyard); a pot of chicken soup was simmering on the stove. He suggested, "Elise, why don't you get out your art supplies while I talk to Mommy?"

Elise went to the lower cabinet in the laundry room that Jenny had designated for arts and crafts, retrieved her crayons, and chose a coloring book. She carried them to the kitchen table, climbed into a chair, and began leafing through the pages until she found a picture she wanted to color.

Sean was shaking his finger at Jenny.

"Don't!" She smiled at him. "I took a nice nap, ate some of the crackers—and thank you, by the way—and drank quite a bit of water. This soup was *super* easy. I chopped some onion and celery, I already had some cooked and shredded chicken, I opened a carton of broth, and I used a bag of mixed vegetables from the freezer. I thought this would be good on a hot summer day and also that it would be easy on my stomach."

Sean was speechless. He hugged his wife, stepped back, and smiled at her. "You are an amazing woman. And I love you so much."

Jenny smiled back. She had heard the garage door open when Sean had left and realized she felt much better. She rose from the bed and walked to the kitchen to begin preparing supper for her family. Sean had arrived back home a few minutes after she had finished assembling the soup.

Sean leaned back against the counter and asked, "Were you able to learn anything from your research?"

"Yes."

"Let's go sit in the living room," he suggested as he cocked his head in that direction.

They sat where they could visit quietly yet could still see Elise easily. Jenny began, "I learned that morning sickness typically begins at about six weeks and usually ends at around fourteen to sixteen weeks. It can happen at *any* time of the day and is usually caused by low blood sugar. Hence, the tendency for it to happen in the mornings. I should take my vitamins, increase my protein intake, and stay hydrated. And this was interesting. It said that morning sickness *may* be a positive sign, an indicator of a healthy pregnancy." Jenny smiled.

Sean could see that Jenny was quite calm. Whether that last sentence was true or not, it had had a good effect on her.

"Well, I think we should go with that. I think we should make the presumption that all will be well—as it was with Elise—and never look back. What do you think?"

Jenny was pensive for a moment. "I know you're right, and I had already thought of that. I'm going to try to only have positive thoughts. But in reality, my emotions can sometimes get on top of my logic."

"Well, that's what I'm here for!" Sean smiled. "If I am at work, call me. If I don't answer, it will be because I can't. You can then try Janice or someone from church."

"Agreed. And I can remember that my pregnancy with Elise was as easy as it gets."

Sean smiled. "We will pray every day for strength, patience, and health for both you and the baby."

Jenny added, "And I don't want *you* running yourself into the ground trying to do everything for me. I will be careful and save any climbing or heavy lifting for you. But the doctor said whatever I *have* been doing, I can *continue* to do."

Sean lowered his head and glanced up at his wife with a wry smile. "Yes, ma'am."

*****

Jenny and Sean were both walking a tightrope. She wanted to have another baby—and knew that Sean *really* wanted a second child—but she was terrified of having another miscarriage. She chose to courageously face each day to the best of her ability, channeling her joy rather than her doubt and fear.

Sean was excited for both of them as well. He, too, appeared to be his usual cheerful self—on the outside. Internally, he was a wreck. He knew Jenny would be devastated if she lost another baby, and the memory of how they had both suffered the last time almost overwhelmed him.

Each was so in tune with the other that they both knew their partner was trembling on the inside. But both of them were afraid to broach the subject for fear of rocking the boat. After about a week, Jenny decided that they needed to confront their negative emotions honestly. While taking her bath before bedtime, she thought about what she would say. After drying herself, she donned Sean's favorite plum-colored nightie and dabbed his favorite perfume on the back of her neck, on her navel, and on the inside of each knee.

Sean was already in bed, waiting for his sweetheart. She crawled under the silky covers and snuggled up next to him, her head on his strong chest and her left hand rubbing his right upper arm. He had dabbed her favorite cologne on his upper abs, and she moaned unintentionally after drinking in the musty aroma.

"I'm going to tell you a secret," Sean whispered.

Jenny was caught off guard. "*What?*"

"You look and smell *incredible!*" He grinned at his lovely wife.

Jenny feigned irritation and gently slapped at his chest. "You are such a goofball!"

The two of them chuckled together. The awkward silence that followed was both atypical and uncomfortable for them.

Jenny took a deep breath and began. "Sean, I know you're being strong for me. I also know that *you know* I am trying to be brave for you. But we're using up a lot of emotional energy and are going to wear ourselves out." Her eyes sought his. In them, she found all the love they would ever need to face anything, together.

He ran his hand up and down her arm as he smiled at this one-of-a-kind woman he had married. When he kissed her forehead, she raised her lips to meet his. Softly, gently, each let the other know of their absolute devotion to one another. They lay together for a few moments, relishing their intense connection.

Sean spoke first. "You are correct. We have spoken before about the need to be honest with one another. I think during the day, in front of Elise and the rest of the world, we should continue with our brave faces. But at night, we need to touch base with one another and confront our concerns."

"I think you're right. We can use this time to release our negative emotions and then recharge and strengthen each other in a safe place."

Sean was impressed. "Listen at you, talking like a marriage counselor!"

"Well, I've been listening to *you* for almost seven years! I would *hope* that some of your clear thinking has rubbed off on me!"

They giggled together, then Jenny began snaking her way on top of him.

"My lady, if you are going to climb into the saddle, you had better be ready for the ride!"

"*Trust me* when I tell you that I can handle *any* stallion." Her hair spilled onto his chest as her mouth closed over his, effectively squelching any retort on his part.

*****

On a Wednesday morning a few days later, Jenny learned she was *not* pregnant. Sean awoke to the sound of her softly crying in the bathroom. He rushed to her and knelt beside her.

"Jenny, what's wrong?" Sean was panicked and shaking.

"I just started my cycle. I'm not pregnant. Sean, I'm so sorry. I know you wanted another baby." She began weeping, and Sean pulled her to him. They both sat on the cool tile and held each other.

Sean kissed Jenny on the top of her head as he gathered his thoughts and chose his words. "My sweet Jenny. There is nothing to be sorry about! You have done nothing wrong! Yes, I think both of us want another child at some point, but it will happen in God's time!"

Jenny was soothed by her husband's words but still felt like she had somehow let him down.

After a moment, Jenny had relaxed a bit, and Sean continued, "Are you sure you were even pregnant?"

"Actually, no. I just presumed when I was sick that day after the trip to the zoo that I was."

Sean was actually relieved that there was no certainty about a pregnancy; he hoped that Jenny had the same realization.

"Well, we were out in the heat all day. Do you think it's possible you may have overexerted yourself or picked up a little stomach virus there at the zoo?"

"I suppose it is. But no one else was sick, so I thought that it must be morning sickness."

Now that they were calmer and more able to think rationally, Jenny realized and shared that according to her cycle, what she had presumed had been morning sickness was actually too early for what was normally expected.

"I can see how you would have thought that it was, especially since we had been talking about and making plans for another child. Dr. Hoffman had said it might take a year to get pregnant after ending birth control. I think we've both been hopeful and perhaps overly optimistic and therefore didn't look at *all* of the picture."

"Yes." Jenny turned her head toward her loving husband and with a look of concern asked, "Are you disappointed?"

"Oh, my love! I know that if it is his will, Heavenly Father will bless us with another child when the time is right. Fortunately, we are both young and healthy, so I don't believe there is any cause for concern. There is plenty of time!"

"Thank you for always knowing what to say!" Jenny said as she rested her head across Sean's warm chest. They cuddled a bit longer then looked at each other and smiled. "Let's get our morning going!"

Sean quickly arose then pulled Jenny's arm to help her up. They rinsed their faces and readied themselves for another day in their wonderful life together.

CHAPTER 18

Sean asked Jenny what she thought about his inviting Tim over for dinner soon so that they could finish their conversation on relationships. "I know he *really* enjoyed your cooking. Would Saturday night be good for you? I'd like to talk to him and then invite him to go to church with us on Sunday."

"I think that's a *great* idea! What if I made a cheesy chicken pasta casserole, a nice crisp green salad with tomatoes and cucumbers from the garden, and some crusty Italian garlic bread?"

"I'll bet he would *love* that! I'll call him later today after he gets off work."

That afternoon while Jenny and Elise were reading together, Sean made the call; it had been almost three months since Tim had asked if he could come over and talk to Sean.

"Hey, Tim! This is Sean. How are things with you?" Sean could tell from Tim's voice that things were not much better than they had been back in April.

"I realize that I've let too much time pass before following up on your previous visit here. Jenny and I would love it if you would come over again. She enjoyed cooking for you because you were so appreciative, and she wants to do it again!"

"I'd like that, Sean. Your wife is a great cook!"

"Can you come on Saturday? She has dreamed up a special meal just for you!"

"That sounds fabulous. What time should I come?"

"We usually try to eat around seven. Why don't you plan to come right after work and we can visit for a while before dinner, like maybe at about four?"

"Sounds good. Should I bring anything?"

"Just your questions or concerns. We can continue to talk after dinner as well if we need to."

"Okay, Mojo. I look forward to it. See you then!"

Sean stuck his head through the doorway into Elise's room and told Jenny to expect Tim at about four on Saturday. She smiled and nodded and then continued reading with Elise.

*****

When Tim rang the doorbell, Elise excitedly ran to the front door and waited for her daddy. For safety reasons, she had strict instructions to never open the door without either Sean or Jenny being with her and to not stand in front of the window—even if she knew who it was. Sean arrived and nodded that it was now okay, and she joyously opened the door and politely asked Tim to come inside. (She had also been given instructions on how to invite guests in, offer them a seat, and ask if they would like something to drink.)

Tim sat on the couch where Elise directed him and told her that he might want a drink later but that he was fine for now. "I brought you something, Elise!"

Elise tried to contain her excitement as she walked slowly with her tiny hands in fists at her chest. She approached where Tim was sitting and smiled up at him. He handed her a bag and told her to look inside.

"A Barbie coloring book and stickers!" she exclaimed. "Thanks, Mr. Tim!" She smiled jubilantly at him.

"Give Tim a hug, Elise!" Sean directed.

Tim leaned forward, and Elise reached her little arms around his neck. "I'm going to go color in it *now!*"

Sean smiled appreciatively as he sat on the couch across from Tim and told him that Elise *really* loved stickers. "So have you thought at all about the things we talked about before?"

"I did. And I know you're right. I'm still struggling with the 'where to find a girl' part."

Sean decided to wait until later in the evening to invite Tim to attend church with him and his family on Sunday after they had had a chance to talk more about developing and maintaining a good relationship.

SHERI KEYES

"So let's assume you have found a quality woman and the two of you have gone out on a few dates. All is going well and you have even considered asking her to marry you. What kinds of things should the two of you be talking about?"

Tim looked confused. "I don't know! Mojo, you ask hard questions!"

"Well, to be sure," Sean chuckled, "I never promised any of this would be easy! But let me help you a little. Some of the more important topics are housing, finances, and children." He used his hands to visually aid his words. "The two of you would need to decide where you would live. Would you save money for a while before you buy a home, would you prefer to just rent, would you live in town or more out in the country? Will you have a joint account or maintain separate ones? Who will manage the bills and where would the money come from? Do you want children? If so, how many? How will they be disciplined when the time comes?"

Tim was staring at Sean with his mouth open. "Did *you guys* talk about that stuff?"

"We did and we do. It is ongoing. As time passes, there is always a new topic that needs to be discussed."

Tim was appalled. "When do you find time?"

"You *have* to. Sometimes we set time aside, like for big decisions. We will even get a sitter or take Elise to Jenny's sister's house. Smaller stuff, like birthday parties, Christmas gifts, and the need to go shopping for clothes or a new lawn mower we handle during pillow talk."

"Gee. I thought you just get up on your day off and take care of stuff." Tim looked defeated.

"That *is* one way to do it. But I have learned that things go better when some planning has occurred first. That way, everyone knows what to expect, and there are no surprises or arguments. It's like when we train for how we will handle a high-speed chase or a hostage situation. Everyone knows the plan and executes it accordingly."

Tim nodded his head in understanding.

"This all falls under the all-important category of communication. None of us are mind readers, Tim, and if two people go into a situation with different expectations, there are likely to be problems."

112

Tim continued to nod.

"Jenny has a friend who was going to go on a weekend camping trip with her boyfriend. *She* visualized a romantic getaway, with lots of hand-holding, slow walks along the river, and lovemaking. *He*, on the other hand, visualized a workout in the wilderness, with lots of walking over rocky trails, climbing hills, and maybe even some jogging. They had the worst argument and nearly ended the relationship over it."

"Wow," Tim responded. "So communication, huh?"

"*Very* important," Sean acknowledged.

"How do I know what things to discuss?" Tim asked with a look of confusion.

"Discuss *everything!* You will either be on the same page and know what to expect, or you will need to have a dialogue. And know that *some* topics, the more difficult ones, may take more than one discussion. At some point, though, you learn enough about each other that you know what to expect, and your interactions get easier. And don't forget, sometimes you just have to agree to disagree."

"Has that ever happened to you guys?"

"No, we've been very fortunate in that regard. Both of us understand we need to listen to the other and approach situations with sound reasoning. Usually, one of us is convinced on the other's stand, and we are quite willing to move to the other side at that point."

"Yeah, but what if there was something one of you was really passionate about and the other had an opposing viewpoint?"

"Again, we try to be objective and rational. I *know* she would never do something immoral or illegal, she is very good with money and is not extravagant, and she is very respectful of our decision to always be honest with and to consult with each other. But if there were *still* a problem, I think I would probably give in to her. Happy wife, happy life!"

The two friends continued to discuss communication, and Sean introduced the idea of compromise. He emphasized that a solution *always* had to be found and that it should never be the same person who constantly gave in to the other.

Jenny walked to the edge of the living room and told the two men that supper was ready when they were. *This* time, Tim had come with an appetite and quite willingly followed Jenny to the kitchen. Sean followed behind, feeling quite satisfied that progress had been made.

As before, Sean seated his wife and daughter, offered a prayer, and served portions of the casserole to his girls before serving Tim; meanwhile, the salad and bread were passed around the table. He cut Elise's food into manageable bites then served his plate.

Tim proclaimed that he thought *this* food was better than the last. Jenny smiled and thanked him for the compliment. Elise told her mommy that she appreciated her for always making yummy food for her to eat. Sean smiled and winked at his wife, who then knew *precisely* what her reward would be later that evening.

After dinner, Sean invited Tim to move to the back porch with him. The two men stepped outside and took seats on the comfortable patio furniture. The sun was beginning to set, and it promised to be another beautiful one—as was typical in New Mexico. Jenny retrieved a citronella candle from the laundry room cabinet, lit it, and carried it to Sean to set on the table between himself and Tim.

"My wife has great talent in the kitchen!"

"Oh yeah!" Tim replied.

"Would you like a drink or anything else?"

"I'm good for now."

"I'd like to talk about something you probably aren't expecting," began Sean.

Tim looked a bit confused but said nothing.

"I am assuming you have relations with most women whom you date."

"Yeah," Tim responded, somewhat embarrassed.

"I'd like to offer you another option to consider." Tim said nothing, so Sean continued, "When I was a youth, my parents told me to be cautious about sharing my body indiscriminately. Not only are there diseases to consider but the relationship changes once you share intimacy." Again, Sean paused to give Tim a chance to respond. Again, he did not. "Many people have told me that it is harder to leave a relationship, good or bad, after they have been physical with one another, that their heart and emotions become more tangled. They have also shared that they are more likely to be careless with how they treat the other person. It's as if becoming physical crosses you over some threshold. Some even admit to becoming quite possessive."

Tim looked out toward the mountains as he shook his head and sighed.

"Tim, I am approaching this, not from a religious or judgmental viewpoint, but from one of prudent decision-making."

"Look, I know *you* fooled around with Jenny before you were married because you told me you did." Tim was showing signs of irritation.

"Yes." Sean nodded. "But after only a few days, I told her that I'd like to stop and wait until we were married to continue. She understood, and that is what we did. She has told me more than once that that made her feel *so* respected, that it showed I cared more about *her* than about having *sex.*"

"Well, I'm not going to agree to anything like that upfront. I will consider it, but in the end, it will be my and the girl's decision." Tim would have been somewhat angry, but he knew Sean was truly trying to help him.

"Fair enough. And I am *not* trying to tell you what to do, I am merely offering a suggestion that I know can have very positive results."

"Sean?"

"Yes?"

"You *still* haven't told me *where* to find a woman."

Sean scratched his cheek, took a deep breath, and glanced to the side as he took a moment to consider his approach. "Well, I'd like to extend to you an invitation to attend church with me and my family tomorrow morning. I know several single women who are usually there. Who knows? Maybe you and one of them might find the other one interesting!"

"I don't know, Mojo, I…"

"Come on, man! Give it a shot! You've tried everything else! Besides, whether you meet someone or not, I've been wanting to invite you to go with us for some time. We meet at eleven, and

Sunday school is during the second hour. We promise not to throw you into the waters of baptism on your first day there!"

Tim chuckled, dropped his head, then took a deep breath. He decided that Sean was right. It couldn't hurt to show up there, and maybe, just maybe, he'd get lucky. And besides, Sean and Jenny had been so nice to him.

"Okay. Do I wear a suit?"

"If you'd like, but slacks and a nicer shirt are fine too."

Jenny opened the door and asked, "Who'd like a nice piece of warm peach pie with a scoop of cold vanilla ice cream?"

"I'm in!" announced Sean.

"Me too!" agreed Tim. Both of them smiled excitedly at her.

Jenny had already prepared the two bowls of dessert and set them on a serving platter with two spoons and two glasses of iced water. She retrieved it from the counter and carried it to the table on which Sean had set the candle earlier.

"Have you already eaten your dessert?" Sean asked.

"Not yet."

"Why don't you get yours and come sit with us. Elise can come out as well if she'd like."

"Elise played with her stickers and ate a little bowl of ice cream while I cleaned the kitchen. Then I bathed her and put her to bed. I'll get mine."

After getting her pie, Jenny returned to the patio and sat beside Sean.

He looked over at his wife. "You *know* this is my favorite dessert, right?" he asked.

Jenny grinned at her appreciative husband. "I suspected as much. Every time I make it, it disappears really quickly!"

The three of them laughed and enjoyed their after-dinner treats under the stars. They chatted a bit longer. "Tim will be joining us at church tomorrow!" Sean shared with Jenny.

A look of surprise and a wide smile lit up Jenny's face. "That's *great!*"

Tim glanced at his watch. "I should probably let you fine folks get to bed. You have been more than gracious, and I really enjoyed the conversation and the dinner. The dessert was otherworldly good!"

"We enjoyed having you, Tim!" Jenny responded.

Sean added, "I hope I gave you some more things to think about, Tim. And, of course, if you have questions, please let me know, okay?"

"Sure thing! I guess I'll see you guys tomorrow. Eleven, correct?"

"Yes," Sean stated. "I'll text you the address." Sean and Jenny walked Tim to the door and waved as he drove away.

Jenny gathered the dessert dishes and the candle while Sean checked on Elise and left his heart on her nightstand. They met in the hall, joined hands, and smiled at each other as they walked to their bedroom, where Jenny enjoyed a reward that was far better than peach pie.

CHAPTER 19

As they were getting ready for church the next morning, Sean wondered out loud about whether Tim would show up or not. Jenny gently scolded him, "What is it you always tell me? *We must have faith!*"

Sean squeezed his lips together and nodded at his sweet wife, his blue eyes sparkling. He kissed her on the cheek as he left their bathroom to go check on Elise's progress toward getting dressed.

"Hey, sweetheart! Are you almost ready?"

"Yes, sir. I get to wear my new shoes today that Mommy and I got this week!" Elise looked down at her feet and smiled up at her daddy.

"They are very nice shoes!" Sean told his precious offspring. "I'm going to go see if Mommy is ready."

Jenny was exiting their bedroom when Sean came out of Elise's room. Sean looked at his stunning wife with appreciative eyes. (It did not escape her attention that her husband looked quite handsome in his vest and bolo tie.)

The trio loaded into Jenny's SUV and made the short trip to their meetinghouse. They liked to get there early so they could visit with the other members before seating themselves in a pew near the front of the sanctuary.

As they moved toward their usual seats, Sean glanced back at the doors one last time and saw Tim entering the building. He smiled at Jenny and quietly told her, "Tim is here. I'll go get him, and we'll be right back. Save us a seat!"

"Hey, Tim! Glad you could make it!" The two men shook hands. "Would you like to sit with Jenny and Elise and me?"

"That would be great! Thanks."

Sean motioned in the direction they would walk. They quickly made their way to Sean's family. Tim bent to hug Jenny and spoke quietly to Elise then seated himself beside Sean.

After the church service, Jenny walked Elise to her Sunday school class. On her way to join Tim and Sean in the room for the adults, she noticed three young single women talking in the hall. One of them, Kayla, was slightly older. Jenny visited with them briefly then quietly addressed Kayla. "I have someone I'd like you to meet."

The two of them walked to where Sean and Tim were sitting. As the women approached, the men stood.

"Tim, I'd like you to meet my friend, Kayla Barnett. Kayla, this is Tim Wilson." They exchanged pleasantries then took their seats and listened to the Sunday school lesson.

After the closing prayer, Sean hurried down to Elise's room then walked with her to join Jenny, Tim, and Kayla. After a few minutes of friendly conversation, the five of them began walking toward the exit.

Sean stated, "Well, I had better get my family home and help Jenny to get some lunch ready. Kayla, it was nice to visit with you again. Tim, give me a call if you'd like to get together." Everyone said goodbye, and Sean walked with his family to their car.

Meanwhile, Tim was becoming more interested in the lovely Kayla by the minute. Not wanting her to get away without making some sort of plan, he offered, "May I walk with you to your car?"

Kayla agreed, and they strolled slowly across the parking lot. Fortunately, she had parked in a shady spot, and they continued to talk comfortably with each other. Tim learned that Kayla was working on her PhD in statistics. She had never been married as she had been going to school for the seven years since she graduated from high school. She was now working on her dissertation and hoped to be finished in the next one to two years. Her goal was to become an actuary with a major insurance company.

For her part, Kayla was enchanted with the fact that Tim flew helicopters for a living. When she learned that he, too, had never been married, she wondered if it might be fun to spend a bit more time with this tall and handsome man.

The parking lot had cleared. Tim's mind was in a whirl. He was trying to remember all the things Sean had told him over time. He knew that despite the shade, it was hot, and he should not take up any more of Kayla's afternoon.

At the same time, Kayla was wondering what she could do to let Tim know she would like to see him again. She had been raised to be very modest and had spent her whole life being a refined young lady. It was, therefore, not in her nature to make the first move.

After a brief moment of awkward silence, Tim decided to take the shot. "Would you be interested in going out for pizza or a movie next week?"

Kayla could barely contain her enthusiasm. "As a matter of fact, there's a movie coming out this week that I'd like to go see! What day are you thinking?"

"I'm actually on mornings right now, so I'm able to work around your schedule. Do you have any open days on what must be a *very* busy calendar?"

Kayla laughed. "Well, I'm busy all the time with programming computer simulations and writing my dissertation, but except for Monday, I can go any evening this week."

"How about Thursday?"

"I think that would work just fine!"

Kayla retrieved her keys from her purse and moved toward the driver's door. Tim moved with her and reached to open the door for her. (She was impressed.) She sat, started the car, and turned on the air conditioner. Then she rolled down the window and closed the door. "Whew! I'm glad I was in the shade!"

Tim squatted beside the car to speak to her one more time. "If you'll tell me your number, I'll dial it, and then you will have mine."

Kayla recited her number as she reached for her phone. It began ringing, and she immediately added Tim's name in her contacts.

Tim continued, "I really enjoyed meeting you, and I hope you have a great evening. Why don't I call you on Tuesday evening and we can finalize our plans?"

"That sounds great! I hope you have a good week and that you stay safe while flying around up there!"

"Oh, I'm always safe! Maybe I can give you a bird's eye view of Albuquerque one day soon!"

"I'd *love* that!" Kayla had never even considered riding in a helicopter, but at this moment, it sounded extremely appealing.

Kayla fastened her seat belt, backed out, and began to drive away. She waved at Tim as he stood and waved back. Once she turned onto the street, Tim moved to his car. He was sure his feet had wings on them.

*****

The following evening, Sean's phone rang, but he was enjoying weekly family time. Each Monday after supper, they turned off the TV and spent time together discussing topics, such as having a good character, being a good citizen, developing a relationship with God, and being kind to and serving others. They usually had a dessert on those days and took pleasure in activities like drawing pictures or working on various other crafts, taking walks or bicycle rides, reading stories, or even role-playing with some of Elise's dolls and stuffed animals. Once they finished, Sean returned the call.

"Hey, Tim. I was busy with the family. What can I do for you?"

"Sean, I wanted you to know that Kayla and I are going to see a movie on Thursday evening."

"That's *great*, Tim! So you two must have hit it off, huh?" Sean looked over at Jenny and winked. She smiled.

"Yes. She is beautiful and sweet and smart and *so much better* than those other girls I have dated. Sean, thank you." He was trying to hide his enthusiasm but was only partly successful because he was chattering like a magpie.

"Oh, I'm *so* happy for you! I'm glad she was there and that Jenny introduced the two of you!"

"I tried to use as much of your advice as possible. I walked her to her car and opened her door for her. Sean, it felt really good! When I questioned her about a movie, I actually *asked* rather than just *telling* her. And she is *such* a lady, Sean. I have a much better idea about the things you've been telling me. I want to…I don't know…

take care of her! Sean, is it possible, could I be in love?" Tim's voice was, by now, shaking.

Sean cleared his throat, which gave him time to choose his words carefully. "I think it is, Tim. I fell in love with Jenny very quickly." He wanted to offer advice but opted instead to wait for Tim's response.

"I can't wait for Thursday. I want to call her right now! I told her I'd call her tomorrow so we could discuss our plans. Would it be okay to text her?"

Sean chuckled. "I know people say to not be overly anxious. On the one hand, you show too many of your cards. But on the other, the other person might think you're not interested enough if you *don't* call."

Tim asked, "What would *you* do?"

"Well, I don't like all those head games, so I'd text her. But keep it friendly and light. Just wish her a good evening and tell her you are looking forward to seeing the movie she suggested. Otherwise, stay with your plan of calling her on Tuesday."

"Okay. I'll do that. Thanks, Sean. I think I might not be able to make it until Thursday!" Tim was nearly breathless he was so excited.

"Keep your wits, lad. And maybe spend some time thinking over some of the things we have discussed. Call me anytime, and let me know how things go, okay?"

"Sure thing, Mojo. Later, man."

"Good luck!" Sean ended the call and continued to sit on the couch in the living room. He smiled quietly. Jenny was walking past him on her way to the laundry room and stopped.

"What's going on with Tim?"

Sean turned to face her. "He has a date with Kayla on Thursday night to see a movie, and he's very excited about it."

"Oh, that's *wonderful!*"

"If things go well, and I know he'll let me know, then we'll have to have them over for dinner."

"Oh, *absolutely!*"

Later that night during pillow talk, Sean told Jenny he thought she was a genius for introducing Kayla to Tim. "How did you know they would hit it off so well?"

"Oh, I've had some experience with couples who are really good together," she teased. Then she rolled over to Sean and let him know what *really good* was like.

Chapter 20

It was Monday evening, and Tim wasn't the only one who wanted to text or call; Kayla fought off the same urges but managed to stay the course her parents had taught her. But that didn't keep her from wishing that *Tim* would contact *her!*

So when her phone signaled that she had received a text, Kayla quickly grabbed it from the table in anticipation. "Yes!" she squealed in delight. Her calico cat, Maggie May, raised her head and glared in disbelief at the audacity of the offending noise that woke her.

Heeding Sean's advice, Tim had written:

> I hope you are not working TOO hard! I watched a trailer for the movie and it looks really good. I'm looking forward to seeing it!

He believed the text was friendly and light, as Sean had suggested. However, he hoped that by not mentioning tomorrow night's call, it left the door open for Kayla to respond in *some* way. Moments later—and much to *his* delight—he heard the familiar *ding* from his phone. He almost couldn't bear to look for fear that it wouldn't be Kayla. He reached for his phone and only partially raised it, fully prepared to slam it face down on the sofa beside him if it weren't her.

His smile nearly lit up the room.

> Hi, Tim. I've been working on my
> simulations—again! I'm glad you're
> interested in the movie. I've heard
> some good things about it.

He wanted to write back immediately. "Slow down, stud" he reminded himself. "You don't wanna run *this* one off." Hearing his master's voice, Vladimir, his Doberman pinscher, stared at him intently. Tim rose from the sofa, opened the back door so the dog could go outside, and went to the refrigerator for a beer. Once there, he changed his mind and filled a glass of water instead. He was pretty sure that Kayla didn't drink alcohol and realized he was reaching for one more out of habit than of desire for one. Besides, he wanted a clear mind right now.

He stepped outside, glanced at the stars that were beginning to shine in the dusky sky, and hoped that *maybe* they were lining up for him this time. He threw a tennis ball for Vladimir a few times, then the two of them returned to the living room. He picked up his phone. Only three minutes had passed. He thought about starting a load of laundry, doing some push-ups, or even eating a bowl of cereal but then realized that to hold off purposefully was equivalent to playing head games.

Remembering that he wanted a relationship like Sean's and Jenny's, he sat on the sofa and decided to just be honest. Recalling Sean's words, he opted also to be supportive. He began typing but stopped. He had noticed that Kayla began her text with a greeting. Though it had never occurred to him to include such a simple act of courtesy, he realized that this very thing was a great example of what Sean had spoken about—of making the other person feel acknowledged and important. He erased what he had typed, pushed his sleeves up, and restarted.

> Hi, Kayla. It's good to hear back from you. Just think, every time you do another one of your simulations, you get one step closer to finishing. That must be exciting for you!

Kayla had no such concerns about head games as she had not dated much due to being so busy with school. To her, they were just sharing friendly dialogue. She realized that this was a good way to get to know one another better without spending time getting dressed up or money on an expensive date. She pulled her hair into a ponytail and began typing.

> Thanks, Tim, for your words of encouragement! Sometimes late at night when I'm writing programs and waiting for them to run or I'm analyzing the results, I feel like I'm all alone in this world!

Tim read her response and realized that all he wanted to do was take care of this beautiful and smart lady. He thought for a moment before typing again. *I hope I can get better at this stuff Sean says to do so that it is just automatic,* he thought. *I don't like having to think about every single thing I say and do!*

> Well, Kayla, any time you feel that way, just text or call me! I have to admit that sometimes I feel the same way. Maybe we can become friends and lean on each other in those times.

He read and reread the message before sending it. Deciding it was a good mix of being supportive and honest without being overly eager, he pressed the send arrow.

Tim and Kayla continued to text for about an hour. Toward the end, he reminded her that he would be calling her tomorrow evening and asked what time might be good for her. She indicated that any time between seven and ten would be okay. They both sent a final text with a "TTYL" and a smiley face.

Tim realized he was smiling. More importantly, he realized he was happy, and he hadn't felt that way in a long time.

*****

Because Elise had already made the decision to begin public school that fall, there had been no need to have Alicia spend the night. Nonetheless, both girls had asked if they could still have a sleepover at Elise's house. Sean set up the tent and brought a long extension cord into the backyard so he could plug in a fan to blow on them as the temperatures in July were quite warm. He also cleaned the firepit and readied it with a small amount of wood so the girls could roast wieners and marshmallows. Jenny bought the necessary ingredients, made pink lemonade, and baked snickerdoodle cookies—simply because they were Sean's favorite.

The four of them sat around the firepit and enjoyed freshly roasted hot dogs, icy cold lemonade, and gooey s'mores. Sean and Jenny each shared their favorite "scary" story from their childhoods, and then the group played a short game of charades. Lots of giggling could be heard coming from the Wallach property.

Jenny had placed construction paper, scissors, coloring books, markers, and stickers in a lidded plastic container on the picnic table in case the girls wanted to have something to do. Sean put fresh batteries in three different lanterns and two different flashlights so the girls would not find themselves in utter darkness.

After hugs and kisses were shared, the adults went indoors to watch a movie, leaving the two girls to brave the wilderness of the fenced backyard. Before the couple went to bed, Jenny turned on small lights in the kitchen and hallway in case the girls decided to come inside. Sean went out and checked on them one final time then opened the window in their bedroom slightly so he could hear any concerning noises arising from the campers.

Sean arose around two in the morning, peeked into the tent, and saw that the girls were both sleeping peacefully. He used the art supplies from the table to draw a red heart and placed the paper next to Elise's sleeping bag.

*****

Tim called Kayla at a little after eight the next evening. She answered brightly, and Tim decided that *this* was a woman to whom he could see himself being married.

"Hi, Kayla. Do you have a minute?"

"Sure! How was your day?"

"Oh, it was great. I want to arrange the details for our movie excursion on Thursday."

"Okay. I looked up the times. There is a showing at four thirty and another at seven. I can do either, so which is better for you?"

Tim considered the options and responded, "It might put me in quite a rush to make the four thirty. Would you like to grab a pizza or something fairly quick and then aim for the seven o'clock showing?"

"Oh! On Sunday, you had said pizza *or* a movie. Are you changing your mind?"

"Well, we both will need to eat supper, and I think it would be nice to have some time to chat *before* the movie, and then we can visit *after* it as well if we want to."

"That sounds *great*, Tim! Do you have a favorite pizza place?"

"I like that place over on Central that has wood-fired pies."

"*Oooh*, I like that one too!" Kayla's voice was full of joy; Tim was not sure he could wait until Thursday.

"Why don't I pick you up at a little after five. I want to allow plenty of time for traffic and a crowd at the restaurant or theater. Does that work for your schedule?"

"Absolutely! I'll be ready!"

Tim knew he had over-allotted the amount of time needed, but he also knew that he wanted *every* minute he could get with Kayla. He knew, too, that he wasn't ready to end the phone call just yet, so he asked Kayla about the computer programs she wrote.

And thus began a nearly four-hour conversation. Kayla finally told Tim that she knew he needed to get some sleep before getting up early the next day to go buzzing his helicopter around town. He begrudgingly agreed.

The next day after work, he went to a florist shop and ordered a dozen deep red roses to be delivered to Kayla's duplex the following day.

Was it too much, too soon? He didn't care because to him, Kayla was worth it. He didn't even need Sean's advice for *that* decision.

CHAPTER 21

Tim's next conundrum was what to wear on his date with Kayla. With *any* other woman, he would have worn his usual stylish yet comfortable clothes, carefully chosen to accentuate his physique and accessorized to give just a hint of "bad boy." He hated that he had gone from being self-assured to having to call Sean for nearly every decision. But he knew Sean was a good friend and was quite willing to help him as much as he was able. And since Sean knew Kayla from church, Tim thought his friend could offer insight into what would be appropriate to wear on a first date with a classy lady.

Kayla, having never dated much, was similarly uncertain. She called Jenny and asked for her advice on what to wear on a first date on a weeknight that was neither overly prudish nor too inviting.

By the time Tim arrived at Kayla's duplex, they had both worked themselves into quite a frenzied state of mind. He stood on her porch, giving himself a pep talk for a moment before he pressed the doorbell. On the other side of the door, Kayla glanced one final time in the mirror, took a deep breath, and forced a smile. She opened the door to find a handsome man wearing jeans and a tucked-in, button-down shirt that accentuated his blue eyes.

"Good evening, Kayla!" Tim's broad smile immediately made Kayla feel comfortable.

"Hi, Tim. Please, come in!" Kayla motioned with both hands for Tim to enter her home. "I was *so* surprised when the roses were delivered earlier today. They are just *splendid!*"

Kayla walked to her small dining table, and Tim followed. She bent to smell the luxuriously rich red flowers. "These are the most gorgeous color I have *ever* seen!" She turned to face Tim, her eyes sparkling.

"You look…" Tim shook his head and shrugged, "just beautiful!" Kayla had chosen a simple floral dress of purples, blues, and greens. At five feet ten inches, she was quite tall for a woman, so she tended to wear sandals. For this evening, she had chosen a blue pair.

"*Thank* you! *You* look really nice as well!"

Tim did not like awkward moments of silence, so after thanking her for the compliment, he asked, "Are you ready to eat some pizza?"

"I sure am!" Kayla smiled back. "Just let me grab my purse from my room."

While he waited, Tim noticed that Kayla's home was clean and orderly. (This was a big improvement over the last girl he dated.) She had many paintings in different mediums and of different sizes. He moved to look more closely at a watercolor beach scene and noted that it was signed "Kayla."

As she reentered the living room, Tim motioned toward the painting and asked, "Did you paint this?"

"Yes. I used to paint a lot, but I've been so busy with my dissertation that I haven't even gotten my supplies out in quite some time."

"So did you do *all* of these?" Tim had a look of amazement on his face while motioning with outspread hands toward the walls.

"Almost all of them. My mom painted the mountain scene over the fireplace. She prefers acrylics." Kayla pointed at the paintings as she told Tim about them. "My dad did the fruit still life there by the kitchen. He swears by the forgiving nature of oils."

As she spoke, Tim moved from one painting to another, examining them more closely and growing increasingly impressed with each one. "I'm no artist, but these are *very* good." Tim turned his head to face Kayla. "Did your parents teach you?"

"There was no *formal* training, but over time, I learned quite a bit from each of them just from watching their techniques—how to mix colors, how to load the brush with paint, and different brush strokes."

"What about these watercolors? Did you take lessons for those?"

"No. I used what I knew and just kinda…taught myself the rest!"

"These are just *amazing!* I had no idea! You hadn't mentioned it during any of our conversations."

"Well, thanks!" Kayla would have been a bit embarrassed, but Tim seemed to be genuinely fascinated. "I'm sure you have plenty of talents we have not yet discussed as well!"

"Why don't we move on to the restaurant so we won't feel rushed getting to the movie?"

"Okay!"

Tim smiled and motioned with his hand for Kayla to move to the door. She reached in her purse for her key as she walked. Once on the front porch, Tim quietly asserted, "Let me get that for you." She allowed him to take the key from her hand and use it to lock the dead bolt. (*Sean would be proud of me for that one*, he thought.)

Tim walked with Kayla to the passenger side of his car and opened the door for her. He waited as she seated herself and then closed it. *Wow!* Kayla thought. *This guy knows how to treat women!*

"I really like your car!" Kayla offered once Tim was seated.

"Thanks. I got it a little over a year ago. It's a lot of fun to drive." Tim had wanted a Camaro his whole life. Once he started working, he saved so he could pay for one outright as he did not want to have a monthly note to pay. Of course, he got the biggest engine available, the leather seats, and all the other niceties that money could buy.

Tim began the drive to the restaurant on which they had decided on Tuesday. "What toppings do you like on your pizza?" Tim asked.

"I usually just get the one with pepperoni and some vegetables. How about you?"

"I get the same! What kind of crust do you like?"

"Just regular, hand-tossed. Not too thick or too thin. And you?"

"Oh my goodness! This is going to be an easy order! I like the same!"

The two of them smiled at each other. Both were growing more at ease with each passing moment.

Tim pulled into a parking space, and just before he killed the engine, he said, "Let me get that door for you." As he walked around the car to Kayla's side, he realized he felt oddly comfortable with being more of a gentleman. *I'm going to owe Sean big time!*

As Kayla stepped out, Tim took her hand to help her rise. "*Thank you!*" She smiled brightly at Tim's unexpected attention to her.

Tim reached for the handle and held the door open as Kayla entered the restaurant. A sign read, "Please seat yourself."

"Do you have a preference?" Tim inquired.

"I think it's fascinating to watch the cooks prepare the pizzas. Would it be okay to sit near the action?"

"Sure! I love how they throw the dough in the air!" Tim held Kayla's arm as she climbed onto a stool at the corner of the counter near where the pizzas were thrown, assembled, and cooked in the wood-fired oven. Then he sat on the stool at a right angle to her.

When the waiter came to take their drink order, he stood at Tim's side. Kayla asked for water with lemon. Normally, he would have ordered a beer, but Tim decided to follow suit with his date. He asked the waiter for his name.

"I am Vinnie."

"Okay, Vinnie. I think that the lady and I are ready to place our order." He glanced at Kayla, who smiled and nodded. "We would like to share one of your twelve-inch Testarossa pizzas."

"Great choice, sir. Can I interest either of you in a salad?"

Tim looked at Kayla and asked, "I know they are really large here. Would you like to split one?"

"I just *love* their Caesar salad. I think splitting one is a *great* idea."

Tim looked back at Vinnie. "Are you able to separate a salad onto two plates?"

"Certainly, sir," Vinnie answered, bowing slightly at the waist. "And you would like the Caesar?"

"Yes. Thank you."

"I'll get those salads right out for you, sir." Vinnie turned and walked away.

"Do you go to movies often?" asked Tim.

"Not really. Maybe twice a year? Sometimes a few of us grad students get together and go out just to force ourselves away from all the focus and pressure. How about you?"

"I've never been a big movie watcher. I like them, I just don't have a habit of keeping up with what is currently out."

Since there were few customers at that early hour, Vinnie was able to quickly bring the drinks and salads to Tim and Kayla. He served them and asked if they needed anything else. Tim was trying very hard to think about how Sean would handle each situation, so he asked Kayla if she needed anything. She smiled and shook her head "No," so Tim thanked Vinnie and told him they were fine for now.

Tim remembered the first time he ate at Sean and Jenny's house and how Sean waited for everyone else to begin before he took his first bite. To keep things from feeling weird, he slowly unwrapped his utensils, placed the napkin in his lap, and casually took a sip of his water.

Fortunately, Kayla dove right into her salad, and proclaimed, "Ummm! This is *so* good!"

Tim smiled at her, nodded his head, and took a bite of the crisp greenery on his plate. "Ohhhh yes! The dressing here is just fantastic!"

They were just finishing their salads when Vinnie arrived with the pizza. He asked if he could take their salad plates; both of them smiled and responded affirmatively. Vinnie placed a clean plate in front of each of them and then served a single slice of pizza to each. "Does everything appear to be correct?"

"It all looks delicious!" Tim answered. "Do you need anything else?" he asked Kayla.

"This smells amazing! I'm just perfect!" Kayla's shining smile was both quick and infectious.

Tim smiled back at her before telling Vinnie that all was well.

Kayla took a bite, squeezed her eyes closed, reared her head back, and moaned her approval. Tim chuckled and was smiling at her when she looked at him. He then took a bite, groaned, and nodded at Kayla. "*This* is why I like to come here!" she decreed.

As they ate, Tim asked, "Where did you hear about this movie?"

"My advisor's wife is a huge movie freak. She brought him lunch one day recently and told us about it. She had seen the previews at a recent visit to the theater."

Each time Kayla finished a piece of the delicious pie, Tim used the spatula to serve her another. She stopped him after the third one by waving her hand. "No, no! I'm stuffed!"

Tim also stopped after three pieces and stated, "It looks like you will be having pizza for lunch tomorrow!"

Kayla's forehead wrinkled and she said, "Oh, I think *you* should take it!"

"I'm on mornings, and it's really hard to eat lunch while flying. I've already got some leftovers I need to use for supper, so *you* take it home with you!"

"Okay. Thanks!"

Vinnie was clearly an experienced waiter. He appeared at Tim's side with a to-go box just as they finished. He asked if Tim were ready for the check then placed it on the counter beside him. Tim removed a credit card from his wallet and placed it in the holder. Vinnie appeared, and the entire transaction was completed very quickly.

Kayla thanked Tim for the delicious dinner.

"You are *more* than welcome! I've been looking forward to it all week!" (Tim had been excited about both the meal *and* Kayla's company; he hoped she understood the double meaning of his statement.)

He glanced at his watch. "Do you want to go ahead and let's start making our way over to the cinema?"

"Sounds good! I know one thing is for sure. I won't be wanting any popcorn at the theater because I'm *stuffed!*"

The two of them chuckled as they stood to exit.

Chapter 22

Tim once again seated Kayla in the car, and once they arrived at the cinema, he helped her exit. She was aware that not very many guys did this anymore and was very appreciative of it. To her, it was a good indicator of his character and his respect for women.

"We've gotten here a bit early. Would you like to go to the restroom or get a drink or anything else?" Tim was feeling more and more proficient at this new way of treating women that Sean had proposed. He was aware that even *he* felt better about *him*self by treating his date with kindness and respect.

"It's probably a good idea to do that while we have time. Then we can go into the theater and chat for a bit before the previews start!"

The two of them strolled to the restroom area. Tim went as fast as he could so that he would be standing outside to meet Kayla when she exited. He somehow knew that Sean would *never* leave Jenny standing or walking alone in a crowded cinema.

They walked to the appropriate theater, and Tim directed her to the seats he had chosen at the time he reserved their tickets. He thought briefly about how in the past he would just walk to the seats and assume that the girl would just follow him.

Once seated, Kayla asked him, "You got to see my paintings. I'd like to know what *you* do in *your* spare time!"

"Okay. As a teen, I learned to play the guitar fairly well. In fact, sometimes Sean and I get together and play. Did you know he plays the piano, the guitar, *and* the drums?"

"Jenny had told me about the piano they bought for him, but I didn't know about the other two instruments."

"Sean's an incredible guy. He's *so* smart and *so* talented yet is the friendliest and most helpful man I know. He has even taught me some things I didn't know about helicopters. We all love him at the department." Tim paused briefly. He knew what he wanted to say next, even if it did sound corny. "I'm especially glad he invited me to go to church with him. Otherwise, I'd probably be at home tonight with my dog instead of enjoying pizza and a movie with a really nice lady!"

Both of them blushed. Kayla was touched by the somewhat awkward compliment; Tim was hoping that what he had said wouldn't send Kayla searching for the nearest exit.

"So when you learned to play, did you take lessons?"

"No!" Tim laughed. "Like so many other teens, a bunch of us just got together and started sharing anything we learned or figured out. Of course, each one of us had dreams of becoming a rock star!"

Kayla laughed. "Did *any* of you make it?"

"One guy did some session work on the drums for a while. Another one plays with a couple of different bands at street dances and stuff like that."

"What do you do *now* when you aren't working?"

"Well, I enjoy a round of golf every week or so, I jog with my Doberman, Vladimir, nearly every day, and like most guys, I like video games. But I've been taking a hard look at what a waste of time and money that is. I'm open to suggestions for an alternate activity."

Wow! That *was not obvious* at all, *stupid!* Tim silently wished he could take that last sentence back and hoped that Kayla didn't rear back and slap him.

"Do you like to read or work any type of puzzle? What about bowling or camping and hiking?"

Tim was so rattled by the forwardness of his statement that he had to *really* drag his head back into the conversation with Kayla—who apparently took it at face value and was responding to it as such.

"I'm not against reading, I just don't seem to ever do much of it. I could probably enjoy most puzzles, but again, I've just never bought any. Camping sounds good. When I was younger, my parents took my brother and sister and me several times, but I never bothered to buy the equipment once I was on my own. Do *you* do any of those things?"

"Well, when you're a grad student, you had *better* like to read because you have to do so much of it! Puzzles are a nice diversion as you are still using your brain, but it's for fun rather than for some adviser in a dusty room in a far corner of a building!"

Tim laughed at Kayla's good-natured manner of dealing with the stressful life of a grad student. "Do *you* go camping?"

"Like you, I went with my family when I was younger. I've always thought that I'd like to do it again but just never seem to find the time."

Tim continued, "You mentioned bowling. Do you do much of that?"

"Like I said earlier about going to the movies, sometimes some of the grad students get together and make an evening of it at the bowling alley. None of us are very good, but we really enjoy ourselves. Sometimes we name the different pins with names of things we don't like."

Tim chuckled. "Like what?"

"Well, I always have trouble getting the ten-pin to fall. So I name it the 'Behrens-Fisher' pin because that is one of the classic problems in statistics. One guy who is a leftie doesn't like his adviser, so he calls the seven-pin by his name."

"*That's* creative!"

"Yeah. You should see us when one of us gets a strike or even a spare! We *way* over-celebrate! But we're all tired and stressed and frustrated, and it's just fun to let your hair down and get crazy sometimes!"

"I'd love to be a fly on the wall and watch!"

"Maybe you can come with us some time!" Kayla offered.

Tim smiled. "I think that sounds like a lot of fun!"

People had been filing in and taking their seats as Tim and Kayla visited. Suddenly, the lights went down, and most of the talking stopped. Soon the ads, reminders, and previews began playing. When the movie finally started, Tim and Kayla smiled at each other.

*****

The movie was a hit for both of them. They stayed to watch the credits at the end—partly because neither wanted their time together to end but also because they both wondered at what locations the filming had been done.

They were the last in the theater to leave.

On the way back to Kayla's duplex, Tim asked, "Would you like some ice cream?"

"I'd *love* some!" she answered. Her face lit up with joy at the thought of extending her evening with Tim.

"Is 'Cold Stone' okay?" Tim wanted Kayla to know that he wanted to give her a voice in decisions.

"It's one of my faves!"

The table in the corner was open, and Tim asked her if it was okay. She smiled and nodded, so he pulled a chair out for her and then helped her scooch in. They looked at the menu board and learned they mostly liked the same things. They decided to get different desserts and then taste each other's choices.

They shared stories from their childhoods as they enjoyed the rich, creamy concoctions. They were quite lost in each other and probably would have stayed all night. One of the workers approached their table. "I'm *really* sorry, but we closed ten minutes ago." The young girl was truly embarrassed.

"*Oh!* I'm so sorry!" Tim said as he glanced at his wristwatch. He stood and quickly moved behind Kayla's chair to pull it back as she stood.

"We lost track of time!" Kayla explained.

"It's okay," said the girl. "But my manager will be worried if we don't lock up soon!"

"No problem!" Tim replied. "We're on our way now!"

Tim seated Kayla in his car, and after he sat, they looked at each other and belly-laughed.

"Well, that's a testament to the fact that we have plenty to talk about!" Kayla offered.

"Indeed!" Tim smiled. "I guess I'd better get you home so we can both get some sleep before our busy day tomorrow."

When they arrived at Kayla's duplex, Tim once again opened the door for Kayla and extended his hand to help her rise from his low-slung car. They walked slowly to her door. (Both *wanted* to hold hands, but both were afraid to reach for the other.)

On her porch, Tim stated with authority, "Hand me your key, and I'll get that door for you."

Kayla did as she was told. As Tim unlocked the door and opened it slightly, Kayla struggled with whether or not to invite him in. They faced each other, and both felt awkward about what to do next.

Fortunately, Tim was able to fall back on Sean's training. "I should probably say good night now. But I would love to call you tomorrow evening if that's all right."

"Yes, I would love to hear from you and find out how your day went," Kayla answered, relieved that Tim had broached the subject.

"When is a good time for you?" he asked.

"I should be back from working on my programs by about six o'clock or so."

"Why don't I call around seven? That'll give you time to get comfortable, feed Maggie May, and relax a bit."

"Sounds great!" There was another uncomfortable moment of silence. Kayla tilted her head to the side and offered, "I had a *really* great evening with you, Tim."

"This has been a *wonderful* evening for me as well," he responded. Tim looked into her sparkling green eyes and smiled. "May I get a little hug?" (He was accustomed to getting a lot more, and he did *not* have a habit of asking first.)

"Sure!" Kayla bent toward Tim. They hugged for a moment, and just before they parted, he kissed her lightly on the cheek. It was a good thing it was dark because they both were blushing.

"I hope you have a productive day tomorrow!" Tim declared. "I'll call you!" He then turned and walked away.

"Be safe tomorrow," Kayla called after him.

Back in his car, Tim's hands were shaking, and he was so excited he could barely stay in the seat. "I've gotta call Mojo," he said out loud.

Kayla walked into her home, a dazed look on her face. She stood there quite a while, smiling and recounting the evening. Maggie May wound herself around Kayla's legs and pulled her out of her reverie.

*****

140

Once he got home, Tim picked up his phone.

"Hey, Mojo. This is Tim."

"Hey, buddy! How was your date?" Sean and Jenny were just getting ready for bed.

Tim rapidly gave his answer. "Oh my gosh, Sean! I asked you the other day if it was possible that I was in love. I'm not wondering anymore. I pretty much *know* I am! She is *so* nice and *such* a lady."

"That's *great*, Tim. I'm happy for you! So is there another date in your future?"

"I've asked if I could call tomorrow after she gets home from school. I'm supposed to call around seven. Sean, I just can't believe it! I did all the stuff you said to do, and it *worked!* And I didn't kiss her or even go in her house after I dropped her off. We just hugged, and I even *asked* for that! I gave her a quick peck on the cheek. Oh my gosh! My hands are shaking like crazy!"

"Aw, man, I'm *so* glad to hear it went well!" Sean was genuinely happy for Tim.

"I don't think I'm gonna be able to sleep tonight!"

"Well, try to since you will be flying tomorrow!" Sean felt like a father advising his son.

"Sean, thank you *so* much! I had my doubts, but, as usual, you were right!"

Sean chuckled. "Any time, Tim. Take care."

Sean shared the news with Jenny. She smiled and stated with great finality, "They'll be married within the year."

Sean grinned at his wife then slid under the covers with her. "Here's to *great* relationships!" he said as he began kissing his wife's delicate neck.

*****

After ending his call with Sean, Tim realized his cheeks were sore from smiling so much.

Since he was so energized, he decided to take a late-night jog with Vladimir. Afterward, he showered. Once he finally fell asleep, he dreamed about going camping with Kayla.

Chapter 23

Jenny was rinsing the dishes from her and Elise's lunch when the doorbell rang. *I wonder who that could be?* She dried her hands and walked to the front door. Through the window, she could see that it was George. She smiled, unlocked the door, and opened it partially.

"Hi, George. What brings you out this way today?" Normally, she wouldn't have been particularly welcoming, but after all, Sean *had* invited him to their home for their party in April.

"Oh, I had to deliver some tools out to a site north of here. Since I was close, I thought I'd stop by and say hello to Sean and you."

"Okay. Well, Sean is at work right now." Though Jenny wasn't completely comfortable with inviting a man into their home when Sean wasn't there, she didn't want to be rude. "Why don't you come in and we can visit for a short bit."

"Great! I'd like that." George stepped into the house, and Jenny closed the door behind him.

"It's hot out there. Can I get you a cool drink of fresh lemonade?"

"That sounds wonderful. Thanks!" George realized he *was* thirsty.

Jenny began walking toward the kitchen, and George followed, appreciative of the opportunity to visit with the charming Jenny. "Just have a seat there at the table and I'll make each of us a glass," she directed.

George chose the chair that afforded him the best view of Jenny in the kitchen as well as the rest of the house. He watched her as she reached into the cabinet for two glasses. She sensed his gaze and smiled at him, albeit somewhat nervously. He quickly returned a friendly grin. *This should be okay*, she thought. *He seems harmless enough. Besides, Sean has always encouraged being kind to others and opening our home to everyone.*

Jenny filled the glasses with ice, opened the refrigerator door, and bent to reach the lemonade. George thought Sean was a very lucky man. She filled the glasses and walked around the peninsula to join him at the table.

"Here you go! This ought to be refreshing if you've been out working in the heat."

George sampled the welcome beverage. "I have, and it is!" He smiled appreciatively as he raised his glass toward her.

Jenny wanted to keep the conversation light so as to discourage a lengthy visit. "Have any of the police departments that you have applied to called you back?" Jenny took a sip of her lemonade.

"I've heard from three of them. One wants me to come in for an interview, one gave me a date to show up for a physical, and the other said they didn't have any positions currently available." (He hoped his answers sounded believable.)

"Well, I'm sure you'll find something soon enough. In the meantime, are you enjoying your current job?" she inquired.

"It pays the bills, and I get to travel all around the area. New Mexico is truly a beautiful state in its own way. I think *Land of Enchantment* is a good nickname for it."

The two of them continued chatting. Then Jenny's phone rang. She scrunched her nose and said, "Excuse me, it's my sister." George smiled at her and nodded.

Jenny stood and walked into the kitchen as she answered her phone. "Hey, Janice. What's up?"

"The kids and I are out running errands. We just bought a new movie, and Alicia wants to invite Elise over to go swimming and to spend the night. We're not too far away. I can come pick her up if that's okay."

"Oh, I bet she would *love* that. I'll help her get some things together. *Thanks*, Janice!"

"See you in a few!"

Jenny picked up the plate of gingerbread cookies she had baked that morning and walked back toward the table where George was sitting. "My sister's daughter has invited Elise to come over. They will be here in a few minutes to pick her up. I need to go help her pack a bag. In the meantime, feel free to enjoy some freshly made cookies! I'll just be a few minutes. Can I get you anything else?"

"No, I'm fine. Take your time!" George waved his hand from side to side to indicate he didn't need anything.

Jenny took a deep breath, smiled slightly uncomfortably, and exhaled as she nodded her head. (Truth be told, she had hoped he would recognize she was busy and just leave.) Then she proceeded to Elise's room. In a few minutes the two of them emerged, just as the doorbell rang.

"They're *here!*" Elise announced excitedly. Jenny stood behind her as she pulled the door open.

"Hey, Sis!" Janice grinned as she reached to hug Jenny. She saw the man at the table, and her eyes remained on him as she stepped back.

"Janice, this is George." Jenny motioned toward him. "Sean and I met him at karaoke one night. We invited him to our last party. He was in the area and stopped by to say hello."

"Hi," Janice said, somewhat uneasily as she was caught off guard by his presence.

"George, this is my sister, Janice."

George stood and flashed an easy, friendly smile as he greeted Jenny's sister. "Nice to meet you, ma'am."

Relieved by his relaxed manner, Janice nodded and returned, "Likewise." Then she turned back to face Jenny. "I guess we'd better get going. The kids are clamoring to get in the pool right away!"

Jenny squatted to hug Elise. "Remember to use your best manners and to follow all the safety rules at the pool. I love you. Daddy will probably call you this evening."

"Okay, Mommy!" Elise kissed Jenny on the cheek and dashed to Janice's van to join her cousins.

Jenny stood. "I'll come get her tomorrow. What would be a good time?"

"Oh, let her stay at *least* until after lunch. We can touch base at midmorning."

Jenny hugged her sister. "Thanks, Janice. I'll talk to you soon!" She watched as Janice checked to see that Elise had fastened the strap on her car seat correctly, then waved to everyone as the van backed out of the driveway and rolled down the street.

Jenny closed the door, smiled uncertainly at George, then moved toward the table where he sat. She chose the chair adjacent to him which was open to the rest of the room. *From here, I can move away quickly if I need to,* she thought.

"These cookies are *delicious!* Are they homemade?" George appreciated that she had given him a snack.

"Oh, yes. I really enjoy cooking and baking for my family!"

"You'd better take 'em away! I've already eaten three of them!"

Jenny laughed. She had eaten two herself while making them and decided that *that* was enough for the day.

George realized that Jenny was slightly uncomfortable now that the two of them were alone together in the house. Hoping to put her at ease, he quickly asked, "So how long have you and Sean been married?"

"Almost seven years. Elise was born about eleven months after the wedding, so we became a family pretty quickly."

"I see. Well, you are a great mom." George smiled warmly as he patted Jenny's forearm, which was resting comfortably on the table.

Jenny nearly jerked her arm back at the unexpected touch from another man, but then reconsidered. *That was just a…friendly, confirming touch,* she reasoned. She smiled at him a bit less nervously than before.

George was glad that she seemed to be relaxing a little. "Tell me about your wedding ring. I've never seen one like that before."

Jenny shared the story of the day she and Sean designed and ordered their rings. She decided to save the tale of the day Sean placed it on her finger while in the helicopter for another time when he could also be there.

"Well, that's very interesting." George reached out to touch the overlaid silver of the thunderbird figure. Of course, his large fingers also touched Jenny's. (In fact, he made *sure* to touch her hand more than was necessary, and he also lingered there *just* shy of too long. He watched her face for any signs of discomfort.) Again, she would have withdrawn her hand, but he truly seemed to be interested in the story and the design. *He's just looking at it. There's nothing wrong with that.*

He raised his eyes to meet hers and again smiled warmly. Jenny was slowly relaxing, as George was behaving very much like a gentleman.

"What time does Sean get off work?"

"They're trying out a new shift this month. He should be home for supper." Jenny was intentionally ambiguous just to be on the safe side.

"I see. How is it working out?"

"He's liking it. He doesn't have to get up too early, and he doesn't get home too late."

"Well, I'm sure *you're* liking that as well!" George cupped and squeezed Jenny's upper arm as he grinned affably.

Jenny decided that George was just a very touchy-feely kind of guy and opted to stop trying to analyze his intentions every time he touched her.

Their conversation rolled on easily. Jenny continued to lower her defenses as George was giving no indication of having any devious plans and kept the conversation focused mostly on what Jenny considered "safe" topics. *After all,* she surmised, *he stood like a gentleman when he met Janice, he has had an easygoing demeanor, and his smiles have been very genuine.* (George noticed *two* things: Jenny was not responding to his advances, but neither was she asking him to leave.)

"So what's your husband getting for supper tonight?"

"I have some white chicken chili in the Crock-Pot. It's a little less heavy than regular chili, so I sometimes make it in the summertime."

"Is that what I've been smelling? I'll bet it's *delicious!*"

"Oh, it is. Would you like to try a bite?"

"Could I? It sounds *fantastic.*"

"No problem!" Jenny said as she rose from her chair. She retrieved a bowl from the cabinet, a ladle from the drawer, and moved to where the Crock-Pot was situated in the deepest part of the kitchen on the opposite side of the peninsula—a fact that had not escaped George's attention.

His hands touched the sides of her arms. Quickly and with force, he turned her to him, and before she could think or have time to speak or react, he smothered her with a burning kiss.

Everything inside her head screamed *No!* even as everything in her body responded to his heated attentions to her. She could feel his need pressing against her torso.

His kisses trailed down to her neck, and he breathed warmly in her ears while tightly holding her arms at her sides. Her lack of resistance encouraged him. One of his hands moved to her breasts and roughly groped them.

He was *much* rougher with her than Sean had always been. The suddenness and intensity of his touch and kiss struck something deep within her. He pulled back to get a read on her. Unintentionally and unwittingly, she sought his lips.

He knew then that she was his. "Come on," he said gruffly. He grabbed her hand and pulled her toward the hallway and into her bedroom. He roughly pushed her into Sean's bed and began unzipping his pants.

She began to shake her head "no," so he quickly bent over her and filled her mouth with his tongue as he pushed her dress up to her waist. She could smell the gingerbread on his breath.

"I just *love* these skimpy little panties you housewives wear," he said with disdain as he jerked them down her legs and threw them to the floor.

Quickly, he moved over her. Though she initially tried to resist him, he overwhelmed her first with strength and then with sheer lust. He was not a gentle lover, and the startling difference between him and Sean did not escape her notice. She gave up all fight as he roughly violated all her body, causing sensations she had never before experienced.

He rolled off her and lay sweating and breathing hard next to her. (She was glad she had taken her and Sean's honeymoon quilt to the dry cleaners earlier in the day.) No cuddling, no pillow talk. She was not sure what to do. The reality of what had just happened began slowly seeping into her mind. She turned her head to look at him.

"You *needed* that," he taunted as he reached over and squeezed her nipple, hard. (George knew that right now, while she was still overwhelmed by and off-balance from what had just happened, was his best chance at controlling her mentally. He knew she would be in a state of confusion between good [pleasure] and evil [broken vows].)

She flinched. He laughed at her. "See? You didn't pull back." He laughed again then turned to face her. "When do you want some more?"

She was horrified at the conflicting thoughts that she shouldn't want it but that she did. She began to tremble.

"Don't be such a baby. You're a full-blown woman, desperately in need of some good lovin' like only I can give you. Just tell me when is the next time I can come over." He grabbed her arm, rolled her to her side, and slapped her forcefully on her butt cheek.

Her mind was frozen, and her lips couldn't move.

"Does your skirt-wearing husband work tomorrow?"

Almost imperceptibly, she nodded her head.

CHAPTER 24

He stood and dressed himself, then bent to give her a final rough grope on her breast as he once again forced his mouth on her, thereby squelching her cry of pain. He stood looking down at her, smirked, and commanded, "Gimme your number. I'll call you tomorrow about a time to come over."

She hesitated. He grabbed a handful of hair from the top of her head and yanked down, forcing her to face him. "I *know* women like you," he said through gritted teeth. He looked over her body. "You *think* you're a good girl, but you *like* it—the rougher, the better. Your kilt-wearing husband can't give you what I can." He clenched his jaws. "*Now tell me your number!*" There was a brutality in his voice that scared her.

As she called out the numbers, he typed them on his keypad. When her phone began ringing, he quickly grabbed it and entered his name into her contacts. He chuckled then thought, *That oughta put some more stress on her!* (He knew that more stress meant throwing her more out of sync and, therefore, the more control he could exert over her.) He gave her a final fierce stare then turned and walked away.

She was horrified. *What have I done?* She raised to a sitting position, hugged her knees, and rocked as she cried. Suddenly, Jenny glanced at the clock and sprang into action. She pulled on her dress, quickly stripped the sheets from the bed, and practically ran to the laundry room to wash them. After adding detergent she paused, then added some more. She switched the setting on the washing machine from warm to hot water.

Jenny hurried back to her room, grabbed a clean set of sheets from the bathroom cabinet, and placed them on the bed. Wailing mournfully, she quickly got in the shower, turned the water on as hot as she could take it, and cleaned herself thoroughly. After toweling off, she brushed her teeth and put on fresh clothes, hoping that Sean would be appreciative, as always, of clean sheets and a nice-smelling wife. *If he notices that I'm wearing different clothes than when he left this morning, I'll just tell him I spilled something on my dress*, she decided. Jenny was just dabbing on cologne when she heard the garage door open.

As Sean entered, he called out cheerily, "Hey, honey, I'm home!" He rounded the corner and smiled at his wife, who was just stepping out of the laundry room after moving the sheets to the dryer. They walked to each other and kissed. "Mmmm, you smell good!"

Jenny returned his smile. "I've got supper ready!" She moved toward the kitchen, and Sean followed. The bowl and ladle were still resting on the countertop.

"I see you are all prepared here!" Sean leaned into her as he teased hopefully, "You must have been wanting me to get home!" He turned his face to nuzzle her cheek.

Jenny raised the lid and stirred the chili as her eyes flirted with him in return to his comment.

"Wow! *That* smells good too!" Sean kissed her cheek and beamed at his wife. "You really know how to make a man want to come home at the end of his day!"

Jenny smiled coyly at her husband. Inside, she was as nervous as a cat caught in a net. "Let me serve you a bowl of this chili. I kinda nibbled on it and also some fruit as I cooked, so I'll just sit with you while you eat."

"Awww, are you sure? I don't want my sweetheart to wither up and blow away!" He had his arm around her waist with his hand resting on her hip.

"I'm fine. Oh! I made you some cookies for dessert!" She purposefully did not say "gingerbread" because that would make her think of *his* breathy kiss.

"Mmmm. You are going to *spoil* me, Jenny Wallach!"

Jenny cut a slice of corn bread from last night's leftovers and placed it in the microwave. As it heated, she ladled some chili into the bowl and topped it with a bit of shredded Monterey jack cheese and some chopped cilantro. She placed the bowl on the plate beside the corn bread and handed it to Sean. "Here, take this to the table. I'll bring you a spoon and some raspberry lemonade."

"Are the raspberries from our garden?"

"Yes. Elise and I picked them this morning. OH! Speaking of Elise, Janice called, and Alicia wanted her to come over and swim then watch her new movie. She's staying overnight. I told her you would call her later."

"I'm glad those two girls get along so well and that we live close enough for them to see each other often. I'll call her after I eat."

Jenny smiled at Sean as she placed his drink and spoon on the table beside his plate. She sat in the chair Sean had pulled out for her, then he sat, and they bowed their heads in prayer.

Sean began eating his supper, oohing and aahing as he went. "Jenny my love, if I didn't know better, I'd think you were guilty of something and were trying to distract me with your beauty and your delicious cooking!" He winked at her.

Jenny gave a flirty smile to her husband even as she thought her stomach was going to turn inside out. She decided she needed to tell Sean about George's visit—or at least part of it—especially since Janice and Elise had both seen him.

"Guess who stopped by today?"

While Sean loved trivia, logic, and problem-solving, he hated *that* type of question. There were too many answers and no clues to go on. He looked at Jenny and turned both of his hands palms up.

She giggled at him and said, "George."

"From karaoke?" Sean was slightly shocked but not particularly concerned.

"Uh-huh." Jenny shrugged. "I guess maybe he thought you'd be home."

"What did he want?" Sean took another bite of chili. As always, they looked at each other as they spoke.

Jenny was purposefully acting as nonchalantly as possible. "Just to visit. He had delivered some stuff near here. I told him you weren't home, but I didn't want to be rude, so I invited him in for a glass of lemonade since it was so hot outside."

Sean nodded as he looked at Jenny. He immediately felt a little warm fuzzy for his wife and her kind heart. He was also comforted by his knowledge that Jenny would have been very much a lady during George's visit.

"How long did he stay?" Sean continued eating, glad that he and Jenny were always completely honest with each other.

"He was still drinking his lemonade when Janice called. I brought the plate of cookies to the table and told him to enjoy a few while I helped Elise pack an overnight bag. Janice got here just as we finished. She saw him sitting at the table, and I introduced them. She and the kids left, I came back inside, and we talked a little while. I asked him about his prospects at the departments he applied to. He said he's heard back from two of them. He left not too long after Janice did."

"Well, I hope he is successful in finding a job. That was a brave move to quit one department and relocate to a new state without having something else lined up."

Jenny noted, "Brave...or maybe not too bright!" They both chuckled. "Why don't you load up a movie? I'll go take the sheets out of the dryer and fold them, then we can enjoy a quiet evening together on the couch." Jenny cast a demure glance at her husband.

"Aaah, my lady." Sean raised his eyebrows and nodded at his wife. "That sounds *wonderful!* But why did you change the sheets again? Didn't you do that in the last day or two?"

"Yes, but we got kinda sweaty last night, so I thought I'd just replace them again." Jenny knew *just* how to use her eyes and body to tease and flirt with Sean.

He decided to choose the shortest-playing movie they owned and couldn't wait until it ended.

Jenny put the sheets away, and Sean had the movie ready to go. They sat together on the sofa, and he put his arm around her. Sean pushed PLAY on the remote, and seconds later, Jenny's phone rang. She nearly jumped out of her skin.

She stood and moved into the hallway to see who was calling. It was Janice. "Hey, Sis. What's up?"

"Alicia wants to know if Elise can stay another night. They are having *so* much fun, and they are *even* letting Adam play with them. And, of course, that makes it easier for me and Tarak to spend a little time together!" Janice giggled nervously.

"Oh, Janice, I only packed her bag for one night!"

"Well, if *that's* the only problem, I've got *plenty* of clothes here she can wear."

"Okay. Let me ask Sean real quick. Hang on."

Jenny stepped back into the living room and asked if it were all right for Elise to stay a second night with Alicia.

Sean shrugged. "Sure, if it's okay with you."

"Janice, that'll be fine if you're *sure* you don't mind."

"Oh, it's no problem! We can talk the next day about maybe meeting halfway or something. I'm sure I'll have shopping to do!"

"Okay. *Thanks*, Sis. I know the girls will have fun! Give all the kids a hug for me and say 'hi' to Tarak!"

"Will do. Oh! Do you want Sean to talk to Elise while we're on the phone already?"

"Sure! I'll put him on."

Jenny handed her phone to Sean, and Janice handed hers to Elise.

"Hi, Daddy!"

"Hey! How's my little girl? Did you have a big day swimming with Alicia and Adam?"

"Yessir! We watched a movie, and now we're playing with dolls. Adam has his cars in Alicia's room, and he's driving some of them around."

"Well, you have a good time, sweetheart. Be nice and mind Aunt Janice and Uncle Tarak. I love you!"

"I love you too, Daddy. Don't forget to leave me your heart!"

"Oh, I could *never* forget that, baby! Do you want to say hi to Mommy?"

"Yes, please."

Sean handed the phone to Jenny and reversed the movie back to its beginning while she told Elise that she could stay another night with her cousins. After finishing the call, Jenny repositioned herself next to her handsome husband.

"Is everything okay?" Sean asked as he wrapped his arm securely around his sweet lady. He was keenly in tune with Jenny and noticed anytime something was even slightly different. It was part of how he tried to keep his wife happy.

"Sure!" she answered brightly. "Why?"

"You really jumped when your phone rang. Are you nervous about something?" Sean was also wondering why she took that call in the hallway; having nothing to hide, both of them normally answered their phones in each other's company. *Maybe she didn't want to disturb me from watching the movie.* He decided to just let that question lie.

"No, no. I just wasn't expecting it." Jenny looked up at her husband with googly eyes. "I was really relaxed and looking forward to snuggling with you, that's all."

"Okay." He grinned as he glanced at her. "Well, now we have to make up for lost time!"

The movie was a mere formality, an excuse to wind down from the day and spend some quiet time together before going on to the more physical part of the evening. About midway through its showing, Sean began gently stroking Jenny's hair and then caressing the side of her neck. He pulled her closer (translation: practically in his lap) and began tempting her with his soft, warm lips.

They didn't last until the end of the movie. Sean was glad he had remembered to activate the auto shut off on both the Blu-ray player and the TV.

They made soft, sweet, slow love then slept deeply and in each other's arms. The sunbeam slithering across the floor was their alarm. They awoke refreshed and at peace.

Until Jenny remembered.

She quickly rose from the bed. "Be right back!" she exclaimed. She washed her face, put on fresh clothes, and brushed her teeth. When she exited, Sean was sitting on the edge of the bed.

He was staring straight ahead and stated matter-of-factly, "I'm halfway thinking of calling in today." Then he looked up at his beautiful wife and whined, "I love my job, but I just want to stay here with you!"

Jenny smiled as her mind raced. If Sean stayed home and George stopped by again, it *could* cause Sean to be suspicious. "Why don't you go ahead and get ready for the day, and we'll see how you feel when it gets closer to the time for you to leave?"

"You're right. Okay, my love. Sean Wallach here, at your service!" Sean stepped into the bathroom and did as he was told. When he exited, Jenny had just finished brushing her hair. He helped her straighten the sheets. "Where is our quilt?"

"I took it to the dry cleaners yesterday morning for its annual cleaning." They walked together to the kitchen to prepare breakfast.

Jenny was relieved that Sean seemed to think everything was normal.

*****

George sat shirtless on the edge of a dirty bed in a dirty motel room; the integrity of the mattress was long gone, given the weight and movements of its various users over time. A slick layer of sweat covered him. He picked up the phone and dialed the front desk.

"The air conditioner in my room is *still* not working," he boomed. "You said you'd finally have it fixed *today*."

He listened to the excuse of the day then cursed at the operator and slammed the phone onto its receiver.

He used his foot to push open the lid on the cooler sitting nearby. "Great. No AC, no beer."

He gathered his keys and wallet; at least he could do something about the second problem.

Upon returning, he tried leaving the door open, but that just made things worse. The smell of the hot pavement and the sound of the cars whizzing by on the interstate were worse than the still, stale air. He rose and slammed the door.

He reached for the remote, turned on the TV, and began scrolling through the channels. He stopped on a *Jerry Springer* rerun. "Maybe some little slut will show her tits."

He wanted to be with Jenny, right now. But he knew Sean would be there. "Damn," he said as he bobbed his head, turned it to the side, and snorted derisively. He was envious of Sean, his job, his affluence, and his relationship with Jenny. "He can't give her what she needs." George had a habit of speaking his mind even when no one was there to listen.

For his part, George knew lust when he first saw Jenny months ago at the karaoke bar. When he learned she was married, he knew that he would have to be very careful, very patient, and very conniving to achieve the object of his desire.

The first step was to gain her trust—and that meant gaining Sean's. He was pleased when he was invited to their house. That accomplished two things: he knew where they lived, and he could watch them interact.

His talk with Sean that night after they sang together did not yield the information about him and his schedule that George had wanted. Instead, it had nearly been disastrous. "That Sean is a smart one."

George was a master chameleon and a skilled manipulator. Since that night, he had tried to lay low, be friendly, and bide his time. He purposefully did not go to the bar each time the group met as that could have made him appear overly anxious. He went often enough to keep himself in the loop with the group. But more importantly, he wanted to keep himself in a position to learn more about Jenny.

Now that he had reached his goal, he wanted more. *Lots* more. "I can have *loads* of fun with her." Then he laughed at his unintended double entendre.

Chapter 25

Sean and Jenny frequently cooked together, and they worked well as a team. They quickly whipped up scrambled eggs, bacon, and pancakes. After prayer, Sean served Jenny's plate. They made small talk during the meal.

"Jenny, is everything okay? You seem a little…distant."

"No, I'm fine. I'm just very relaxed and comfortable."

"Well, I'm *happy* about that, but you've hardly eaten anything. So I'm going to ask you again, is everything okay?"

Jenny knew she had better straighten up and act normal or Sean would stay home to keep an eye on her. She forced a smile on her face and renewed energy in her demeanor. "Yes! I'm actually thinking about the dining room. I was wondering if we might want to go ahead and go to Santa Fe to look for a nice dining table and chairs." *That should do it*, she thought. *I didn't say anything definite like needing to weed the garden. He'd notice whether I got that done or not. Just keep smiling and get him off to work*, she told herself.

"Yeah, we kinda have let that slide for quite some time. Do you have any idea what style you're interested in?"

Jenny was relieved. Sean seemed to have bought her story. And *fortunately*, she *had* somewhat recently thought about the look she wanted in the dining room. "I definitely want something older and fairly substantial…a little masculine?" Jenny narrowed her eyes and scrunched her nose. "Maybe with a bit of Spanish influence?"

"That sounds nice. When would you like to do this? And do you want to look here in town or make it more of a day trip to Santa Fe with Elise?"

"We can *try* some stores here, but I think an antique is going to be what we want. Have you ever restored any furniture—in case we find something that needs a little 'love'?"

There's my Jenny, thought Sean. *She looks and sounds much more like herself now. She doesn't normally get that distracted. But she seems okay now.* "My dad did a little bit of that sort of thing, and Colin and I always loved to watch him as he puttered around out in his little workspace."

Jenny's mind was racing. She was walking two *very* thin lines and playing a *very* dangerous game. "Why don't we tentatively think about driving up there on your next day off?" *That way*, she thought, *even if George comes over, we won't be here.*

"All right then. Let's clean up our breakfast mess, and you can tell me what you're going to do today while trying not to miss me too badly!" Sean loved teasing his wife like that.

Working together, they quickly took care of bringing order back to the kitchen. Jenny shared that she couldn't decide between researching furniture restoration techniques, shopping online for seeds and plants for their fall garden, or reading the new book she had recently purchased. *Nothing tangible in those activities*, she surmised. *That will buy me a little time.*

"Well, I guess I'll go to work after all. I don't like to use up my sick days, you seem to have a full agenda, and besides, it's a beautiful day for flying." Sean went to their room to change into work clothes. While there, he saw something on the floor just under the bed and reached to pick it up. After determining what it was, he set it on the top shelf of his side of the closet.

Jenny's phone rang. She stepped out onto the back porch to see who it was. The screen read "George." She quickly declined the call and then deleted it from her "Recents." She changed the setting to "vibrate only" then pocketed it and walked back inside.

Sean came around the corner of the hallway. "Who called?" he asked brightly.

"It was just spam," Jenny answered while shaking her head.

"Why did you take it outside?" His face showed he was more than just curious.

"Sean, you are acting very distrustful! I was just glancing at the garden to see if it needed watering right away or if I could hold off for a little while!"

"Well, *you've* been acting kinda strange!"

They were several feet apart, and both stood in an aggressive stance with a challenging facial expression. Suddenly, both of them realized how foolish it was to be bantering like this. They quickly moved toward each other and hugged.

"I'm sorry, baby. You just seemed a little off last night and this morning, and I got a little scared." Sean rubbed Jenny's back as he held her.

"I know," Jenny responded. "I'm sorry. I've got a lot of ideas swirling around in my head. I haven't even talked with you about some of them yet. I should slow down!" She leaned back from his embrace and smiled up at him.

Sean held Jenny close and inhaled the scent of her hair. A groan escaped him.

Jenny noticed and pulled back slightly. She glanced at the clock on the wall then looked up at her husband alluringly. "Wanna get in a quickie?"

"You betcha!" Sean had once again fallen victim to Jenny's ability to beguile him.

Afterward, as Sean was redressing for work, Jenny pointed out, "We've never had to have 'make-up' sex before!"

Sean laughed. He bent to kiss her forehead, winked at her, and told her he loved her. On his way out the door, he hollered, "See you this evening!"

Jenny lay in bed, hugging Sean's pillow and drinking in his manly smell. She heard her phone vibrate in the pocket of her shorts on the chair. She raced to retrieve it. It was a text from George.

> Don't ignore me like that again.

Her heart was racing. *What have I done? I know this is wrong, but I can't quit. What is it about him? He already has such a hold on me! I'm afraid of what he might do*, she thought.

She was standing naked in her and Sean's room with tears running down her cheeks when the phone began vibrating from an incoming call.

"Hello?" she answered breathlessly. She hadn't even looked to see who it was.

"Hey, babe. I forgot to tell you. They are changing me back to morning shift starting tomorrow. I thought I had better let you know in case that affects your household activities at all."

"Okay. Thanks, Sean. I'll adjust our meal schedule. Fortunately, we've been doing this for a while, and I already know how to handle it!"

"Right. Okay, well, have a good day, sweetheart."

"I will. Bye, Sean. Be safe. I love you."

"I love you too, Jenny."

Just as the call ended, the vibrating started again. This time, she knew who it was. She took a deep breath and channeled all the confidence she could muster. "Hello?"

"It's about time. Has that husband of yours left yet?"

"Yes." Jenny's voice was lustier than she had wanted it to be.

"What time is he due back? I wanna know how much time I have to play with you."

She hesitated.

"And don't mess around and give me some range of time. Guys like that follow the clock. You *know* when he'll be there. Now tell me!"

"About seven thirty."

"I'll be there in twenty minutes. Why don't you have some food ready for me. I'm bringin' some beer. Put on something sexy."

Jenny opened her mouth to speak, but the call ended. She grunted in frustration at how quickly he was assuming control.

She was *still* standing there naked, but now she was shaking with a strange mixture of rage and desire. She looked in the mirror. She wasn't sure she knew the woman standing there.

*****

The doorbell rang, and Jenny raced to open the door. He was fifteen minutes late. George marched straight in, what was left of a six-pack of longnecks under his arm. He didn't say hello, he didn't smile at her or hug her. He simply ordered, "Next time I come over, have the door unlocked so I can just walk in." He opened the refrigerator, set the three beers inside, and stood upright. His eyes scanned over her.

"I guess that'll do for today. I'd be willing to bet you got somethin' a lot sexier in that closet o' yours. I'll pick somethin' out later for next time."

She was still standing at the door, angry at him for being late but relieved that he was there. She stared down into the abyss she knew she was falling into. She didn't know what to say or what to do.

He strode to her, grabbed her arm, and commanded, "Come on." He jerked her roughly and walked so fast she had to almost jog to keep up with him. Once in the bedroom, he shoved her onto the bed like he did yesterday. She immediately sat upright.

She was breathing hard—more from fear, confusion, and passion than from exertion. Her eyes sought his. She wanted him to service her like yesterday, to bring her to that new level of fulfillment. She found no connection with him, as he was snarling at her, contemplating what he was going to do to her.

"You were late," she stated defiantly.

He laughed. "It's good to know you're so anxious to be with me!" His face turned serious. "I had to park down the street, stupid, and walk here. I can't risk your helicopter husband seeing my truck in his driveway." (He frequently referred to Sean in order to let her know that he was not only taking her *for* himself, but also *from* Sean.)

"I'd like to take this belt and whip you good so you'll know who's boss around here. But I suspect that panty waisted husband of yours would notice the stripes and cause a lot of problems."

She gasped at the notion of being spanked with a belt. Her dark eyes were smoldering embers.

He laughed. His face took on a sinister look. "You know you want it. Say it!" he commanded.

She continued glaring up at him.

He stepped to her and raised his fist to backhand her.

It took everything she had to not flinch.

He lowered his hand and chuckled. "I like that in a woman. I like 'em when they're hard to tame. It makes the fall even sweeter. Women like you *always* end up being the most obedient."

By now she was shaking. But she had not moved.

He squinted his eyes and leaned toward her. "I gave you an order. I *expect* obedience."

Something rose up in her—a rebellion she could not deny.

He grabbed a handful of her hair and jerked her head back. She grimaced silently. "You are *going* to say 'I want it' even if I have to beat it out of you. Now open that pretty little mouth of yours and say it." He pulled down even harder on her hair. Again, she grimaced, and again she managed to not utter a sound.

"I want it," she mumbled.

He jerked her hair with even more force. This time a small squeal escaped her. "I can't understand you!" His teeth were clenched in rage.

"I want it," she said clearly but quietly.

He yanked her head to the floor, and her body followed. "You are gonna learn that I am *much* easier to get along with when I am obeyed." He knew that she would enter a state of compliance if he could quickly cause her enough pain to fear more of it.

"I want it!" she yelled. The trembling had stopped. Now she was incensed.

That is precisely where he wanted her. Angry people did what they were told, in some weird way of proving that they could stand up to the person in control.

"Why don't you raise up and unzip my pants?" he growled.

She obeyed.

He glanced down at her. "Now stand and unbutton and take off my shirt. And don't you *dare* throw it on the floor." He jutted his chin toward the two chairs by the window. "Set it nicely on that chair over there, the one your *husband* sits in."

Again, she did as she was told, admiring his tanned and muscular body as her hands ran across his shoulders. She noticed a long scar on his left side but said nothing.

"Now I want *you* to get undressed." He was spitting his words out and leaning toward her. "And I want you to do it like the little tease you are. *Make me smile.*" He straightened and reared his head back haughtily.

She pulled off her shirt first, then her shorts. Both were tight, so a good bit of wiggling was required to get them off. She was wearing nothing else.

He grabbed her arm and pulled her to him. He pulled one of her arms behind her back with his opposite arm and used the other hand to lift her thigh up his leg. He kissed her. Hard. She could taste the beer in his mouth. He ground himself against her. He released her leg but continued to hold her arm tightly behind her as he bent to nibble and kiss her neck, chest, and abdomen. He was relentless in his assault. He could tell it was taking a toll on her. She was ready for him.

"Get on your knees," he ordered with a raspy voice.

She willingly obeyed.

CHAPTER 26

He pulled his pants back up and zipped them. She remained on the floor, her eyes staring blankly at it.

"Stand up."

She obeyed. Her eyes remained downcast.

"Put on a robe or somethin' and then get in the kitchen and fix me somethin' to eat."

As she turned to walk away, he caught her arm and growled, "Don' even think about tryin' to get away with somethin' tricky." Then he pinched her hard on her bottom.

She could sense the warmth of his face next to hers, smell the beer as he exhaled, and feel his hot breath blowing on her face.

"Step it up, girl. I'm hungry. Don' make me wait."

She went to the closet, pulled a simple sundress over her head, and walked into the kitchen. He followed closely behind her.

"Gimme' some o' that chili you were s'posed to give me yesterday. And bring me a cold beer while you're heatin' my food."

She put some chili in a disposable bowl, set it in the microwave, and turned it on. She reached into the refrigerator and then delivered his beer to him.

He intently watched her every move and took long gulps of the beer. "I ain't eatin' outa' no *paper* bowl. Serve me up in your good stuff." Keeping her back to him, she took a deep breath, vowing to herself that she could take anything he could dish out. She reached into the cabinet for a ceramic bowl.

"What kinda toppings you gonna use? I *know* you put stuff on *his*. Make mine pretty."

She was glad she still had a bit of grated cheese in a container in the fridge as well as more cilantro. She emptied the heated chili into the bowl and topped it with the extras. She pulled a spoon from the drawer and walked the food to him.

He ordered her to sit with him as he ate. "Bring me another beer," he said with a mouthful of food. When she returned with it, he ordered, "Open your mouth." She did, and he shoved a spoonful of chili into it. "You're a purty good cook. I like that." He laughed at her as she chewed.

Suddenly, he leaned toward her and snarled right in her face. "You need to say thank you when I'm kind enough to give you somethin'!"

"Thank you," she whispered with pouty lips. She was staring upward into his eyes.

He leaned back. "You...are...a...*sexy* little thing. Too bad your 'man' can't give you what you need." He smirked as he shook his head from side to side. "If you were mine, I'd keep you on a short leash." He narrowed his eyes and nodded as he spoke. "Anything you got, you'd have to earn, including food. Pleasing me would be your one job." He stared at her with cold eyes.

She sucked air through her open mouth and shivered with fear and desire as she envisioned life with him. He took note of the effect his words had on her.

When he finished eating, he pushed his chair back and instructed her to sit on his leg. He reached under her dress and touched her. Everything he did was rough. He watched her face and laughed when she grimaced as he explored her.

"Ya got any more of them cookies? I'll bet you do. Be a good girl and get me some." He slapped her on the bottom as she walked away.

She went into the kitchen, put two cookies on a napkin, and brought them to him.

"Don't try to get stingy with me. Go back in there and bring the whole plate!"

She could hear him chuckling as he watched her walk away to follow his order.

He touched each cookie, using the hand he had used under her dress, grinning up at her as he did so.

"Well, I'm ready for some more of that lovin' your husband is so fond of. And I know *you* want it, too, cuz you already *told* me you did." He reared his head back and laughed out loud. "Let's go to our little *love nest*!"

He told her to start walking. Then, because he could, he said, "Stop. Get me another beer. And raise that dress up so I can watch you walk in front of me."

She obeyed his commands. After she gave him his drink, he ordered her to turn with her back to him. She waited as he gulped part of it down.

He pressed himself hard against her from behind; she actually had to push back slightly to keep from being pushed forward—which is what he wanted. He spoke directly into her ear. She could smell the chili and the beer and the gingerbread. "See how easy things go when you do as you're told? I'll bet your husband can't control you like I can. Now walk."

She heard him belch as he walked behind her.

Once in the bedroom, she stopped, awaiting further instruction. He stood close behind her, reached up and stroked her hair, and pulled it back away from her face. He breathed into her ear. "I like how you're wanting and waiting for my command." With his other hand, he grasped and then smacked her buttock.

"Get on the bed, girl! I'm gonna give it to you good! We got *lots* of time!" He gulped down some of his beer.

He began working her over as he removed both their clothes, and he knew what he was doing. She was beginning to hate him, his brute nature, and his stench. But he had a way of finding the yearning inside her. And he knew when she was ready.

He scooched back and taunted her. He wanted this woman— and all others for that matter—to beg him. He wanted them to beg for what he was going to do anyway.

"Tell me you want me."

She grimaced and could not bring herself to say it.

He moved closer so his face was right beside her ear. Though he spoke quietly this time, there was a hate-infused fervor that made her adrenaline rush. "Am I gonna have to retrain you on followin' my command?" His breath was smelly from beer and hot with lust.

When she didn't respond, he touched her roughly. "I'm *gonna* have my way with you. So you may as well do what I say. I *know* you want what I got. Now just tell me."

"I want you."

"Oh, really? Whatta you want?"

She rolled her eyes.

Instantly, he was above her. He grabbed a thick handful of hair and yanked her head back, got in her face, and screamed at her. His spit flew from his lips and onto her cheeks and mouth. His face was red with rage. "Don't you *ever* disrespect me like that again, do you hear me?"

She cringed. "Yes."

He backed away, his naked body kneeling above her. She could see that he wanted her. *Maybe if I just do what he says, it will end sooner.*

She opened her mouth and stated what he wanted to hear.

He finished off the beer, set the bottle on the nightstand, and gave her what she had said she wanted.

She didn't want to enjoy it. But he was fierce in his passion, thorough in his attack on her body, and able to manipulate her as he wanted.

Like the day before, he lay beside her afterward, sweating and panting. No cuddling, no caressing, no sweet kisses.

Suddenly, he sat up. "Well, you've satisfied me, fed me, and satisfied me again. Now you're gonna clean me up. Come on, let's take a shower."

She rose and followed him into the bathroom. She stood nearby as he adjusted the temperature of the water in the shower.

"Get in."

She did, and he followed her. "What are you waitin' on, girl? Get after it! I wanna be squeaky clean."

She began to rub the bar of soap over him.

"Don' miss any spots. And do an extra good job down there. I don't wanna smell like some *tramp*." He said the last word with such contempt that she almost believed it to be true.

When she finished rinsing him, he had her dry him off. By then, he was ready for more action. They walked out of the bathroom.

He picked her up and tossed her onto the bed. She landed on her stomach.

He straddled across her. She tried to turn over and fight, but he overpowered her. If she thought he had been rough before, then this was all-out brutality. He was done with games. He wanted to take her ruthlessly. And this time, he didn't care if she wanted or even enjoyed it.

She had never before been sodomized. She cried out. He told her to shut up. When she didn't stop screaming, he grabbed her hair, turned her head to the side, and shoved part of a pillow in her mouth.

Once he finished, he sat on the edge of the bed and ordered her to get him a warm, damp washcloth. She came out of the bathroom and tried to hand it to him. He laughed at her. "Don't you get it? You're here to serve *me!* Now clean me up."

She began the task, but he grabbed her hand and stopped her. "I said *warm*, you stupid little whore! Go back and try again."

She did as she was told with shaking hands, completed the task, then went to the bathroom to use soap and water to clean the cloth.

When she came out of the bathroom, he had finished getting dressed. "I know you need some time to hide all the signs of me being here. I know you'll miss me, but I gotta jet now. And I shouldn't have to tell you to keep that sexy mouth of yours shut real tight about this. If your wuss of a husband finds out, it will mess up my plans with you."

He reached for her and pulled her to him. As he had on the first day, he kissed her roughly. However, this time she tried to fight back. He held her tight and continued with his mouth on hers. The harder she fought, the rougher he got. Ultimately, she began to relax, mostly out of sheer exhaustion. When he finally pulled back, she could barely stand. He grabbed her hand and moved it to his groin.

He looked her up and down and grinned like a madman. "You remember this, you little c———. You *wanted* what I gave you. From my first kiss, you wanted all I had to give. You *told* me I could come back. You dressed for me, you hungered for me, you fed me, and you cleaned me. You *know* you need it the way only *I* can give it to you."

He pulled her to him again, wanting to drive home his point. He rubbed his hands over her as he kissed her over and over. When he heard her groan, he knew he could come back again. He released her slowly and was curiously gentle in helping her to remain standing.

"Does your sweet little husband work tomorrow?"

Against her will, she nodded as she wiped her mouth with the back of her hand. Her lips were swollen with passion, and she was glaring at him with upturned eyes.

"Same time?"

"No. Morning shift."

"Seven to three?"

She nodded.

"I'll be here at seven-thirty." He thought for a moment and remembered something. "Let me look in your closet for an outfit for you to wear for me tomorrow. Come with me."

He filtered through her clothes, finally settling on a short, flouncy jean skirt and a tight-fitting, midriff-baring blouse with buttons down most of the middle. "Don't button these after you put it on. I'll need easy access to you if I'm going to please you again…*like only I can*."

As he said those last four words, he looked over at her and made eye contact. He emphasized them and nodded as he stated them. He knew that as long as he could make her believe she needed him, he could continue to entertain himself by using her body.

"Gimme a last li'l kiss." He stood a bit away from her, forcing her to either disobey him or move to him willingly. Still reeling from his last attentions to her, she tiptoed to kiss him. He hungrily accepted her mouth. As he explored her with his tongue, he touched her roughly. She tensed but continued kissing him in return. When he pulled back, he gave her two quick little slaps on her cheek. She gasped and raised her hand to her face.

He leaned toward her and spoke right at her face. "Don't you forget about me or what I can do to you."

She was panting through her open mouth, her eyes lifted up to his.

"I'm leavin' you all stirred up *on purpose* so you'll keep thinkin' about me." A surly half-smile spread across his face. "Have fun with twinkle toes tonight," he taunted then cocked his head back. "By tomorrow, you should be needin' me pretty bad."

He snorted at her derisively then turned and walked away.

CHAPTER 27

H er mind was in a whirl. *What time is it? Three o'clock. Sean will get home around seven-thirty. Four and a half hours.* She tried to make a mental list of all she needed to do, but she was weak from having not eaten much breakfast or even supper the night before. She was physically tired from her encounter with *him* and from fighting him, and emotionally wrung out from what he had put her through in order to control her. And, of course, she had also loved Sean *twice* in the last twenty-four hours.

Spiritually, she was a mess. *I need to pray,* she thought, but then shook her head. *Heavenly Father must be very angry with me right now.* A sob escaped her. *This is all my fault. I should have told him no. Now I don't know* what *to do!* Her body shook as she cried.

Mostly, she just wanted to be in Sean's loving arms. *I can't let him find out! It will kill him!* She collapsed into the bed. She wanted to rest, to heal, to sleep, and to make it all go away. She smelled *him* on the sheets. Her body jerked involuntarily as she thought of their time together. She knew she wanted more sessions with him, even while knowing how very wrong it was.

Her phone vibrated on the nightstand.

"Hello."

"Are you missing me yet?" *he* taunted.

"Maybe."

"*Maybe?* Sounds like I didn't give you enough of what you want so badly. Tomorrow I'll have to make sure you are *so* satisfied that you can't wait to start again."

She was too tired and too confused to respond.

"Are you there?"

"Yes."

"Touch yourself."

"Why?"

"Because I told you to, you stupid little b———!"

She was silent.

"Are you doing it?"

"Maybe. How will you know the difference?"

"Ahhh, yes. You're one of those smart ones. That just means I'll have to work you harder. You *will* submit to me. Mark my word."

She wanted to tell him they needed to stop, but the call ended—yet another power move on his part.

Jenny glanced at the clock and realized she only had about four hours left before Sean got home and about five hours' worth of things that needed to be done.

She rolled out of bed, slipped into the sundress, and went to the kitchen to get an apple. *This'll give me enough energy to get some things done.* As she ate it, she thought of all that needed to be completed. *Prioritize*, she told herself. *Do the* most *important things first* then *figure out the rest.*

Jenny decided that the sheets *had* to be washed, dried, and put back on the bed. Sean would notice if they were a different set. So she stripped the linens and loaded them into the washer.

Next, she rinsed the bowl and spoon from George's lunch and put them in the dishwasher. She realized she would have used a glass for a drink, so she grabbed a glass from the cabinet and loaded it into the dishwasher as well.

Remembering the soiled cookies, Jenny decided on a solution. She dropped the plate on which they were stacked to the floor, then quickly swept up the shards from the plate and the crumbs from the cookies. She dampened the mop and swabbed a large area to remove any stickiness. If Sean asked about the cookies, she would tell him she accidentally knocked them off the counter while working in the kitchen. She would stress that there were tiny particles of glass all over the cookies, and she was afraid for her family to eat them for fear of ingesting one of the little splinters.

Jenny retrieved the bathroom cleaner and a sponge from the shelf in the laundry room. *Thank goodness I normally keep a pretty clean house. Maybe Sean won't recognize that I will have cleaned the shower again so soon.* She wet the sponge, sprayed the walls of the shower with the cleaner, and wiped them down. She took the soap to the lavatory so she could rinse it carefully as she checked to make sure that none of *his* hair was on it. She replaced the soap on the shelf in the shower stall then used the sponge and spray cleaner to disinfect the floor of the shower, again checking carefully for foreign hairs.

Jenny decided that she would go ahead and give a quick wipe down to the vanity area—just in case a stray hair found its way there. She gathered the soiled washcloth and the towel she had used when drying *him* and walked to the laundry room.

The washer was just finishing up the spin cycle on the sheets. She moved them to the dryer then put the towel and washcloth in the washer and started it. (Jenny didn't want to wash them with anything else.)

In the kitchen, she opened the refrigerator to make sure *he* had removed his beer carton. She moved some items around so that the blank space he had created in which to set it no longer existed. She wiped the countertops and also the breakfast room table.

Jenny knew she needed to have supper ready for her sweet Sean. She glanced in the freezer. *Yes!* She was happy that she routinely froze leftovers to be used for spur-of-the-moment meals. There was a container with about four servings of Sean's favorite vegetable lasagna. She also saw that there were two slices of garlic bread wrapped in foil. She set both items on the counter so that they could begin to thaw.

Next, she glanced in the trash can. There, right on the top, were two beer bottles. Jenny knew a third one was on her nightstand. (*He* had purposefully left them there, knowing it would create an added bit of stress for her in deciding what to do with them.) She quickly went to her and Sean's room to retrieve the longneck as her mind worked overtime. *I can't throw them away here! Sean is so on top of things! He will either see them, hear them bumping against each other, or smell them when he takes out the trash.* She determined the only way to get rid of them was to put them in a bag with a few other things, including the paper bowl in which she had heated *his* food, place the bag in her SUV, and drive to a convenience store to use the trashcan outside their door.

What if Sean notices my car has moved? What if someone sees me out and about and mentions it to Sean? She decided she would buy some ice cream for her and Sean to eat after supper. *I never shop there! It's too expensive, and Sean knows that.* She quickly justified the decision: since she only needed one item, she didn't want to go all the way to the grocery store. Besides, it was a last-minute thought to indulge him, and she didn't have time to wander through the store and wait in line at the register.

Satisfied with her solution, she knew she could resort to teasing Sean with her eyes, smile, and body if needed in order to distract him.

She hated the person she was becoming. And she was beginning to realize the amount of control *he* was exerting over her even when he wasn't with her—both in her thoughts and in her actions.

Jenny checked the sheets to see if they were dry enough to put on the bed. Because she had selected the hottest setting (she wanted to kill off as much of *his* filth and stench as possible), they were. She set them on top of the dryer so she could insert the towel and washcloth and begin drying them. *I might just get this all done*, she thought.

She quickly made the bed then jumped in the shower for a thorough cleaning. She didn't have time to dry her hair, but since it was so hot outside, she knew it would be okay. As she dried herself, she noticed the shorts and shirt that she had been wearing when *he* arrived lying on the floor. She shoved them and the sundress she had donned under some other laundry in her basket in the closet. *If Sean wonders why I have so many dirty clothes, I'll just tell him the shorts were getting a little snug and that is why I resorted to the sundress. That would also explain my not eating much. I'll tell him I had put on a few pounds and wanted to cut back.* Jenny smiled. *I'll flirt with him and tell him it's for him.*

"This is all getting to be very complicated and exhaustive," she said out loud.

Jenny dabbed some cologne on the back of her neck, in her cleavage, and at her navel. She slipped into Sean's favorite floral dress and buckled on a pair of sandals.

She fetched a grocery bag from the pantry, put the three beer bottles in it, and covered them with some of the trash from the can. She tied the bag and set it by the door leading into the garage.

She got her wallet and keys from their closet, her phone from the nightstand, and picked up the beer bottle trash on her way out to her car. *Oh! I almost forgot the things in the dryer!*

She quickly walked to the laundry room, removed the towel and washcloth, and folded them. *We don't know what people have gotten on towels at hotels. We just assume they are clean and use them. I'm just not going to think about these,* she thought as she put them away in the bathroom cabinet.

Jenny drove to the nearest convenience store, nonchalantly deposited the bag of trash in the can outside the door, and went inside to buy a pint of Sean's favorite mint chocolate chip ice cream.

The clock on her dashboard read five thirty as she pulled into the garage. Once inside, she put the ice cream in the freezer. Then she walked through the house, trying to remember precisely everywhere *he* had been. She looked for any clues of his presence and decided that she had done a good job of covering up their tryst.

And she hated herself for having to do that.

Chapter 28

The final part of Jenny's smoke screen was to create the illusion that she had been busy all day, as was her norm. *What did I tell Sean I was going to do?* She knew she would need to begin getting supper ready around seven; that meant she had roughly one and a half hours to generate about eight hours of busyness.

Jenny got her computer and a notebook and pen from the dresser in their room and brought the items to the table. She opened the website where she typically shopped for garden supplies. *Fortunately,* she had previously put some thought into what she wanted and how she would lay it all out. She made a quick sketch of the garden and drew arrows pointing to the different rows, noting what she intended to plant in each. Below it, she rapidly jotted prices of seeds, plants, and other items she would need. *If Sean questions me, I'll just tell him that this is the first run at it and that I will double-check everything before placing an order.*

While she was on the computer, she hit several furniture-restoration websites. She spent virtually no time on any of them. But now they were in her history, and she could show them to Sean if it came up in conversation.

Finally, Jenny sat on one of the sofas and reached for her recently purchased book which was resting on the coffee table. *I'll just speed-read through a few chapters. If Sean asks about it, I'll be able to tell him a little something about the characters and the plot. If necessary, I'll tell him it wasn't very good or that I just was having a hard time getting into it.*

She wanted to cry at the mess she had gotten herself into, but Sean would notice if her eyes were red. *This is crazy! I've never before had* anything *to hide. Now it feels like I have to lie about almost* everything! *Where is that strong girl Sean always talks about and loves so much? I feel like a blithering idiot!*

She set the alarm on her phone to go off at seven so she could get supper ready then forced herself to focus on the book for the time she had remaining.

*****

Jenny was setting the table when she heard the garage door open. She rushed over to the door at the end of the hallway to greet Sean.

"I missed you today!" she said as she hugged him close.

"Well, we will have to make up for lost time then!" he replied as he looked down at her and smiled. He was happy that his wife was back to her normal good spirits.

"Why don't you get changed while I finish up with supper?"

"Okay. It smells wonderful, and I'm hungry. I'll be quick!"

Jenny removed the lasagna from the oven, put the garlic bread in its place, and then reached into the refrigerator for the salad she had made of red cabbage, green apples, pepitas, walnuts, and Craisins. She placed the tongs in the bowl and carried it and the Italian dressing to the table. As she was putting ice in the glasses, she heard Sean coming down the hall. She poured the last of the raspberry lemonade into the two glasses and set them at their places at the table.

"What can I do?" he asked.

"I'll put the trivets down if you'll carry the lasagna to the table."

"Got it!" he responded cheerfully.

He pulled Jenny's chair out, seated her, and then himself.

"Why don't you offer prayer this evening, my love?"

"Okay." Jenny was somehow aware that he was trying to gauge her mental state by his suggestion. She smiled at him and bowed her head.

Sean must have been satisfied that all was well because he seemed content all evening. They sat on the couch together and discussed the minutia of life. When she showed him her ideas for the garden, he indicated that he was pleased with what she had chosen. She opened the furniture-restoration websites on her computer and had him look over them while she served the ice cream in small sundae glasses.

"Would you like a little squirt of whipping cream on top?" Jenny called from the kitchen.

"Of *course!*"

As they ate their ice cream, Sean playfully put a dab of whipping cream on his wife's nose. This led to him gently wiping it off which, of course, led to a make-out session which, of course, led to early retirement to the bedroom.

While holding her afterward, Sean told her he was the luckiest man in the world to have a wife like her. Jenny smiled, told him she loved him, and fell asleep—exhausted from the intensity of her day.

*****

Because they went to bed early and slept wonderfully, it was easy to get up at the alarm's beckoning. As Sean showered and got dressed, Jenny heated two egg casserole "muffins"—an idea she had conceived when his parents had visited years before. He could easily eat them as he drove to work. She wrapped them in foil and filled a lidded cup with orange juice. She also packed an apple and a granola bar for him to snack on since eating a regular lunch was nearly impossible while piloting a helicopter.

He wrapped her in his arms, kissed her longingly, and told her he couldn't imagine having a better wife to come home to each day. She smiled shyly, patted him on the bottom, and told him he'd better get going or he would be late.

"Okay, but I can't wait to get back home to you this afternoon! Do you think Elise will be here by the time I get here?"

"I'll have to talk to Janice."

"How about I bring home some pizza this evening? It will work whether Elise is here or not, and you deserve a break from cooking all the time!"

"Hmmm. Sounds *great!*"

"Done. I need to run, but I love you more than you can ever know, Jenny. Miss me!"

"I will. Be safe. I love you, Sean."

They kissed one last time, and he left.

She stood in the living room for a moment, wondering how long she could keep up this double life and regretting she had entered into it. Then she remembered the state *he* had left her in yesterday before he departed, so she rushed to the front door to unlock it—as she had been told to do—and then to her closet to change into the clothes *he* had chosen. She also brushed her teeth, dabbed on a bit of cologne, and made the bed. Finally, she checked in the refrigerator to make sure there was enough leftover lasagna in case *he* told her to make something for him.

By seven twenty, she was sitting on the couch, tapping her foot nervously. She was full of anticipation and longing for the intense feelings *he* brought her to. *I'm going to enjoy* him *today, but I've got to find a way to quit him. I can't keep this up. And I can't bear the thought of hurting Sean. If I can just end it before he finds out, I will just carry the secret to my grave.*

The clock read seven forty-two. *He* had said that he'd be there at seven-thirty, and she thought she might throw up from being so nervous. She got up to look out the window. Nothing. She looked out the back door at the garden. The plants needed watering, but she didn't want to miss his entrance. She decided she would just wait until after he left.

She paced into the kitchen and looked in the refrigerator. She realized she needed to make more lemonade. She didn't *dare* consider being busy with something so mundane when *he* arrived. She thought she heard something out front and rushed to look again out the window. Nada. While there, she closed all the shutters just in case he wanted to parade around the house naked. The time was seven forty-eight. *Oh my gosh! Only six minutes have passed! I can't stand this! Where* is *he?* She was so keyed up she was now trembling.

She had not eaten this morning, telling Sean that she would have something a little later after making the bed. Now she was regretting that decision because the hunger and nervousness together were causing her stomach to flip-flop. *At least that* wasn't *a lie. I* will *eat something at some point, and it* will *be after I made the bed.*

She couldn't believe she had resorted to such shady tactics.

CHAPTER 29

At eight thirteen, the front door opened. Though she didn't *want* to feel relieved, she was. At this point, she couldn't bear not having her daily fix with *him*. If she could figure out how he had such power over her, she would know how to stop. But all reason flew out the door when *he* stepped in.

She rushed toward him but stopped when he held up his hand like a traffic cop. Her eyes showed disappointment, and he laughed out loud. She could smell stale beer on his clothes and fresh beer on his breath. His eyes scanned her over, and he nodded in approval.

"Put these beers in yer fridge."

As she carried the partially full 12-pack of cans to the kitchen, she recognized what a reversal this was from Sean not allowing her to carry hardly *any*thing.

"Well, come on, girl. Let's get this party started! Bring me one o' them beers."

She turned back, retrieved a can from its box, and walked to her current obsession. When she extended it to him, he stood there looking at her. She raised her eyes to his with a questioning look.

He stepped closer to her so that he could literally be over her and look down on her. "Maybe you're not so bright after all. Are you too *stupid* to remember that you are to *serve* me?" His eyes were flaming with rage, and his volume had steadily increased with each word, causing her to flinch slightly. He laughed at her again. "Open the damn can, dumba——!"

I should have thought of that! Maybe I am stupid! She pulled the tab and once again extended the can to him.

"That's more like it. You'd best get yer mind in gear, or I'm gonna hafta do some extreme training on yer a——. If *that* has to happen, I won't have time to give you what you need so badly." He reached between her legs and roughly grabbed her—just in case she needed a reminder of what that was.

Just as he expected, her face showed near terror, not because of the possibility of punishment, but at the thought of not receiving what he could give her. He knew she was falling into his clutches, just as all the others had.

He knew what to look for in a woman—they had a certain look about them, especially in their eyes—and he knew how to treat them, both in order to gain their trust and then to dominate them.

And, of course, he knew how to please them.

He took a long drink of the cold brew. "So what's it gonna be?"

"I'll be more careful," she whispered with pouty lips. She was so ashamed at having displeased him that she couldn't bring herself to look at him.

"Speak up!" He reached out, stuck his hand inside her unbuttoned blouse, and wrenched her breast unforgivingly.

"I'll be more careful!" she squealed.

Just to make sure she knew what he could do to her to control her, he backhanded her across both breasts. When she cried out, he grabbed her face roughly, brought his face within an inch of hers, and through clenched teeth rebuked her, "You haven't yet earned the right to scream or cry. You'll have to take a *lot* more than that!" He glared into her eyes and saw all the emotional elements he needed: pain, fear, and confusion.

He grabbed a handful of her hair to use like reins on a horse with his left hand, stated "Lead the way," and motioned with his right hand, his middle finger extended as a pointer. (Of course, the remaining fingers firmly grasped his requisite beer.)

As they entered the bedroom, he smugly quipped "You made the bed for me! *That's* the kind of service I'm talkin' about!" He yanked her hair which brought her to a stop, then he pulled on it until she backed into him.

Still grasping her hair, he bent his head down and around until his mouth was right at her ear. Very quietly but using a voice dripping with threat, he breathed into her ear, "I don't want you doin' anything for *Sean* you ain't doin' for me. I expect the same royal treatment you give him, you understand me?"

"Yes."

"*Yes?*" He pulled down hard on her hair, forcing her face to point upward.

"Yes, *sir?*"

"There ya go." Then he put his mouth over hers and began his blitz on her body. When he pulled back, he continued to hold her hair as he gulped the remainder of the beer, then he crushed and tossed the empty can onto the floor in the bathroom. He belched loudly. He could feel her trembling.

"Get undressed, real sexy-like, right here beside me." He released her hair.

She did.

"Take my clothes off. Maybe give me a little attention while you do it."

She found his arrogance repulsive even while wishing to please him more than ever before. She unbuttoned his shirt while arching her back and jutting her breasts upward toward him. Her mouth was open, and her tongue danced from side to side, the tip occasionally peeking out onto her upper lip. She gazed at him with upturned eyes. When she got to the bottom button, she kissed his navel and moved up his abdomen to his chest, lingering there a bit, giving extra attention to his nipples. He was watching her with glazed eyes. She continued to his neck, rubbing herself against him. She used her hands to knead his arms and shoulders as she removed his shirt.

By the time she got to his pants, it was clear that he was ready.

"Hurry up."

She gently pulled his pants down, being careful not to cause him discomfort, then kneeled and held them down at his ankles so he could step out of them. He used her head for balance as she removed first one sock and then the other.

"You've done this before, I see." He leaned over, put his hand on the back of her head, and hurriedly pulled her mouth to his, hungrily searching for her tongue.

Just as suddenly, he pushed her shoulders back with both hands, causing her to have to twist and fall over on her hands and knees.

"Get on the bed." As she crawled onto it, he swatted her hard on her exposed backside, pleased to know that *that* one would leave his red handprint for a while.

She was so ready and wanted him so badly she didn't even mind.

He climbed over her to the middle of the bed.

"I'm tired o' doin' all the work. *You* ride *me* for a while." He had a good buzz going, but he was not so drunk as to not be able to read her body and handle her as he saw fit.

She was more than happy to mount up.

This was her favorite, and very quickly, she was close to her reward. Sensing it, he ordered, "Get off o' me."

A whimper escaped her, but she obeyed.

"I want your mouth. Finish me."

She did as she was told but was desperate for her own release. She swallowed hard and looked at him with pleading eyes. He laughed loudly.

"Go get me another beer. And this time, wipe off around the rim. I don't want any crap gettin' in my drink."

She walked toward the closet to get a robe, but he stopped her.

"What are you doing?" His voice dripped with disgust.

She told him, but he ordered her to go naked.

He noticed her worried look and grinned. *I'm going to be able to get this li'l gal to do almost anything!*

She returned with a cold beer and a dampened paper towel, wiped the rim, and popped the top.

"Why don't you take a swig?" He lay on the bed, his hands under his head.

"Bu—" She stopped herself, knowing he would exact a high price for her insubordination. But she also knew that if she drank, Sean would know.

He was savvy to the situation. "Just one swig. It'll be long gone before your little lover boy gets home."

She took a deep breath and cautiously sipped from the can.

"Come on! Attack it like you just did me!" he encouraged.

She gulped down three big swallows. She had not had a beer since the day before she had met Sean. No longer accustomed to it, she nearly instantly felt its effects.

"See? You learn real quick when you set your mind to it, which is probably good for you because I was in the mood to *really* lay into your behind today. You woulda known I'd been here when you tried to sit down!"

She wasn't afraid of the possibility of pain; she knew she could handle just about anything. Her fear was of Sean finding out. If she had bruises or welts, he would immediately know about her lack of faithfulness.

"Gimme that!" He reached out, and she placed the can in his hand. He sat up and gulped down most of the remainder.

"I gotta go to the head. Why don't you come hold me while I do?" He moved to the edge of the bed. "By the way, that's an *order*, not a question."

They walked into the bathroom, and she directed the flow as he relieved himself. He finished off the beer, crushed the can, and tossed it onto the floor, a sinister sneer on his face.

He sat on the edge of the bed. "You're gonna need to start me up. Get on your knees."

She positioned herself on the floor between his legs and began working on him.

Suddenly, he stood. "Stand up and lean over the bed."

She followed his order, and he met her. He was close, and she had lost her edge, so he finished, again leaving her in anguish. He laughed as he stood upright and backed away from her.

"Come here."

She stood and faced him, desperation clearly showing on her face. She had wanted as much of him as she could get—and the accompanying reward for herself—but so far, all she had received today was frustration.

He grabbed one of her nipples and brutally pinched it. She somehow managed to not cry out. "You're gonna need to feed me if I'm gonna be able to keep this up. We're gonna go in there bare-assed, and you're gonna treat me like I'm your king. Ya got any high heels?"

She nodded.

"Put 'em on."

She went into the closet, got the stilettos off the shelf, and came back into the bedroom to put them on.

She put a shoe on one foot, rested it on the edge of the bed, and bent over to fasten the thin strap, highly aware that he was enjoying the show. She hoped this would earn her the reward she sought. She did the same with the other foot. This one was a little more difficult because she was having to balance the other leg on the daggerlike heel. He used this opportunity to touch and squeeze her until she yelped. He wanted to backhand her for that but knew that it might leave a bruise.

"Thanks for the show, you dirty little slut. Face me."

She obeyed. He wrenched her nipple so hard she thought he may have ripped it off. She grimaced, twisted her body, and screamed.

"That's for yelping before. I *told* you, you haven't yet earned the right to make noise." He gave her a moment to process what he had said then did the same to her other nipple. He laughed as she tried desperately to swallow her pained scream. "And *that's* for the last scream. I don' like a lotta hollerin'. See to it that you obey me."

She looked into his cold, dead eyes for the slightest sign of humanity and found none.

He told her to lead the way to the kitchen. She knew he would watch as she walked, so she made a point to give him something to look at in hopes of finally gaining his favor. She heard him mumbling in appreciation behind her.

He sat at the breakfast table, his bare bottom in Sean's chair. She opened her mouth to comment, but the evil look on his face let her know it would be best to hold her tongue.

"What's for lunch?" he bellowed.

"I have lasagna and salad."

"No bread?"

"I can toast some regular bread."

"Do it. Sprinkle a little garlic powder on there. And bring me a beer."

She reached for a can and took several steps toward him, then remembered that he wanted her to clean the top first.

She delivered his drink to him, opened it, and set it on the table. He reached between her legs and tweaked her until she moaned.

"Go get my food ready."

She prepared his plate and brought it to him, along with silverware and a napkin.

"You got any o' that lemonade?"

"No, we ran out."

He rolled the hairs of his mustache at the edge of his mouth between his thumb and forefinger. "From now on, you will refer to me as 'Master.'"

When she did nothing, he widened his eyes and jutted his head toward her.

"Yes...Master." That act of submission was *extremely* difficult for her, and he knew it. That's what he was counting on.

"Stand here beside me in case I need somethin'."

"Yes...Master." She could feel her face flushing with shame.

She could smell his food and realized she was hungry. She looked down at his plate and felt like one of Pavlov's dogs. She swallowed.

"What're you lookin' at?"

She jerked her eyes forward.

"Answer me!"

"I'm hungry, Ma-Master."

He stood, knocking the chair over backward as he did. He grabbed her by the back of the neck and shoved her face into the salad. "*First* of all, you start out with 'Master,' you hear me?"

"Master, yes."

"Second, *what the hell is this s——on my plate?*" He picked up a handful of the salad and threw it across the table onto the floor.

"Master, it's salad."

"It ain't no salad like I ever ate. Now clean up that mess on the floor."

She stooped to pick up as much of the salad as she could then went into the kitchen and dampened a paper towel in order to clean up the tiny pieces and the dressing.

"Throw that away and get back over here."

"Master, yes."

He put his hand between her legs and rubbed down her calves and up her thighs on both legs. He roughly rubbed into her. She grimaced and twitched but managed to keep her feet planted and her mouth shut. She was hungry, weak, and embarrassed, and her feet and legs were hurting. Walking in stilettos is one thing, but being forced to stand in them is quite another. She began to tremble. She desperately wanted the reward she had been waiting for all morning.

Meanwhile, he shoveled the lasagna into his mouth, chewing noisily and grunting his approval like a hog.

Suddenly, he shoved the plate away from himself. "What's for dessert?"

"I don't have…"

He pinched her as hard as he could. He roared, "Aren't you forgetting something?"

"Master, I don't have anything," she screeched in pain.

"What about them cookies?"

"Master, I accidentally dropped them all on the floor yesterday, and glass got all in them, so I had to throw them away."

"You got any candy, ice cream…?"

"Master, I have a small amount of ice cream, but I was…"

"You were saving it for that spoiled husband of yours, wasn't you?"

"Master, yes."

"Bring it to me. All of it. Put it in a nice bowl. And if you got anything to put on top of it, do it. And take this plate outa my way."

"Master, yes." She did as she was told.

He ate the ice cream then told her to face him. The struggle was evident on her face, and he liked it.

Her feet and legs were screaming in agony. Her lip began to quiver. She glanced at him.

He looked up at her. "I sure do like those pouty lips o' yours."

Her lips parted to speak, but she changed her mind. Nothing she could say would matter to him anyway. He was in complete control of her, and for the first time, she realized it.

"Bend over here and remind me how good you are with 'em."

Again, she obeyed.

After a few minutes, he pulled her by the hair off of him. He leaned back in the chair, stretched, rubbed his belly, and belched loudly. "Bring me another beer."

After cleaning and opening the can, she was ordered to drink more. She guzzled about half of it before stopping. He smirked at how easy she was to control.

"Let's get back to what I'm here for. Lead the way."

CHAPTER 30

As they entered the bedroom, he glanced at the clock on the nightstand; it read ten fourteen. *Lots of time left to play,* he thought. *But I wanna raise the stakes.*

"Don't you guys have a daughter?"

"Yes…I mean, Master, yes." She looked at him with eyes widened in terror.

He chuckled slightly at her discomfort. Then his face fell, and all she saw was coldness. "Where is she?"

"Master, please. Not her, *please!*" Tears welled in her eyes.

He waited for a while before responding. He wanted her to struggle. He watched her closely. "Don't worry," he finally said, "I'm not a pedophile." In a rare move of tenderness, he lifted her chin with two fingers. "I was just wonderin' where she was."

She was so relieved she almost couldn't stand. She looked at the floor. "Master, thank you."

He gave her a moment. *Damn. What a buzz kill. And now I prob'ly gotta start over with her.* But *she did stay in character and remembered her training. I'll give her that much.*

"Where is she?"

She was not sure if she could trust him. *He* did *show a moment of concern,* she thought. *I have to believe him. God help me.*

"Master, she is still at my sister's."

"What's her name again?"

She looked up at him, searching his eyes for the slightest sign of… anything. But he was a master at what he did to people, especially women. "Master, may I ask why?"

"I think you should call your sister and find out when your kid is comin' home. I don't think you want me here when they show up again."

"Master, her name is Janice."

He picked up her phone from the nightstand. "Gimme your password." He stated it matter-of-factly, knowing she would tell him. And if she didn't…well, he would enjoy the training that followed.

"Master, it's 8-6-7-5-3-0."

He chuckled at the cleverness of her passcode. "Is she in here as Janice?"

"Master, yes."

He found Janice's name and opened her screen then set the phone down.

"Well, let's see about gettin' you a little pleasure, shall we?"

"Master, yes." As an afterthought, she added, "Please."

He chuckled. *Too bad this one's married. I'd like to have her around the clock. We could have lots of fun.*

"Get in bed."

He crawled in next to her and lay there for a few moments, working out the details of his plan. Then he turned to her and started working her body over from her head to her toes, both softly and roughly, with his mouth and his hands. She was a pressure cooker in no time.

He climbed onto her and began the final leg of the journey. She could not hold back her moans.

He slowed the pace, reached for her phone, and dialed Janice's number. "Here, talk to your sister."

Again, her eyes widened, this time in disbelief. She shook her head from side to side then heard the ringing begin. He placed the phone against her ear then began working her *very* intentionally.

"Hello?"

"Hi, Janice. How are the kids doing?" She squeezed her eyes tightly shut and grimaced from the difficulty in not being able to moan and fully enjoy what he was doing to her.

"Oh, they're great! In fact, I was just about to call you. I know it's kinda last minute, but is there *any* way she can stay *one* more night? Alicia is near tears over her going home."

Her body was in rhythm with his, and her eyes were closed. "Yes, Janice, I think that's okay. Sean and I are enjoying a bit of, umm, unstructured time in the evenings." She was so close she almost couldn't remember words.

"Oh, *thanks*, Jenny! Adam and Alicia just *love* it when she is here."

She grimaced again. She was having to concentrate with all she had on two completely different things.

He was ready to finish her and was beginning his crescendo.

"No problem, Sis. I-I, umm, appreciate you having her over."

"Is everything okay? You sound…distracted."

"Oh, I'm…playing a game on my, umm, computer. It's really hard." She was nearly needing to scream.

"Okay. Well, I'll let you go. We can talk tomorrow, okay?"

"Sure, Janice. Talk to you later. Bye!"

She quickly ended the call, and a low moan began rising from her. It rose in volume and pitch until she ran out of air. She whimpered as she tried to breathe in enough air and retrieve her body down from the clouds.

He finished on her abdomen and chuckled at her total loss of control. *What a woman!*

He lay on his side looking at her. He tweaked her nipple. "*That's* for saying your husband's name in my presence."

Her face contorted, she twitched, and then she looked over at him. "But you *made* me talk on the phone!"

He smiled at her. Then he tweaked the other one. "Your job is to figure out how to please me. Not my problem."

Her eyes flashed with anger.

He laughed. "You are so easy to control. I know you better than you know yourself!"

He raised to a sitting position in the middle of the bed. "What we need here," he glanced back at her, "is another beer. Be a dear and bring two."

She was *so* tired. Too much intense physical activity and too little food. Nonetheless, she knew he was only here for a short while, so she, too, sat up. "Master, yes."

"I don't like the way that sounds. We're gonna go with beginning *and* ending with '*Master*,' kinda like they do in the army, except they use *sir*."

She looked over at him with tired, confused, and exasperated eyes. "Master, yes, Master."

He kicked her bottom playfully as she crawled out of bed.

She came back with two beers, cleaned them, and pulled the tab on one to hand to him.

"Ladies first. I gotta tell you, I *am* impressed with the ability you exhibited when you was on the phone." He jutted his chin toward her. "You drink that as a little reward for a job well done."

She sighed. "Master, thank you, Master." She drank thirstily and deeply, this time nearly two-thirds of it.

He grabbed the other can from her hand, pulled the tab, and raised it in the air in a toast. She knew he expected her to finish hers. Besides, though it wasn't food, at least it was *something* in her stomach. She turned the bottom up and polished it off.

She closed her eyes and felt the alcohol enter her bloodstream and her brain. In a mere moment, she heard the crushing of his can. He grabbed her empty can, crushed it as well, then threw both of them into the bathroom.

Then he released a belch that rattled the windows.

*****

It disturbed him that he was actually beginning to admire her. He *hated* women. Ever since his mother first burned him with her cigarettes and later beat him with electrical cords—or anything else she could pick up for that matter—he wanted to pay back every woman he saw. His mother was not shy about having sex with any of her different "boyfriends" (i.e., tricks) in front of him, either— sometimes more than one at once. She would call him into her room. He would watch, stone-faced. When the men climbed off her, he would go back to his room. To him, women needed to be kept in line through pain and fear of it, and then punished with sex—even if they happened to enjoy that part. That he was good at the second part was how he made sure he could return again and again.

In junior high school, he was skinny and awkward, and all the kids avoided him. But he talked a girl into going under the bleachers with him in the gym. "We can just kiss," he told her. But once they got started, he wanted more. She tried to fight him off and to get away, but he overpowered her and ultimately raped her. She had three older brothers, and she told them what had happened. They took him under the same bleachers and beat him senseless. A few weeks later, he confronted two of them as they were walking past his house. They agreed to meet him in the field at the end of the road. George pulled out a knife, but the larger boy wrestled it from him and cut him deeply on his left side. The two brothers panicked and ran, leaving George for dead. He somehow stumbled and crawled home. His mother took him to the emergency room. He had to have surgery and was in the hospital for several days.

The day he was discharged, his mother made him help her pack their few belongings and load them into their ramshackle car. They moved to another state so as to escape the bill collectors. His mother returned to prostitution. He never finished school. But he had learned that to get what you want—especially from women— you had to control them.

He traveled from state to state, taking odd jobs in order to pay the bills. He could always find a woman in any town. Some were married, some were not. He found young girls, older ladies, rich "kept" wives, and poverty-stricken whores. But they were all the same. They wanted him to "tame" them. Doing so made their ecstasy more intense when he serviced them because training them stripped away all their hang-ups and phobias. The "prescribed methods" they demanded from their husbands were forgotten. It was just him, and he was *very* good.

Women who didn't enjoy sex with others drooled on themselves to get to spend time with him. Women whose husbands were inadequate vowed they would divorce them if he would just stay.

Those who could gave him money. Others, like Jenny, fed him. It was a crazy life, but it was one he enjoyed. As he saw it, he wasn't really hurting anyone—except maybe a few husbands. *At least I'm not a* murderer. He shrugged his shoulders. *They shoulda been better at taking care of their women.*

But *this* one, this Jenny, she was different. She was, of course, beautiful. And she was *just* feisty enough to be interesting. And responsive didn't even begin to describe her. She was a Ferrari among Volkswagens. He decided he *might* have to deviate from his usual game plan with her.

*****

"Are you hungry?"

She sighed, clearly at the end of her strength. "Master, yes, Master."

He crawled out of bed and grabbed her hand. "Come on."

He led her to the kitchen. "What do you have in here that I can quickly make for you?"

She stared at him with disbelieving eyes. In fact, between the beer and the hunger, she couldn't really even comprehend what he was saying.

"Jenny, I know you need something to keep your strength up. What can I make that you would eat?"

"Peanut butter sandwich?" Suddenly, she realized she had forgotten to say "Master." Her eyes showed a brief moment of terror.

"Don't worry about it. Peanut butter's in the pantry, where do you keep your bread?"

"In the microwave."

"Sit down. I'll bring it right to you."

She did as she was told, zombielike.

He grabbed the two items, found the drawer that contained the silverware, and spread the peanut butter. He made a stylized little swirl as he finished. He had seen where she kept the plates, so he retrieved one, put the sandwich on it, and hurried over to her.

"Here you go."

She looked up at him and smiled slightly.

"Here, let me take those shoes off of you. Your feet must be really hurting." He bent to unfasten the straps.

She slowly took a bite and began chewing. She set the sandwich back on the plate.

"What's wrong? Did I make it wrong?" He was standing beside her, watching her, ready to serve her.

"No, I just can't eat much right now."

"Well, take a few more bites, okay?"

Shocked but encouraged by his tenderness toward her, she ate three more bites. When she set it down, she shook her head at him, indicating she couldn't eat anymore.

"All right. Do you feel better?"

She nodded yes then raised her eyes to him and smiled again.

"Let's go have some fun! Let me get a beer."

She stood and began moving toward the hallway.

He trotted into the kitchen, grabbed the next-to-last can, and patted her on the fanny as he raced past her.

He was sitting on the bed when she entered, guzzling the last few drops of the brew he had just shotgunned.

She knew the tender moments were over when she looked at his face. His eyes were glazed over and his jaw was set hard.

"Git in the bed, b——."

She rolled her eyes. "Master, yes, *Master*," she replied snarkily. Now that she had eaten a few bites, she had a little more energy to stand up to him.

Before she could make a move, he grabbed one of her arms and the other hand and pulled her across his lap, facedown, as he sat. He held her in place with one hand as he spanked her buttocks with his other one *hard* at least twenty times before the fury began to subside. Then, because he could, he landed about ten more.

He pulled the hair from the top and back of her head, yanking her head back so he could yell right in her ear. "You *will* respect me, do you hear me, you f——whore! Don't you *ever* use that tone with me again!"

He had hit her so hard he was panting from exertion and anger. She had probably screamed, but he never heard it. His mother's words were sounding in his ears. "*You will do* what *I tell you* when *I tell you, and you* will *be respectful when you do it!*" He could almost feel the sting of his mother's electric cord on his own buttocks.

Once his breathing and heart rate slowed a bit, he could hear her sobbing. She had struggled mightily to free herself. But he was larger, stronger, and meaner. *This* is one of the reasons he worked out—the other being to attract the women in the first place.

As he stood, he tossed her onto the bed, facedown. He quickly grabbed something from the floor.

She knew what was coming next and tried to escape. But his blood was boiling, and he had no trouble holding her down as he got into position. He sodomized her, more with the intent to hurt her than to please himself.

After her first scream, he held the dirty and smelly sock he had picked up from the floor within a few inches of her face. "Scream again, b——! I'll stuff this whole filthy thing all the way down your throat!"

She was terrified. The pain was like nothing she had ever experienced. She bit so hard into a pillow she thought she might break a tooth, and tears nearly squirted out of her eyes.

He finished on her buttocks. He liked the contrast of the red handprints and the whitish cream. He rubbed it into her skin then collapsed beside her.

*****

He continued to come over on each of Sean's workdays for about two weeks. As his dominion over her was nearly complete, he could manipulate her into doing whatever he wanted. Though he humiliated her and inflicted great pain on her, her reward was the intense pleasure he provided her. Sometimes, in order to make her more desperate, he even withheld *that* until the end of the session.

Some days he was so rough with her she nearly cried. But she refused to cave. It was her strength and ability to never back down from his threats, demands, or punishment that appealed to him. She was obedient but always with an air of rebellion about her.

During the second week, Sean was unexpectedly moved to the night shift for four days because the other pilot (Tim) was out of town for a funeral. Sean knew having someone up in the air over the city during the night was critical, so he accepted the change without complaint. This played well into the lover's trysts. Since it was summer, school was out, and Janice had a pool, Elise was gone on all the nights except one. *He* came over anyway; the only thing that changed was that they had to stay in the bedroom, and they had to remain reasonably quiet. She somehow managed to handle those few days with *very* little rest.

To help her have more energy, one night *he* brought her some cocaine and forced her to snort it. She outright told him he had crossed a line and was prepared to accept any punishment he meted out for her insurrection. But instead, he calmly apologized and said he wouldn't do it again. His respect for her grew. But he continued to manhandle her.

CHAPTER 31

On one of the days that Sean was home, Jenny ran a variety of errands including going to the dry cleaners to pick up their honeymoon quilt. She placed it on a shelf in the closet, hoping Sean wouldn't notice. But she felt even more strongly about not leaving it out for *him* to soil.

On another day, the Wallachs traveled to Santa Fe to look at dining tables in some of the unique stores there. They really liked one that met all of Jenny's criteria, but it was just too big to fit in the room with the baby grand piano. As Jenny and Elise continued to peruse the store, Sean quietly spoke with the owner, who indicated he had just received a shipment. They walked to his storage area.

At the very back, under some blankets, Sean saw one that he knew Jenny would like that would fit in the room (he had measured the area before they left home). He pressed the man for a price, then offered about 20 percent less, indicating that it hadn't been cleaned and readied for the showroom. Sean pointed at one of the table legs. "This is loose." Then he bent to look underneath. "This hardware is rusty and will probably need to be replaced. And these chairs will need to be reupholstered."

The owner, who had instantly liked the kilt-wearing Scotsman, grinned at Sean and agreed to accept his offer. "I'm short on time and long on inventory!" he stated cheerfully.

Sean quickly took care of the payment and arranged for delivery then found Jenny and Elise in another part of the store looking at wind chimes. With a coy smile and upturned eyes, Jenny let her husband know she wanted to buy one.

Sean looked at his wife yearningly. "How can I refuse you when you look at me like that?" He grinned. "Which one do you want?" he said with resignation.

Jenny asked Elise which one she preferred, and they agreed on the largest one. Sean removed it from its hook and walked it to the cash register. After paying for the new addition for their back porch, he suggested, "Ice cream, anyone?"

Elise and Jenny looked at each other with surprise and then smiled at the man in their lives. "*Yes!*"

*****

The two of them lay for about twenty minutes, not together as a couple but on the same bed as people who had shared an encounter. They were both exhausted. He was drunk and demented, she was weak from too little food and not enough sleep, and she was in pain. Despite deviance and immorality, both had experienced *incredible* pleasure.

Quietly, he asked, "When does your husband get home today?"

She turned her head to face him. Since he wasn't speaking derogatorily about Sean, nor was he using a loud or gruff voice, she assumed that "the game" (as she had begun to mentally refer to their encounters) was over.

But her rear hurt in more than one way, so she surely didn't want to incite his anger again. "Master, three thirty, Master."

"You can stop all o' that. I'm spent." He reached over and moved some strands of hair away from her face.

"Look, Jenny, I know you're tired, and there is less time remaining before he gets home today than normal. Is there anything I can do to help you?"

She was pensive for a moment. There were sheets to wash and replace, dishes to rinse and put in the dishwasher, beer cans to pick up off the bathroom floor where he usually threw them, and then they had to be taken away to a trash receptacle. She also needed to make certain to open all the shutters to their normal positions, water the plants, and make the refrigerator look normal on the inside. She was so tired she didn't even want to think about trying to make it look as if she had been busy all day. Maybe she could just tell Sean she was tired because of where she was in her cycle. (Then she realized he was probably more familiar with it than she was.)

"It would be great if you got *any* sign of beer out of here." (He had continued to make her drink some as he liked it when his women were a little "sloshy.")

"*Oh my gosh!*" She jumped out of bed and ran into the bathroom. She brushed her teeth and then gargled with mouthwash. When she stepped back into the bedroom, George was sitting on the edge of the bed and looked almost sad. She dropped her shoulders and tilted her head to the side. "Are you okay?"

He shrugged. "Yeah. I just feel kinda bad. I was pretty harsh with you today."

"I'll be all right. I just hope there aren't any bruises. That will be hard to explain to Sean." (He had spanked her again because she had refused to let him take her on the back porch; she was worried about the possibility of being seen by neighbors.)

"I don't think there will be. I kept my hand flat." He lowered his head, and when he looked back up at her, there were tears in his eyes. "I'd love it if you would let me make love to you. Just a nice gentle and caring experience. You're special, Jenny. You're not like any other woman I've ever met."

She *wanted* to believe him. She *almost* even wanted to take him up on his offer. But he had switched like Jekyll and Hyde on more than one visit, and *she* was the worse for it. Besides, "the game" was over, and she was no longer under his control. Now she was Sean's wife, and she *had* to have the strength to turn George down.

"I think maybe we should just try to clean up and move on."

"Can I come again tomorrow?"

The part of her that he could control stirred in her. She looked down. He took that as a moment of weakness and stood to hold her in his arms.

Jenny winced and jerked away slightly. He could tell her energy was different. He didn't want to push her, so he stepped back. She wrinkled her face to keep from crying. Though George was neither kind nor funny nor intelligent nor spiritual nor a leader nor talented in so many things like Sean was, they nonetheless *had* shared some sort of connection. Most importantly, though, he was not Elise's father. And she was savvy enough to know that he must have had an abusive childhood to be able to treat women that way. She started to shake. She looked up at him just as a tear rolled down her cheek.

George didn't have Sean's gentleness or deep understanding of the delicacy of women's emotions, but he knew that they needed to be held when they were crying. So he again stepped to her. This time, she didn't push back but rather folded into his arms. He kissed her on the forehead and cheek. "Let's get dressed," he said quietly.

He put on his clothes and shoes while she stepped into the closet to choose a summery dress. "Let's go out to the living room," he softly directed.

Jenny hated that he was being so…nice. That made things much more difficult in her head as well as her heart.

"Let me just remove these sheets and get them in the washer." As she did so, she very gratefully remembered that she and Sean had decided to go out for Mexican food tonight, so she didn't have to try to get dinner ready.

In the kitchen, George got the beer carton from the refrigerator. He went into Jenny's bathroom to get the empties off the floor and put them in the box. He walked back to the kitchen where Jenny was rinsing off his dishes and wiping the countertops. "If you want me to take these away, I will."

Jenny looked over at him, smiled, and said, "Yes. That will help. Thank you."

He watched her wistfully as she returned the shutters to their original positions. He knew he would never meet another woman like her.

They both knew that something akin to love had entered into their relationship. For him, it was no longer about the pain, the punishment, and the control, as he had begun to admire her. For her, it was no longer about being controlled by what had begun as a near-rape, as it had morphed into a full-blown affair—complete with anticipation and feelings of empathy.

"I have to go out in the backyard and water my garden." She was thinking, even hoping, that he would just leave.

"May I come with you?" His body language was neutral, his face was calm, and his eyes were kind.

"Okay." *I can always spray him down with the hose if he tries anything.*

As she watered the various plants, he asked her about them. He was impressed with her knowledge and the fact that they *really did* use the food produced in the garden and on the trees.

She finished, squinted up at the cloudless sky, and said, "Let's go back inside. I can make us some lemonade."

"I'd like that."

George sat at the table and watched her move very efficiently about the kitchen. Soon Jenny was sitting with him, and they were both sipping on a refreshing glass of cold homemade lemonade.

"Your husband is very lucky."

She smiled at him. Sean frequently told her that.

"Look, Jenny, you deserve a good life. You are beautiful, you're a great cook, you're smart, and you have *such* strength. No matter *what* I threw at you, you stood up to me, you took it, and you came back for more. You're the only woman I've ever admired. Plus, you have a great husband. He clearly takes good care of you. I wish I could get as lucky as him, but I don't think that's in the cards for me."

She wanted to tell him he might, but she would have been lying. So she just smiled again.

In a voice barely above a whisper, George stated, "I'll never forget you."

Jenny looked down, and a small sob shook her. She forced a smile and looked back up at him.

George stood and picked up the box full of beer cans. "Does Sean work tomorrow?"

"I think so. They just changed his shift again, and I fell asleep last night before we had a chance to talk about his workdays."

"If I were to stop by for a moment, would that be okay?"

Jenny was torn. She *wanted* a final session—even a gentle one as he had described. Rough could be good too. But the timing was right for him to go *right now*. To prolong the end would just make it hurt longer and in more varied ways.

"I'd love to see you," she whispered, mostly because it was the best she could muster, given her physical and emotional status.

Also, she knew it was true.

But she knew she wouldn't be home.

She offered her cheek as he bent to kiss her, then he left.

CHAPTER 32

Jenny was happy she was so tired and so weak. That kept her from pacing the floor and losing her mind. She had just sent away someone who could somehow go someplace in her head and do things to her that she could never have imagined.

And now she was alone. Elise was once again at her cousins' house. Sean was zooming around in the air over Albuquerque. She sat at the table, dazed, as if she had been struck by lightning. She remembered the sheets and hurried to move them into the dryer. While she was up and moving around, she walked through the house again to make sure all signs of *him* were gone.

Sean was due home in about an hour and a half. *I've got to keep going, at least until after we get home from the restaurant.* She ached to be safely in Sean's arms, sleeping soundly. *I wish I could just permanently erase the last two weeks.*

Jenny decided to take a shower; by the time she was finished, the sheets would be dry, and she could replace them. Then she would get dressed for her and Sean's dinner date. She hoped that the water and the physical activity would energize her enough to make it through the next five or six hours. She was afraid Sean was going to notice—if he hadn't already—how tired she had been lately. She was grateful that she would now be able to return her life to its normal routines.

She stepped into the refreshing spray of warm water. The fresh fragrance of the soap further livened her senses. More alert now, her mind began working a bit better. She was appalled to learn that the numbing effect of anticipation for her next tryst was gone. Guilt set in. *Why did I let that happen? Sean has been a* perfect *husband and father. He makes it so I never have to worry about anything, and he takes* great *care of me. And he has always been an incredible* lover. *So why,* why *did I let another man seduce me?* "WHY?" She realized she was crying. She leaned against the wall of the shower and slowly slid down it, moving her head to the side so the pulsing water didn't hit her directly in the face. Shame was beginning to consume her.

She knew she would tell Sean. She just wanted to wait until… until what? "Until I get the nerve," she said to no one. *When will* that *be?* she wondered.

Jenny knew that her affair was going to cut Sean to the core. He would probably never be able to trust her again. Their lives together would probably never again be as good as they had been. "And it's all my fault. I should have said NO," she lamented out loud.

Suddenly, she realized—for the first time—that Sean *might* not want to stay married to her. She had made the assumption that they would reconcile their relationship and then life would be returned to normal. Panic gripped her. She nearly hyperventilated. She stood, afraid of drowning from the cascading water or from the newfound fear that was already beginning to overwhelm her.

She was panting. She hastily turned off the water. She stepped out of the stall and grabbed the nearby towel. With shaking hands, she wrapped it around her as best as she could, then she attempted to walk to her chair in the bedroom. She had to hold onto the wall, the bed, the dresser. She sat, depleted. Her hair was dripping great drops of water to the carpet.

"Get a grip, woman!" Jenny said out loud to herself. She didn't want her eyes to be red and swollen from crying. That would most *definitely* bring on a conversation that would surely divulge her tremendous sin.

Then another problem crept into her consciousness. Her cycle was late. Her body shifted from hyperventilating to barely breathing.

Jenny was sure of this: her time with *him* had caused her to learn of a strength inside of her that she did not know she possessed. And right now, she *needed* that strength. She needed to wash her face, pull herself together, make the bed, and get dressed. She needed to make a plan to get through the evening.

Her mind found a new gear. *I'll go to dinner with Sean, come home, make sweet love to him like never before, and get some rest.*

Tomorrow, when I can think more clearly, I will figure out Sean's days off, arrange for Janice to keep Elise, and think about how I will tell him and what I will say. She was pretty sure Sean worked tomorrow, so she would use that time to map it all out.

She nodded. "Good plan, Jenny."

She pulled the sheets from the dryer and made the bed, got the quilt from the shelf in the closet, and placed it back on the bed. She went into the bathroom, unwrapped the towel from around herself, and hung it neatly on the towel bar. She rinsed her face and looked deeply into her hand-held mirror for signs of having cried. She had *definitely* looked better, but if Sean mentioned anything, she would just say she was tired, which would be the truth. Just maybe not the *only* truth. She missed the days when all she had to do was just be honest.

After she dried her hair, Jenny stepped into the closet and searched through the rack for *just* the right outfit. Her eyes lit on a blouse she had recently bought but not yet worn. It was lavender in color, it fit snugly, and it was *much* lower cut than what she normally wore. She knew Sean appreciated that she didn't usually wear clothes that were too revealing, but tonight, she wanted to distract him. She wanted him focused on anticipation, on getting home to be with her, and on loving her. Her new push-up bra would help to entice him even more.

She chose her *best*-fitting pair of capri jeans, poured herself into them, and viewed herself from several angles in the dressing mirror on the door. She smoothed her hands across the material. *Nice.* She stepped into a pair of purple heels with ankle straps and a cute little bow on the back and consulted the mirror again. Sean always loved to admire her calves. Tonight, he would be well-rewarded when walking behind her. She dressed her upper half, stepped into the bathroom to view the vanity mirror, and liked what she saw.

Though Jenny didn't often wear makeup, she decided a bit of mascara and a trip around her lips with a sparkling lip gloss would be in order. She smooched at the image of herself. "You go, girl!" A few dabs of cologne, some silver jewelry, a quick swipe of the brush through her hair, and she was ready.

She stepped into the kitchen and drank a small glass of cool water. As she was moving to sit on the couch, she heard Sean's truck pull into the driveway and the garage door open.

She stood at the entrance to the hallway, her left upper arm resting against the door facing, and her right hand propped on her hip. She cocked her left leg and dropped her head so that her eyes would be looking up at Sean when he entered.

The door leading into the garage opened. One glance, and Sean dropped his backpack, grabbed her around the waist with both arms, and buried his face in her neck. "Jenny," he whispered. He was pretty sure she had *definitely* lost a little weight because she felt even smaller than normal. But right now, he didn't care. She was in his arms. The past couple of weeks had been a little tense, what with extra days of work, multiple schedule changes, and the resultant difficulty in getting enough sleep; of course, there were also concerns about Jenny's behavior and health. But tonight, she clearly had him, and only him, on her mind.

He was close to tears; whether for joy for the future or for sadness because of the past, he was not sure. But he knew this: tonight, he would love her until they both could stand no more. He would hold her tight against him through the night, and everything would be right.

Jenny found great comfort in being held against his strong chest. *Tonight* was going to be epic.

As he pulled back, he grabbed her hand and spun her around. He shook his head, unable to believe that anything or anyone could look and smell and feel this good all at the same time. His eyes landed on her necklace. He touched the tiny hummingbird and smiled. He also noticed the earrings he had bought her in Santa Fe on their second date. He gave her a soft kiss, which led to a wet one, which nearly caused the cancellation of their dinner date.

"I'm hungry!" she said as she pulled away and looked provocatively up at him.

"I hope for me!" he quipped.

She held his eyes with hers. As she slowly ran the tip of her index finger from his collarbone to his belt buckle, she lustily directed, "*You*, my dear, are dessert!"

Sean moaned out loud. Had she not indicated her hunger for food, he would have carried his Jenny straight to their bed where he would have satisfied *his* hunger for *her*. Staring deep into her eyes, he asked, "Are you ready?"

With sultry eyes and a hoarse whisper, she told him all he wanted to know. "More than…"

Sean stared at his stunning wife. *Her mouth is a thing of beauty.*

She had to pull him out of his trance by patting him on the chest and telling him, "Come on. Let's go!"

*****

Sean had no idea what he ordered or if it was any good. All he saw was the object of his desire. He uncharacteristically watched her chest as she breathed, often having to force himself to look up into her eyes. He hoped that what Jenny had told him—that it was good luck to see a hummingbird before important events—would hold true tonight.

She gazed at him and delivered that Mona Lisa smile through-out much of their evening. At one point, he seriously considered that he might need to ask her to drive them home, as he didn't think he could remember how to find the way.

Her stomach had shrunk from the past weeks of not eating much, so she couldn't even eat half of her meal. When the waiter asked Sean if they needed refills, more chips, or a box, all Jenny's entranced husband could do was look up at the lad.

Jenny rescued him with a "Yes, please."

Sean had no idea if he wrote $5 or $50 for the tip on the charge ticket. No matter. Some things were more important—like getting home to be with his luscious wife.

*****

It was a good thing that no patrol units were running radar on their trip home because Sean was *definitely* exceeding the posted speed limit. Once in the garage, he literally ran around his truck to

Jenny's side, opened her door, and lifted her as gently and as quickly as possible into his arms. He kissed her hungrily as he walked to the door and twisted the knob. He pushed it open with his leg then kicked it closed with his foot. Down the hallway they traveled toward their beckoning bed, locked in a scalding kiss.

Sean carefully placed his striking wife on the bed; she rolled to her left and then right as he pulled the quilt and sheet back. He slid in beside her, his eyes finally able to enjoy her without the interruption of waiters, food, or traffic.

"You look 'Wonderful Tonight,'" he sang to her. She responded with a sleepy smile—*just* the one he liked.

He began a barrage of heated kisses to her neck and chest. Jenny was near delirium and moaned primally. He tenderly began to undress her as he continued to enjoy increasing amounts of her soft flesh.

Without words or any type of signal, they both sat up. She gazed directly into his eyes as she slowly unbuttoned his shirt. Both were breathing heavily, their heated bodies warming the room. With soft hands and a firm touch, she pushed his shirt back off his chest and shoulders then held it as he wriggled his arms out of the sleeves. Her eyes went to his very masculine chest, and she groaned.

With one hand behind her neck and the other around her waist and back, he lowered her to the pillow. He continued exploring her with his mouth as he used his hands to finish removing their clothes.

He moved his body close to hers. They were both trembling with desire. "May I love you?" he managed.

She whimpered. He covered her, and they were as one. Their ecstasy had never been sweeter. Both vocalized sounds that were echoes from the past.

Sean remained in place, panting as he gazed down at his reason for living. He had one arm under the small of her back, and the other was holding his weight off of her.

Jenny continued firmly rubbing his back, shoulders, and arms. Her head was thrust back, her eyes were closed, and she was gulping in deep breaths of air.

"We are going to have to invent some new words, because 'incredibly fulfilling' doesn't even come close," she breathlessly informed him.

Finally, she brought her head around to the side and opened her eyes. She turned her face to look up at her strikingly handsome and *very* capable lover.

Neither wanted to move or separate from the other. She exhaled a final moan. He whisper-kissed her face and lips then eased to her side. He slid the arm that had been under her back to under her neck, and the arm that had been supporting himself was now wrapped around her torso.

Sean was worn out from his recent zany work schedule; add to that the stresses of worrying about Jenny, and he was ready for some serious slumber.

Jenny only had enough energy remaining to whisper, "I love you, Sean." Her eyes fluttered, and she was finished.

Sean mimicked her sentiment and hoped that she had heard him as she drifted away. Then he joined her.

Chapter 33

Sean and Jenny were both so tired and so happy to have loved each other the way they had in times past that in their deep sleep, they never moved. When Sean's alarm sounded, he reached to his night-stand to silence it then rolled back into position beside his sweet-heart. He was careful to leave his other arm under his still-sleeping wife's neck.

She wiggled slightly and snuggled up even closer to her loving husband, a sexy, groggy moan escaping her as she nuzzled his chest. "Throw that noisy thing down the toilet," she said in a raspy voice.

He kissed her on the cheek. "Just one more day, my love." He carefully moved his arm from under her and pulled her pillow under her head and neck. Then he sat up and replaced where his warm body had been with his pillow.

Without opening her eyes, she sleepily teased, "You can't fool me. This is too soft."

He chuckled and bent to kiss her mouth. "Sleep, my love. I'll call you later."

She reached out to gently stroke his face. "I love you." She flut-tered her eyes open, and his heart nearly melted on the spot.

"I love you too, Jenny. I'll see you this afternoon."

*****

Jenny awoke about three hours later. She got dressed and made her way to the kitchen. Though she was still groggy, she felt guilty that she had not cooked anything for Sean to eat. She glanced into the freezer and saw that he had taken one of the breakfast sandwiches she had previously prepared for him. Happy that he was not going to go hungry, she moved to the cabinet to reach for a juice glass.

She smiled. Now it was *her* heart's turn to melt. Sean had drawn a red heart on a sticky note, and knowing his wife loved to drink juice in the mornings, he placed it on the cabinet door. She took a picture of it and sent it to him. She didn't know when he'd get a chance to check his messages, but she wanted him to know she had found and appreciated it.

She sat at the table and began to try to decide when, what, and how she was going to tell Sean about what she had done. She was immediately distracted by thoughts of…*him*. She shook her head. Just one more day of Sean being at work, then she would tell him. If he would agree to stay with her, she would re-devote all her time and attention to him and their daughter.

Suddenly she remembered—*he* wanted to come by to see her. She gulped down her juice, rinsed the glass, and put it in the dishwasher. Then she hastily made her way to her closet to get her wallet and keys.

She quickly backed out of the garage and made tracks for the interstate into town. Her plan was to get lost in it. She knew she couldn't see *him*. *This is best*, she thought.

Jenny decided to run a few errands that had been unattended to during her many days of torrid sex with *him*. She went to the pharmacy, the dry cleaners, and the home-improvement store where she chose some fertilizer for the garden and found the gloves Sean had asked her to get. She also went to a stationery store to choose upcoming birthday, graduation, anniversary, and new baby cards for several different friends. On her way back to her SUV, her phone dinged. It was Sean, responding to her text with a little cupid. She giggled out loud. The phone dinged again. This time, he sent an image of chopsticks and a flag from China. While she was typing a response, it dinged again. He had attached a link to a menu from a restaurant they liked. She clicked on the link, and as it was loading, she heard the familiar ding yet again. She tapped her messages icon, and her heart stopped.

It was *him*.

She gasped and covered her mouth with her hand. Her pulse, breathing, and blood pressure all increased dramatically. She stared at the screen with widened eyes. She was terrified to open the message but couldn't bear the thought of *not* doing it. She and her heart had to negotiate an agreement that it would stop beating so wildly. In return, she would remain calm. Familiar with the failed treaties of the 1800s in the American Southwest, she doubted that either party was going to uphold its end of the deal.

With shaking hands, she clicked on the message.

> Where ARE you?

Overwhelmed with excitement, fear, anxiety, and a sudden longing for something she hadn't anticipated wanting, she dropped her head in her hands and cried. Her body shook so hard she could feel the car rocking.

After several moments, she leaned her head back and wiped her eyes. She was breathing like a Thoroughbred after a race. *What am I going to do?*

"Tell the truth," said Jenny's mind to her heart. She began typing.

> I needed to run some long-overdue errands and pick up some groceries. I also need to go get my daughter and bring her home.

The last part wasn't true because she had not yet spoken with Janice, but she planned to at the very least go visit after she bought groceries. She decided it was close enough to the truth. So she shrugged slightly and pressed the send button.

Nearly immediately, *he* responded.

> I miss you.

Jenny grimaced and closed her eyes to keep the tears from falling out. She put her hand over her mouth as if to silence herself. *Now is the time to use some of that strength*, she told herself.

It's better this way.

After she typed the words, she stated them out loud so that she couldn't deny that the words had been spoken.

She immediately returned to her home screen and looked at the picture of Sean and Elise in the mountains.

Her phone dinged. Strengthened by the image of the two most important people in her life, she opened the message.

Can I PLEASE at least call you?

Jenny knew the relationship with *him* simply *had* to end. And of legitimate concern, her time with him may have already done irreparable damage to her family. She had no other option but to try to salvage as much of it as she could. Step one was to quit George.

Ok, but let's keep it short.

Her phone rang nearly instantly.

"Hello." Jenny tried to sound calm and in control.

"Hi, Jenny. It's good to hear your voice. I miss you so much."

"George, I'm *married*. I have a daughter. I truly enjoyed our time together, and I know I will smile with a tiny bit of sadness when I think of you. But it will just cause *more* problems if we keep dragging this out."

"Look, I know I seem like an ass, and I am, most of the time, anyway. But you...you..."

Jenny could hear his voice breaking.

"You made me realize there *is* hope and there *are* good people and especially there are good *women*. Before I met you, my purpose seemed to be to hurt as many women as I could, by whatever means, through…well, sex."

Jenny grimaced in pain for this person who, in a different set of circumstances, may have turned out to be a normal guy. "I'm glad you told me that."

There was an extended pause.

"George, I know you must have had a terrible past. And I saw the scar on your abdomen. But help is available. I know there's a great guy under all the garbage you endured as a child and all the baggage you're carrying around."

Jenny could hear him sniffling faintly.

He took a deep breath. "Would it make you too uncomfortable if I showed up at the karaoke bar sometime?"

"George, I don't know where I stand with Sean right now. We may never go there again. We may even split up. I just don't know. I have to put all my efforts into helping him get past what I've done to him."

"Would it help if I talked to him for you and explained things to him so he would understand?"

"I haven't yet told him. I'm waiting for his days off so he won't go up in his helicopter and crash or something. But I know him. This is going to be bad. He trusted me, and I violated that."

"You're an incredible woman, Jenny."

"Thank you, George. I know that under your rough exterior, there's a hidden gem. Try to find it, George. It's there. You may be damaged, but you still have working parts."

"How can you say that? You saw what I can do and say to women!"

"George, I also saw and heard the other side. You don't do it much, so it isn't comfortable for you. But try to be kind and gentle more often. You *will* get better at it. I promise! And who knows? Maybe you'll find someone who can see that little diamond down there amongst all that coal!"

"I think I love you, Jenny." She could hear that he was sobbing.

"George, I love you as a fellow human being. But I love my husband, and I want to put all of my energy into preserving our relationship. We have a wonderful daughter we are raising together. I don't want her to now be in the middle of a separation or divorce."

"Jenny?"

"Yes?"

"Is Sean a good lover?"

She paused, trying to decide if it would be appropriate to share such an intimate detail. She decided that in this case, it would. For some reason, he wanted to know. She thought that right now, while he was peering down into the trash can of his life, searching for the little bit of goodness to be found among the stinky parts, it would help him to know the answer to his question.

"Yes, he is. Excellent, in fact."

"Then *why*, Jenny? *Why* did you allow me to seduce you?"

She took a deep breath. He wanted the answer to something *she* needed the answer to. She just hadn't yet had time to think about it.

"I'm still working on that answer. But...perhaps...for the excitement? Maybe to fulfill some primal urge? The heightened sensations?"

"So it wasn't for lack of love?"

"Oh, heavens, *no!*"

"Were you attracted to me?"

"George, like I said, I have a husband that I love very much. I wasn't *repulsed* by you. But I just don't look at other guys. You seemed rather nice to me, or I would have never let you in."

"Why did you let me kiss you?"

Jenny blushed. "Well, you kinda held me pretty tight. And it was so sudden. I was just overwhelmed."

"Jenny, I'll never regret coming to your house that day. You kinda saved me."

She thought she better not open that can of worms—not because she didn't care, but because she *had* to think of Sean now. Whatever she may have been able to do for George was done.

"Well, I hope you can continue to move forward." She paused to choose her words. "Do you go to church?"

"Nah. I ain't got no use for all that superstition." George was trying desperately to shift into his confident, tough-guy persona.

"George, God won't bang on your door. But he will answer the slightest tap at his." There was an awkward silence. "If you're still in town when you decide you'd like to find out more about him, I can set you up with an appointment to talk to some people who would just love to share their experiences."

"I'm gon' be honest with ya. That ain't likely to happen."

"I understand. Everyone has their own timeline. I will only ask you to keep it in mind on the back burner. He will wait. And he will be there when you get ready."

"A'ight. Well, thanks for talkin' to me. I want you to know that I'll never forget you."

"I won't forget you either, George. I am going to, in the weirdest way, think of you as a friend. I *do* want to ask a favor though."

"Go ahead."

"It is already very hard to tell you goodbye because I *actually* care about you. But I'm going to ask that you don't contact me or my family. I just know that is how it needs to be. Can I trust you to do that?"

She heard him breathe in sharply then exhale as if he were sobbing. When he spoke, she knew she was right. "Yes."

"Can we tell each other that we had a special moment, that we have feelings for the other, but that our time must end?"

He was still crying. "Sure."

"Our paths may cross again someday, somewhere. I hope the next time I see you that you have a wonderful woman at your side and maybe even a kid or two. And I hope that our mates can respect that our two ships once passed each other in the night."

"Okay."

"Take care. I'll always remember you too."

She ended the call.

For several minutes, and for reasons she did not understand, Jenny sat and cried. Maybe it was for the loss of a lover with extraordinary talents? Maybe it was because she had strangely fallen in love?

Maybe because she wanted to "save" him and now her chance was over? What *mattered* was that *it…was…over.*

She decided to *choose* her reasons for crying. "I cheated on my husband, and I am guilty of lying, of breaking my vows, and of violating my loving husband's trust. I have, therefore, lied to God. Furthermore, my selfishness, my shirking of my responsibilities as a wife and a mother, and my lack of self-discipline are going to hurt not *just* my husband but our relationship and, therefore, our family, maybe past the point of no return."

Stating these things out loud felt oddly right. It was like an alcoholic admitting his illness. She wiped her eyes, grabbed a tissue from the glove box, and blew her nose. Jenny cleared her throat and said a few words out loud to make sure her voice sounded normal. She decided to call Janice.

"Hello?"

"Hi, Janice. I'm in town running errands. I still need to get groceries, but I was thinking I should probably come and rescue you from Elise! Does that work for you?"

"Yeah. They are just having so much fun together. Alicia doesn't have many friends here in the neighborhood. She and Adam are the youngest."

"Well, I know Elise loves it there. And while we're chatting, I'll go ahead and tell you. Sometime in the next week or so, I'm going to need to ask you to watch her if you can and will. That's why I thought I should come get her today. And Sean and I miss her!"

"I understand. And sure! Just let me know when. What's going on?"

"Oh, Sean and I are wanting to spend some sustained time together, no interruptions. We may even try to get away somewhere."

"Okay. Sounds great. I'll have her get her things together. When do you think you'll be here?"

"Probably between one and one thirty."

"Great. See ya then!"

"Bye, Janice! You're the greatest!"

After she ended the call, Jenny drove to her favorite grocery store. Normally, she had daily menus and a list of items to be purchased with her, but she felt like she could probably ad-lib this week. She focused on buying staples and items that were versatile enough to be used in several ways. She also bought a Pokémon coloring book for Alicia, a battery-powered police car with flashing lights and a siren for Adam, and a new book of puzzles for her sister; Janice was a puzzle-solving fanatic.

Her final item was found in the health-and-beauty department. After making her choice, she stuck it under some of the other items. She did not want the prying eyes of friends and neighbors she might encounter to start asking a lot of questions or making assumptions.

She paid for her things, loaded them in her SUV, and began the short drive to Janice's house.

"Mommy!" Elise enjoyed being with her cousins, but she really loved her mother. Jenny squatted to hug her and talk to her and then greeted Alicia and Adam. She also handed them the gifts she had purchased for them. Janice stood by, smiling.

Jenny stood. "I don't know how I can ever repay you for all the times you have watched Elise for us!" Her face showed sincere appreciation.

Janice laughed. "It's *really* no problem. With her here, mine aren't so much underfoot. It's actually *easier* when she's here!"

"Well, sweetheart, we'd better leave! We need to get home, unload our groceries, and get cleaned up. Daddy is taking us out to dinner tonight!"

"Oh, *goodie*! Where are we going?"

"It's a surprise, but you've been there before, and you liked it!"

Elise answered with excitement, "Okay!"

Janice and Jenny hugged. Jenny lingered just a bit longer than normal.

"You okay?" Janice queried.

"Yeah. I'm just tired. Sean's schedule has been really crazy the last couple of weeks. Trying to make everything work has just sapped both of us."

"Well, you be careful! Let me know when you need me to keep Elise again." Janice and her two children stood on her porch, ready to wave to Jenny and Elise as they drove away.

"Will do! Thanks again!"

Chapter 34

Jenny and Elise quickly brought in the day's purchases. Jenny sent Elise to her suite to take a bath and put on fresh clothes as she put away the various items she had bought. Then she took her shower. She loved looking and smelling fresh for her husband!

In order to pass the time, mother and daughter began assembling a jigsaw puzzle on the large coffee table between the two couches. They had just finished connecting all the edge pieces when Sean came through the door. He kissed and hugged his ladies, then he, too, cleaned up for the evening.

The little family enjoyed delicious Chinese food at their favorite buffet. Once home, Elise asked if they could watch *The Lion King* together. She sat on one side of her daddy, and Jenny sat on the other. Elise had played hard while at her cousin's house, so she quickly fell asleep against his arm. Sean carried her to bed then returned to the living room to sit on the couch with Jenny. He cleared his throat. "Can we talk?"

"Okay." Jenny exercised *massive* discipline to control both her emotions and her facial expression. *What can it be?* she wondered, full of fear for the worst.

Sean drew a deep breath then sighed. "My supervisor called me into his office today."

Jenny turned toward him; her face showed concern (which she thought seemed appropriate).

"Don't worry, it's nothing bad." He smiled. "He wanted to offer me a deal."

Now Jenny just looked confused.

"He told me he appreciated my willingness to help out when Tim was out of town. He also was thankful for my patience when they kept changing my schedule around so frequently. He said they were trying to maximize the effectiveness of the department's schedule as a whole and wanted to try some different things."

Jenny's face relaxed, and she smiled at her husband, proud of him for having been recognized as a good employee. "So what is the deal?"

"He asked if I would be willing to work five more days on evenings, then he would give me ten days off in a row, without using any of my vacation days."

"Oh, Sean, that's like a paid vacation!"

"I told him that I tentatively agreed, but that I would need to ask you. I know these last few weeks have been difficult for *you* as well. I told him if you balked, I would call him first thing in the morning. Otherwise, I said I would show up for work tomorrow."

"I think it sounds like a good deal. *You* must feel the same since you almost already accepted it."

"Yes, I do. You and I need to spend some time together when we are both not so tired."

"I agree." She tried to look and act calm even though her nerves were acting like Mexican jumping beans inside of her. "At least it's evenings, so we can sleep a little late in the morning!"

Sean raised his eyebrows and nodded. "Indeed." He reflected for a moment and then shared some recent updates with Jenny. "In other news, Tim has called and texted me a few times. He and Kayla have gone on several dates. He told me they went bowling."

"Bowling?" Jenny laughed. "I've never been. Did they have fun?"

"He said they were terrible but that they had a blast. He's really falling for her. In fact, he has told me that he thinks he loves her."

"That's great! I'm happy for them. Maybe we should have a double date. I bet it would be a lot of fun!"

Sean smiled, nodded, and grunted in agreement.

"All right then. I can now make *my* plans so I can take care of you!" she said brightly.

Sean noted "Well, you can start *right now!*" as he winked at her.

They retired to their room, where they loved each other slowly, intensely, and thoroughly.

*****

The next morning, they were awakened by Elise knocking softly on their door. "Mommy, I'm hungry!"

Jenny jumped out of bed, threw on a robe, and walked with Elise into the kitchen. "Do you want to help me make pancakes for Daddy?"

"Yes, ma'am!" she said gleefully.

Meanwhile, Sean showered and got ready for the day. *Just five more days*, he thought. *Then I can spend some time talking to Jenny.*

Poor Sean, thought Jenny. *He has been working so hard. It's a good thing he really loves his job! But now I need to use this time to think about how I'm going to tell him about the awful things I did.* She shook her head from side to side.

Elise saying "Mommy?" brought her back from her thoughts.

"Yes, sweetie?"

"I was talking to you, but you weren't answering me!"

"I'm sorry, baby! I've got some things I'm thinking about. What did you need?"

"Can we put strawberries on our pancakes?"

"*Sure!* I think Daddy would like that a lot!"

Sean emerged from their room about the time his girls were putting the food on the table. "My, my, but you two ladies have prepared a *beautiful* and delicious-looking meal!"

Later, the family worked together on the jigsaw puzzle. Before Sean left for work, Jenny made him a sandwich with a homemade pickle on the side (Sean's mom had given them the recipe). She also packed a snack that he could take with him. Jenny and Elise had leftover quiche with roasted zucchini from their garden for supper and then went to the living room to work more on the jigsaw puzzle.

After Elise went to bed, Jenny finally had some time to think about what she was going to say to Sean in a few days. Several times she had to force herself to stop thinking about *him* and focus on the problem. *I miss him*, she finally admitted to herself. *But I* know *what I want, and that is Sean. He and Elise mean* everything *to me. I've got to stop thinking so selfishly.*

*****

The next four days of Sean's going to work passed quickly. Jenny struggled at times with memories of George and even desire for him. Sometimes while Elise was playing in her room, Jenny found herself pacing the floor like a heroin addict in need of her next fix. *What is wrong with me?* she asked herself, her mind in tremendous turmoil. *Sean loves me, takes care of me, adores Elise, and is a* great *lover. I couldn't ask for more.*

On the fourth day, the solution hit her: ask Heavenly Father for counsel.

After Elise had been tucked in for the night, Jenny knelt at her and Sean's bedside and began. "Dearest Heavenly Father, I should have come to you long ago. I have been a *terrible* wife. I know that through your Son, I can be forgiven. But before that, I need help in telling Sean about what I have done. I ask also for your support in helping him to understand how much I love him and want to be with him and how badly I feel for having hurt him like this. I know also that families are important and that you want us to be together. I pray that you will guide and direct us." She paused, unsure of whether or not it was appropriate to say what she had in mind. Realizing that God *knew* what was on her mind, she continued, "Heavenly Father, I also ask that you send your Spirit to whisper in George's ear. He is in desperate need of guidance to be able to forgive those who have hurt him from his past and also to direct his future. He needs the help that only you can give him. In Jesus' name I pray, Amen."

Jenny was ashamed that she had broken her vows, had strayed so far from her Heavenly Father in thought and deed, and had not even prayed about it until now.

But having turned to him, she felt better already.

The next day, she took Elise to Janice and Tarak's house. The summer was drawing to a close, and the cousins wanted to get in as much swimming as possible. This time, Jenny packed plenty of clothes and a few books. She also stopped at the store on the way, and she had Elise point out to her what drinks and snacks were everyone's favorites. She bought two cases of Gatorade, two family packs of assorted chips, a large bag of oranges, and some grapes. She also picked up a bulk package of hamburger meat and two bags of hamburger buns. *Maybe Tarak can fire up the grill and they can all enjoy some yummy burgers and then have leftovers the next day.* Finally, she bought a family pack of soap, a bottle of shampoo, and three different blow-up toys the kids could play with in the pool.

The kids rushed out to greet Jenny and Elise. Elise excitedly shared with Alicia and Adam that her mom had bought some new pool toys. They scrounged through the bags, found them, and ran inside to begin blowing them up.

Janice helped Jenny carry the other items inside. "You didn't have to do this! It's not like we're poor or anything! Tarak makes good money!"

"I know, but you can't begin to understand how much we appreciate your helping us out all the time. I am quite certain that our marriage is stronger because you have given us so many opportunities to have couple time."

"Well, like I told you before, when Elise is here, my life is actually calmer! I'm glad you guys live so close!" Janice wrapped her arm around her older sister's waist and hugged her. "Are you sure everything is all right? I just sense some…I don't know, maybe sadness in you?"

"We're fine. I need to find some time real soon to come spend a day with *you*, li'l Sis!"

"I'd like that! You guys have fun. We'll be fine here. We'll call you if we need to, but otherwise assume all is well!"

*****

Sean got home late that night as he had some extra paperwork to complete. He called Jenny and told her she could go to bed if she wanted to and that he would be quiet when he came in.

"No, I'd rather wait up for you. I took Elise to Janice's, so we won't have any time constraints or interruptions for the next few days."

"Okay. But promise me that if you get tired, you will go ahead and get in bed."

"Oh, I'll be in bed all right! I just won't be asleep," she taunted.

Sean grinned and blushed as there were other officers in the room who were completing *their* paperwork. (There had been a big car chase for several miles, and the perpetrator had done a lot of damage to property and other cars along the way. They all agreed that the insurance companies were going to be busy for weeks on this one.)

"I'll be there as fast as I can. Love you."

I hope all the good times we have had in the last few days will help Sean as he struggles with what he will soon learn. Jenny sighed and said out loud, "I'll just have to trust that Heavenly Father will help us."

Jenny was too nervous to read, so she decided to make a casserole that could be heated tomorrow when they got hungry. It didn't take long to prepare, so she knew she still had quite a bit of time on her hands. She decided to give herself a pedicure, complete with nail polish. *Sean will like this. He notices everything...*

When he finally did arrive, she could see the exhaustion on his face. But she had already baited him over the phone, so she felt that she needed to fulfill that agenda. She decided she would do all the work so he could just enjoy himself.

He took a quick shower. Afterward, because the weather was so hot, he put on his kilt. When he stepped out of the bathroom, she was sitting on the edge of the bed.

"Umm! Easy access!" Jenny teased.

He sat beside her and put his arm around her. They smiled at each other and kissed.

Jenny stood, turned to face him, and made sure he was happy to be home and with her.

*****

They both had a great need for some deep and restful sleep. It was nearly noon when Sean checked his wristwatch. Jenny felt him stir and turned to face him. Her stomach was in a knot, but her resolve was strong. *Today. No matter what.*

They made their way to the kitchen and decided on a light breakfast of fruit and granola bars. Jenny told Sean about the casserole she had ready to go for later when they got hungry.

Sean knew they needed to talk. He had observed too many unusual things in Jenny's behavior. He wanted to get to the bottom of whatever was going on. He stared coolly at his wife, who was sitting across the table from him.

Do it, NOW! she told herself. She returned his gaze and took a deep breath.

"I need to tell you something." There was no going back now.

"That you've been having an affair with George?"

Jenny's widened eyes and open mouth answered the question for him.

"I've got to go." He strode to their closet to get his keys and wallet. Jenny followed him.

"Sean, please, let me explain," she pleaded. She even tried to grab his arm and turn him to her.

He looked at her with a coldness that made her shiver—despite the August heat. Then he spun and stomped to the garage. In a mere moment, he was gone.

Chapter 35

Sean drove like he had on the day Jenny was in labor. He didn't care if he got pulled over, and he would deal with it if he did. He headed north toward the mountains. He had no idea where he was going, nor did he pay any attention to where he went. He found himself on a dirt road and ultimately reached a secluded area. He pulled off to the right. On the other side of the road, the terrain dropped off sharply. He walked to the edge and stared out into the vastness. His breath quickened as his emotions washed over him. The tears came, but they did nothing to help. He screamed, loud and long, until he had no air left. Then he screamed again, forcing his lungs to empty. His abdomen ached. He dropped to his knees, coughing and sobbing. Now his head hurt, right along with his heart. Time passed, even though he was sure that his life had ended.

He didn't know where he was, what time it was, or what to do. He sat, his legs spread before him, his back and shoulders hunched over in defeat. Time continued to pass. He still didn't know what to do. He leaned over and laid on his side.

The sun continued across the sky, and the shadows began to grow long. He sat up and looked around. Somehow, he realized that he should begin trying to find his way back to civilization. He walked back to his truck and turned it around. Because he was a pilot, he had a good sense of direction and was able to make his way back to roads he recognized. When he reached Bernalillo, just north of Albuquerque, he decided to check into a motel.

He turned the key and opened the door. The room was dark, even with the overhead light on. *Perfect. This suits my mood.* The bed had a sunken spot down the middle that was so deep he could see it from where he stood at the door. *Probably from two people on top of each other, cheating on their spouses.* The carpet was stained, and when he turned the air conditioner on, it smelled so bad he almost turned it back off. *Just like my life right now.* In the bathroom, years of dripping faucets had left hard water stains in the sink and bathtub. *Even so, it's still better than going back.* She's *stained, just like everything in this room.*

Then he thought of Elise. His precious, dark-eyed baby girl. His lip quivered, and the sobbing began anew. He sat in the chair in the corner. One of the arms was loose, and the legs weren't all the same length. But it appeared to be the cleanest thing in the room. *What am I going to do?* "What am I going to do?" he yelled. He didn't care if anyone heard him through what were most likely *very* thin walls.

The clock on the nightstand was blinking "12:00"—probably as it had been doing for days or even weeks. He stood and pulled back the heavy curtain to glance outside. It was fully dark. *That means it's probably at least ten o'clock.*

He realized he was hungry. Again, he looked outside. Down the road, he could just make out two yellow arches. *It'll have to do.* He grabbed the room key and his keys and wallet.

The dining room was closed, so he turned into the drive-thru lane. "I'm sorry, we are closing in four minutes," said a female voice.

"Is there *anything* I can order, or is there another place you can tell me about? I just found out my wife is cheating on me, and I haven't eaten all day. I have a daughter..." Realizing he probably sounded like a crazy man, he stopped.

There was a long pause, then a male voice said, "Pull up to the window, please." Sean moved forward.

The teenage girl could see that Sean had *clearly* been crying. After she had heard Sean's story, she went to ask the manager what they could do.

She reported to Sean, "My boss said we can make some fries and a couple of kid's hamburgers. Would you like cheese on them?" Sean could see that behind her a man was pouring frozen French fries into the basket above the deep-fat fryer and dropping them into the hot grease. He moved to the cooktop area and placed two frozen patties on it.

"Yes, please. That would be great. I really appreciate this." He reached for his wallet in his hip pocket.

"It's okay." The girl waved both hands in front of her. "Don't worry about paying. We've already closed the registers."

Sean reached into his wallet anyway. "Here are a couple of twenties. That will pay for the food, and you can consider the rest a tip."

"Sir, I can't take your money!"

Sean motioned toward her with the two bills in his hand. "I insist. I had an apple this morning, right before my wife…" He had to stop so he wouldn't cry again.

The girl reluctantly accepted the cash and quickly walked to speak with the manager. She came back with an unopened bottle of Coke and offered it to Sean. "We had already broken down and cleaned the drink machines. I had brought this with me to work today, but you are welcome to it if you'd like."

"Thank you. Thank you so very much." He opened the bottle and drank thirstily.

The girl walked to the back again and in a moment opened the window and extended a bag toward him. "I'm so sorry about your situation." Her face was wrinkled in concern. "I hope things get better for you."

"Thanks. I really appreciate your kindness. Please tell your manager thank you." Sean waved at her and pulled away.

Back at the motel, he pulled the food from the bag and held it in one hand as he flattened the bag with the other so he could use it as a plate—or at least a barrier between his food and the table, which probably had a disreputable history. He ate fast, afraid he would lose his appetite. As he finished the last bite, he regretted the decision as his stomach let him know that it was not happy.

He went into the bathroom and flushed the toilet to make sure it worked. It did, but several minutes later, he was aware that the water was still running. He removed the lid to the tank and nearly vomited from the stench of the mildew and slime growing inside. He wiggled the handle and could see that it was going to work now. He quickly replaced the lid and made a mental note to wiggle the handle if he had to use the facilities. *I'd be better off pissing in the parking lot,* he thought with disgust.

His physical requirements met, he sat to face his emotional needs. Try as he might, he could not focus. He looked in the drawer of the nightstand. What was once a notepad but was now two pieces of stained paper on a cardboard backing would have to do. The pen had bite marks all around it. He walked to the bathroom and washed it off in the sink. He didn't know whose mouth it had been in, but he didn't want any part of wherever else that mouth had been.

Though he was a resolute problem solver, at the moment, he felt that he had encountered an unsolvable problem. *Think, Sean!* He wished out loud that he could talk to his father. Immediately, he was prompted to pray. The act itself calmed him. He asked for a clear mind and a forgiving heart. When he finished, he felt peace wash over him.

"Okay. Let's break this down." He absentmindedly drummed his fingers on the tabletop. He picked up the pen and drew a line down the middle of the page, separating it into two columns. Above the column on the right, he wrote STAY; he wrote GO above the other one. His mouth flew open as he stared at the two words. He set the pen down. "That's it!" he said out loud, his outstretched hands before him indicating the obviousness of the solution. *I don't have to have* reasons *for one action or the other. I only have to* choose *one of them.* "So which will it be?"

Sean thought of the day he met Jenny. He remembered riding out to the canyons with her behind him on his Harley, her long hair billowing out behind them. He visualized the first time he made love to her. He swallowed. Memories came flooding into his mind: designing their wedding rings, how she looked at him as they vowed their love to one another, making love to her on the floor of their new house, how beautiful she was as she held Elise right after she was born...

He knew the answer to the question. He couldn't imagine not making more memories with this woman who had surpassed any rational ideas he had for a mate. He didn't want to have to sell everything he had worked for and start over. He couldn't bear the thought of having "visitation" with his daughter.

Besides, up until now, Jenny had been a *superb* wife and mother. This was not an ongoing or recurring problem. Whatever their life was going to be like from here on, he knew it would be better *with* her than without her.

Suddenly, he was more tired than he had ever been in his life. He pulled the coverlet off the bed and, fully clothed, crawled on top of the sheet. The bed embraced him on either side as he slipped into a coma-like sleep.

*****

When he awoke, he regretted not having put on his watch or picked up his phone before he left. He quickly peeked out the window and saw that it was probably around ten in the morning. He used the worn-out toilet and waited to make sure it shut off, then grabbed his wallet and keys and headed south.

Sean parked in the driveway and used his key to enter the front door. Jenny was on the couch, her legs curled to the side. She was hugging a pillow and rocking. She had not slept. To keep herself from going crazy, she had created a puzzle for Sean because he loved working them. She jumped up and ran to him.

Sean held up both hands and stepped back. Jenny stopped, her open mouth and wrinkled brow showing the confusion she was feeling.

She had never looked worse. Her face was swollen, her eyelids were puffy, and her eyes looked like those of a drunk on a Sunday morning.

But she was his wife.

His.

"I am here." Sean paused as he scowled at her intensely. "But we need to have some serious conversations."

Jenny closed her mouth, swallowed, and nodded her head.

He walked to the kitchen for a glass of water. He gulped it down and refilled it. He drank it as well. He filled it one more time and carried it to the table. "Come have a seat."

Jenny walked to the table. She was quivering.

Sean wanted to take her in his arms and stop the shaking, dry her tears, and love away her fears. But he was revolted at the thought of touching her.

Nonetheless, he was a man of manners, and she was a woman. He pulled a chair out for her and then sat across from her. He was leaning over, his forearms resting on the table and his hands lightly clasped. His head was lowered a bit, and he was staring coolly across at her. Jenny could see the pain and anger in the intensity of his glare, but she could also see that he had a tight grip on his emotions.

He spoke quietly. "I want you to begin at the beginning. I want the truth. If I tell you to stop, then stop."

"Okay," she nodded. "But can I ask three questions first?" Deep lines of worry marked her forehead, and her eyes were full of concern for him.

Sean jutted his chin and rubbed his teeth with his tongue. He sighed. "What are they?"

"Where did you go?" She had lain awake all night, imagining multiple worst-case scenarios.

"I have no idea. I slept in the filthiest motel in all of New Mexico. Next."

"Are you okay?" She would be willing to do *anything* if she could remove even a tiny part of his pain.

"No. Next."

"How did you know?"

Sean took a sip of water. "The day after George visited, I found a pair of your panties on the floor just under the bed. They were all rolled up like they had been pulled off, not fluffed like coming out of the dryer. I know that's not concrete evidence, but I found it odd. That same day, you started being unusually jumpy and distracted. You started taking calls privately and had *never* done that before. You weren't eating normally, and you even lost weight. Most importantly, you kept changing the sheets. And in the bedroom, while it was as good as ever, you just didn't seem to be into it like you always had been."

Jenny dropped her head in shame. She had known all along— but had chosen to ignore—that Sean would see the signs. She had been caught up in the excitement of how *he* controlled her mentally and how he brought her physically.

She told Sean the story. All of it. She even included the things she did to attempt to cover up her lying and cheating. At times, tears streaked her cheeks as the realization of the pain she had caused deepened within her.

Occasionally, Sean would have to ask her to stop. He sat there, stone-faced, breathing hard and staring at the table as the agony of visualizing his wife with another man roared through him. A few times his upper body would convulse; whether he was sobbing or near vomiting was unclear to her.

Twice he rose from the table and walked onto the back porch. The first time, Jenny went to him after a few minutes. "Leave me be," he commanded, never looking at her. The second time, she remained in her chair.

Now she understood how hurt Sean had been when after her miscarriage, he had wanted to comfort her, and she would have no part of it. She put her head down on her arms and wept.

He came back in, and she finished the story, including the phone call she and George had shared when she was in the parking lot of the stationery store.

> Sean,
> I know you love puzzles,[1] so I created one for you. I hope it brings you joy in multiple ways.

---

[1] Solution is in the final chapter.

WILL YOU LOVE ME AGAIN?

Clues

1. Keep it s____ple
2. Insane
3. Round_____, by __ __ __
4. Respect _____rself
5. _____ you still love me, tomorrow
6. It is missing in this puzzle and in my life; _____ make me feel like a natural woman
7. It's what the world needs, now
8. Keep on rockin' ____, baby
9. When will I see you _____

I hope the answer you figure out is the one I want to hear.

CHAPTER 36

As Jenny shared the various encounters of her affair, Sean felt like knives were stabbing him in his heart, his gut, and his brain. He felt a myriad of emotions: confusion as to *why* Jenny would be interested in another man in the first place, as he had been a good husband; anger at the man for touching his wife; jealousy that she admitted to in some strange way having feelings for the other man; disgust with the things she allowed the man to do to her; and fear that it could happen again.

They sat for a long while, neither of them speaking. They were emotionally wrung out. With no tears left to cry, Sean finally spoke. "I want a new bed."

Jenny nodded; she understood. She opened her mouth to ask if he wanted to shop for one today when Sean suddenly stood and exploded.

"I *cannot believe* you let me make love to you and then sleep with you in your and his *filth!*" He was enraged, and spit flew from his lips. His breath and heart rate were as rapid as if he had just run a sprint. "I am *disgusted* at what may be on me!" He turned to walk away then stopped and faced her. "And you were with him in our *shower* too!"

Jenny's lip quivered, and she dropped her head in shame.

"I'll be using the guest shower for a while. Or did he leave his mark there as well?" Sparks of rage flew from his eyes. Of everything he had learned today, this was the worst. She had allowed *another man* into his domain and had *willingly* permitted him to degrade her. Then she had let him wallow in *their* pool of lust. For the first time since she had known him, Jenny heard Sean use profanity as he walked away.

Sean was in the shower for a long time. He soaped up twice then stood under the hot running water, allowing it to massage his body. Physically, at least, he felt better. He wrapped himself in a towel then went into their room to choose some clean clothes. He kept his back to the bed; he couldn't even bear to look at it. Then he thought of something.

He marched into the living room, where Jenny was sitting on the couch. From an aggressive stance, he spat out, "Did you let him romp around with you on the quilt I bought for you?"

She turned her head to look straight at him. "No," she declared as she shook her head vigorously.

"Did you wear the jewelry I'd bought for you when you were with him?"

"No!" Tears were filling her eyes.

"Was the plate you broke with the cookies on it one of the ones I bought for you on our honeymoon?"

"No!" By now her face was contorted, her eyes were closed, and her head was completely lowered.

Her answers notched Sean's anger down. His shoulders dropped a bit, and he went from leaning toward her as if in battle to standing more upright. That felt even better, still. He took in a deep, cleansing breath and let it out slowly. "Why don't you shower so we can go look for a bed," he said in a *much* calmer voice.

"Okay." Jenny stood. She opened her mouth to say more, then decided it might be best to remain quiet.

She emerged from their bedroom wearing a modest knit dress and comfortable sandals. She found Sean in the kitchen. She walked haltingly in his direction.

"Come here," Sean directed.

Jenny timidly approached him but kept a respectful distance.

"What you have done was wrong. You broke your promise of commitment to me, you trampled on the trust I freely gave you, and you disrespected yourself *and me* by bringing another man into *my* home, *our* home. The one I bought for you and for us and for our family." He paused to take a deep breath because what he would say next was going to be difficult for him at this time. "But that does not give me the right to be rude or hurtful to you, and I have. I'm sorry."

He held his arms out toward her and quietly said, "Come here."

Jenny could not get close enough to the man she loved. His warm arms were like a blanket of peace, love, and security around her. She fought the urge to cry, but a *few* tears of joy *did* escape her. Sean felt their wetness on his chest and turned her face up to him.

"I can't kiss you yet," he whispered as he gently wiped her cheeks, "but soon, maybe."

Jenny shook her head while telling him it was okay. "I understand."

They held each other for many minutes, allowing their hearts and minds to begin to reconnect. By the time they drew apart, they were much more at peace.

*****

Jenny was increasingly ashamed of her infidelity and was, therefore, increasingly timid. She rode with Sean in his truck to the furniture store to choose a bed but had no input on which one to purchase. "Whatever you like," she said with a forced smile. (In reality, she was falling apart on the inside and was just bravely trying to appear normal.)

Sean was mildly frustrated by her timidity, but he understood that she was feeling remorseful for having shredded his emotions. He made a mental note that he would have to encourage and help her to once again find her confidence. But first, he had to again find his dignity.

A bed was chosen. Sean was prepared to pay extra to get it delivered that night, but the salesman told him they always had same-day delivery on beds. "Most people want that good night's sleep right away!" he said.

*****

When Sean didn't come home after leaving when he had learned of her affair, Jenny moved the casserole she had previously prepared to the freezer so she and Sean decided to go to a local favored hamburger joint. Sean purposefully chose a small corner table so that they would have no choice but to sit close to each other. He knew that their reconciliation and his recovery were going to be somewhat like falling off a horse; it was important to get back on quickly and *force* steps toward what was once familiar. Though they normally conversed easily, tonight they were both silent.

His forearms were spread before him on the tabletop; her hands were tightly clasped and resting on the table in front of her. He was surveying the crowd; she was staring at her wedding ring. As they sat waiting for their food to be prepared and their name to be called, he lowered his head and adjusted his hand slightly to gently touch her hand with the back of his index finger. His eyes looked up at her to see her response. A little bit more of his frozen heart melted as she raised her head and turned her face to him, smiling sweetly.

They were reestablishing their connection with each other. Without a word, they both leaned in toward the other. Sean was contemplating giving her a quick peck, but he heard his name called on the loudspeaker. He stood to retrieve their burgers.

When he returned to their table with them, Jenny was sitting more upright and was smiling easily at him.

*****

The man at the furniture store told them it would be after nine o'clock before the bed would arrive. As they left the restaurant, Sean glanced at his wristwatch.

"We've got a bit of time. Why don't we go somewhere and buy some new pillows and sheets and a new mattress cover?"

Jenny understood that this was a need for Sean; quite frankly, she thought it would be good for her as well. "Sure!"

"Do you have a store in mind?"

"There's a good place about two miles up here on the right."

They parked, and Sean went around to open Jenny's door as he always had. *I wonder why it feels so foreign?* he thought. He offered his hand to help her down from his truck. *This almost feels like a first date.*

Jenny smiled and looked up at her husband. "Thank you!" She knew he was struggling mightily. She wondered what more she could do to ease his pain.

They walked slowly, both of them secretly wishing that the other would reach to hold hands. Jenny decided now was the time for action. She "accidentally" stumbled slightly into Sean and their hands brushed each other. Both of them took advantage of the opportunity, then smiled weakly at each other.

One baby step at a time, they thought simultaneously.

Once inside, they found the bedding department. Sean, always full of creative ideas, said, "Why don't we both choose something we like, then we will compare. We might even get both."

"That's a good idea," Jenny agreed.

They walked in separate directions. Sean made a selection fairly quickly. Being taller, he kept an eye on Jenny, watching to see when she had picked up a set. When he saw that she had, he began walking toward her. As they approached each other, they burst into laughter; they had each chosen the same thing!

"Are we meant for each other or *what?*" Sean exclaimed. (He realized that he was forcing himself a little, and it felt corny, but he also knew that if they were going to even approach the fabulous relationship they had had before, they would *have* to take those baby steps. They would *have* to put aside their negative emotions and at least *act* like they were enjoying each other's company. He knew that if they were diligent, they could get through this and hopefully emerge even stronger because of it.)

Jenny preferred having at least two sets of sheets, but she didn't feel like she had the right to ask Sean to buy anything. However, he was aware that it made sense to have two sets.

He offered, "Why don't we go ahead and get another set. That way there can be a backup set at the ready."

"That's a good idea." Trying desperately to be the confident girl Sean admired, she suggested, "Why don't we get a solid-colored set that coordinates with this pattern? That way we can mix and match and will effectively have three different ways to make the bed. We can get an extra package of pillowcases as well."

Sean couldn't help but smile. *There's my girl!* "What color do you think would work?"

They quickly found what they were looking for. They also picked up some new pillows and a mattress protector.

Once home, Jenny quickly unwrapped one set of sheets and got them in the washer so that they would smell fresh. *At least I won't be having to change sheets so often now*, she thought. She found that to be both humorous and guilt-inducing. She chose to chuckle.

Sean walked past at that very moment and saw her smiling. He stopped and looked at her questioningly. "What's so funny in there?"

She looked up at him and bit her lip. *Honesty always!* She took a deep breath and looked down, trying to decide how to tell him. She didn't want to ignite his pain or anger.

He stepped near her and quietly ordered, "Tell me."

Again, she looked up at him then stared straight ahead. *Just tell him the truth!* "Honestly, I was just realizing that I won't have to be washing sheets so often anymore." She looked back at him; this time, her face held a look of hope.

He grinned. He was proud of her for trying to find some humor in a bad situation. "When you get finished here, let's talk while we wait for the deliverymen."

"Okay. I'll be right there."

Chapter 37

Sean had filled a glass of water for each of them and was sitting at the table when Jenny joined him. She took a deep breath, nodded, and smiled at him, letting him know she was ready.

"When the deliverymen get here with our new bed, they're probably going to expect that we have moved the other one." He paused. "I can't do it, Jenny."

Jenny was considering trying to move it herself so that Sean wouldn't be further traumatized, but she wasn't sure she was physically able.

"I'll pay them, tell them they can have it *and* the old sheets… whatever it takes."

"Okay," she nodded.

"Once the sheets are dry, I'll help you put them on." Sean closed his eyes and took a deep breath. "I want us to have an understanding," he exhaled, "about…bedtime." When he opened his eyes, they were sad.

Jenny wasn't sure what he meant. "Ooo-kaaaay."

Sean looked at his wife, drew in his lips, and shook his head. "Jenny, I can't…I can't…*be* with you yet."

She dropped her head. "I understand."

"Jenny, look at me," Sean stated with great authority.

She looked up, trying to keep her face neutral.

"I know I still love you. And I *want* to be with you. But I just can't yet get past the images in my mind."

"I understand."

"Tonight, I'll lie with you, but please know that I'm not sure that I will be able to hold you or even touch you."

"Okay." Jenny nodded because she understood that Sean was doing all he could. And she trusted him to be able to, as always, fix things.

"I'm working on it, but I am open to suggestions as well."

"Why don't we pray?"

Sean smiled and nodded. He knew she was right.

"Let's go in the living room and kneel at the couch," he directed. As he walked, he remembered all the nights he, his brother, and their parents had knelt at the timeworn couch in the tiny living room of the home in which he had grown up.

Once there, he waited for her to get comfortable, then he kneeled next to her. He looked over at her as he took her hand in his.

"Dearest Heavenly Father, we come to you tonight seeking your counsel. Transgressions have been made, and we need to seek forgiveness from you, from each other, and from ourselves." Tears were streaming down his face, but he was able to keep his voice strong. "We know that families are important and have chosen to recommit ourselves to ours. We need to heal the rift in our lives. We ask that thy Spirit will whisper softly to us, guiding and directing us as we work to strengthen the tattered bonds between us. Heavenly Father, we love you and know that you love us. You have blessed us with a precious daughter, and we pray that we may continue to always consider the importance of raising her as you would have us do. Please help us to replace negative thoughts with positive ones, jealousy with love, anger with calm, confusion with clarity, and fear with peace."

He sniffled, turned his face toward Jenny, and whispered, "Would you like to add anything?"

She nodded. Seeing Sean's tears caused hers to begin. "Heavenly Father, I have sinned. I have hurt my husband, jeopardized our relationship, and ignored the potential impact that my actions may have caused to our daughter and our family. I ask that you free my husband's mind from the terrible images he is bearing and ease his heart from the dreadful pain this has caused him. I also ask that as I turn my heart and mind back to you, that you help me begin to have relief from this terrible guilt. I pray that I may from this time forward always seek to follow the teachings of your blessed Son, that I may have helpful hands, a loving heart, and a charitable spirit. I pray also that I may join my husband in raising our daughter in your house. We are grateful for the infinite blessings which you have given us and pray that we always remember to seek your wisdom in our lives. We give these thanks, and we ask for these blessings in the sacred name of our Lord and Savior, Jesus Christ. Amen."

Sean turned to Jenny and held her closely; tears were flowing freely from both of them. Once he regained enough composure to speak, he quietly said, "God has begun to wash our pain from us." They remained there, consoling each other for several more minutes.

Ultimately, Jenny stood first. "I need to move those sheets to the dryer so we can go to bed tonight!"

A few minutes later, the doorbell rang.

Sean was able to convince the men (with the help of US Grant) to take the old bed and all the bedding with them. He hoped that one of them had a wife that would be well-pleased to have a high-end king-size bed in excellent condition, along with three sets of good quality sheets and several pillows.

He and Jenny worked together to put the mattress protector and sheets on the new bed. Then they decided it would be a good idea to play a board game—something to lighten the mood and take their minds off the troubling truths of the last few weeks.

They moved once again to the table. Sean set up the board for Monopoly as Jenny made popcorn and lemonade.

They appreciated the diversion that the game provided; a sparkle even made an appearance in each of their eyes as they laughed together and enjoyed each other's company.

Later, as Sean put the game away, Jenny stored the leftover popcorn and turned out the lights in the kitchen. They moved to the couch to watch a bit of TV. Both of them knew that they were avoiding the inevitable uncomfortable situation they would face in the bedroom.

Once they both began to yawn, Sean stood and said, "Come on. Let's get it over with." Sean checked all the doors, and they both got ready for bed.

He waited for Jenny to get in first. Then he positioned himself in such a way that he was not touching her but could turn and reach for her when he was ready.

They lay together, neither able to sleep. Jenny spoke first. "Sean, I know you probably know it, but I haven't actually said the words." She turned her face in his direction. "I'm *so* sorry for what I've done and, more importantly, for how it impacted you. I was being selfish. And I didn't even have a good reason to do it. In fact, I had *every* reason *not* to." She paused to collect herself. "But I can't change it. So I want you to know that I regret my actions more than you can know. I'm *so* sorry. And just so you know, I love you."

Moments later, Sean felt the bed shake from her sobbing. He *knew* he should comfort her, but he just couldn't.

Then he had a realization.

He was being selfish in choosing to wade around in his pain and victimhood. Here lay his wife, trying desperately to do the right thing, and he was ignoring *her* pain. *Maybe we can soothe each other*, he reasoned.

He reached for her shoulder and gently pulled on it. She was wrapped in his arms in an instant. He knew it would be a while before he could again make love to her. But this felt right.

After many minutes, and with as much positivity as she could muster, Jenny said, "Sean, I think that, in the end, the day went well." She had her hand on his chest and could feel his heart thumping. "Everything has been exposed. No more hiding, no more lies. We got the new bed, and we prayed—together. I know *I* felt immediate relief, and I hope you did as well. And now in less than forty-eight hours from hearing everything, we are here, trying our best to rebuild our relationship. I'll say again how sorry I am. But right now, I feel like I am in heaven here in your arms. I won't pressure you for more. I'll give you time. Just know that I am yours, and *only* yours, when you get ready."

"Thank you," he said quietly. "And I love you too." Jenny fell asleep moments later.

*****

Sean stared at the ceiling for hours. *Why?* he thought. *I tried to do everything right.* He was troubled by the lack of an answer.

At a point, he walked out to the back porch and sat looking at the stars. It was still hot, but the dry night air had cooled from the overwhelming heat of the daytime. He realized he was but one tiny speck of pain in a whole universe of others feeling the same way. *We had it figured out*, he thought. *We were* so *happy that others were jealous of us. And now this. If I could just understand. If I just had some answers.* The problem solver in him was thwarted until he had something to work with. He went back inside.

Jenny had felt him leave. She had tried to go back to sleep but couldn't. Once he was settled in bed again, she asked, "Is there anything I can say or do to help?"

"Actually, yes."

She sat up. "Name it and it's done."

"I want to know some things."

There was a long pause. She was torn between giving him what he wanted and telling him that she didn't think it was a good idea to bring those images freshly back into his mind. Ultimately, she realized that her husband was a man who knew his limits. "Okay. Do you want us to lie here comfortably? Do you want to sit up? Do you want the lights on, off? Do you want to go to the living room or kitchen?"

"Here. In the dark."

"Okay." She lay back down. She wanted him to hold her, but she didn't want to press her luck. She knew he would reach for her when he was ready.

CHAPTER 38

Sean's confusion was compounded by the fact that he didn't really know what questions to ask to get the answers that might help him to understand why his world had fallen apart. The simplest one, of course, was "Why?" But he doubted that even Jenny herself knew the answer to that.

He lay on the bed, the arm closest to her under his own head. *Pain, I can deal with,* he thought. *But confusion...that's not something I can tolerate. On anything.* That was the nature of a problem solver. He realized that their life *had* been good partly because he had found solutions to problems, sometimes even before they appeared.

He sighed. *Well, it'll get the conversation started at least.* "Why?"

Jenny was lying on her side. Somehow, being able to see her husband by the moonlight pouring through the windows was better than facing the ceiling. "Why...did I have the affair?"

"Yes."

"Sean, I wish I knew the answer to that."

"Okay. *What* did you gain from it?"

"A lot of pain for you." She wasn't trying to be funny; she was stating the obvious. But she knew that Sean was frustrated, and *that* answer wasn't helping. "Okay. Ahhh...stab in the dark here...excitement?"

She instantly regretted her use of that phrase; she knew Sean felt she had stabbed him in the heart—in the dark or otherwise.

"Terrible idiom to use given that we are lying here in the dark." He decided not to add any reference to the "stab" part. *At least one of us thinks of the other's feelings,* he thought.

He instantly regretted having *that* thought. He sighed. *This is going to be a snaky pathway.*

Both of them were experiencing devastating torment. Jenny rose and walked around to Sean's side of the bed, knelt, and softly put her hand on his arm. He twitched, thinking to pull away from her touch, but decided that there were going to have to be some uncomfortable moments in this journey.

"Sean, I'm sorry for that. It was thoughtless, but I didn't mean it that way. I *know* I have hurt you to the core. That statement didn't help, intentional or not."

Sean lay silent. Her hand on his arm was a firebrand to his already tortured soul. But it was also oddly erotic, reminiscent of times past when he enjoyed her warm body—all of it.

"Sean, do you remember when you came back from Scotland after your father's death?" Jenny began lightly stroking his arm and drawing little patterns on it as a means of soothing him.

"Uh-hmm."

"We were struggling in our relationship because of my shunning your love and attention after I lost our baby."

"Yeah." Though he was following her, he had no idea where she was going with this train of thought. Nonetheless, he decided to try to hang in there.

"You tried to hold me, in there in our bathroom." Jenny nodded her head in that direction. "I tried to get away. But you held me tightly and kissed me. No matter what I did, you overpowered me—though you were very gentle. I told you that I *did* want us to be together but that I just didn't know *how*."

"Umm-hmm," Sean grunted.

"Then *you* said that you didn't know how, either, but that you knew we could do it, together." Jenny paused to let those words sink in.

"Sean, I understand why you wouldn't want to touch me or be touched by me. I've really messed things up. If I could, I would hold you and kiss you to help you remember what we had. But I can't overpower you. *My* approach has to be different than yours was."

Right there, on that new bed, right next to her, lay the man she loved more than anything else in the world. He was hurting. She couldn't do anything about it, and it was ripping her apart.

She gently moved her shaking hand to his chest. She could feel the rise and fall of his breathing. She could feel his heart beating. She wanted him so badly she could barely stand it—not so much for the sexual act itself as for the physical closeness and spiritual connection.

Sean did not move away from her.

"Do you remember a conversation we had some time later, when we agreed that we never wanted to go through times like that again? I said that we had to have faith in God and trust in our love for each other."

"Uh-huh." Sean had not moved since he had returned to bed from being outside.

"Do you remember the code word I came up with to remind ourselves of that?"

"Unity," he declared as he rolled toward and reached for her.

She quickly crawled into the bed beside him. She could hear his ragged breathing, feel his body sobbing.

He had wrapped her in his arms. One of her hands massaged his strong chest, the other gently stroked his face.

After a while—after his breathing calmed—she continued, because she knew Sean. She knew he wouldn't stop pursuing the answers to his questions. Without the answers, their relationship was going to be on the rocks. If she could help him to understand, they could commence the reparation of their battered ship. She decided to dive into the deep, dark water to begin the task.

"Sean, I didn't mean my life *lacked* excitement. Being married to you is *way* beyond exciting. It was more like…the excitement of the moment, maybe?"

She felt him nod slightly.

"When he grabbed me…then kissed me…it was all so sudden. I was caught off guard. And I remember that he held me very tightly; I couldn't have gotten away. But once he let me go, I *should* have slapped him, kicked him, screamed, run…*anything*."

"Yep," Sean interjected.

Only her intense love for her husband kept Jenny going. "But he had…awakened my desire… That sounds impossible to me because I love you so much, and you are the *only* man I want."

"Well, the logical response to that is 'Apparently not,' but I'm trying desperately to believe you." Sean knew that the two of them needed to be *brutally* honest with each other. There was no place for tiptoeing around this issue.

"I know you are, and thank you." Jenny took a moment to think about what she would say next. "He had seemed so nice, so gentlemanly. We had even invited him to our party, remember?"

"Biggest mistake I ever made."

"When Janice came to get Elise, he stood. I remember thinking of you and how that is something you would have done. And when he patted me on the arm, I thought that maybe he was just one of those 'touchy-feely' kind of people."

"Well, he was."

"Sean, I don't want to hurt you further…"

"What hurts is not understanding how this happened. I need you to be honest with me. Please."

"Okay. This isn't easy for me. I feel like I'm stabbing you all over again." Jenny was near tears.

"You are, but I have asked for it." Sean was in a "safe" place in his brain, a place where logic and reason ruled. As much as was possible, he detached from his feelings so he could make sense of what had happened between his wife and the other man.

"His kiss was intense, and his hands knew where and how to touch me."

Sean knew well how responsive Jenny was to his touch. But apparently not *just* his.

"Sean, he just…overwhelmed me. He pulled me into our bedroom and then shoved me onto the bed. I had never been handled that roughly by *anyone*. It was so different from you. You are so gentle but so…effective."

"Let me ask you this. If you had fought him, do you think he would have raped you?"

"Absolutely. It was almost rape anyway. He was so rough."

"I could kill him."

Jenny pulled back from him slightly. "Sean…" She shook her head. "You're not that guy."

"Over you, I am."

Jenny shivered. She folded herself back against Sean's chest.

"I think his roughness is what...what excited me. It was something different and made him very successful in achieving his goal. And it created fear, which gave him the power to control me mentally."

Jenny thought for a moment and then added, "Actually, I *did* try to resist him. He simply overpowered me."

"So at what point did you stop fighting?"

"Oh, Sean." Jenny's face contorted at the thought of having to say the next words.

"Just tell me."

"He got me all...stirred up."

"So fear, dishonesty, lying, cheating...*none* of those entered your brain? Only lust?"

"I'm sorry, Sean! I'm just trying to answer your question!" Her voice was squeaky because she was crying again.

Sean patted her on the shoulder. "I'm sorry. I shouldn't ask for something and then punish you for delivering it."

Sean knew this was terribly uncomfortable for Jenny, but he was past caring about anything except trying to find a way to fix his relationship with her—whatever it took. *Then*, he thought, *we can smooth over whatever damage* that *causes.*

"Did you enjoy it?"

"Well, I...climaxed."

"Did you invite him to come back?"

"No! He demanded that I tell him when you would be at work."

"And you answered him? You could have lied."

"I was...afraid. Partly, anyway. Also, he was so...fierce. He was rough and loud and forceful. I...I...didn't...Sean, I wasn't able to think. It's like he brought me under his spell or something. He was in control."

"But you are *strong*. How could you let him dominate you like that?"

Jenny was frantically trying to answer Sean's questions so they could restore their marriage to the enchantment they had formerly known.

"He got up in my head too. *Right* after, he told me, 'You needed that.'" Jenny mimicked the tone of his voice and his facial expression. "Then he pinched me—hard. I didn't pull back because…because I was trying to show him I wasn't going to let him win. Then he asked me when I wanted more and told me I *needed* what only he could do."

"What about the phone calls and texts? Why didn't you just ignore them?"

"I felt *so* bad after. I was ashamed. And I didn't know if he was really going to show up the next day or not. When he called, I declined it. I was *terrified* that he would call back and you would notice. I knew you would learn what had happened, and I felt partly responsible."

"Jenny, to be honest, you partly were."

"I know. So then there became this whole 'keep it all hidden from Sean' thing going on." She took a moment to remember what happened next. "He texted after you left for work. It said, 'Don't ever ignore me like that again.' I was so scared. Then he called and gave me a bunch of commands. I guess I just kinda went into 'prevent more damage' mode."

"You're saying he *mentally* controlled you?"

"Yes. I can't believe it happened, but it did. And *very* quickly." Jenny was fighting through her tears.

Sean's breathing was heavy. Jenny was concerned that he may have reached the limit of what he could take.

"He pulled my hair…*a lot*. It's kinda like being beaten because it hurts, really badly. But it doesn't leave any marks. And one time he was talking, and he told me something like 'angry people do what they are told because they want to prove that they can stand up to their oppressor.'"

"Did you start looking forward to him coming over?"

Jenny took a deep breath and groaned. "In the strangest way, yes. I'm sorry, Sean. I can't believe the control he exercised over me." She turned her face into his shoulder and shook as she sobbed.

"Was he better than me?"

"Sean, *please* don't make me answer that!" She sniffled.

"Answer me," he said gruffly.

"No. Physically, I was satisfied, that's true. But with you, it's... it's on a whole new level. With him, it was very...primal. I enjoyed it but only sexually. In every other way, I knew I was in the wrong. He hurt me, and he made me feel like I was some kind of whore. *You* build me up. *He* tore me down."

"Did you think of just leaving the house before he was supposed to get there?"

"That's what I ultimately did. And I want to add something. I am *certain* that had I not cooperated for every single thing that we did, he would have physically forced me to do it."

Sean took a deep breath. "I need time to process all of this."

Jenny raised her head to look at him. "Okay. What can I do to help?"

"I'll let you know." He rolled away from his wife, stood up, and glanced outside. "The sun will be coming up soon. I'm going to go for a drive." He looked at Jenny, who was now sitting upright. Even in the dim light, he could see that her face showed fear. "I'm not leaving. I just...think better when I'm flying or driving."

"Okay. Will you be hungry when you get back? Do you want me to make you anything or do anything for you?"

"Just be here. We can talk more."

CHAPTER 39

New Mexico has beautiful sunrises and sunsets in its deserts and mountains. Sean decided to drive east on I-40 toward Santa Rosa. After climbing up and through Tijeras Pass, the road descended as he traveled through Edgewood and Moriarty then began to ascend again before it reached Clines Corners. A steady drop in elevation carried him into Santa Rosa.

After the pass, he engaged the cruise control, and his truck gobbled up the miles. He was in Santa Rosa in just over an hour and a half. The sunrise had been brilliant.

Initially, his mind was swirling with vile images, evil thoughts, and negative emotions. They were like scattered lumber at a construction site after a tornado. By the time the road began its final descent, he had calmed down enough to begin making some sense of the things Jenny had told him. In Santa Rosa, he pulled over to get gas and use the restroom. The sun was rising quickly behind him as he turned back to the west to head home.

Sean had spent his life training his brain to solve problems. Like a carpenter picking up first one board and then another in order to build a structure from the scattered pieces, he arranged the various components of the affair into a framework so that he could further analyze them. In this way, he could put everything in perspective and begin to heal from the effects the devastating storm of the affair had had on his heart, mind, and soul.

He breezed into Albuquerque around eight forty-five. He stopped at a bakery and bought two caramel pecan rolls. He pulled into his driveway and parked in the garage.

Jenny met him at the door. Though she had showered and put on one of his favorite floral sundresses, he could see the worry on her face and tiredness in her eyes. He wondered if he looked any better.

"I brought us some breakfast," Sean announced as he held up the bag.

"Oh! Thanks, Sean. That was thoughtful of you! Do you want me to heat them now, or do you prefer to wait?"

"I'm hungry now. I would imagine you are as well."

"Yes, I am. I've got a fresh gallon of milk in the fridge if you'd like some."

"Great," he said. "Would you like some as well?"

"Yes, please."

A visiting stranger would consider them to be a happy couple, with both of them being helpful and kind. But they both knew they were each forcing all this friendliness.

Jenny was ashamed and felt that she would need to spend the rest of her life somehow atoning for what she had done to her husband. *But if he will just stay with me, I'll be happy.*

Sean was still hurting—and maybe always would—but he wanted to be married to his wife and raise his daughter in their home. *If I could just understand* how *this happened, I know that the two of us can make it back to our loving relationship.*

Neither was able to envision the life and love they had once shared happening anytime soon in their future.

After breakfast, Jenny quickly rinsed their plates and glasses and put them in the dishwasher. As Sean watched her, he thought of all the times he had sat in that very chair, viewing her with eyes full of love. An image of the other man—standing by the sink and holding his wife tightly as he kissed her—began creeping into his mind. He shook his head as if he could make the vision tumble out of his brain.

Jenny rounded the corner of the peninsula and questioned, "Are you okay?"

"Just tired I guess." Then, "That's not true. I was trying to delete the image of him in our kitchen holding and kissing you."

A worried look crossed her face, then she tried to smile at him.

"Jenny, I don't want to live like this! How are we going to get past this?"

"Honestly, I think right now we are both too fatigued. We're not going to be able to make much progress if our brains and emotions are so strained. Personally, I think we should close the blinds so the room is nice and dark and then lie down and rest."

Sean nodded. "I know you're right." He wanted to say something but couldn't remember what. "Let's do it."

*****

They had both fallen asleep quickly and rested well. Around two in the afternoon, Sean's eyes popped open. He decided to take a shower. He quietly gathered some clothes and went to the guest bathroom.

Feeling *much* better, he walked into the living room to find Jenny sitting on one end of the couch looking at a magazine.

Jenny had decided that she was going to, as much as was possible, be the person she had been before...*him*. Instead of being in turmoil (and looking worse for it), she would relax, smile, and take care of Sean. If he refused her tenderness, she would act normal and give him time. She would be the woman he fell in love with. "Feel better?" she asked cheerfully.

"Much." Sean could see in Jenny's eyes that she felt better as well. He sat on the opposite end of the couch from her. "You look more rested than you did earlier this morning."

"Thanks!"

Sean noted that her smile seemed genuine.

"What are you reading?" he asked, trying to get a conversation started.

"Janice had this travel guide listing all of the state parks and other places to go to in New Mexico. It shows pictures, lists fees and restrictions, and tells about things to do and see. She thought we might enjoy it, so she gave it to me since they never go camping."

"Sounds like a good thing to have. Do you have any trips in mind?"

"Well, the area around Angel Fire is always beautiful. Elise *loves* to go camping, and it's been a while since we went. What do you think?"

"I think we should consider it. It *would* be a nice distraction."

True to her resolution, she continued, "You still have seven days left of your vacation. We could get a trip in before school starts."

Sean was nodding his head as he contemplated the timing. He wanted to spend more time talking with Jenny now that he had had a chance to cool off and collect his thoughts. He knew they needed to lay the groundwork for how they were going to proceed with their lives in their "new normal"—the one that included his wife having cheated on him.

With that in mind, Sean directed, "I'd like to spend some more time talking today."

Jenny closed the magazine and set it on the coffee table. "Okay. What's on your mind?"

"I'd like to start by telling you where I am right now in my perception of…what happened."

"Sure. But first, I set out that casserole I had made earlier to begin thawing. It will need an hour in the oven before we can eat it. So when you start to get hungry, let me know and I'll take care of that real quick." She smiled at her husband as she would have…before.

Sean *truly* appreciated that Jenny was trying to act normal. It hurt him to see concern or fear in her face. He reasoned that she must have spent some time doing a bit of "emotional engineering" during the times that he had left the house.

"Sounds good. And thank you." He looked over at her. *Just start*, he told himself. He took a deep breath, drew in his lips, and exhaled slowly. "I've thought about the things you have told me. I don't know his initial intentions when he stopped by here that day. Maybe he *truly* did want to visit with me. Personally, I rather doubt it. Based on what you told me about his background, I suspect he was going to take advantage of an opportunity if it presented itself, if not *that* day then *a different* day. Even though he was seemingly well-behaved at first, you *probably* should have found a way to get rid of him." Jenny nodded in agreement. "By being allowed to stay—even though the two of you were having a 'pleasant conversation'—he was able to make his move."

Sean looked at his wife. Jenny had quietly accepted his chastisement and continued to look at him attentively. He continued.

"He was *dead* wrong to approach you—and he'd *better* not try to again." Sean's eyes flashed pure hate for a brief instant. "So the fault of initiation lies squarely on his shoulders." Again, Jenny nodded in agreement. "However, when you had the chance, you did nothing to try to stop him, initially at least. You *allowed* him to seduce you."

Jenny took a deep breath and forced herself to continue to hold her head high. Sean needed to see that she was attempting to put the whole thing behind her and move on.

"I know he restrained you. And I believe you when you said he would have raped you even if you had fought him. So again, he was *completely* in the wrong."

Though her insides were beginning to feel a little shaky, her outward appearance indicated that she was calling on her inner strength to stand up to Sean's judgment.

"Had that been the only time he came over, I would have been angry and hurt, sure, at *both* of you, but I would have felt like he should have carried the bulk of the blame. I would probably have considered, overall, that you had been raped and would have tried to be very attentive to you, keeping *my* pain more on the inside and dealing with it in due time. I feel like *you* would have needed more healing than me."

Jenny was amazed at Sean's ability to clearly perceive a situation and analyze it straightforwardly. Again, she nodded in agreement with him.

Sean rose and took a seat on the couch opposite from her. "But he came back. I understand he had gained some mental control over you, and as such, you gave him your phone number. But why didn't you tell me? I could have taken care of the situation. I have an entire department of friends who would have seen to it that *his* decision would have been to leave town."

Jenny looked up as she searched for an answer. "I told you. I felt partly guilty...mostly because of having...you know, *enjoyed* it. And

I was afraid…though I now can see that I was only afraid because he *had* gotten in my head."

"Fair enough. I'm sure you were doing the best you could, given the circumstances. In the future, however, know that your husband can *and will* protect you."

"I know. Thanks."

"Here is the problem. You began to *want* him to come back." Sean was staring intently at Jenny with cool, blue eyes.

Jenny wiggled uncomfortably in her seat, glanced down, then quickly back at him. That was unnerving, so her eyes quickly darted away from him, back down, then back at him. She knew she had to face him.

"Answer me truthfully. Do you believe that, from that point, there was *something* you could have done to end it?"

Jenny again looked down, took a deep breath, then looked directly across at her husband. "Of course."

Sean looked up, exhaled deeply, and bit at his upper lip. "So I'm going to say that he is 100 percent guilty of *initiation*. But the two of you share in guilt for the *perpetuation* of this affair. I'd say, maybe, sixty-forty, him to you." To Sean, problem-solving began with organizing, analyzing, and quantifying data. "Would you agree?"

Jenny had trouble meeting Sean's piercing gaze. But she forced herself. "I don't know how to assign a number to it, but, yes, I agree with you."

Sean's shoulders dropped as he began to relax. Somehow, it was important to him that she admit her guilt. His eyes were much softer now. Their eyes met. "So what now?" Sean asked with upturned hands.

Jenny half-shrugged. "I think we just have to move forward even though we may not know what the road ahead holds for us. I told him that it's over and asked him to not bother us." Then she quietly, gently, yet emphatically stated, "I believe him when he said he wouldn't."

Sean's lip twitched involuntarily. He had no faith whatsoever in a man who would take another's man's wife—in the husband's bed, no less!

Jenny continued, "You told me you wanted us to be together if for no other reason than for Elise. I want to be with you as well. And not just for Elise either. You are my *husband*, and I love you."

Sean nodded. "I don't know what the future holds, Jenny. I don't know how long it will take me to heal from this. *You* probably have some unaddressed feelings as well. I suspect we will have good and bad days. Some days, I probably won't want you near me. Others may even feel like those from times past. We're going to have to be *very* understanding and *very* patient with each other."

"Do you want to see a marriage counselor?"

"No," Sean quickly replied. "We had it figured out before. We just need to heal and get back to what works for us. Besides, we have all the counsel we need right there." He looked up as he pointed skyward.

Jenny smiled and nodded in agreement.

"Why don't you put that casserole in the oven then come back in here."

The next hour was spent on the couch and began with holding hands, which led to cuddling, which ultimately led to kissing. The healing had begun.

Chapter 40

The oven timer sounded, and the couple moved to the kitchen to eat an early supper. After cleanup, they discussed plans for a camping trip.

Jenny began, "You could gather the equipment and load it while I run to the grocery store. We could pack our bags tonight and get a good night's sleep and then start out early in the morning. We could pick up Elise on our way out of town." Jenny was excited about their little family spending time together outside in the beauty of nature.

"Aren't you quite the trip planner!" Sean smiled at his wife with a bit of admiration. *Maybe things* can *work out after all*, he thought.

In reality, Sean had spent a lifetime *choosing* a positive outlook. He *chose* to see the good things in people and situations. Admiring one's wife is better than criticizing her. Building each other up produces better results than nitpicking at each other. Surely, this habit would help him through the rough times ahead.

"How many days would you like to spend there?" Jenny asked. "I need to know how much food to get. Also, is there anything in particular you would like for me to plan to cook?"

"How about four days? I think burgers would be easy for the first night since they don't take long. Of course, we *have* to have s'mores since they are Elise's favorite. And I always like your camp stew. Maybe you could make that one day?"

"Sounds great! I'm excited! I'll call Janice and tell her we will get Elise tomorrow around...do you think eight is too early?"

"Maybe nine o'clock would be better for Janice? We don't want her to have to clamber out of bed early just to accommodate us. She's done so much for us already."

"Agreed! I'll call her and then make my list."

The two of them tended to their respective duties and later went to bed. As before, Sean kept space between them. But during the night, out of habit, he moved to her and wrapped his arm around her. Her face broke into a smile when she awoke as the sun was breaking on the horizon.

*****

Sean pulled into Janice and Tarak's driveway, and the two of them quietly knocked on the door. Alicia opened it, with Adam close behind her.

She informed, "Elise is taking a bath. My mom thought it might be good for her to start out smelling good."

"Well, that will be great! Thank you, Alicia. Have you kids had a good time together?" asked Jenny.

"Yes, ma'am. My dad says we swim like fish."

Adam added, "We played dolls and cars!"

"Did you? That's great! Is your daddy at home?"

"No, ma'am. He's at work."

Sean, ever mindful of the high cost of air conditioning, directed, "Why don't we all step inside and close the door?"

Elise had finished her bath and was getting dressed when she heard her parents' voices. She came running into the living room to jump into her daddy's arms. That beautiful smile of pure love that children possess shone brightly on her face.

Meanwhile, Jenny walked into Alicia's bedroom to find Janice hovering over Elise's suitcase on the bed and packing the last of her clothes (she had washed and folded them last night after the kids went to bed). "Oh, Janice, you are *so* wonderful! I don't know how to thank you!"

Janice stood upright. As the two sisters hugged, Janice whispered, "Is everything all right?"

They stepped apart and grasped each other's hands. Jenny tilted her head to the side and smiled as she answered, "Yes."

Janice could see in her sister's eyes that Jenny seemed much less apprehensive than she had for the last few weeks.

"I'll need to come by one day soon, and we can catch up."
Janice smiled, "I'd *love* that!"

*****

The little family headed north and east for the three-hour drive
to Angel Fire. Because Elise was older and, therefore, more capable than the last time they had camped, she helped her daddy erect
the tent. Meanwhile, Jenny set up her "camp kitchen" and began
making sandwiches from the smoked turkey and bacon spread[2] she
had created the previous night. After lunch, the three of them took
a four-mile hike. Elise loved nature and pointed out various birds,
butterflies, and flowers.

As suppertime approached, Sean built a fire in the portable grill.
Jenny sliced tomatoes, onions, and lettuce for the burgers and had
Elise help with making the patties. Sean carried their sleeping bags,
pillows, and clothes from the truck to the tent.

After the delicious supper, the three of them played *Sorry!* as the
daylight was fading. Sean lit lanterns, and they played some of Elise's
favorite card games. Once it was fully dark, they sat in their chairs
and looked up at the stars. Sean pointed out constellations to his
ladies, and they even saw a meteor flash across the sky.

Sean retrieved his guitar from the truck and sang softly with
the chords he strummed. Elise fell asleep in her mommy's arms. Sean
carried her to bed then returned to sit by his wife. "Good day!"

[2.] To make this delicious smoked turkey and bacon sandwich spread, prepare the
following:

1 pound smoked turkey breast, cut up then processed into tiny bits
8 slices bacon, cooked until crisp and crumbled
1 stalk of celery, sliced thinly
1/4 cup sweet pickle relish
1/2 cup mayonnaise

Mix all ingredients in a bowl. Store covered in the refrigerator. It tastes great
on homemade bread. Serve with bread and butter pickles for a real treat! All
ingredients are to taste; use as much or as little as you desire of each.

"Yes," she agreed. "Thank you for cooking those burgers. They were *delicious!*"

"Thank *you* for getting everything ready!"

"I was enjoying the music. Would you mind singing a few more?"

"Not at all, especially for a lady as beautiful as you."

Jenny could feel his gaze. She turned to him and smiled that Mona-Lisa smile he loved so much.

"I love you, Jenny."

"I love you too, Sean."

Sean picked up his guitar and played the Eagles' "Love Will Keep Us Alive."

*****

The family continued to enjoy their short vacation. They ate hot dogs that they skewered onto long sticks and held over the fire and then made s'mores over the embers. Jenny cooked the stew that Sean had requested, and Elise got to see grazing elk, circling hawks, and even some hummingbirds. That night at the campfire, Jenny told Elise the folklore her grandmother had told her about hummingbirds.

During the drive home, Jenny asked Elise about the coming school year. "Are you excited?"

"Yes! Alicia and I are going to have a contest to see who can get the best grades."

"Oh, that will be fun! Will the winner get a prize of some sort?"

"Yes! The loser has to take the winner to the movies and buy her popcorn."

"That sounds like a great idea," Sean commented while looking in the rearview mirror at his sweet daughter. "Do daddies get to join in, or are we just the chauffeurs?"

"You can come with us. Maybe you can buy us some sodas to go with our popcorn!"

"Sounds like a *wonderful* deal!"

*****

The Wallachs arrived home, unloaded the truck, and returned all the equipment to the proper locations. Suitcases were unpacked, laundry was started, and Jenny emptied the cooler.

The next day, Jenny and Elise went shopping for a few more clothes and any remaining needed school supplies. Sean began working some of the plants that had finished bearing vegetables back into the soil in preparation for their fall garden. That evening after supper, Elise modeled her new fashions to her daddy. As usual, he thought she would be the prettiest girl at school.

Jenny awoke early the next morning. She tiptoed into the bathroom so as not to wake her gentle husband. Later that morning, she would call Janice and ask if Elise could come over for a couple of days since they were the last of Sean's vacation.

CHAPTER 41

Sean loved Jenny's breakfast tacos, so after getting dressed, she quietly closed their bedroom door and moved to the kitchen. He and Elise emerged from their rooms at almost the same time, probably because of the delicious aroma of bacon in the air.

Jenny smiled sweetly at her family. "Good *morning!*"

"Good morning, Mommy!" Elise hurried to set the table. She had quite an appetite because of all the swimming, playing, and hiking she had been doing recently.

"Good morning, my love," Sean said as he kissed his wife's cheek. "Would you like me to pour some juice?"

"Yes, please."

Soon, everything was ready and on the table, and the family bowed their heads for prayer. Once everyone began eating, Jenny asked, "Elise, would you like to go to Alicia's today and tomorrow?"

Sean suddenly looked up at Jenny with a slightly bewildered look on his face. *We didn't talk about this*, he thought.

"*Yes!* We won't be able to swim once school starts except on weekends. This will be fun!"

Aware of his confusion, Jenny looked at Sean as she told Elise that she would call Janice a little later in the morning. "Daddy only has two more days of his vacation remaining. He and I *might* try to have a date night or something."

"I hope she says yes. Alicia and I need to talk about what we're going to wear to school on the first day and who we want to sit with at lunch and stuff."

Sean smiled. *Girls sometimes think of the weirdest things*, he thought.

"Mommy, can I pack my own suitcase? I know what to put in it."

"Sure, honey. I'll just peek at it once you finish, just to make sure."

"Okay. I'll do it right after breakfast."

Jenny started to tell her to wait until she found out if it was okay but changed her mind. She and Sean smiled at each other.

Jenny called, Janice said yes, and Elise was overjoyed. Her suitcase was packed perfectly. Soon, she and Jenny were on their way to her cousin's house for a final summer swim.

*****

Though he was appreciative to be having two days alone with his wife, Sean was also curious about what Jenny had in mind. *I hope she lets me have some idea soon and doesn't keep me on edge all day*, he thought. He was rather shocked to realize that if she were going to "play" with him, he might be okay with that. *That* may *be what needs to happen*, he realized. *I am just not yet ready to be the initiator.*

All his fanciful thoughts vanished when Jenny walked through the door. He could see that she had been crying even though she bravely tried to smile. They had been together long enough—seven years—to know each other *very* well. Additionally, as all their friends pointed out, they shared an intense connection.

Sean's shoulders dropped. "What's wrong?"

"I need to tell you something."

"You've said that twice before. The first time was to tell me you were pregnant, the second time was to tell me...you know." It was difficult for Sean to say "George," "affair," or anything else that reminded him of...the dark time. His mind was racing, and he was trying *desperately* to keep *that* thought out of his head—the one that she was about to tell him.

"I'm pregnant." She smiled, and the tears began. This was supposed to be a happy announcement. They had been trying for well over a year.

Sean *truly* wanted to take her in his arms and comfort her. But first, the question: "Do you know whose it is?"

"I can't be sure." She sniffled.

Both of them knew the obvious answer: no birth control all that time, and no baby; a different man, and now pregnancy.

Sean turned away. *Is there no end to this?* He was breathing hard and fighting the urge to run, yell, or put his fist through a wall. He was so angry, so shocked, and so hurt. "Is this confirmed?" he commanded.

"I took a test this morning. I'm two to three weeks late." Her voice was weak.

Suddenly, Sean turned to her, his face and eyes red with anger, his voice booming. "When does this all end, Jenny? What other secrets are you keeping from me? How much more must I bear? I did *everything* right! Yet I'm having to bear all the pain!"

Jenny remained standing, motionless and silent. Her tears had stopped. She wasn't sure if she should be afraid of this ranting man. She, too, was breathing hard.

Sean narrowed his eyes, gave her a final glare, and walked out the front door.

He walked, with no purpose other than to release the whirlwind of emotion and energy that consumed him. He reached the end of their cul-de-sac and continued on the pathway created by other walkers and cyclists. He walked until the trail disappeared. Standing among mesquite trees, desert willow, and cacti, he realized his shirt was drenched with sweat.

He looked to the heavens. "Why, God, *why?*" A distant thunderhead rumbled over the desert. Nearby, a rabbit scurried for better cover.

Sean had expended the bulk of his rage-like energy. *What now?* he wondered. He stood there for many minutes. One sob shook him, then another. He dropped to his knees. The sand quickly absorbed his dripping tears. From behind him, the thunder growled.

He was struck with an irrefutable prompting to consult the scriptures. He reached into his pocket and pulled out his phone. He looked at several[3] and was humbled in the knowledge that the Lord is always with us and will always help us. He bowed his head, asking for strength to be a good husband and a good father, to love others unconditionally, and to follow the Lord's commandments.

He stood, dusted the dirt from his legs, and began his walk home. Lightning crashed nearby as he opened the front door.

*****

Jenny's elbow was resting on the table, and her forehead was resting on her hand. She was numb; thinking about what she should do next was beyond her current ability level. Even breathing seemed to tax her brain.

One thought played in her head like a looping audio file: *Sean has left again. I can't believe he'll come back now. He has suffered so much and at* my *hand. It's one thing to come back to a cheating wife but quite another to come back to one who is pregnant, maybe with the other man's baby. Sean has left again...*

She heard the lightning crash and saw the light come through the front door as Sean opened it. In her tortured state, she thought

---

3. Sean was prompted to read these scriptures:

"Have not I commanded thee? Be strong and of a good courage. Be not afraid neither be thou dismayed for the Lord thy God is with thee whithersoever thou goest" (Josh. 1:9).

"And the Lord, he it is that doth go before thee. He will be with thee, he will not fail thee, neither forsake thee. Fear not, neither be dismayed" (Deut. 31:8).

"Yea, though I walk through the valley of the shadow of death, I will fear no evil for thou art with me. Thy rod and thy staff they comfort me" (Ps. 23:4).

"Likewise, the Spirit also helpeth our infirmities for we know not what we should pray for as we ought, but the Spirit itself maketh intercession for us with groanings which cannot be uttered. And he that searcheth the hearts knoweth what is the mind of the Spirit because he maketh intercession for the saints according to the will of God. And we know that all things work together for good to them that love God, to them who are the called according to his purpose" (Rom. 8:26–28).

the lightning had blown the door open. *It would serve me right to be struck by lightning.*

Sean was shocked that she hadn't even looked up when he came in. He approached the table, pulled out a chair, and sat across from her. He cleared his throat.

Her head jerked up, and she sat more upright, gasping in air as she did. The two of them looked at each other like strangers stuck on a subway together at the end of a long day after wrapping up a tough week. Jenny could not hold her eyes on his.

Sean was out of answers. He, too, looked away.

Many minutes passed.

Sean was the first to speak. "Jenny, do you want me to be your husband?"

Jenny raised her eyes to his. His question seemed so bizarre to her that she wasn't sure how to answer it. She shook her head, squinted her eyes, and licked her lips. Her mouth moved as if to speak, but no sound came out.

Suddenly, her eyelids felt very heavy, and she began leaning to the side. Her upper body slumped onto the table.

Sean immediately arose, placed his arms under her, and used his lower leg to kick her chair out of the way. He quickly carried her to the bed and placed pillows under her shoulders and head. Moments later, he was wiping her face with a cool damp cloth. Nothing. He called her name. Three times.

She gasped and opened her eyes. "Sean!" she said weakly. Her face told of the shock she felt that he was there. She tried to smile but wasn't very successful.

Sean was torn. Here lay his wife—the girl who had captured his mind the instant he saw her and his heart soon after, the mother of his child, and the woman who took care of him. But she had also recently been with another man, violating everything he stood for. And *now* she is pregnant, possibly as a result of her two-week affair.

The Sean who had moved from another continent to be with her ached to hold his wife, longed to comfort her. But the Sean whose heart had been trampled was having to fall back on the manners his father had taught him. And *that* is why he was there, trying to revive her.

"I'm going to get you some water and crackers. Stay here."

Sean returned and offered the glass to her lips while helping her hold her head up. "Here. Eat a few of these crackers."

She shook her head, still too weak to speak.

"You need to eat something for some strength. Come on now, just a few."

Even munching the cracker was almost too much effort for her. He again helped her drink some water then held out another cracker.

"Do you need to go to the hospital?"

She again shook her head. "I'm okay," she managed.

Sean remembered Jenny's extreme tiredness at about this point in her pregnancy with Elise. "Rest. I'll be right here."

His last four words were a sedative to Jenny. As she slept, he sat in the chair and thought deeply about their life together.

*****

When Jenny awoke, she was much more alert. Sean rose to stand beside her and feel her forehead for a possible fever. She seemed fine.

"You passed out on me."

Jenny seemed shocked. "Really?"

"Yes. I had to carry you in here."

"Oh my. I'm sorry."

"Here, eat another cracker and drink some water. If you feel like it, we'll move to the table and I'll get you some juice and maybe a sandwich or something."

She did as she was told.

"Do you think you can stand?"

"I think so." She sat upright.

"Don't rush. I'm not giving you a trophy for going fast."

Jenny laughed slightly. Her head felt much clearer. She swung her legs to the side of the bed, touched her feet to the floor, and stood carefully. Sean was nearby to catch her if necessary.

"Can you walk?"

She took two cautious steps. "Yes, I think I'm fine."

"Here, hold my arm—at least at first."

269

The two of them made their way to the kitchen table. Sean poured her a glass of orange juice then spread a slice of bread with some peanut butter. He put the snack on a small plate and placed it in front of her as he took a seat across from her.

"Do you remember what I asked you?" Sean inquired.

"When did you get here?"

Sean smiled slightly. "I'll take that as a no. I think maybe you were nearly passed out and then finished when I got here." He raised his eyebrows and tilted his head toward her. "I have that effect on women, you know."

Jenny giggled.

"No matter. I withdraw the question, Your Honor." Sean's eyes were almost sparkling, and his voice sounded normal.

That he was attempting to be lighthearted made Jenny feel better.

"As you slept, I did some thinking. But before I share, do you have anything you'd like to say or ask?"

"No. I'm anxious to hear your thoughts though. They're always good."

"All right. I see it like this, Jenny." He paused to push his hair back away from his face. "We had previously talked, quite a bit. The decision was for us to stay together and try to rebuild our relationship. It was a fairly easy choice to make because...well, I love you, Jenny. Being hurt and confused doesn't change that. And we both understand that we need to be together to give Elise a strong family life. So far so good?"

"Yes."

"Today, you thickened the plot." Sean was trying to be as gentle as possible, but they needed to come to an understanding.

Jenny's head dropped in shame.

"Jenny, look at me."

It took her a moment as it was difficult for her, but she raised her gaze to meet his, biting her lower lip as she did so.

"You are carrying a baby inside you. This is a gift from God, no matter the circumstances."

Her lip quivered.

"Is there any way to rule out one of us as the father?"

She dropped her eyes and shook her head.

"Are you *certain* of that?"

Looking directly at him, she responded, "Yes."

"Then it *could* be mine."

Her hesitancy to respond told Sean that she was thinking the same thing that he had—that given their history, the baby was *more* likely to be…*his*.

Several moments passed. Jenny was afraid to speak. It felt like everything she had said or done for weeks had caused her husband pain.

Sean took a deep breath and continued, "Okay. So we're staying together and will work to bring about a better future. The question now is, do you have the baby or not? Can you agree with that *question?*"

Jenny squirmed uncomfortably in her chair. She told herself, *Just answer the question, no more, no less.* "Yes."

"For me, there is no need to consider the 'not' option," Sean declared.

"Agreed." While Jenny knew that Sean did not approve of abortions—nor did she—on the inside, she was still relieved because this was a sticky situation, and it was *their* situation to figure out.

"So *now* the question is do we *keep* it or not? Can you follow my *logic?*" Sean pointed his finger in the air to emphasize the last word.

"Yes."

"I don't see you carrying a child to term and then me forcing you to give it up for adoption."

Jenny looked at Sean and blinked several times. *Did he really use the adoption word?* she thought. As her brow wrinkled, he realized that perhaps she had not understood him.

"To be clear, I would *not* ask you to put the baby up for adoption."

Jenny breathed a sigh of relief.

"So now the question is…well, it's not even a question actually. The situation is practically carved in stone. We will love and raise the baby as our own because God tells us to love one another."

Tears were pooling, and her face was contorting.

"Come here." Sean patted his thigh.

Jenny walked to his side and sat on his leg. Her eyes were closed because she was trying to dam the flood of tears.

Sean patted her on the small of her back and looked up at her. "Jenny, I love you. I *want* to be with you and Elise. This new baby doesn't change that. We have several months to work hard at repairing the broken parts of our relationship before it's born."

All she could do was nod. But she was beginning to shake.

"Come here." Sean put his hand on her far shoulder and pulled her to him.

Her face on his strong shoulder was like a switch for the floodgates to open. She wept for several minutes. As the overwhelming emotions began to subside, she whispered, "Sean, I love you so much. I don't deserve you."

He held her tightly with one hand and patted her with the other, remembering his mother's words from long ago: "When a woman cries, you shouldn't 'shhhh' her or tell her that everything is okay—because it might not be. Sometimes a woman just wants security and the knowledge that the man is with her and her only, and that he will love and protect her."

Finally, Jenny sat upright and smiled at her incredible husband.

Sean reasoned, "It's quite simple really. There have been *far* more good times than bad ones. What you did was a one-time thing. I have already forgiven you. I just have to work at…living with the memory of it. And this baby here"—Sean patted Jenny's tummy—"will grow and be born. It will need love and care just like any other child. We are good parents. We can do this."

Jenny smiled again, not quite able to believe that things were going so well after she had messed up so badly.

"I need to apologize to you for my outburst. I was wrong to use such harsh words."

"I deserved it," Jenny said, her head shaking from side to side.

"No, you didn't. And I normally wouldn't allow myself to explode like that. But we all make mistakes. And I'm sorry."

A few moments passed, and Sean added, "And another thing. I was wrong to say that I was the one bearing all the pain. I can see that you have born a great deal as well. We will strengthen each other as we have in the past. We will get through this, Jenny, I know it."

Jenny put her arms around Sean's neck and shoulders and hugged her husband. "You're my hero." He carried her to their bed.

Dog-tired from the past few weeks but relieved by the day's progress, they slept.

Chapter 42

One of life's most wonderful pleasures is to get to sleep until you wake up on your own—*especially* if you have a job and/or children. Sean and Jenny were able to do just that. Feeling energized, they quickly arose, showered, and dressed in comfortable clothes. As they made the bed, Sean suggested, "Why don't we go out for breakfast this morning?"

Jenny's face showed her surprise; early in their life together, they had agreed that trips to restaurants would be infrequent and usually only on special occasions. They knew that they would not only save money but that they could eat more nutritiously. Besides, Jenny was a *great* cook. Also, when they *did* go, they could, therefore, afford to splurge and patronize the more high-end establishments.

"Are you *sure?*" she asked. "We've been eating out *a lot* here lately."

"I know." Sean smiled at Jenny in appreciation of her having followed their game plan without a single complaint over the years. "But it *is* my last day of vacation." He paused to consider his words, not wanting to start the day on a negative note. "I'd like to treat you to something special, then come home and spend some time with you. We probably need to converse about a few more things."

"Okay!" she answered cheerily. "What are you hungry for?"

"I was thinking brunch at Fogo de Chão."

Jenny's mouth gaped open. "Well, *I'm* underdressed!"

Sean laughed. He was happy to see Jenny's sense of humor returning. Just as importantly, he was happy to realize that he was able to enjoy it.

Jenny knew that Sean was having difficulty with intimacy—and she understood his reason. She also knew that in order to restore their bedroom relationship to its former glory, she *might* need to "jump-start" it with a day of teasing him and building his anticipation. Going to brunch at this particular restaurant was the *perfect* setup for her to enact her plan. And now, before her baby bump began to show, she could wear the new dress she had found—on sale, of course—for just this purpose.

Jenny changed while Sean made reservations. When she exited the closet, he gasped. He slowly enjoyed the scenic route over the landscape of her body. He took an extra detour at the slit that ran up her left thigh. Their eyes met. He exhaled quickly, nearly in disbelief. "Wow. You will *definitely* be the most beautiful woman there." He unconsciously licked his lips.

She walked toward him, her eyes locked on his. The black dress hugged her tanned body, and the neckline plunged to *just* before too much. The silver chain holding the luxurious amethyst pendant Sean had bought for her on her birthday was the perfect length and was guaranteed to hold his attention. She had bought new stilettos as well. Faux crystals ran the length of the heel from the ground to the sweet little bow at the top. Any man would know that a woman wearing *those shoes* was neither sweet nor innocent.

Sean's reaction had shown that he was clearly appreciative of Jenny's efforts to entice him, so she draped her slender arms across his shoulders. He swallowed, *hard*. His mouth was partially open, and he was panting slightly. He looked at her lips and wanted them. He closed his eyes and shook his head.

Jenny had the ability to look completely innocent while asking very simple questions but in a voice that caused Sean's loins to stir. "Don't you think the amethyst is a perfect accessory for this dress?"

Though Sean made it his habit to be respectful and look only at Jenny's face, her invitation was too tempting. His eyes slowly followed the warm silver chain to the gemstone lying provocatively at the top of her cleavage. A groan escaped him. He swallowed again and brought his eyes back to hers. His lips were swollen with passion for his wife.

With upturned eyes that never blinked, she watched him. She knew that with little effort, she could make him surrender all his willpower and anything else that was keeping him from taking her right there.

He knew what she was doing. He blinked as he considered whether or not to kiss those lips he knew were both warm and waiting.

With exquisite timing, she brought her lips to his and delivered the softest of kisses that left him aching for more. She smiled slightly as she pulled back. "Let's go eat." Her voice could not hide the fact that she, too, was full of passion for her man. She continued to hold her lock on his eyes. "But I want to finish this conversation when we get home."

Sean chased her lips when first she moved from him. His head was spinning, and the only thing he could see were her eyes and mouth. He knew that, at that moment, if she kissed him like that again, he *could*, in fact, be with her.

And *she* knew he was there as well. She turned to move toward the hallway, knowing that he would watch her.

His jaw jutted to the side and his tongue rubbed against the back of his upper teeth as he watched her walk. "I wish I had a tuxedo. Anything less and I feel like *I* am underdressed compared to you."

Jenny tossed her hair back as she turned to face him and grinned. "Just change into your new suit and that tie that you wore at our reception." She struck a coy pose. "Do you need me to help you?"

Sean shook his head and laughed. "No, my lady. If you touch me now, we will be late for our reservation." He drank in the vision of her once more, then moved to the closet where he quickly changed into the attire that Jenny had suggested.

At the doorway, he reached for her hand. The walls of the hallway provided needed guidance; without them, they may have ended up in Toronto as their eyes never left each other's.

*****

At the restaurant, the task of managing the details of tending to Jenny mostly kept Sean's mind off their upcoming "conversation," but it didn't keep him from enjoying the view. He longed to kiss her slim, tanned shoulders…

"Sean?"

He jerked his head as he snapped back into reality. "I'm sorry. What were you saying?"

Jenny laughed. Now she knew how other women felt when their husbands were watching football on TV or a pretty girl walking by. Given that Sean *never* did that to her, and that she was *purposefully* putting him in that position, she didn't chastise him. "I was wondering if you wanted to try a bite of this soup. It is *delicious!*"

"Yes, please."

She pushed the cup toward him, and he dipped his spoon into it. His eyes widened, and he nodded as the silky texture and subtle spice warmed his mouth.

"That is *excellent!* I'll bet you could figure out how to make it."

"Oh, I've already got a recipe forming in my head. I can't wait to make it for you."

As Jenny talked to him, Sean couldn't help but notice the subtle movements of her body, the slight tilt of her head, and the enticing look in her eyes. Her allure was stronger than ever. Had it not been for embarrassing her, he felt certain that he could have taken her, right there, on the table—and to hell with the other patrons.

Sean had finished his first plate of meats, cheeses, and fruits. He watched Jenny as she finished her fruit, salad, and soup. As they waited for their omelets to be delivered, a realization struck Sean. His lips parted, and he stared at her as the impact of it wound its way through his thoughts.

"Sean?"

Once again, he jerked his head and apologized for his distant demeanor.

Jenny's brow was wrinkled. "Is everything okay? You were really far away!"

"Yes, actually. In fact, I am…" Sean sat more upright and looked to the side then quickly turned his focus back to his wife. "I am… very well."

With twinkling eyes and a slight smile, Jenny asked, "Can you share?"

Sean's mouth was open, ready to speak, but no words were coming out. He looked at Jenny, adjusted himself in his chair, and smiled. He looked away again. He had been holding his breath, trying to find the right words, but his body wanted oxygen. So he exhaled quickly.

He drew a deep breath, looked at his wife, and with a wrinkled brow simply said, "I love you…Jenny." It was almost as if he had realized it for the first time ever.

"I love you too, Sean!" Jenny's brow again furrowed and she tilted her head to the side. With a playful demeanor, she stated, "But I think there must be more to tell!"

Jenny could easily see that *whatever* thought had struck Sean was game-changing. She locked eyes with him. "Right now would be a really good time." She nodded as she quietly spoke, encouraging him to share his revelation.

He leaned back in his chair and sat motionless. Jenny could see in his eyes that he wasn't ignoring her but that some notion was zooming around in his brilliant brain. When he looked back at her, she knew that all had been restored to normalcy. All signs of pain and anxiety were gone.

Suddenly Sean rose, walked to Jenny's side of the table, and pulled her chair back. He helped her stand then held out his arm for her. He quickly spoke with the first server he found and gave him *more* than enough money for their food and taxes as well as a generous tip.

The trip home was rapid, with Sean looking at his beautiful wife as much as he safely could. Though she was confused, Jenny knew that Sean would ultimately tell her everything because that is what they did with each other.

Sean hurriedly parked and helped Jenny from his truck. Though he was *keenly* aware that she had on the stilettos—and that it was difficult to walk rapidly in them—he nonetheless grabbed her hand and tugged her into the house. In the living room, he pulled her to himself and held her close. He buried his face in her neck, drinking in her intoxicating scent. He drew back and looked at her with appreciative eyes as if for the first time in a long while. He smiled, shook his head from side to side, and began.

"You didn't do this *to* me. As I have encouraged, you *allowed* him into our home and generously served him food and drink. You were friendly, which I have also encouraged, even though you were uncomfortable with his presence. You even tried to justify his behavior by trying to view him through eyes of neighborly love and kindness."

He reached for and held both of her hands. "But then you got caught up in something that you didn't ask for, you didn't start, and wouldn't have done. He overpowered you physically. You were seduced, that's true, but I honestly believe he *would have* raped you. So it's almost as if you were in *survival* mode. You played along with him in his twisted game to minimize the damage he might cause. Then he quickly overpowered you mentally. You were in a state of *mind control*, not *passion*."

As he spoke, Jenny was fighting back her tears. Not only had Sean realized the true nature of what had happened, but he was able to articulate it in simple, understandable terms. That was something even *she* had not been able to do. But most importantly, he held her virtually blameless.

When he finished speaking, Sean raised his hands to her cheeks and stared deep into her eyes. Then he wrapped her in his arms and kissed her like a doughboy canoodling with his best girl after returning home from overseas.

They walked, now slowly, to their bedroom. They took turns removing their clothing from one another. Sean led Jenny to bed then slid in next to her.

Had that been all Sean could have managed, Jenny would have been the happiest woman on earth. But he continued to kiss her, to hold her, and to tease her. She was ready for him, but more importantly, she knew *he* was ready for her.

Just to be sure, though, she asked, "Will you love me again?"

In his eyes, she found the answer as it had always been.

CHAPTER 43

Epilogue

Elise and Alicia

Because of his tremendous work ethic, Sean returned to work the following day. But he took the next day off to accompany Jenny in taking Elise to her first day of school. Once back home, they held each other and shared a few tears as their "baby" entered a new stage of her life.

That weekend at her birthday party, Elise and Sean played perfectly the piano duet they had been practicing. Everyone there, including Jessie and Lucy and Tim and Kayla, clapped and whistled with gusto at their performance.

Elise *loved* getting her allowance each week. Sean helped her set up a spreadsheet where she could practice managing her money. There were columns for tithing, savings, and a special one for setting aside a portion of it for things she wanted to buy.

At the end of the semester, both Elise and Alicia had straight "As" on their report cards. Even though there was no clear-cut winner, Sean took them to the movies anyway and bought popcorn and soda for both of them.

Lucy, Peggy, and Jessie

Peggy was promoted to manager at the grocery store where she had been working. With the increase in salary, she was able to move herself and her kids to a newer and larger home.

Lucy applied to and was accepted at a cosmetology school in Albuquerque. Additionally, she was awarded a grant which covered almost all her tuition. She stayed with Sean and Jenny, who welcomed her help with cooking, cleaning, and babysitting. Upon graduation, she was hired by a popular salon and quickly became one of their most sought-after stylists. She was soon able to get her own apartment.

Before Jessie and Cassandra got married, they were baptized and became members of the church. Soon after the wedding, they began their own family. Their firstborn was a son; they named him Sean.

A few years later, Jessie was able to get special permission, and he took his mentor for a flight over the desert in an Apache helicopter.

Sean wore his kilt.

Tim and Kayla

The couple continued to date. Due to many long conversations with both Sean and Kayla, Tim became increasingly interested in the church and was soon baptized.

When the weather cooled in the fall, they bought tents and went on a camping trip to the canyons in northeastern New Mexico (where Sean and Jenny had had their first date). While there, Tim dropped to his knee and proposed to Kayla, who, of course, accepted.

Tim asked Sean to be his best man. Standing at the front of the sanctuary beside the groom, Sean could barely tear his eyes away from his lovely and very pregnant wife, Jenny—even as the bride walked down the aisle.

Kayla submitted her completed dissertation, and it was accepted. She received her PhD at commencement and the next day learned that she, too, was pregnant. Tim had to once again consult Sean—this time for advice on being a father.

Sean and Jenny

Sean and Jenny continued to lead a busy life. They took walks, maintained their garden, and supervised Elise as she cared for her chicks—which soon became hens who laid eggs! Sean ran alongside Elise after removing her training wheels, and she quickly became a competent cyclist. The family loved riding their bikes together through the neighborhood.

*****

The Wallachs enjoyed a wonderful Christmas. Elise received the microscope she had wanted and created and viewed slides of everything she could get her little hands on. Janice helped Jenny prepare a feast for their two families and also their brother, Jack. They enjoyed it on the antique table Sean had secretly bought in Santa Fe. Once it had been delivered, Sean worked at restoring it to its original state, using tips from the websites Jenny had found. Jenny reupholstered the seats of the chairs with a fabric they chose together.

That night, after everyone left for their own homes and Elise was in bed, Sean asked Jenny to sit on the couch while he went to the bathroom. They sat together, staring at the lights of the beautifully decorated Christmas tree and discussing their plans for a New Year's Eve party. He pulled his wife close to him, and she snuggled into the crook of his arm.

Suddenly, Sean pulled a small present from his pocket. He had kept it hidden away as he wanted to give it to her privately. With a look of confusion and frequent glances to her loving husband, she slowly pulled the ends of the awkwardly tied ribbon.

Sean, embarrassed by the amateur-wrapping job, smiled at her and promised that the gift inside would be better.

Jenny opened the long, narrow box and discovered a creased and stained piece of paper. She unfolded it slowly. She brought her hand to her mouth and looked at Sean with tear-filled eyes.

I	M		Y			
	A	B	O	U	T	
	D		U			
			W			
A	G	A	I	N		
			L			M
			L	O	V	E

Answer:

I'm	mad	about	you.	Will	you	love	me	again?
(1)	(2)	(3)	(4)	(5)	(6)	(7)	(8)	(9)

Missing word from clue 3: Y-E-S.

It was the puzzle she had created for Sean the day he left after he learned of the affair. She had never given it to him but had absent-mindedly stuck it in his underwear drawer. During the emotionally intense weeks that followed, she had forgotten about it.

"I carried it around in my wallet for a few weeks and never really looked at it. One day, a severe storm came up at work, and I was grounded for a couple of hours. I pulled it out and worked it. I *loved* that you did this for me!" Sean looked up to allow his tears to find their way back to where they belonged. "You are"—he shook his head from side to side—"the *only* woman for me, and I will love you, and only you, forever."

Jenny curled up next to her wonderful husband with her head on his chest. She was still holding the puzzle in her hand. The two of them had spent many hours talking and praying about their relationship; as such, things had returned to normal, maybe even better.

"Why don't you look a little deeper in that box?" Sean suggested.

Jenny raised to look at Sean, her eyes questioning his.

Sean picked up the box and handed it to her.

She pulled back the layer of soft fabric and found a small piece of folded paper, which she quickly opened.

I CHOSE THE LAST ONE, BUT YOU SHOULD MAKE
THE CHOICE THIS TIME.

WITH A NEW BABY, YOU WILL NEED THE UPDATED
FEATURES FOUND IN A NEW CAR.

LET'S GO SHOPPING TOMORROW!

Jenny squealed with joy and wrapped her arms around Sean's neck, hugging him tightly. She pulled back to look at him. "Are you sure? Can we afford it?"

"Don't you worry about that! This is one of the reasons I work that extra job!"

"Oh, Sean! Elise will be so excited!" Then she hugged him some more.

*****

When she was about six months pregnant, Jenny decorated the nursery. She and Sean told Elise that she would soon be getting a baby brother or sister, and she was elated. "I can help take care of it while we ride together in the back seat of our new car!"

The family attended church regularly, and both Sean and Jenny were called to positions of responsibility. They continued to have parties at their house, and everyone in attendance was always welcomed warmly and fed well.

The couple began again to attend the karaoke bar with Sean's friends from the APD. Sean had some of the men try to learn of George's whereabouts, but it was decided that he had left town for good.

*****

On the first of April, Jenny gave birth—once again *very* quickly—to a son. They named him Johnny (which was a blending of their names) Elan ("friendly" in Apache).

When the pediatrician informed the parents of Johnny's blood type (AB), Sean quietly moved to the hallway to quickly research blood type information on his phone. He knew he was type B and Jenny was type A; nearly a year ago, George had coincidentally told him at the karaoke bar that he was type O. Sean chuckled. It seemed as if he and Jenny were the fools on this day.

Sean walked back into the birthing room with tears in his eyes. He kissed his radiant wife, and then gently kissed his son's cheek as he lay sleeping on his mother's chest.

ABOUT THE AUTHOR

Sheri Keyes taught junior high and high school math for twenty-two years. Now retired, she is able to pursue her varied interests—including painting and drawing, crafting recipes, creating and solving diverse types of puzzles, and writing.

Will You Love Me Again? is a sequel to her first novel, *May I Love You?* Her second book, *A Charm Bracelet of Stories*, retells many events from her life and also includes some of her poems and short stories (as well as a few of her recipes!)

She is "proud to be a Texan and happy to be retired!"

CPSIA information can be obtained
at www.ICGtesting.com
Printed in the USA
BVHW071810211122
652433BV00001B/20